THE FALLEN KINGDOMS

WELL OF EIDA

KB BENSON

This is a work of fiction. Names, characters, places, and incidents either are the product of the author's imagination or are used factiously. Any resemblance to actual persons, living or dead, events, or locales is entirely coincidental.

Copyright © 2022 KB Benson

All rights reserved. No part of this book may be reproduced, distributed, or transmitted in any form or by any means, including photocopying, recording, or other electronic or mechanical methods, without the prior written permission of the author, except in the case of brief quotations embodied in critical reviews and certain other noncommercial uses permitted by copyright law. For permission requests, please contact the author at kbbensonbooks@gmail.com.

Map Design by Stardust Book Services in collaboration with Fred Kroner.

Cover Design by Franziska Stern at Cover Dungeon

WELL OF EIDA

PRAISES FOR WELL OF EIDA

"*Well of Eida is a page-turning fantasy adventure with a rich story and characters to root for!*" ~ Casey L. Bond, author of House of Eclipses

---

"*Benson absolutely delivers with a fierce heroine, edge-of-your-seat action, emotional betrayal, deliciously morally grey characters, a gritty world, and swoon-worthy romance.*" ~ Rachel L. Schade, author of Empire of Dragons

---

"*This is unlike any other fantasy book I've read, and it was super unique, with a fresh twist on all the things we love in fantasy. Trust me, you'll want to read this one as soon as possible. Benson delivers on everything a YA fantasy should be!*" ~ Emily Schneider, author of Scales of Ash & Smoke

OTHER BOOKS BY KB BENSON

Call of the Sirens Trilogy ~ YA Fantasy

The Harvest
The Hunt
The Harrowing
The Harbor

Would you like to read a copy of The Harbor (a Call of the Sirens novella) for FREE?

Join KB Benson's newsletter and get an exclusive digital copy of THE HARBOR plus be the first to get access to cover reveals, advance review copies, exclusive giveaways, and all things bookish from KB Benson. If you'd like to join, you can join here:

https://www.kbbenson.com/newsletter.html

WE
HAVEN
Ghora
ABANDONED
BLOOD DESERT
THE MARKET
Arautteve
Ei

ELL OF EIDA

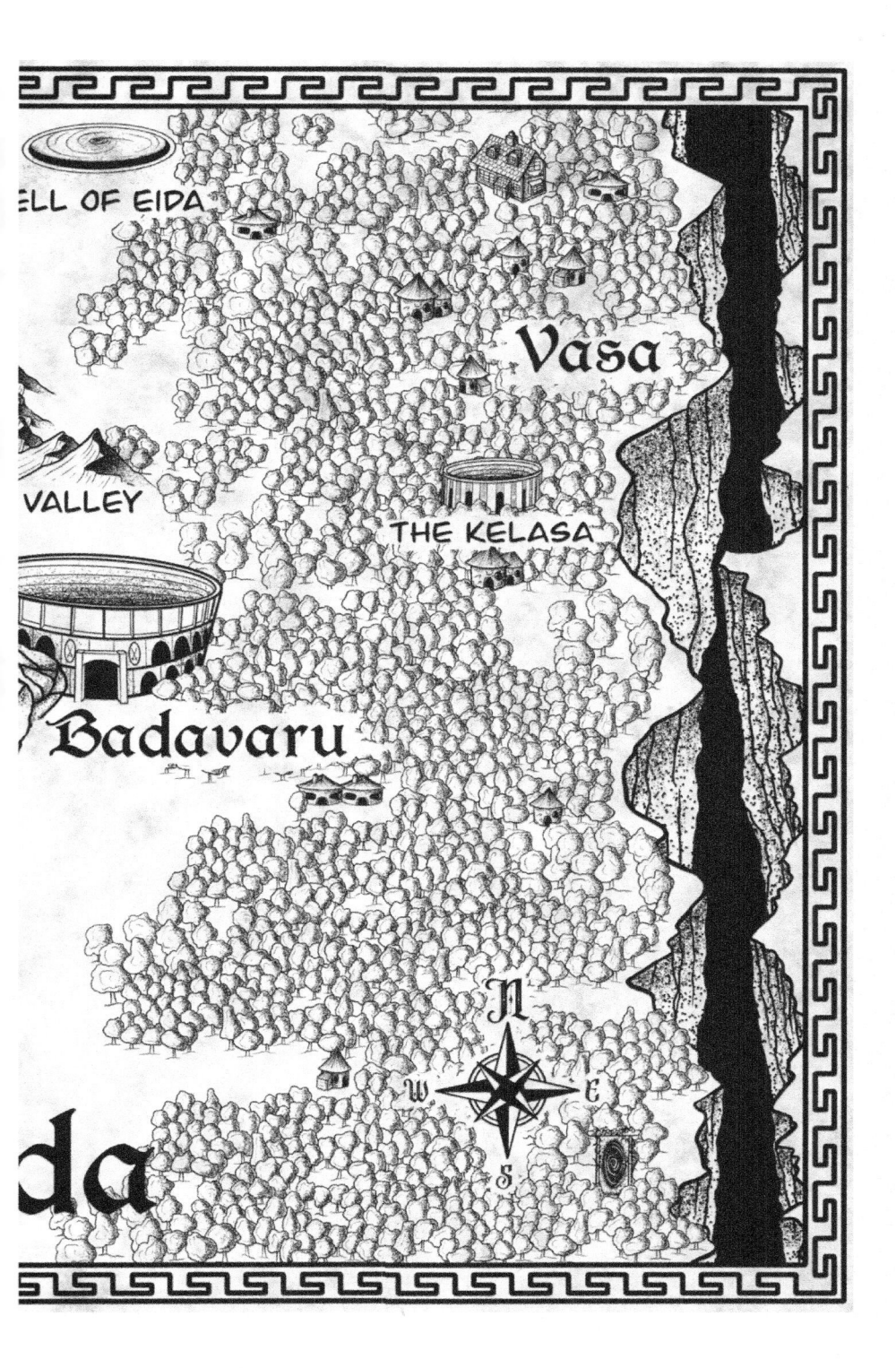

VALLEY

Vasa

THE KELASA

Badavaru

da

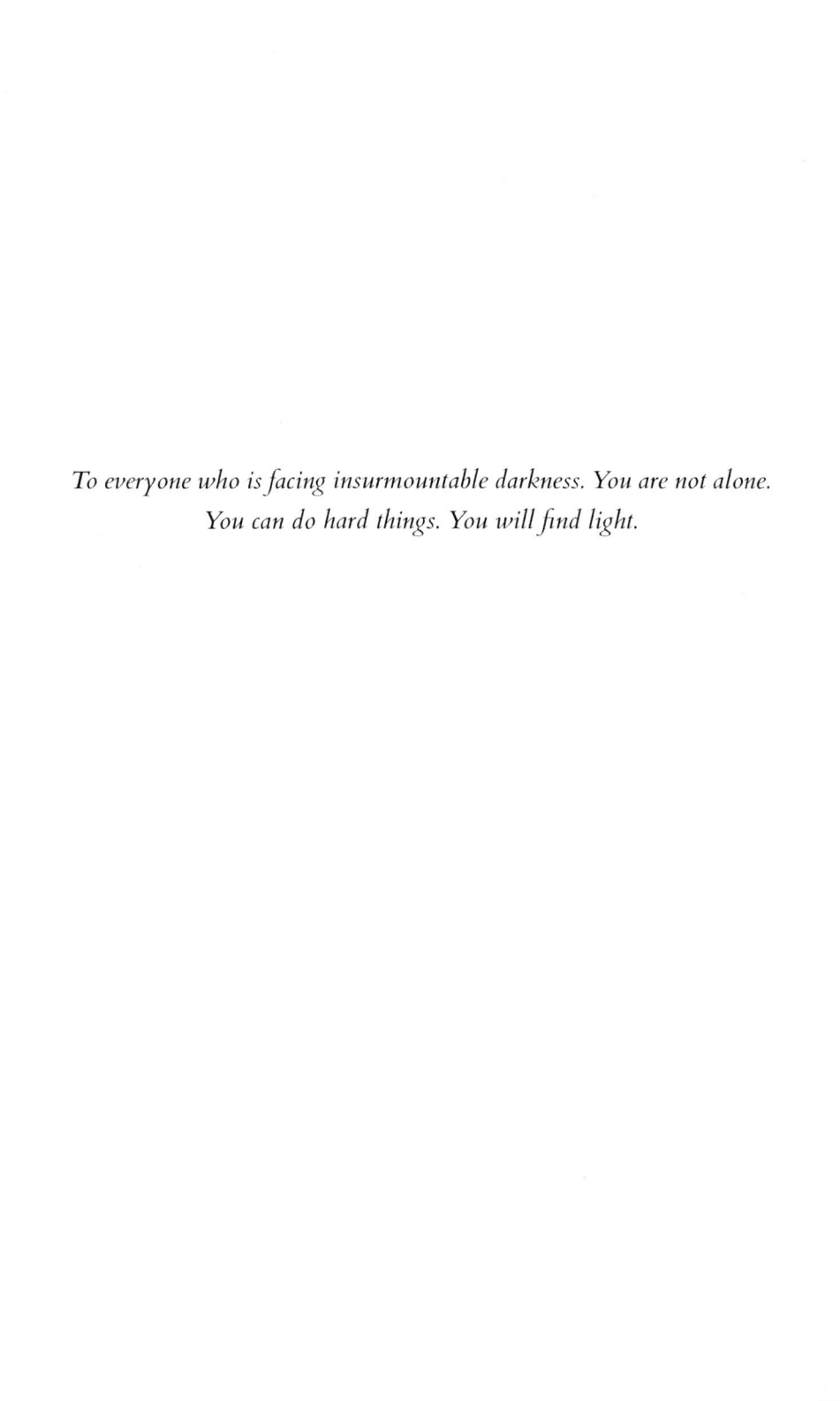

To everyone who is facing insurmountable darkness. You are not alone. You can do hard things. You will find light.

PRONUNCIATION GUIDE

PEOPLES IN EIDA	DISTRICT	DESCRIPTION
SEEKER	Ghora	People from the human realm who enter Eida seeking to fight for their heart's greatest wish.
MARKED FALLEN	Arautteve	People taken by the trolls to fight against Seekers and keep them from receiving their wishes. Marked Fallen have unleashed their inner monsters and train with a master.
UNMARKED FALLEN	Haven	People taken by the trolls to fight against Seekers and keep them from receiving their wishes. Unmarked Fallen have not unleashed their inner monsters and avoid it at all costs.
TROLLS	Vasa	Cursed magic-wielders banished to live in the realm of Eida.

Person
Caelum (CAY-luhm)
Isla (EYE-luh)
Chorin (COHR-un)
Inaara (ee-NAHR-uh)
Graeden (GRAY-dun)

Place
Eifelgard (EYE-full-gard)

Arautteve (Ah-rah-OO-too-vay)
Ghora (GOHR-uh)
Eida (AY-duh)
Vasa (VAH-suh)
Taiatum (TAY-uh-tuhm)
Idrium (Ih-DREE-uhm)
Kelasa (Kuh-LAH-suh)
Badavaru (Bah-dah-vah-ROO)

Other
Jivanna (Ji-VAHN-uh)
Aerin (EHR-in)
Sulika (Soo-LEE-kuh)

CHAPTER ONE

Tib would never get me killed.

Even still, my heart pounds into my sternum with each shallow breath that fills my lungs. An unfamiliar wave of nausea roils in my stomach.

"Aribelle..."

I scrunch my nose and shove my anxiety deep inside myself. "Formalities will get you nowhere, *Tiberius*."

He hasn't used my full name in years. Standing outside, Tib leans farther in through the rough worn window, holding the curtain to the side. His shaded features are nearly impossible to see against the backdrop of night.

"I would do almost anything for you, Tib." I rub my arms to smother the night's subtle chill. Or maybe it's the vision of what he asks of me that crawls over my skin. "But not this. It goes against Bridgewick's laws."

"And since when has our village's laws stopped us?" Tib baits, his voice hushed.

Never. The answer presses against my lips, but I force a hard swallow. "This is different. It's dangerous."

The dozens of stories the elders told our village slam into my memory. Vicious, blood-thirsty beasts. Brutal murders. Death's cold, bitter end. Entering the Enchanted Wood is a death sentence. Unless the elders commission a villager to travel there, it's strictly forbidden.

Tib lifts his hand and presses his palm against my cheek. Despite myself, I lean my face into it. We've been betrothed for four years, and his touch still sends heat through my skin. Though, it took every moment of those years to forge our friendship and for that friendship to grow into something stronger.

I'm not entirely sure when this forced arrangement turned to love, only that it did. My skin tingles, and I swallow. A new wave of heat courses through my cheeks. Thank the stars for the cover of darkness.

"And even if you don't die," I glance over my shoulder toward the darkened house where Mother sleeps and lower my voice, "the elders would imprison you for getting one of their trained fighters killed in the forest."

"Who says we're going to get killed?" Tib lowers his hand and gives my shoulder a light push. "Besides, we've all trained to defend Bridgewick and one day face the dangers of the Well. If you die, there's more where you came from."

"Why Tib, do you charm all the girls this way?" My knees ache pressed against the stiff mattress beneath me, my bed wedged beneath the window. Shifting my weight, I slip my feet under my thin blankets. "As tempting as near-certain death sounds, you should leave."

Tib's smile slips, and the shadows swathing his face deepen. A veil of melancholy fills my thatch home.

"What is it?" I whisper.

Tib drops his head until his eyes are hidden from mine. Not that I could see them anyway with the moon at his back.

"It's my mum." Tib's hushed voice cracks, a sound as sharp and as brittle as the edge of a broken sword. "She's ill."

My reluctance snuffs out like a dying candle. My fear. My anxiety. It's gone, a flame capped without any oxygen to feed it. "Why didn't you tell me?" I whisper.

"It's not for the village to know."

Rolling back to my knees, I lean toward Tib, leaving only a foot or so between us. I inhale deeply, waiting for his scent to encircle me like a wave of cinnamon on a frosty eve, but it doesn't come. I try to lift Tib's chin to meet mine, but he closes his eyes and turns his head away. The moonlight cuts a jagged line over his lips.

"I'm not the village, Tib. You should have told me," I say. "What is she ill with?"

Tib sniffs, but I can't see if tears fall. "I don't want to talk about it."

"If I'm to travel to the Well with you, I need to know why."

Tib's body stiffens almost imperceptibly. His lips flatten into a hard line, his fingers clamping tighter around the curtain. "Is it not enough to trust me?"

My chest tightens, and I grit my teeth.

"The stars have no war with us," Tib recites. "But if they did, we would not fall. Hand in hand. In light or darkness. Together. Isn't that what we always say?"

I frown and drop my gaze to my fingers knotted together against the windowsill. We made the oath years ago just after our betrothal. It's frivolous and nonsensical. Yet, it's brought me peace more than once to remember we aren't alone. Not really.

"Please don't abandon me, Ari." Tib's voice falters, broken and afraid.

My thumb brushes my *ndoa*—a tawny mark encircling my bicep. A symbol of my vow to tie myself to Tib.

Since I was ten, I've wielded a blade and trained to protect those I love. Every youth in Bridgewick has. My life has been a series of clashing steel leading me to battle. I wipe my slick palms against my worn blankets. I didn't think battle would come so soon, but one never does.

I glance over my shoulder at the gauzy curtain that separates my room from Mother's. She stirs softly beneath her quilt. If Mother finds Tib at my window, she won't hesitate to give him a ripe beating with Father's old rod. In the shallow moonlight streaming through my window, I can barely make out Mother's silhouette and the empty space next to her where Father should be.

My throat tightens as my gaze sweeps that empty space. He's gone. So is my sister. My jaw tenses, and the sting of tears burn behind my eyes as I trace the shadows where their silhouettes should be. The subtle shimmer of their memories has nearly faded. A heavy ache settles in my chest. How could I forget the contours of their faces after only a few years?

Setting my jaw, I smother the emotions. I know how. It was either barricade the memories or be consumed by them. I swallow against my dry throat.

Now, Mother and I only have each other. I glance at Tib. And we have him.

When my world burned, he held my family together. The boy who has seen the hideous ghosts of my past and never left my side. Shutting my eyes, I bury the memories of that night.

My resolve hardens, and I know what I'll do no matter how stupid or foolish it may be. Tib has stood with me through everything. Now, I'll stand with him. No one should travel to the Well of Eida, and they especially shouldn't travel there alone. If Tib truly plans to bargain with the trolls, I will walk with him as far as I can. In the end, though, he's the one who must pay. Every wish at the Well comes with a price.

I roll my shoulders, forcing them to relax. Tib and I will do this together. He keeps me safe, and I him. I won't break our vow.

"Why didn't Caelum talk you out of this?" I ask.

Tib's twin brother should have at least tried. I sigh. Ever since I rejected Caelum's offer of marriage for Tib's, things changed between us. They changed between Caelum and Tib, too. Caelum always looked at us with an envy I tried to ignore. I don't bother waiting for Tib's answer.

"You realize you'll be indebted to me, right?" I shove aside my growing nerves and try to muster some playful teasing into my voice. It falls flat. Traveling to the Well is not done lightly.

It shouldn't take long to find, nestled at the heart of the Wood, but you never know what the trolls will claim for their price when you arrive. You must be prepared to give them anything.

"I wouldn't expect anything less. A few days?"

"Try for life."

Tib scoffs and rolls his eyes—or I assume he does. I can't see anything but his silhouette and the faint curve of his lips.

"For you," I say, sobered. "And for your mother."

The tension slips from Tib's body, and he creeps away from my window into the darkness. I pull on a pair of calfskin trousers and snatch a few of my blades. No one travels into the Wood unarmed, not anymore. I strap my blades into garters and tighten them against my thighs.

After wrapping my furs around my bare arms, I grab a few waterskins. I swing my leg over the windowsill and pause. Mother's quiet snores fill our small home like a beehive. She won't lose anyone else. I'll return before morning's light. She'll never know I left. I blow her a silent kiss and slip out after Tib.

Tib's footsteps are quiet against the tightly-packed dirt. He darts from one hut's looming shadow to another—me at his heels—until we reach the edge of Bridgewick. The Enchanted Wood sparkles beneath the moon's silver light.

Pausing where Bridgewick's hard earth meets the Enchanted Wood's lush soil, I stroke a delicate leaf hanging from a silver branch. Residue coats my fingers like stardust, and I smile. It has been too long since Tib and I have dared venture into these woods. We used to visit them daily—they belonged to us. Until, one day years ago, a village elder discovered the Well. He went in, and never returned.

Legends had told of a mortal world that once held magic you could wield. A world we were no longer a part of. We thought magic had been taken from the human realm long ago. Then when the Well arrived, we realized the magic had never left.

The Bridgewick elders commissioned half a dozen men to find him, hoping to learn something. Anything. Only one reappeared years later, but not a day older. His young face was battered and broken; his eyes lost in time. He returned with enough of himself to describe the horrors within the Well, but it wasn't long before he withdrew from the village and took his own life.

I've often wondered where the Well came from, but none in Bridgewick know. And when the news grew too fearsome of the trolls guarding the Well of Eida, our village stopped looking for answers.

My smile slips. Tonight, I have no idea what we'll find.

My eyes trace the shimmering trees. Regardless of where our journey ends tonight, the excitement whirring through my veins is palpable. I'd almost forgotten how the Wood calls to me at its edge. A piece of its ancient heart tied to mine.

I step over the line separating Bridgewick from the Enchanted Wood, and a familiar warm embrace smothers the remnants of fear in my veins. I sigh, my earlier anxiety evaporating from my skin. Tipping my head to the sky, I imagine my fear floating away—iridescent beads disappearing among the canopy of colored leaves. Soft pinks glow in front of the moon, lavenders twinkle as though made of starlight themselves, vibrant teals sway in the light breeze like the sea. I soak it in.

I have missed the Enchanted Wood.

Tib doesn't stop to admire the Wood as I do. His steps lack his usual carefree stride and instead are placed with purpose and efficiency.

I wonder what we'll find at the Well. Monsters? Bones? Tension ripples through my arms. Maybe we'll meet an elderly troll waiting near the portal accepting tokens for passage. I force a smile through my apprehension. Surely our journey would never end at something so docile. Besides, we all know the trolls have no need for money.

Everyone who seeks a wish from the Well must pay a different price. Maybe the youth of your skin, or a year from your life. You pay for passage into Eida with parts of yourself you can never get back, and then you fight for your heart's greatest desire. If you return alive, the Troll King will grant your wish.

My gaze slides to Tib weaving along the trail at my side. He hikes without pause and with a confidence I haven't seen in him before. But my heart races too fast, beats too unsteady. Despite the Wood's calming enchantment, my heart thrums anxiously. This journey only ends one way: with Tib entering the troll realm. My heart shudders and skips a beat. I worry it won't end well for him.

Our village prays for those few the elders send to the Well to receive a wish to protect our people and way of life. Only that one has returned. The others have not. Before he died, the man who returned shared pieces of his tale, but the stories were vague and often muddled by his fractured mind. Bloodshed, starvation, illness... and time. Endless amounts of time for those trapped inside. If Tib enters the Well, I don't know when I'll see him again. Or if I *ever* will.

He shouldn't be doing this. I shouldn't let him. My jaw ticks, and I force the tightness in my throat to ease. It's not up to me. He'll travel to the Well whether I'm with him or not.

I bite down on the thoughts stringing together in my head until they unravel. The *ndoa* weighs heavy against my arm. I vowed every part of myself to Tib, including my loyalty. Tib is not my husband yet, but still I won't let him walk this path alone. I can't. Not after what he's done for me.

Tib must believe he's ready to face what waits for us at the Well and within it. A flutter of unease brushes my skin. I'm not so sure.

"What weapons did you bring?" My voice spirals into the darkness, a lone sound among the hushed wildlife.

"Enough." Tib's tone is clipped as he places one foot in front of the other.

I grimace at his tone. He may walk with confidence, but his voice tells another story. "You know, we don't have to travel to the Well. Surely there's something else we can do for your mother. You have nothing to prove. I think it's foolish to risk traveling to the Well if we don't need to."

My fingertips brush against the hilt of one of my blades, and I cast a sidelong glance into the trees. Just checking. There is honor in traveling to Eida and fighting to protect our people. It's not without risk, though, neither within the Well nor in these woods.

The moonlight flashes across Tib's face. His cerulean eyes are darkened with shadow, roiling like a storm-filled sky before the rain. A shiver laces through my spine. The Wood's shadows elongate his nose and deepen the swells around his eyes. He's never looked more like Caelum.

"The Troll King won't grant just anyone's wish, you know." I run a hand through my hair. "You must earn it. You must kill for it. Are you ready to have that blood on your hands if there's another way?"

A muscle ticks against Tib's jaw. "This *is* the only way."

Tib shakes his head before disappearing farther down the path. Tension as thick as sap tightens in my chest. I pin my glare on his shrinking form. Why won't he see reason? A sharp sensation burrows into my stomach, festering and vile. I shove it away.

I can't imagine the stress bearing down on Tib's shoulders tonight. With a sobering inhale, I follow his rigid footsteps deeper into the Wood.

The trail steepens, a slight ascent carving a path ahead of us, when an arctic chill weaves through the Wood. Its icy hand crawls over my skin and reaches my bones. The leaves rustle through the treetops. The hair rises on my arms. I search for the warm embrace I felt when I entered the Wood, but any such feeling has disappeared. Instead of whimsical magic clinging to the surrounding bark, it's riddled with fear. Rather than cloaks of wonder buoying my heart, I feel Death's caress.

My gaze snaps toward where Tib climbs, his feet digging small furrows in the earth.

"Tib," I say, breathless. "We need to leave this place."

"Are you scared?" Tib's voice holds a darker tone, and I'm not sure if he's teasing.

"Of course, I'm scared," I spit. "Only a fool wouldn't be. We can find another way to help your mother. These woods have become dangerous." I glance over my shoulder as the wind quickens, the leaves a symphony of secrets.

Grabbing Tib's cloak, I tug him back toward the path we've already traveled. He whips his arm toward me, breaking my grip.

"I can't go back!" Tib's lips are tight, his glare hard and unrelenting. A single breath, and his irritation disintegrates. His shoulders slump forward. "I can't leave."

"What's your plan?" I hiss. "We make it to the Well, you pay the price to enter Eida, and then what? You die in vain trying to save your mother. And then she'll die, anyway!"

I regret the words the moment they leave my mouth. The Wood's frosty breath creeps down my spine, and silence swells between us. I swallow the bitterness climbing up my throat. Tib's doing the best he can—I know that—he always has.

"Your mother wouldn't want you risking this." Barely restrained panic trembles beneath my resolve to help. Heat climbs into my cheeks. "The trolls are lethal and violent." How could Tib forget the lessons we have learned for ages? The one central truth we all follow? "Have you forgotten the most important lesson the elders have ever taught? That my father taught?"

Tib remains silent, his scowl burning a hole at his feet. When he doesn't respond, I answer my own question.

"Survival, Tib. Survival. You live, and you die. Once you die, you're done. That's it. So long as we're alive, that's all that matters."

The night air strokes my skin and makes it crawl. I smother a shiver.

He isn't going to leave.

Taking a deep breath, I press my palm against Tib's heart. His body stills. His heart thumps against my skin, the steady beat increasing with my touch. The light breeze rustles the leaves surrounding us, a strand of my dark hair floating around my shoulders. Tib stood at my side during the darkest night of my life. He cradled me in his arms for days, my tears staining his simple tunics and pooling against his shoulders. As the life I knew went up in flames, Tib was immoveable.

I rebury the dark memory deep inside my soul.

"We are in this together, you and me," I say. "Even had the elders not betrothed us years ago, the stars have aligned for us. You never must face your monsters alone. But I don't think we should face them here."

"This is the only way," Tib grunts.

A muscle works in my jaw. This isn't like Tib. He's not usually so stubborn. My gaze roams over his stiff posture, waiting for my answer. He's different in the Wood tonight, but so am I. I'm never this cautious.

The stars have no war with us, but if they did, we would not fall. Hand in hand. In light or darkness. Together.

Only Tib knows our vow. Only he would recite it to me. Whatever change has wrought in him, it's still Tib. Frowning, I nod.

"Thanks, Ari."

With resigned determination, I gesture towards the trail, and Tib starts off again. The soil shifts to loose gravel beneath my boots as we carry ourselves deeper into the Wood. A cold sweat trickles between my shoulder blades. No matter how fast my blood pulses, I can't shake the chill in my bones. The icy whisper that says we shouldn't be here.

Forcing the thought from my head, I place my steps with precision, still losing at least half the ground I gain with each footfall. The gravel clatters down the steep slope, an unintentional warning for all the surrounding creatures.

If our intent was to surprise the trolls, we've failed. They'll have heard us from miles away. A restless anxiety sinks deep into my stomach.

Before long, we reach a sharp turn in our path. Instead of following the trail, Tib presses forward through the trees. I stalk after him, restraining the thick branches from snagging my cloak and tugging at my hair. This grove of trees curves inward, their trunks twisting and mangled. I make a mental note of their shape so I can find my way back to Bridgewick when we finish here. I swallow the lump forming in my throat. Tib won't be returning with me.

It doesn't take long before we emerge onto a new path, the gravel replaced by violet soil. The clamor of color from the Enchanted Wood's edge has all but disappeared as we are submerged into an array of violets. Wisteria hangs in long strands from the treetops. Violet orchids and irises line the mauve soil we tread on. Even the patches of sky peeking between the trees carry a lavender tint.

Tib stalks onward, his gait not once slowing to admire the Wood. I crouch near the edge of the trail and caress a blossom between my fingertips before brushing it aside. The shadows behind it seem to sway back and forth like switchgrass, the lighter parts reflecting the violet tint of the Wood.

I've stepped into a fairytale.

An aching nostalgia loosens the ever-tightening knot in my chest, if just for a moment. For a single heartbeat, I'm back in the Wood as it was years ago—magical and exotic. Tib and I used to hunt for fairies among these trees, though we'd never traveled this particular path before.

I glance to where Tib presses ahead. The nostalgia ripens and rots as reality crashes around me again. The woods still glisten like the fabled memory from my past, but my light-hearted anticipation has grown heavy with dread.

We don't speak as we follow the trail, as though this part of the Wood is too sacred to defile with words. The path carries us from a world of violets through a tunnel of greens, a forest made up of every shade of red, and a river crossing as orange as the sunset. Only when the colors dull and become muted, do our footsteps halt.

Shadows bathe a wide, round meadow. A creek trickles around stones and past long blades of sedge grass, gurgling quietly in its calm passage. A small garden bridge arches over the creek.

This meadow could be beautiful if it weren't for the Well sitting at the other end of the meadow at the head of the brook.

My heart thunders, and my ears drum with its laden pulse. My head swells as the blood rushes to my brain.

We shouldn't be here.

I place my warm palm against my clammy forehead.

Magic froths from the Well like water, pouring softly into the creek and meandering beneath the bridge. One whispered wish, and the portal will open for Tib.

I shiver, and my throat grows dry.

"Tib," I whisper, resting my hand on his arm.

Tib rolls his arm out from under my touch. His shoulders rise to meet his ears as he draws in a heavy breath and releases it. Without offering any encouragement to me, he steps down the pebbled path.

When Tib whispers his desire into the Well, he'll have to pay the price to enter Eida to fight for it. No one knows what the cost to enter will be until after the wish has been made. By then, it's too late to change your mind.

My blood crawls through my veins, thick and frozen. I strain to hear snapping twigs or labored breathing, but all I hear is the pounding of my own heart. This is wrong.

Tib climbs to the center of the garden bridge that overlooks the meadow and rests his hands on its railing as though overlooking a beautiful kingdom. His knuckles drum against the wood mindlessly. Once. Twice. Three times. Where is his fear?

I follow much slower, keeping an eye out for trolls lurking in the shadows. The bridge creaks as I step onto the wood, but I don't dare climb to its peak. Tib's eyes flicker to mine, irritation and sadness painting his ashen irises. Ashen, not blue. I suck in a breath.

The price at the Well could be anything—even the color of your eyes.

"Tib?" I ask, my nerves electrifying. My feet slip from the bridge's slick wood, and I step back onto the soil. The air in my lungs is sculpted from ice, cracking and spitting under the pressure of my panic. My words rush out in a breathless exhale. "Have you been here before?"

He doesn't get the chance to answer.

A loud clap splits the air. The small creek explodes, and a torrent of water cascades around us like a waterfall. My eyes widen, my breath completely stolen. Grey, dimpled skin covers the troll who has materialized from the creek. He gathers his footing, and my own legs tremble as he climbs from the creek, shaking the earth beneath his heavy steps. A scrap of muddied cloth covers his torso and legs.

My gaze locks on the creature. He towers over Tib and me as he climbs the bridge, his body a few feet larger in every direction than a man, and I'm frozen with fear. I swallow against the desert forming in my throat. I'm here for Tib. I'm here for his mother. I won't leave him alone in this. With a shaking hand, I draw my sword.

"You have returned?" The troll bellows.

"Returned?" I whisper. Tib *has* been here.

Tib ignores me and stares at the towering troll. "I have brought the price you have asked. A girl with fire in her blood."

My heart turns to stone. What type of deal requires him offering the color of his eyes and… me?

The troll's meaty hands grasp onto the bridge's railing—the wood moaning beneath his weight—and he leans over to me and inhales deeply through his nose.

I step back from the troll, too paralyzed to do anything more.

"I'm sorry, Ari," Tib whispers, unable to look at me like the coward he is.

The troll grunts. "Is this her?"

"No," I whisper. Tears gather in my eyes. He would never get me killed and yet, *hand in hand. In light or darkness. Together.* He's brought me to the Well. An aching, crushing weight collapses onto my chest. Everything he said was a lie.

"Yes," Tib says.

My fear shatters. I spin on my heel and bolt for the tree cover, but it's too late. The troll snatches my wrist, and in a single movement throws me into the meadow. Wind claws through my hair. The small stream's spray is an icy bite against my skin as I smash into the bank and skid through the water.

My lungs burn, but I can't suck in a decent breath. Panic thrums through my chest, but I can't think. Can't breathe.

The air crackles and snaps around me. More trolls materialize into the meadow. I scramble for a solid footing to run, but it's fruitless. Thick-skinned hands grope my body. Cold. Ruthless. I gulp a strangling breath, and a raw scream tears from my throat. Dozens of hands are over me. They tie ropes around my wrists and legs and fasten a gag between my lips.

I scream anyway.

Tears roll down my cheeks, and I scream for help. I scream at Tib. I scream because despite all my training, I know I'm going to die.

My blurred vision finds Tib's back at the edge of the meadow. He's returning to the Enchanted Wood.

He's abandoning me.

One of the trolls lifts the rope attached to my feet and coils it around his hand. With a sharp tug, he drags me through the creek toward the Well. I thrash against the restraints, but I'm not strong enough. My screams turn into whimpers.

Trolls fizzle from thin air until they surround the entire Well. Their voices chant low in a language I don't understand, growing louder with each passing moment. Rough hands chafe my skin as I'm lifted from the ground.

My breathing grows shallow, and my panic sets in. I thrash against their iron-shackle grips and scream. It does nothing. Soon, I'm suspended above the Well's mouth, flashing lights pulsing within. The trolls' chanting cuts off.

Silence fills the meadow, haunted by the echo of their voices. Slowly, the hands tilt toward the Well, and I slip.

A scream tears from my throat, and I tumble straight into the troll realm.

CHAPTER TWO

Two Years Later

"It's as hot as the Nether Winds." Sweat trickles down my back, and I resist the urge to wipe it away.

I lift my gaze to the sky hovering above Badavaru—if you can call it a sky. There is no such thing in Eida. No sky. No sun. Only clouds that churn like the ocean. Yet only Eida's arena district seems to boil like a furnace.

Turning my hands over each other, I wrap a stained cloth around my knuckles. The cloth has never been white, not even when I stole it from another fighter. My gaze traces the blackened smudges, but I don't let myself dwell on them. It would do me no good to know where they came from. I'm just grateful for the added protection.

"Bless our King." "Bless our King." A group of trolls scurry around me from the promenade hall and slip into Badavaru's arena. Each of the trolls looks different from one another—different hair, different body types. They're almost human-like in that regard. Except they're all vicious beasts.

The Troll King. Of course, he's to praise… or blame. I refrain from rolling my eyes. As a self-sustaining world, Eida gives the entire realm life. The Troll King gives it power. If only the realm could give us some rain once in a while. I say, *Curse Eida! And curse the Troll King!* My tongue slips between my cracked lips. Heaven knows we could all use a fresh rainstorm.

Heaven doesn't exist in Hell, though.

Shoving the thoughts aside, I tie the cloth in knots around my palms. Daggers are sheathed against the outside of my thigh, hidden within the folds of my faux leather skirt. Another blade hangs at my waist against the fitted girdle. It's not much, but it's all I have to protect my major organs. Besides, anything more would only slow me down.

I straighten the straps of my animal hide top and tighten the worn bracers wrapped around my forearms. In this arena, I'd rather be swift than protected. Armor can only shield you so much, and if your enemy can't catch you…

Sweat already dews on my skin, and I stifle a moan. More than the speed, it's too hot in this district to wear any thicker armor.

Adrenaline builds in my stomach as I step into the short tunnel blocked by the arena's portcullis. Light floods the stadium beyond the latticed grill. Any moment now, the gate will rise, and before I know it, I'll find myself standing over the corpse of my opponent

— a Seeker seeking a wish from the Troll King. I tighten my fist around my sword.

They come from everywhere, seeking the Well of Eida within the Enchanted Wood. Just like I did. My nostrils flare, and I return my attention to the arena.

Eida's games have three rounds. Round one, a Seeker fights a Fallen. I stretch my neck and unsheathe a blade. Round two, they fight a Fallen with the strength of the Fallen's inner monster. My fingers curl around the gate, and I squint from the darkness into the arena. If the Seeker still lives, we enter round three. The Seeker faces the Fallen's monster, and the monster alone.

It could be a basilisk or an ogre. Some have even fought serpents with multiple heads. Many Fallen and trolls alike hope one day to watch a dragon fight in the arena. A smirk toys with my lips. As if they were real. They're myths. Bedtime stories told to children to get them to close their eyes. No one has ever shifted into a dragon since Eida began. It doesn't keep people from imagining, though.

Regardless of the creature, they're all savage animals focused on one thing: blood.

My gaze drops to my blood-stained bracers. That's why I ensure the Seekers I face never make it to round two. I couldn't shift. The trolls would discover I'm Unmarked—a Fallen who refuses to unleash her inner monster. A Fallen who can't shift. Then, they'd rip the beast out of me to fight for them.

I may kill those who attack me, but I won't become a monster. How could I ever face my mother again if I did? Leaning forward, I peer through the gate. If I win enough battles, I'll find my freedom and my way back to her.

Shaking the thought from my head, I focus on the task ahead of me. If either the Seeker or I lose consciousness, the round ends and we'll move into round two. I stretch my shoulder. I won't leave the Seeker conscious, let alone breathing.

Hundreds, if not thousands, of trolls fill the stadium benches towering over the arena. Their sneering noses and paunches pour over their seats for a better look at their fighters. They shove each other, their laughter cackling around them. Gnarled fingers point at me and my opponent as the trolls huddle together and wager on our fight.

The trolls live off the land. They have no need for money, so I have no idea what they trade. Probably whatever pieces of the Seekers they claim as the price for entering this rathole. I glance at the Seeker but can barely see him through his own portcullis. Not that it matters. Small or large, it will be his blade on the ground when this ends and my name the trolls chant.

An ili scurries past my foot into a dark corner, and I hiss. The small rodent's stomach protrudes from hunger, its ribs flaring with each breath. Coarse, wiry fur sticks out as though it has been struck by lightning. Or magic. It stares at me with its slit eyes, a low growl building in its belly as it protects the blood staining the floor beneath its body. My lip curls as the creature scrapes its fanged teeth against the dried splatter.

Filthy.

The mutated rodents gather around blood stains and the decaying bodies of those Fallen who lose their fight in Badavaru. They scrape thin layers from the carcasses before the bodies are carried away to Eida's beast.

A shudder ripples through my spine. It will never be my corpse they taste. Not if I have anything to say about it.

The portcullis clangs, and my attention returns to the arena. My chest rises with an inhale, and I grip the hilts of my two full-length swords. Today, I will show another Seeker how terrible this realm can be. Gears shift, and the gate creeps up the wall.

The ili bares its unnatural fangs at me once more as though it expects me to fight it rather than take my place in front of the Seeker. I swipe my foot into the creature, and it skids into the arena's light. The creature squeals as it writhes on its back, burns melting away the bald parts of its flesh. Its small, clawed feet scramble against empty air. I watch it struggle. I watch it suffer without batting an eye. Is that not what we're all here for?

To fight? To die?

The ili rights itself as its wiry coat begins to sizzle and darts into the shadows. If only I were so lucky to have an escape...

Kill or be killed. It's simple. No matter what else happens this day, once I step into the arena and face my Seeker, only one of us will walk out again.

My body moves of its own accord into the stadium's light, and the false sun blinds me temporarily. A clang echoes throughout the grounds as the portcullis locks into place, sealing me between these walls. Against the burning sky, the trolls' silhouettes cheer, their fists pumping the air. As my eyes adjust to the unnatural light and the trolls' ugly faces take form, I force my gaze to the opposite portcullis.

A slender man steps foot over foot toward me as though he's practiced his footwork all day. His bare chest barely has the tell of manhood—no contoured muscles, no hair. He may even still carry some of his baby fat.

What is he doing here? My remorse evaporates the moment I feel it. Anyone standing on the opposing side of the arena from me deserves what's coming. They chose to come. They chose to fight to the death. And they're choosing to die.

Even still, at least he doesn't die in the name of the Troll King like the Fallen. Like me. He dies fighting for his heart's greatest desire. My nostrils flare, and my grip tightens against my blades.

I draw circles in the air at my side with my swords. Their sharpened steel reflects the false sun, and I focus on the light. It's about to get very dark in here. I refuse to squirm as I already know exactly what it will feel like when my sword ends his life. Quick, yet painfully long. Relief marred with guilt. Another fracture splintering my soul.

The man carries a small buckler shield that, if anything, might protect his wrist and part of his forearm. My swords feel heavy in my hands. I guess a buckler shield is better than no shield. Unless you're me.

The man bangs his sword's hilt against his small shield, baiting me.

Bang! Bang! Bang!

I don't so much as flinch against the clatter. His strategy is obvious: evoke my fear by announcing his lack of it. The thing is no one is unafraid, especially in the arena.

Bang! Bang! Bang!

He's daring me to attack, likely hoping I'll retreat instead. He has no idea what he's asking.

Focusing on the pulse of my blood, I center myself in a memory not lost in my hatred. The starlit sky spreads over my head, the village gathering and settling at my feet. Drums beat into the crisp air, clapsticks slap against each other, and beads rattling in their gourds breeze around me. I open my arms to the sky and dance. My feet hit the ground in rhythm with the drums, my face tilted to the sky. For once, I felt free.

Tib's smiling face interrupts the memory as it had done in reality. Only now, instead of a teenage flutter in my stomach, something rots inside my gut. My anger burns through my peace, hot and ugly, and my eyes flash open.

Rolling my shoulders, I run my thumbs along my swords' pommels and break into a run. The distance between my rival and me shrinks. A guttural scream tears from my throat, and I allow my consciousness to dissolve into the back of my mind. I watch through fogged glass as my body—trained and experienced—takes control.

Our swords clang, the vibrations traveling up my arm. We spin away from each other before our swords meet again. The man swings his shield through the air, and I duck below his arm, sweeping his feet out from beneath him and sending him to his back. His blade skids against the ground, out of his reach. I stab my left sword toward his chest, but he rolls out from beneath the blow, and my steel digs into the earth. Grunting, I slash my other blade in his direction as I tear the first from its hold.

As I recover from my misplaced aim, the man shoves his foot into my knee. My leg gives out, and I fall. The man doesn't spare a breath. He leaps forward in a daring attempt and snatches my arm. He stretches it to the side, too far. Pain burns through my shoulder. The man shoves his shield into my forearm. I scream. My second sword clatters to the ground, my fingers shaking from the nerve damage, but adrenaline blocks the pain. Running my tongue over my teeth, I slash my spare blade between us, and the man lurches back and scrambles for his fallen sword.

Red bleeds into my vision. Tightening my grip on my lone sword, I yell a battle cry and charge the man. He blocks my blow, and our swords clang as though we perform a well-rehearsed act. Again. He blocks, and the only sound I hear is the melody coming from our swords until he misses a beat. My sword slips past his, and soft flesh succumbs to the sharp steel.

He grunts, anger curdling his features. Withdrawing my blade, I leap back as the man slashes his toward me. One step. Another. I raise my sword between us, and his gaze gets lost in the smeared blood coating it. He stumbles. His brow creases, and he presses a hand to his abdomen. Blood paints his palm.

His arm falls to his side, and the Seeker drops to his knees.

He stares at me, and I watch as his life flickers in his distant gaze. Dread seeps down my spine.

You had no choice, I think, but the words feel wrong.

The man collapses onto his side and then rolls to his back, sucking in short, haggard breaths. Blood gushes from his wound, and I step back. I must have hit something important. The man's skin pales, and his furrowed brow deepens as though he's confused that he lost.

My own shallow breaths match his as I stand over his body watching him bleed out. The short wisps aren't enough. The stale air in this hell will never ease the darkness of watching a life slip away. Blood pools around the man's body. I did this. I killed him.

A muffled applause breaks through my reverie. It rings in my ears. I tear my gaze from the dying man and glance at the stadium seats. The trolls stamp their monstrous feet and snarl into the air, spit snapping from their teeth as though they themselves are victors. They cheer for me and for the man's death at my hands.

I dare one more glance at the pallid face, unremarkable in his death. He knew the risks when he visited the Well of Eida—we all do.

One more breath. Deep. Penetrating. I shove the guilt gnawing against my lungs deep inside and don the glory of my victory like the mask it is. I raise my weapons, and the crowd becomes voracious for blood.

Lowering my arms, I pump them into the air again, but the frown carved into my lips is impermeable. This mask is the only way I have survived the last two years.

The portcullis creaks as it lifts once more to allow me my sole exit. I wipe the back of my hand over my lip. Blood coats the already tinged cloth. I unwrap the gloves and ball them in my fist. One kill closer to my freedom.

Or what the trolls call my *pardon*. I roll my eyes. A pardon, as if we truly are prisoners. The trolls can't possibly believe any of their Fallen slaves could slay four thousand Seekers in exchange for their freedom. But then, that's the kink, isn't it? They don't expect anyone to. It's all a bunch of false hope.

Those of us taken by the creatures of Eida will fight as their slaves, only allowing a Seeker to receive their wish with our deaths.

It's not so easy to defeat Eida's warriors, however. I scrape dried blood out from beneath my fingernail, and a hollow pit forms in my stomach.

We are the Fallen. And we *are* monsters.

CHAPTER THREE

THE BITTER CHILL BITES my skin, angry and unrelenting.

Closing my eyes, I hug my knees into my chest and huddle deeper beneath a thin scrap of fabric. Its three frayed corners are tied to obsidian turrets—it's not much of a tent. But then, Haven's also not much of a respite.

This narrow strip of tents is a haphazard fringe on the edge of Ghora, nestled against the wall that separates the Seekers' district from the Marked Fallens'. Since I am neither a Seeker nor Marked, I hide here with the others. Neither a part of Ghora nor Arautteve.

Technically, Haven doesn't exist. Neither do we.

The icy air cuts through to my lungs with each inhale, and I cherish the moment of solitude. It tastes of frost and lightning. Like a storm brewing on the night-capped horizon. The clouds will never bless this district with snow or rain, though. Right now, I'd settle for a little of Badavaru's heat.

I blow a breath of warm air into my hands. But as it is, I'm stuck here, and the weather doesn't shift from region to region. Magicked, is my guess by the same awful trolls who put us in the arena. I'd bet coin on it if I had any.

I draw a waterskin from the shadows, nestled safely out of sight.

The sheep hide is soft against my touch, but much too light for my liking. Unscrewing the cap, I upend the bag over my lips until it's dry. It's not enough. It never is.

A year ago, I stole this treasure from the market and have kept it my secret since. My throat tightens, and I lower the lightweight skin. It doesn't hold much, but fresh water is hard to come by in Haven. The only place I've found it readily available is in the Market. I assume they get it from one of the ever-flowing rivers not found on this side of the border. I swipe my dry tongue over my teeth. A droplet, that's all I need. Rarely, though, does anyone return from a raid with full urns, and now I'm out.

An aching burn claws up my throat, biting and relentless. I stare into the shadows of Ghora just beyond Haven. At least the Seekers suffer, too. The Troll King rarely puts them into the arena without weakening them first. We may have little, but the Seekers have less.

I lick my dry lips. I've been thirstier before. If I don't get more water soon, though, I'll be too dehydrated to be of much good anywhere.

Tucking the waterskin into the garter against my thigh, I sigh. I guess tonight will be my turn to raid the market myself.

I settle onto the threadbare blanket spread across the cold, hard ground. At least here in Haven, I have a canvas over my head and a somewhat private place to think and incinerate my guilt. The Seekers have nothing.

My gaze sweeps the expanse outside my tent where dusk settles against the sky. Upon entering the Well, Seekers are dropped into the vast shadows of Ghora. No light. No food. No water. All they have is time to either wait for their turn in the arena or die.

A shuddered breath slips through my nose. Seeker or Fallen, there's only one difference: they chose to come here.

The trolls say we aren't prisoners. But we are. They may not guard us, but then again, there's nowhere to go. If we fail to fight and are caught, the Troll King will sacrifice us to his beast. If we die in the arena, we meet his beast. If we run and hide, eventually we'll die. No one escapes Eida.

The only way out of this realm is through my pardon. The death of four thousand souls. I swallow against the lump forming in my throat. I'll survive however I must in this realm until I've killed them all and can leave it. My throat dries as my thoughts wander back to my mother. Alone in Bridgewick.

I never meant to abandon her there.

Pressing my lips together, I lie back on the blanket and wad my one extra pair of clothes beneath my head.

My thumb brushes the soft flesh on the underside of my wrist. So many Unmarked Fallen have been taken by the trolls, sold, and branded as slaves to a master. Most of which I've seen are human themselves. Maybe it wouldn't be so bad. The Marked Fallen have food, warm beds, and medical care.

For a moment, I bask in the memory of home. The way my hot bath rolled over my skin, or when Mother brought me a blanket hung by the fire after a long winter night of hunting. I could bundle near the hearth for hours.

The memory sours, as I imagine a pair of vicious eyes raking over my body, and I cringe. It's not hard to imagine what a master would seek from his slave.

Haven is safe—for the most part. When the trolls roam through, we scatter just like the Seekers. Still, I'd take this over being Marked.

Resting my arms over my stomach, I let my eyes slip closed. The day's battle plays through my memory. The stiff vibrations that traveled over my arms as our swords met, the tremble that now accompanies my fingers with every move because I let his shield find my wrist.

Who brings child's armor into Eida's arena?

My thoughts linger on the thin resistance of his belly against my blade as I ended our battle in Badavaru. I squeeze my hands into fists. The memory of blood gushing from the Seeker's wound, his pallid skin and fading gaze is too fresh.

I recoil from the images, but his blood speckles my fingers. An ever-present reminder. I'm not even sure when during our battle it happened. Snatching the soiled cloths I'd tied around my palms; I scrape his blood from my skin.

"Kill or be killed," I whisper into the small space. With nothing to echo the sound, the words disappear into the chilled air.

Survival. That's all I want—what we all want in this world. It always comes at a cost, though. One I have no choice but to pay if I'm ever going to see my mother again. I swallow against the impossibility. I must cling to something even if it is unrealistic.

My gaze wanders back to the stained cloth. A life for a life. And if I must choose between my life or a Seeker's, I choose mine. Every time.

The arena slips back into my mind's eye. The flash of steel. The man toppling onto his side, expression torn with disbelief. The growing pool of blood. I shut my eyes against the memory, every drop of blood like a barrage of arrows. My stomach clenches as the man's eyes glass over in my memory, and his body slumps against the ground.

Guilt...

Squeezing my eyes shut tighter, I focus on my breaths before the pain can spill over.

Murderer.

My jaw tightens, and I grind my teeth.

Monster.

Tears burn behind my eyes. They will not burn. One of us had to die in that arena. I won't show remorse for someone who would have killed me had I not killed him first. I refuse to meet Eida's beast.

My emotions simmer until the hate-filled words are replaced with one: *Survivor.*

A sense of calm floats through my blood like a meandering river. Peaceful and numb. I stare ahead at the darkness, willing the serenity to remain with me.

Tib stole my life two years ago. An ache crawls through my chest. I was only sixteen. I refuse to let anyone else steal what little control I have left. I may fight for the trolls of Eida, but I do not belong to them. I will not be their monster.

I blink, and tears cling to my lashes. If only I knew how to avoid becoming one. What would my mother think if she saw me now? I wipe the back of my hand over my eyes and inhale a steadying breath. The violet sky softens with night on its way, and my breaths fall into a calm, rhythmic lull.

Once I used to lay beneath stars, tracing their patterns and imagining traveling among them. I grimace. I haven't seen a star in years.

Before my mind dips into a dreamless sleep, a solemn knell rises over the camp. My eyes flutter open. Exhaustion tugs at my bones, but I shove it away. After checking that the waterskin is still at my hip, I crawl from my bed and onto the path between our tents.

"Night falls!" A man's gritty voice cries, his lengthy build towering over the other Fallen.

Night never truly falls in Eida with neither a sun nor moon, but the rolling violet clouds that crackle with magic dim at the day's end, when trolls no longer draw power from its reserves. I glance at the sky, a wine-soaked tapestry.

People scramble over the slick ground to gather around the Fallen and his handbell. Bodies shuffle into mine, many wiping the sleep from their eyes. My chest tightens, and I resist the urge to shove the Unmarked off me. A yawn stretches in my throat. Pinching my lips, I swallow my exhaustion. If the bellringer is to send me to the market, he must believe I have the energy.

"Six hours," the man says. He spins in a slow circle to meet each of the Fallen who've heard his call. He points his handbell to the dark clouds above us. "Six hours until light. Who will go to the market this night?"

The men and women surrounding me hesitate, their gazes falling to their feet and their hands preoccupied with their worn clothing.

"I believe it's my turn." A woman with a thick midnight braid swishing against her thighs steps forward.

"I am with you," says a man sidling up to the woman.

"It's too dangerous!" A sharp voice cuts through the crowd, and its owner pushes her way to the front. "If you're caught, you'll be Marked for sure. They'll rip out the monsters inside you."

The bellringer turns on the woman, his dark gaze pinning her in place. A sheen of sweat glistens on the woman's pale brow.

"You must be new to Eida," the bellringer says. His voice is quiet, but his tone is deadly. "It's more dangerous not to. The Troll King doesn't care what happens to us outside of that arena. He only takes care of his Marked Fallen. We show up to fight and maybe one day reach our pardons. Until that day, we raid to survive."

The woman slinks back into the crowd, her gaze boring into the ground.

Two others join the pair. A broad man with sandy hair shorn above his ears and gold glinting along his earlobes that the bellringer calls Erom. The other is a stocky man with a blunt beard that holds its form against the breeze.

"I'll go." My hand rests on the pommel of my sword, and my fingers drum against my waist.

The bellringer shakes his head. "No, not you."

"I'm completely capable," I say, my defenses rising. I swallow against the dryness in my throat. "I've taken down—"

"We know how many you've slain, Fallen," the bellringer says. "You just got out of the arena. You need rest."

I shake my head. Rest is not coming; I need a distraction. I need water. "Don't tell me what I need."

The bellringer watches me as though he's seen hundreds of other Fallen make this same choice. As though he might understand why I don't want to close my eyes tonight. Or why risking my life to help our camp might muffle the memory of the stadium.

"Keep to the path. The Seekers are bound to Ghora, but they wander. Give them your back, and they'll run you through." His lips fall into a flat line, but he hands me an oversized burlap sack along with the other four travelers. "Return before first light. We go back for no one."

The rules are always the same. We may camp together, we may gather supplies to share among us, but we each fight for our own survival. That's the way it is for everyone in Eida.

It's the way I like it. If you can't take care of yourself in this realm, you have no chance of ever escaping it.

Tents flank the edges of Haven, lining the streets, and we tiptoe through the darkness. I tuck my wrist against my side, hiding the even skin tones unbroken by a branding iron. Not that anyone will see us. We should reach the Crossing in under an hour, slip around the denser parts of Araütteve in two. That leaves a few hours to steal what we can and get back to Haven before the trolls awaken.

The obsidian gives way to wilting flowers as we near the Crossing. My gaze skims the horizon for the leafy canopy spread over the towering tree. A tunnel carved through the tree's enormous trunk, the Crossing is the only way into Arautteve and the market. The stone beneath my feet softens with soil.

With an eye on my sandals, I pick my way over brittle shrubs and skirt around the sparse vegetation. Quiet and precise. A drum beats in my ears, a flare of anxiety rippling from my heart. No one should be at market until light, but that doesn't mean it will be empty. My shoulders stiffen, and I glance behind me. My gaze wanders through the shadows, but I'm met with only barren land. Shaking my head, I fall back into line.

The woman's words from camp echo in my head. *If you're caught, you'll be Marked for sure. They'll rip out the monsters inside you!*

My steps are silent against the earth, my ears pricked for any sound of pursuit. All is quiet, hushed. Too quiet. Tension rides the air, and hair prickles along my neck. Slowing my steps, I peek over my shoulder. The others in my company hesitate, too. The man with the shorn hair—Erom—draws his blade, the scrape of steel ringing into the silence with its warning. We stare into the depths of Ghora's darkness. Waiting.

I bristle as nothing happens. The darkness is thick and pungent but still. My chest barely rises with shallow breaths, but as I scan the deadened land I wonder if my senses are off. The tension in my arms wanes. I relax.

"Please!" A man lunges from the shadows toward our company. "Help me!"

I leap away along with the others, drawing my two swords and aiming them at the man. His gnarled fingers clutch onto Erom's arm, dragging himself closer to us. Erom shakes his arm in an ill-attempt to rid himself of the outsider, but the man holds tight.

"You must help me," he hisses. Dark, sweltering circles form under his eyes, his cheeks sunken and sallow.

A stomach-wrenching stench hovers around us. My eyes burn, and I can't breathe. Erom gags before lifting a foot and shoving it into the man's gut. The outsider stumbles backward and falls, his lightweight shirt rising. Bruises paint his pale skin, dark veins trailing over his exposed ribs.

"The Plague!" The stocky man gasps.

The Seeker's expression contorts with rage, his pitiful plea erased in a heartbeat. He stands on unsteady legs, grinding his teeth as his eyes bore into Erom. He withdraws a rusty dagger, his hand trembling. "I shouldn't have expected anything more from a couple of Fallen," the man spits.

He shuffles a step toward us, and I raise my blade. The man is already lost. I don't hesitate. Covering my mouth with the empty sack, I leap forward and slash my blade through the outsider's chest. Blood splatters down his front and across my blade. He groans, the sound elongated and eerily reaching toward the sky for too long.

My gaze flits to the sandy-haired man from our company. Erom stands opposite the rest of us, our weapons standing point between our bodies. The Plague is the most contagious disease in Eida with no remedy or cure in this realm. Its cure lies in the human realm. Once you've been touched, it's inevitable. The fatigue sets within hours. The bruises a day or two. And the barreling scent of death... The Plague will steal your life in less than a week.

Erom stretches his fingers on the arm the plagued man had grasped. He's been touched. He's as good as dead, and he knows it, too. His lips arc into a deep frown, and he nods. A resigned acceptance. Tears blanket his eyes, but he sniffs and blinks them away.

"So it is, mates," he says. He meets each of our gazes, his eyes lingering on the woman with the long braid. He takes all of her in. And when he speaks, it's as if his words are only for her. "It's been a fair bit of time getting to know yeh."

I lower my blade. The stocky man whose name I still don't know stands at my side. He offers a single nod in farewell before he thrusts his sword under Erom's rib cage. A rattled gasp rips from Erom's throat, and blood gurgles over his tongue and pours down his chin.

Erom collapses to his knees, his body retching against the gushing blood. I flatten my lips, but I don't dare close my eyes. A full minute ticks by before Erom tips onto his side and gives a final, ragged exhale—nothing more now than a draining corpse. I stare at his form, a metallic tang and rush of powerlessness tainting the air. His expression slackens, and his skin pales beneath my gaze. My eyes flit to the woman traveling with us. Her jaw is clenched, her chin lifted, but sorrow consumes her glassy eyes.

I force a full breath of that copper-tinged air into my lungs, quelling the twisted knot in my chest. My concern isn't for the man—I didn't know him well, yet something still turns my stomach. Sour and wretched. Erom chose to die. I have no doubt he could have stood against the rest of us, but he didn't. He died to protect us. To protect her.

The woman presses her fingers to her lips and then to her heart before turning away from the lifeless body. My eyes fall on Erom's corpse. I'm not sure I would have done what he did. What if he could have survived? What if there was another way? He willingly gave up his life for the rest of us—and now he's gone.

"Dispose of your weapon," the stocky man orders. "It's contaminated." He tosses his own blade into the shadows behind a wilted bush.

My fingers regrip my sword's hilt, and I tighten my jaw. This was my good sword. I'm better with two. Grinding my teeth, I glance over my shoulder at Erom. My frustration dies in my chest. We just lost an Unmarked. I toss my blade with the other weapon and step back, shaking my head.

Without another glance in Erom's direction, I step into line behind the rest of the company. I grip and regrip empty air, wishing I'd let someone else end the outsider's life. With any luck, someone will have left a spare blade in the market. Otherwise, the first move I make against my next Seeker will be to take his.

As we round a corner, the Crossing's great tree towers over us like a mountain, its trunk wider than a river. I tip my head to the clouds and am blanketed with a leafy treetop. I never get used to seeing the Crossing's magnificence. Braided roots twist upward from the ground, intertwining with one another.

Sprouting from each side of the tree, roots twist together into a tangled wall, one set disappearing east into the shadows toward Badavaru. The other side travels west as far as the eye can see, creating a wall to separate Ghora from everyone else. A wide passage cuts deep into the tree's trunk, and a light mist swirls beyond.

Arautteve.

I lift my hand and brush my fingertips through the mist. Warm and inviting. It's as though a line has been drawn between Arautteve and Ghora, and the Crossing's great tree is the gateway. My fingertips thaw as I play with Arautteve's air. The difference between the two districts is tangible.

Dropping my hand, it swings through Ghora's substantial despair and hangs at my side. The darkness kisses my skin like a friend, its scent tainted by death. A wry smile crawls onto my lips. Death and I have been kindred spirits for a while now.

A quick jaunt along the wall to slip past the Marked Fallen's district, and we'll have the market to ourselves. Erom's lifeless eyes flash in my vision. My throat tightens, and I brush my hand over my neck. We've already lost one. If we aren't careful, none of us will make it back.

Tightening the large sack around my shoulder, I dip my head and cross the Great Tree's gateway. The mist crawls along my bare skin as we slink along Arautteve's edge. I hug the wall, careful not to venture too far into the Marked Fallen's district. In the arena, my bracers shield my unbranded wrists—everyone must think I belong to another. My wrists are bare now, the leather bands left at Haven, still unwashed from my latest victory. If the Marked Fallen discover I'm Unmarked, traipsing through their district… I swallow as a knot forms in my stomach.

The farther from the Crossing we wander, the harder it is to breathe Arautteve's thick air. Fragrant blooms mark nearly every surface, their potent scents smothering the fresh air. I scrunch my nose against the forceful scents. You wouldn't think it by looking at this land, but in some ways entering this district is far more dangerous than entering the arena.

Those in Araütteve and the market want more from us Unmarked Fallen than our lives. They want allegiance. My stomach cramps, and a low rumble echoes through our company. I shove my fist against my abdomen to silence its moaning. Still, I get a few glares from the other travelers.

I chew the edge of my lip to trick my mind into thinking I eat food. Instead, my mind wanders to the spoils we'll gather at the market tonight, and my mouth waters. The soft crunch of an Elderberry scone. The savor of fried cheese stretching over my tongue. My stomach growls again.

The stocky man tosses me a piece of bark. "Quiet that noise, or you'll wake the entire district."

Heat crawls over the back of my neck as the rest of the Unmarked turn their stares on me. Setting my jaw, I give a curt nod and slip the bark between my lips to chew.

Ahead of us, a graveyard of bone-white tents spreads across the horizon. My lips curl into a smile. Aside from the striking fabric, the market is dark and still. Tonight, we'll have hours and full pickings. Our feet barely brush the packed dirt as we creep into the main square. The other Unmarked scatter into the surrounding tents. My pace slows, and I stop in the barest shadow of a large one-armed statue.

My fingertips brush over the pedestal's crumbling stones, its inscription hardly visible anymore: *Eida's first Fallen.* We've all heard of Alec the Brave—the only Fallen to have slain two thousand Seekers before being skewered himself. The trolls honor him for the sheer number of Seekers he stopped from receiving their wishes. Decay and disregard have marred the old hero's stone flesh. Now he's nothing more than a faded memory.

So much for glory.

I draw my sack over my shoulder and cinch it open. Most tents are barren, but not all. And if you know where to look, you'll find no merchant takes *everything* home with him at the end of the night.

With a silent inhale, I slip into the nearest tent.

CHAPTER FOUR

RUBBISH. COMPLETE RUBBISH.

Bowls of low-end baubles. Shelves of pointless trinkets. All litter we have no use for in Haven.

I abandon the tent and disappear into another, the barest of sounds crunching beneath my sandals. One hour. That's all the time we have left here if we expect to make it back to Haven before the merchants return to their shops, and the Marked Fallen flood the streets of Arautteve.

I never want to find myself in their district during daylight. It would be near impossible to reach the Crossing unnoticed once they're awake.

I dart from tent to tent, gathering bits and pieces, but my sack's still too light. My hand twitches at my side. It's not nearly enough. I inhale a steadying breath, and the dry air scorches my parched throat. That sands-blasted thirst! Burning and biting.

Time is running out. I need water. The Unmarked need food. And my sack has barely enough to feed one person for a day.

Picking up my pace, I climb over a storefront's counter and drop inside. Bone chimes clatter and the canvas rustles as it closes behind me. A tribal rug spreads over the dusty ground. My blood pounds in my ears as my fingers still the swaying chimes. Pressing myself against the counter, I listen.

A subtle breeze carries the constant hum from the clouds, but nothing out of the ordinary. I slowly count to ten before rummaging through the shelves built-in beneath the counter.

"Finally, something as good as gold," I whisper, lifting a basket of day-old rolls. Tossing a piece of bread into my mouth, I dump the rest into my sack.

My fingers caress carefully angled urns and test the weight of sealed jugs. The full ones join the other provisions in my sack, and I leave the near-empty behind. No water, though.

Darting to the other side of the tent, my toe catches the edge of the intricately woven rug. The corner folds over, and my heart sticks in my throat. I stare at a trap door.

Every nerve in my body screams to run. I've heard of these doors. A place where Unmarked are imprisoned until they're sold. Crouching next to the trapdoor, I brush my fingertips over the single steel ring. One pull, and I could set them all free.

But what else lies inside with them? There could be guards—Unmarked Fallen fetch a fancy price in the market. Or the Plagued. I draw back my touch, closing my fingers within my fist. As quietly as possible, I replace the rug and retreat. Climbing over the counter, I nearly gasp. The flash of steel strips my breath away. Cold dread seeps down my spine.

A long, curved blade glints beneath the sky's dim light. It scrapes against the hard ground, carving a small furrow behind the troll who drags it. I don't move. I don't breathe.

The troll holds a worn rope in his hands, one end coiled into a noose. His steps are slow and heavy. I balance on the countertop, rooted in place, pleading his gaze doesn't shift in this direction. No matter what these trolls once were, they have become a vicious lot that constantly crave blood. As soon as the creature notices me, it will be my blood.

My gaze slides back toward the safety of the tent. To the trap door I'd now give anything to hide within.

The troll trudges past the tent, his beady eyes mercifully fixed on the path ahead. My hope hangs by a thread as despair settles into my stomach. One glance southward, and I'm dead.

The troll rummages through the tents, not bothering to hide his looting. He drapes beaded cords around his neck and shoves small trinkets into his pockets. Thick, snakelike skin covers his bulging arms, and he bears no marking. This troll is the lowest of the low.

With his attention fixated on his treasures, I slip off the counter and back inside the tent. I loose a silent breath and press my back against the counter's lower shelves.

Sweat beads on my brow, and my palms grow slick. Clay urns scrape against each other outside my tent, and the troll tosses something that lands with a loud thud. Daylight is almost upon us. I can't stay here. A merchant finding me would be no better than a troll.

Tipping my head against the countertop, I peek over into the market square. Something shatters in a nearby tent, and I lock my ear to it as my gaze slips through the fading shadows. A quick dodge around the tent parallel to mine, and I'll be out of the troll's line of sight.

Slipping back into the safety of the tent, I inhale a trickle of courage. The clamor from the market square silences. My muscles tense, and my breaths thin. With no noise, I have no sign of how far the troll has wandered.

I peek over the counter again, and my stomach tightens. The troll stands ahead of me, his beady eyes boring into mine. A sneer crawls across his face. His rotted teeth gnash behind his cracked lips. The troll's large fingers and overgrown nails caress the rope in his hand.

Panic bolts through my veins, and without a second thought, I leap from the storefront. Rolling over my shoulder, and beneath his outstretched arm, I pop to my feet. Before I take a step, a spark ignites in my chest. It rips through the tissue and singes my lungs. I gasp, and the inhale fans the inner spark into a flame.

"Gah!" I press a palm against my sternum and collapse. The flames leap through my chest.

The troll closes the distance between us in a matter of steps, thrusting his large face into mine. A stench rolls off his breath, and I stifle a gag. "Well, what do we have here?"

"Release me." I mean to command him, but it comes out as a plea. If he's trapped me with his magic, I have no choice but to follow.

"Oh, I haven't done anything yet." The troll practically drools, but I can barely register his words. The firestorm claws up my throat, scorching lung and body. Burning, ravenous, ready to consume all flesh in its path. Smoke billows across my vision. The flames blister everything.

"We caught ourselves a little snack, we have." The troll lunges for me, his prickly skin wrapping around my ankle.

Fight back! I know I must, but I can't focus. The heat sears through my body as the troll drags me into the center of the square.

I thrash in a pitiful attempt against the troll's tightened grip. Sharp pebbles dig into my back.

Is this how you want to die!? My hands scramble for the blades at my waist, and I unsheathe a dagger. Raising the blade, my hands shake, and sweat slicks my palms. I curse under my breath for the weakness. The fear. I aim for the troll's wrist and attack. The dagger cuts through the air but halts a hair's breadth above the troll's skin.

I tug at the blade, but it is wedged midair, as though stuck in a stone. The troll releases my foot and steps back. A snort ripples through the empty market, thick mucus vibrating within the sound. My hope sinks like a boat capsizing in a growing storm.

There is a second troll.

His clawed hands curl in front of his bare chest, and lightning sparks between his fingertips. He stares at me from beneath his thick brows, his swollen lips curved into a twisted smile.

My stomach turns. Bitter and vile. Heat burns against my palm. I fight it and tighten my grip around my blade, but the fire on my hand sears. I clench my teeth, and the heat scorches. It's too hot. I drop the red-hot blade, and it clatters to the ground. Cradling my burnt hand against my chest, my hope plummets.

"Rise," the second troll commands.

I drag myself to my feet, my movements not my own. They're stiff, unsynchronized, and I nearly collapse onto my face. My entire body moves at the troll's will.

"Get her hands, Chorin," the troll wielding his magic barks.

The troll who had caught me—Chorin—ties my hands behind my back. The burn smarts against my palm, and I inhale a sharp breath.

Chorin strokes my hair, letting it knot around his fingers, and tugs my head upward to meet his face. "Why struggle, little one?" he says. "You have nothing worth living for now."

I clench my teeth, wishing to spit fire at him, but I already know he's right. They'll strip away what little freedom I have left. The troll slides the noose around my neck, and there is nothing I can do to stop him. He tightens the knot until it brushes my throat then fingers the rope's tail and gives it a small tug. I stumble forward.

Flaming nights.

The trolls drag me behind them through the market, and I can hardly stay upright. At least it's not to Eida's beast, I think to myself. I imagine a large feline creature prowling from the shadows, flames trailing from its back as if it's caught on fire.

I've never met the beast, but the tales have painted a vivid picture in my mind. A magic-starved creature used to dispose of the dead…or the disobedient. It feasts on magic. It craves it. My gaze skims the dark horizon, and a haze rolls through my vision.

The trolls lead me from the market and over a small hill. A moth-eaten tent is anchored into the ground far from any others. Debris of what once was a flourishing shop litters the ground. Shattered earthenware, bowing tent poles, forgotten moments.

A swift breeze stirs the remnants of the shop, and I choke against the stale, musty air.

"What do we do with her, Gunther?" Chorin's high-pitched voice whines. He whips the rope toward me, and its coarse fibers sting my cheek.

Gunther tromps forward and brushes his thick finger over the sting. He grabs my wrist, his coarse skin needling into my flesh. "She is Unmarked." His eyes flash to mine. "She'd fetch a decent price. I say we take her to market."

A cold sweat coats my palms, but I force my face to remain expressionless.

Chorin drops his gaze over my body, lingering on my thighs. His tongue smacks his lips. "She has a bit of meat on her bones still. Could be a tasty snack?"

My eye twitches, and I set my jaw. Or there's that.

Gunther grabs my leg above my knee as though inspecting a slab of pork. His rotting teeth grind together, and he takes a long sniff.

I don't want to be claimed by a master. Or die.

"You're making a big mistake," I hiss.

Chorin jerks away, startled. An amused smile widens his round cheeks, and he points a stubby finger at me. "Oh, it speaks."

"It's not a mistake. You'll make a fine meal." Gunther releases my knee and stands. His head nearly brushes the tent's tattered canvas. "It's been a long while since my pal and I have feasted on something so fresh."

He grabs my wrist and forces me to my knees. Heat burns against my chest.

"I've met my monster," I spit. "You do not want to."

A lie. I've never even felt it stir. Not in Bridgewick. Not in Eida. My monster has always been buried deep.

"You've met your monster?" Chorin giggles. "An Unmarked?" He stumbles backward in a fit of laughter. "Go on, tell us then. What are you?"

My lie snares in my throat. I meant to catch his attention. I didn't think it would work. The trolls strive to unleash every Fallen's inner monster, and every Fallen strives to stifle it. An inner monster unleashed means a stronger fighter in the arena. It also can't be undone. Once you unleash your monster, it becomes a part of you forever.

The troll's laughter ebbs, and I still haven't spoken. His smile fades, and his near-bare brows angle sharply. He gnashes his teeth inches from my face. "Well, what is it?"

"A hellhound," I growl.

Gunther sidles next to him. Lust twists his ugly face, overpowering any concern that I may lie. His lips curl into a grotesque smile. "We've never had a hellhound."

CHAPTER FIVE

I stumble down the ladder and sprawl onto the hard floor beneath the trap door.

The trolls had led me outside the main market to a threadbare tent with no contents other than a worn hatch on the floor. Now, dozens of eyes gleam from the shadows, their hosts pressed against the walls.

So, the rumors are true. Merchants do imprison the Unmarked until sold.

I scramble to my feet and leap for the ladder. Gunther laughs, drawing it out from the cellar. My hand flies to my hip, but my weapons are gone. My longsword's steel sparkles in the troll's grip.

Cursed trolls. I grind my teeth. There goes my second blade.

With a leering smile, Gunther retreats from the trap door. "Don't rough yourself up too much," Gunther laughs. "You are rare, hellhound. We have much need for you yet."

The creaking of aged wood echoes through the cellar, and the world above us disappears. Blood pulses behind my ears. The haggard breaths of the other Unmarked fade. Whimpers and muffled cries cease to exist. Only my scrambled thoughts, urging me to move.

But to where? I can't reach the trap door, and the troll has likely locked us in. A disarming hiss slithers across the top of the door. My step falters, and I hesitate. Violet mists of magic curl through the hatch's cracks. Throwing my arm over my mouth, I retreat into the shadows with the others.

I hold my breath, waiting, watching. The magic curls through the room, lining the ceiling and crawling down the walls. And with its approach, the crowd tightens. A mass of limbs burrowing together and sinking to the ground. Me at its center.

"Quick! Quick!" comes a high-pitched whisper. A woman dressed in shadows, opens her arms as a few of the younger Unmarked scurry into the gathering. She buries their little faces and arms at the center, where they can stay untouched.

"Hush now." Another voice. Rougher, more matronly. "There's no need to fear."

Our breaths share space, heads bowed low and covered by shoulders or arms. A young boy's wide eyes glisten in the dim light shed through the cracks above us. He can't be more than eleven or twelve. Why would the trolls have taken him? A child? Unless… my thoughts sharpen despite the panic laced through the hovel. Was he born here?

The boy's eyes meet mine, fear and fury. His unkempt brows narrow, and his head tilts. I match his expression and try to retreat, but there are too many bodies pressed against mine.

A burning tingle caresses my calf, and I jolt. The magic crawls over us all. My eyes dart among the other Unmarked, watching as they wait for whatever this spell will do. Only does my gaze stop roaming when they settle on the boy's again.

The boy intertwines his fingers with mine and whispers. "It will be okay."

A boy. A child. Comforting me in the face of horror? But I believe him. An unsettling calm stills the adrenaline demanding I hold on. The unnatural peace like a shackle against my own emotions.

The boy doesn't break his gaze—his bold, golden eyes holding mine. The false tranquility robs me of my strength. Exhaustion breeds through every limb, and I'm so very tired. I try to keep my gaze locked on the boy's, but my eyes grow heavy. His do, too. The shadows shift and tilt and teeter forward. Down. Down.

My head swims with nightmares of foolish, hopeful things. A pain worse than despair—that hope you know will never come to pass. A dull ache pulses through my limbs as though I've lied far too long in one spot.

How long was I asleep? My head throbs, and I can't seem to pull my thoughts together. A heavy grogginess steals my energy. A loud, angry grumble echoes through the room as a stab of hunger shoots through my stomach.

Dread seeps into my bones. How long have I been unconscious?

Pushing myself into a seated position, I rub the remnants of the sleeping spell from my eyes and stretch my stiff muscles. We were lucky that's all his spell did. Squinting into the darkness, I scan the room for the boy who'd held my hand.

Bare walls. Empty shadows. A spray of blood across the dusty floor.

"Hello?" My own voice ripples back to me, distorted and trembling. I whip in a full circle. "Hello?"

My heart plunges to my stomach. I'm alone.

I scramble to my feet and stare at the sealed hatch. Bare remnants of light cut through the slats. It's morning.

They're gone. Every single one of the Unmarked that had been with me, taken.

Jumping, I swipe my hand toward the hatch but I'm just out of reach. I slept while the trolls came and stole the others away… The young boy's golden eyes sparkle in my vision. I wonder if he felt fear when the trolls came for him. Or if he tried to fight when they dragged him away from the others. I wonder if he lives.

Sorrow embraces my focus, but I shove it away. There's nothing I could have done for any of them. I'm an Unmarked. We're all on our own in Eida.

A growl stirs in my throat, and I leap again, my fingers brushing the wood. This time, the hatch shifts. I stumble as I land but catch myself against the wall.

The hatch groans as Chorin hefts it open and lowers the ladder. Morning's light floods the darkness. I resist shielding my eyes.

"Hellhound," Chorin says in his high-pitched whine. He points a stubby finger at me and then to his feet.

"Where did you take the rest of them?" My voice betrays me and cracks. I don't care about the others, but I have to know where he took the boy.

His lips screw to the side, his smile vicious with the answer I already know he won't tell me. His smile slips, and he bares his rotting teeth. "Climb out before I drag you out."

I glare at Chorin's ugly sneer. What are the chances I could fight my way out of the market? I clench my jaw. They aren't good. With aching muscles, I climb the ladder.

I hold my hands by my shoulders in false surrender as I emerge into the bustling streets outside the market square. Merchants and patrons scurry toward the market's entrance. My gaze drops to my dagger hugging Chorin's hip. A quick lunge and I could snatch my blade and shove it through his belly. I run my tongue over my teeth.

"Tut tut," Gunther says from behind Chorin, his hands poised in front of his body. He flourishes his fingers, and steel snakes around my wrists, another set shackling my ankles.

"No!" I tug against the bonds and step away from the trolls, but it's too late. A single chain sprouts from the binds at my feet and crawls through the air until it has welded itself to the restraints at my wrists.

The cold steel kisses my skin like a reaper come to steal my soul. My body tingles as Gunther's magic invades my control and takes over. I can't flinch. I can't resist. I've lost control.

I am a prisoner.

Panic surges through my veins as Chorin tugs the chain forward, and I follow like an obedient mutt.

"There is a good crowd of merchants today," Gunther says. His eyes roam over my body. "Some Traders, too."

My breath hitches. Traders. Elite Fallen who were offered the chance to train instead of fight. They have no pardon to reach in this realm, but neither must they ever enter the arena again.

A Trader will buy you and call you his or hers. They train you. They own you. They're fierce and unyielding, reserved to discipline the most savage of monsters.

My gaze skims over the sky as if, for once, I'll find an escape from this realm. But the sky rolls lazily in cloud cover. Unless I reach my pardon, I'll never leave.

The Troll King expects his Traders to train their Fallen to be lethal and unbeatable in the arena. He expects them to unleash the monsters within their Fallen. To control them. A lump grows in my throat. Eventually, someone will discover my lie, and when they do, it'll be my carcass lying at the beast's maw.

Aside from the training, the Troll King doesn't care what happens to his Fallen, be they beaten or loved or ignored altogether. I'd prefer the latter.

The trolls will sell me as a girl with hellhound's blood in her veins, and I'll belong to the highest bidder. It doesn't matter whom they sell me to, though. I won't be anyone's pawn.

"You're a bit scuffed up," Gunther says. "But I don't think it will be mattering. Move."

My feet stumble forward like a puppet whose strings are all the wrong lengths.

We crest a low hill, and noise rises from the market. The cacophony rumbles through the ground, a volcano begging to be born beneath our feet.

Chorin shuffles ahead, and the market spreads before us. Instead of an empty square, there's hardly space to breathe. Trolls lumber between the tents, bouncing into each other, with an occasional Fallen tugged along behind them. Voices argue over the price of goods, others thrust their hands to their hearts in a gesture of trade. It's chaos.

Gunther cuts a path through the hoard, and Chorin and I take advantage of the sparsity left in his wake. He slips through the buyers and sellers with precision, never falling off course for a moment. My gaze wanders among the crowd and dozens of escape routes sift through my mind.

The chains chafe against my wrists. If only the trolls hadn't bound me. I won't get far shackled like this.

My eyes flit among the merchants and buyers, all busy trading coin for goods. Gunther ignores them all.

"You have already found a buyer?" The question tumbles from my lips.

Chorin's gaze trails to mine from the corner of his eye. His lips uptick into a smile. "The most notorious in Eida."

The dense mob thickens, and we press ourselves deeper into the square. Stale sweat weaves around us, and the scent of unwashed bodies coats my tongue.

Gunther halts in front of a large, white canvas. With a flourish of his hand, his control over my body melts like ice in the summer sun. As though he knows I pose no threat in the presence of a Trader. A breeze billows behind the entrance flap, and I catch the scent of burnt woodchips. It's rich and amicable and welcoming. A lie.

A soberness flows through my veins, and my stomach tightens. Nothing good waits for me within this tent.

Gunther lifts the spotless flap—stark in comparison to the stained tents nestled on either side of it—and gestures for me to enter. My blood runs cold. The time to flee is gone.

When I don't move, Chorin rams a sharp finger into my back, and I stumble forward. He slogs in behind me, and the flap folds us into the dimly lit enclosure.

My gaze flits through the haze as my eyes adjust. A small coal oven in the corner. Scattered papers over a desk. A basin of water nestled against the ground. My tongue turns to sand, and I lick my dry lips.

Forcing my eyes from temptation, I settle on the shadow behind the desk. I blink. The shadow takes form—a man. His black leather boots cross atop the large desk, and his legs are stretched long. Tilting his head, the light from a nearby candle flickers across his face. Dark hair brushes his shoulders, and a trimmed beard trails his jaw. Shadows hug his features making his already tanned skin disappear further into the flame's low light.

Removing his feet from the desk, his boots' clasps scrape against each other, and the room fills with the sounds of battle. He stands and steps around his desk. Thick muscle wraps around his bare shoulders, and I can see the firm slope of his waist beneath his sleeveless tunic. I stiffen, and an uncomfortable warmth sweeps over my skin.

His storm-filled eyes wander across my body as though searching every crevice for something. I tighten my jaw and lift my chin. I will not shudder in front of this monster.

"You have found a hellhound, I heard." The man's voice is the sound of a crackling fire and warm butter, of frothy ale. I don't trust him.

He circles me, his steps slow and methodical. His chin dips as his gaze meanders over every inch of my body, and suddenly I wish I'd scraped together more clothing. I'm surprised. Eida's most notorious Trader doesn't look much older than me. I'd expected a man with ash woven through his hair.

"Fifty coin," he says.

Gunther snatches my arm and hurls me behind him. I stumble against his assault, barely catching myself before splaying through the tent flaps. The trolls snarl and bare their yellow teeth. The man doesn't flinch.

"That's robbery. She is a hellhound!" Gunther roars.

The man snatches a knife from his belt and presses its blade against Gunther's neck. Gunther backs down, the tension icing. The man glances at the trolls from beneath a lock of hair. His gaze flicks from their beady eyes to mine.

"Show me."

Gunther scrambles for my arm and tosses me between him and the Trader. "Well, go on. Do it!"

Shallow breaths slip between my paper-thin lips. Lies. My loose tongue has weaved a broken web, one with a single taut thread ready to snap. I lock my eyes with the Trader's. If anything, I hope he'll see indignation rather than dishonesty.

"Enough of this! She's a hellhound, and at the least can warm your bed, Trader." Gunther licks his lips, the thought lingering on his tongue. "Two hundred coin, or she can warm mine."

The man's stare lingers on my face, as though waiting for me to perform. Or, perhaps, he sees the truth of why I don't.

"Good for nothing Fallen! Can't even shift properly," Gunther growls. He raises his hand to strike me, but the man steps into the light and locks a fist around Gunther's wrist.

"You plan to mar and weaken goods you are trying to sell?" The Trader cocks a well-groomed brow at Gunther. "This must be your first time at market, troll. Your incompetence has cost you. One hundred coin, or you can have the girl. Your bed clearly needs her."

Gunther's nostrils flare, his breaths hot and heavy as he glares at the Trader. He grinds his teeth behind his closed lips, his hand curling around my upper arm. "Deal."

With excess force, Gunther shoves me toward the Trader. My feet tangle beneath me, and this time I do fall. The man steps back, and I careen to the ground. He stares down his nose at me as though I'm vermin he wishes weren't thrust upon him.

Gunther and Chorin collect their coin and stalk toward the tent's entrance. Gunther kneels at my side so only I hear his words.

"One week, and you'll be running for Eida's beast." Gunther's eyes flick to the man who sheathes his small blade at his side. "Graeden requires…a great deal."

With a discreet wink, Gunther ducks out from the tent leaving me alone with Graeden. Pressure swells against my chest. The entrance is only a few feet from me. What I wouldn't give to dart through it when Graeden's back is turned. I smother the desire. He would only drag me back in and cause a scene.

"Best get this over with." Graeden retreats to the other side of his desk and draws a fire iron from his drawer. The steel coils in an intricate design no larger than Eida's coin. He sprinkles a shimmering dust over its head.

"What are you doing?" I ask.

Graeden doesn't glance up. He spreads another layer of the fine mist over the steel coil. "Troll magic. It'll keep you in my sights no matter where you go."

My throat tightens, and I swallow thickly. Graeden holds the handle, rotating the branding iron through the air as though practicing. Anger fumes in my chest.

Pushing myself from the ground, I growl, "I will not be your whore."

Graeden's eyes flicker to mine as though he's forgotten he's not alone. His expression remains neutral, if not with a glimmer of irritation. Using his knife, Graeden scrapes burnt flesh from the iron's edge. My lip curls.

"I belong to no one," I seethe.

Graeden's lips settle into a firm line. His jaw clenches, and his eyes flare, golden suns flaming to life. When he speaks, his voice is a low snarl. "You belong to me. Either fall into line or fall to your grave."

My words catch in my throat. I'd rather fall to my grave than climb into his bed, but he's said nothing of his intentions. Graeden shoves the iron's head into the small furnace burning in the back corner. Lifting a steel collar, Graeden storms toward me and pins me in place with his glare. My brain screams to run, but my pride holds my body upright. I won't give him the satisfaction of a chase.

"Don't attack me," Graeden orders, a low grumble vibrating in the back of his throat. "Even while not taking my monster's form, I am swift and, no doubt, better trained than you."

Graeden lifts his hands to my neck and brushes a strand of hair from my shoulder. His fingers trail over the soft flesh, and I close my eyes against his touch. Steel grinds against itself as Graeden locks the collar around my neck. It lands against my collarbone with a heavy thud.

I open my eyes, and my stomach gives a nauseating roll. A chain is fixed to the collar, strung through a small loop at its front. Graeden grabs the chain's two ends and guides me toward his furnace. His movements are purposeful, controlled, as though he's done this dozens of times.

Locking the chains to the furnace's top, Graeden extends his hand. I don't move. Graeden presses his tongue against his cheek, and he inhales a slow breath through his nose. "Your hand."

My hand trembles at my side, and I squeeze it into a fist. Graeden does not own me. Soon enough, he'll understand he'll never break me. Setting my jaw, I burrow my glare into his. Graeden snatches my wrist and rolls it so my palm faces the ceiling. His grip tightens—a shackle of its own kind—and he draws the red-hot iron from the furnace.

"You can scream," Graeden says. "They all do."

His taunt at my strength flames my anger far more than the trolls or even the thought of being his slave. Gritting my teeth, I lock my eyes onto the steam burning through the air surrounding the iron. I will not look away, and I will not scream.

The iron's heat warms my skin like a summer morning as it hovers inches above my wrist. Graeden's eyes flash to mine, awaiting the reaction that surely thrills him with each Unmarked Fallen he purchases. His eyes don't waver from mine as he presses the iron against my skin.

Searing pain scorches my wrist. A bolt of lightning shoots up my arm and sends a wave of darkness across my vision. My nostrils flare, and I inhale long, deep breaths. The blinding pain encapsulates my entire being. A whimper builds in my throat, but I swallow the cry. My gaze flits from my melting flesh and meets Graeden's eyes.

He doesn't grin. No amusement tugs at his eyes. He stares into mine as though evaluating my strength.

I wonder if within them he sees fire. Or if my gaze reflects a child huddled in her mother's arms, watching the world burn. The tent's sharp, woody scent cuts through my reverie, and the flames from my past dissolve.

Sweat beads on my forehead, and I'm unsure how much longer I can hold my tears back. Graeden removes the branding iron roughly, and it peels away from the raw skin beneath it. I gasp as the sharp pain dulls to a biting throb, and the dry air blankets the wound. Reflexively, I tear my arm from his grasp and cradle it against my chest.

Graeden's lips lift into a joyless smile. And when he speaks, venom drips from his words. "You belong to me."

CHAPTER SIX

THE CHAINS HANG HEAVY around my wrists, and shame colors my cheeks.

The Marked Fallen watch me with arched brows and pursed lips. Their eyes bore into my back. I keep my gaze locked anywhere but on them as Graeden tows me through Arautteve.

Unlike Eida's other districts, Arautteve drowns in blossoms. My tongue swipes over my dry lips. The thick, sweet scent is suffocating.

Fragrant roses brush my elbows as we march along flagstone paths. Daisies and pansies curl down from oak rafters. A spray of sunlight scatters among the towering trees, and fruit hangs from their branches. My gaze roams over the grounds and settles on a cluster of mushrooms tucked within a patch of lush grass.

I don't trust this place. Reflexively, I reach for my sword's pommel. The chains tighten around my wrists, and the steel smarts against the freshly burned brand. I close my fingers over empty space, and my heart sinks into my stomach.

It didn't take long for Graeden to pack up his camp and lead me away from the market. We wandered through the district's thick florals for just over an hour before Arautteve's temples dotted the skyline.

My feet ache, but it's a more welcome pain than the flare on my wrist. I turn my arm into my stomach to hide the brand. Not that it matters. No one can see it underneath the shackle.

Graeden leads me around dozens of stone temples, each gaudier than the last. We climb a rounded hill to where at least a dozen training rings spread across the warm sand in a honeycomb pattern.

Not only must warriors fight their opponents within their rings, but they must not step into another's. Wonderful.

Unlike the overpowering florals near the temples, the training yard is barren. Loose sand blankets the land, the life plucked from the ground like the Fallen have been plucked from their homes.

Graeden draws the key to my chains from his pocket. "Marked Fallen must fight. If you cannot do that, you don't belong here."

"I *don't* belong here," I say through clenched teeth, holding his gaze.

Graeden doesn't bat an eye. "Then you belong to Eida's beast."

A pang snaps through my chest, but I keep my mask in place. He'd sacrifice me to Eida's beast? Even with so little magic in my veins? Glancing over my shoulder, I pick at a stray hair clinging to my top as if it's worth more of my attention than his threat. "Maybe. But then you'd be without your shifter."

Graeden glares at me, his jaw tensing. Tearing his gaze from mine, Graeden lifts a sword off a nearby weapon's wall. He brandishes the blade, its sharp edge cutting through the air.

"One chance, Fallen," he says. "You use this weapon to try to escape, and I won't hesitate to end your life. Hellhound or not."

Graeden pulls his own weapon from the wall, a thin blade with a slight curve at its edge. He crouches next to my legs and shoves the key into the lock at my ankles. His face hovers inches from my knee. One swift thrust, and I could launch my knee straight into the side of his head. If I do it hard enough, I could knock him out for enough time to make it close to Haven. My teeth catch my bottom lip.

The chains fall around my feet, and Graeden stands to unlock the shackles against my wrists. His eyes flash to mine. "I won't hesitate."

I roll my neck back to stare him in the eye. I'm not afraid of him.

Graeden hands me the blade along with its sheath and a set of bracers. I tie the thin armor around my wrists and strap the sheath to my waist before Graeden backs me into one of the training rings. I retreat until there's enough space for three Fallen to stand between us.

If I kill Graeden during training, no one will know I escaped. I cleave my sword through the air. Our steel clangs as Graeden catches my blow. He parries my sword, twisting it aside, and I drop to the ground sweeping a leg underneath his. Graeden leaps gracefully over my leg and throws his blade toward my head. I roll out from beneath its edge.

Shock stirs in my stomach, and my jaw drops. "What if I hadn't moved?"

Graeden cuts his sword through the air again, power and anger fueling his movements. I dance out of the way, if only by a few inches. "Then you'd be dead."

My nostrils flare, and I grit my teeth, slashing my weapon toward Graeden with more force. "Lot of good that would do you, *Master*." The word chokes from my throat, and I fill it with as much venom and sarcasm as I can. He will never own me.

"Lot of good you are to me if this is how you fight."

Graeden catches my blade again with his, and pain stings my injured hand from where Gunther burned it. I toss my sword to my non-dominant hand. Graeden draws a whip from his belt. The leather cord cracks the air with a small flick of Graeden's wrist. He snaps the whip toward me, and I raise my forearm, the whip cracking against the leather bracer protecting my skin. I suck in a sharp breath. The bracer may protect my skin from the weapon's sting, but a sharp ache still spreads through my bone.

He drops his sword from mine and lunges. I attempt to parry, but my focus is on my arm. The growing welt pulses in time with my heart, each beat spreading the pain. Clanging steel ricochets against my ears, but my vision tunnels. I lift my blade, and our swords collide again, a jolt trembling up my arm. The singed skin on my hand burns raw.

My feet stumble over themselves as Graeden attacks again, pressing me out of the ring, and I fall onto my rear. Graeden cuts his sword through the air and stops his momentum just as his blade touches my neck. The sound of his sword having clashed against mine disappears into the air. Warmth trickles down my neck. I blink the fatigue and disorientation away. My fingertips brush my neck and come away sticky with blood.

I glare at Graeden, hating the man who calls me his.

Graeden returns my glare, both our chests rising and falling with each other's. I may be the one who ended up bleeding, but a wave of satisfaction rolls through me. At least Graeden is winded, too.

Lowering his blade, Graeden steps back and sheathes his sword. "Araurteve is your home now, Fallen—"

"Ari," I interrupt.

Graeden's gaze darkens as his eyes flit to mine. His slender nose flares, and his jaw tightens. "What?"

"My name is Ari." I push myself to my feet and sheathe my own sword. "You may claim I'm yours, but I'm not a faceless animal. I have a name. And if you expect me to work with you, you will use it."

Graeden stalks forward, a predatory gait, until his angry breath fills the shrinking space between us. He stands a full head higher than me. His chest rises beneath his dark, sleeveless tunic with furious breath. Pinning my gaze to his toned chest, I resist the urge to tilt my head up to look at him like a child.

A rich, musky scent touched with a slight sweetness curls around us. I force my glare to harden. Still, heat rises in my cheeks when I inhale deeper, the scent lingering a little longer than it should. It's been a long time since I've smelled anything so welcome.

Graeden's gaze burns into my face, but I don't meet his eye. "You do not work with me. You work for me. I decide how you eat, how you're punished, how you fare. I will call you what I want. I will call upon you when I want." He leans back enough for his gaze to wander down my body to my waist. He grabs my hip and jerks it against him.

My hand flutters to my blade's hilt, my tongue trailing the back of my teeth. Familiar tension rolls through my muscles in preparation for battle.

Graeden's hand brushes my waist, and his spare hand knocks mine off my sword. His palm folds around its hilt. "You don't get to keep this." A dark smile curls the corner of his lips. Drawing my sword from its sheath, he tucks it into one of his own.

He steps back, and the tension rolls off my skin.

"Watch yourself, Fallen," Graeden warns. "This wouldn't be the first time I trade one of my own Marked to another master. And I may be one of a few left in Eida, if not the only one, who still values virtue."

Graeden whips around and stomps away from the ring. With nowhere else to go, I follow with my scowl locked on the ground.

Graeden's arms cross over his chest, his pointed glare pinned on me again.

I stand at the edge of a large spring on the southeast end of Arautteve. Water cascades down a small waterfall on one end and seeps away from the pool through a small creek at the other. The water is sprinkled with naked Fallen.

"I don't see why this is necessary," I start.

"Get in," Graeden orders.

I close my mouth and huff. The Marked Fallen wash their bodies in the fresh spring, and I can't remember the last time I bathed. I pick at the dried blood beneath my nails.

Small ferns drape their fronds along the clear water's edge, lush plants ooze with pastel petals. A few trees pockmark the pool for privacy interspersed with an occasional crumbling colonnade. It's as though an ancient colosseum had flooded, and they decided to let people bathe here.

"I need to undress." I turn on Graeden, planting my hands on my hips.

"Go ahead."

I glare at him. "Turn around."

"I wouldn't trust you if we stood alone in the Blood Desert with nothing but sand." Graeden doesn't budge. "I'm not letting you out of my sight."

We glare at one another for a long minute. Steam curls up from the spring and coats the back of my legs. Warm droplets trickle over my skin, softening the build-up of grime. My resolve wavers. It's been so long since I've been clean.

Grinding my teeth, I cross my arms over my chest. He won't break me.

Something flares in Graeden's eye, and he smirks.

In a heartbeat, Graeden shoves my shoulder. I stumble, flailing like a newborn, and my feet leave the bank. The bathing pool swallows me, my head slipping under the steaming waters. Breaking through the surface, I gasp and sputter like a fool. Water streams down my face, the high heat tempering to a comfortable warmth as my body adjusts. All for the exception of my injured hand which burns like I hold a raging ball of fire.

Graeden rests his forearms across his knee as he leans over the edge of the pool. His stare doesn't waver from mine. "I said, 'Get in.'"

Hatred boils in the depths of my belly, but I stifle it. Graeden will get his punishment. In the end, we all do.

Sinking until the water laps against my shoulders, I swim away from Graeden's unrelenting eye. Only when I'm sure he can't hear me do I allow a long sigh to escape my lips. The water draws the ache from my muscles. Grime sifts from my clothes and skin and disperses through the spring. I close my eyes and let the steam rise around me.

My sandals dig through the soft earth at the bottom of the pool. The water drifts over my shoulders, and I roll to my back, gradually pulling myself farther away from Graeden. He stands at the edge of the bank, his arms still folded over his chest and his eyes on me.

I rub my hands over my legs, and let the heat soothe the wounds I've worn over the last few years. The burns on my hands sear deeper with the pool's heat, but I shut out the pain. This is a moment to remember.

My back rams into another Fallen, and I lurch forward.

"Sorry," I say, flipping around. "I wasn't paying attention."

A petite girl smiles, her sensual lips the same shade as the rose-colored hair that hangs over her shoulders and pools into the water above her chest. Her pale skin nearly glistens, and pointed ears cut through the veil of her hair. She looks ethereal.

"I see you." Her voice is soft and kind.

My brows raise. "Okay."

"You are troubled, no?"

My mouth falls open to respond, but the words don't come. I peek over my shoulder at Graeden still standing on the bank. Still watching me.

My brows draw together. "Of course, I am. I'm Marked."

The girl lifts her chin, her smile still caressing her unblemished cheeks. "But there's more. You hide a terrible secret."

My stomach turns to stone. The water has lost its lure; I'm ready to leave.

"Don't worry," the girl says. "Your monster will show itself in time. But be warned, you must do more than unleash it."

I eye the girl. "What do you mean?"

"It's not for me to say. In time, you will see, Aribelle." The girl bows her head as she draws herself away from me.

My lips part a hair's breadth. "Ari," I stutter. "How do you know my name?"

The girl's hands brush the water's surface. "I know many things. I'm Isla of Morrey."

Sheer wings sprout from her back and draw her from the water. A gossamer bathing dress clings to her form, shimmering like starlight. She flits from the pool over the treetops, and my eyes widen. A fairy. I've only seen a handful in Eida and always at a distance. I never realized they were from Morrey. It isn't even a part of the human realm.

I swim back to Graeden in a daze. Wringing my hair into the water, I inhale one last steamy breath before climbing onto the bank.

"She was a fairy," I say as we wander back to Arautteve's temples.

"You put that together on your own?" Sarcasm adds an edge to Graeden's voice.

I frown. The Well in the human realm is the only entrance into Eida, or so I thought. The only thing I've ever learned of fairies is the longer they're away from their hollows, the weaker their connection to it grows. Their immortality lasts only as long as they're tied to the strength within their trees. I've never heard of one straying so far. Why would a fairy risk leaving her hollow to come here?

My gaze trails the sky where Isla disappeared. She's thin, her arms straight and small. There's a softness to her milky skin that has no place in the arena.

"What would a fairy even do in Eida?" I mutter the question more for myself than anyone, but Graeden still answers.

"We have uses for many types of creatures. Fairy, goblin, human…"

"The trolls don't throw us all in the arena?" I ask.

"Not every creature is as disposable as a human." Graeden's voice darkens. "As you. That fairy you met? She's a seer. The trolls wouldn't dream of sending her to die."

I narrow my eyes, but let his slights roll off my shoulders. If this Isla is waiting for some type of pardon to free herself from this place, she may die here like the rest of us. Whether or not she ever steps foot in the arena.

"You will live in Arautteve with the other Marked Fallen. I could chain you up again," Graeden's eyes flit to my wrists as though considering it. His dark smile toys with his lips. "I doubt I'll need to. Though, I'd be happy to prove my threat."

I fold my arms over my chest, my burned hand chafing against my damp leather girdle. I frown. It's going to take a while to dry out the armor.

"Clean that up." Graeden's gaze flits to my flaming red hand, and his smile slips. "An injured Fallen is as good as dead."

My stomach sours, and I grind my teeth. "Sure. I'll use all my spare med equipment to heal it right up."

Graeden draws a grungy cloth from his satchel and tosses it at my chest. "Haven't used that in a fortnight. Don't catch the Plague. Can't say where it's been."

My scowl deepens as Graeden turns his back on me. *Thanks for the concern.*

Wrapping the cloth around my hand, I cringe against the dull pain. I step into line behind Graeden as we weave along the flagstone paths toward Arautteve's courtyard. Polished statues tower over us—victors from decades gone by, now all dead… because eventually everyone's killed in Eida. I frown.

Clusters of Marked Fallen blather in hushed tones as we pass. Their laughter quiets. Some point. Some stare. I shift uncomfortably in my damp clothes. No one tries to talk to Eida's new hellhound.

Graeden passes through a set of wrought-iron gates toward an ornate temple. Fluted columns adorn the building's edge like prison bars. A pediment perches atop the columns, moldings carved into its stone face of past battles in the arena. Weapons and warriors and champions. It doesn't show real battle—the blood, the stench, the carnage.

Graeden's boots disappear through the temple's entrance. Whisking through the gates, I race to catch up. We saunter through arched corridors and climb steep steps until I'm sure we must be able to overlook the whole of Eida.

"Your quarters." Graeden stands to the side of a narrow doorway. When I hesitate to enter, he says, "Unless there's someone else's bed you'd like to sleep in. I can track down your troll friends, if you like."

Ignoring him, I step into the ostentatious room. The aromatic scent fills my nose and stuffs my head. The flowers are worse inside the temple than outside. I snap a small white blossom sprouting from the wall and toss it over the balcony.

My eyes sweep through the room. The moment I'm alone, these flowers go. At least the wicker basket stuffed with folded clothing at the foot of the bed is already clear.

Brushing my throat, I swallow heavily. My breath smothers in my chest, and I can't swallow enough air. The flowers are too fragrant, the walls too confining. Everything about this place whispers lies, an obvious attempt to keep the Marked Fallen in their own district.

There are no guards in Eida. The entire realm is our prison. Arautteve's grandeur is a reminder that we can survive if we play by the Troll King's rules. He will feed us and have us trained. All we owe him is our lives—an eternity of killing for him.

My eyes settle on a small porcelain dish covered with aaerin. Arautteve is overflowing with food, and those in Haven starve. I scowl, but my traitorous stomach grumbles. I haven't had aaerin in far too long. I stare at the warm vanilla sauce swirled with bitter chocolate, sandwiched between thin biscuits.

I won't be swayed so easily. Aware of Graeden's eyes on me, I move in the opposite direction of Eida's delicacy. The worn soles of my sandals slip across the woven rug beneath the bed without noise. I rest on the edge of the bed, the deep folds embracing me. My eyelids grow heavy, and my body aches for rest.

The sooner Graeden leaves, the sooner I can change my damp clothes and sleep. And eat. Forcing my laden eyes to focus on Graeden, I say, "Are you finished?"

Graeden's golden skin darkens, and he swallows the light airiness of the room like a black hole. "Now that you're in Arautteve, you have two options: Secure yourself a trip to Eida's beast or unleash your monster and fight. You've already accomplished the latter." Graeden narrows his eyes skeptically, and an insecurity crawls up my spine. "I look forward to a performance at first light."

"Fallen aren't supposed to transform outside of Badavaru." The rehearsed words escape my lips, and I wish I could shove them back in. I've known a few Fallen who have disappeared from Haven only to reappear in the arena stronger, more lethal, and inhuman. I used to chase after them, searching for my friends. Friends that didn't exist anymore.

Graeden glances toward the balcony window. "As that may be, the rules do not always apply to me. I'm training you to be Eida's greatest warrior. You'll be at the rings at first light, ready to shift into your hellhound."

Without waiting for a response, Graeden sweeps from the room. The blood drains from my fingertips leaving behind an icy chill. I tighten my fists as though I can suffocate my cold, rising panic. I don't know how to shift. So, how in Eida's depths am I going to shift into a hellhound?

CHAPTER SEVEN

The sky flashes a particularly brilliant shade of violet over Arautteve's training yard. It's a beautiful day to die.

My blood races as I approach the weapon's wall. My expression is too firm, my arms too stiff. Graeden's going to discover my lie. I inhale another wavering breath, but it does nothing to quell the raging surge of panic in my veins. I spent the entire night plotting a way out of this—some lie I could spin or some ailment I could fake, but I awoke with nothing.

I glance through the training yard.

Today, every ring is filled with sparring Fallen. They dance through their individual rings, never crossing into someone else's. I make a mental note to not let Graeden force me from our ring. He doesn't need another reason to hate me, and if I'm injured in another's ring, he wouldn't hesitate to send me to Eida's beast.

"Staffs." Graeden's dark voice ricochets through the training field. I swivel my head toward him in time to catch the wooden rod he's tossed at me. It hits my palm with a sharp smack, prickles spreading across my skin.

I swallow my relief. At least Graeden doesn't expect me to shift in front of the other Fallen. My gaze flicks to the weapon's wall. Aside from a few rapiers no one has claimed, it's empty. My expression drops to one of disinterest. "I will never choose a staff in the arena."

"Maybe not." Graeden's brows angle sharply as he tightens his bracers. "But once you wield the staff, you can wield any weapon. Once you wield the staff, it's only a matter of becoming accustomed to another weapon's weight. Maces. Scythes. Axes." His dark glare flits to mine. "Any of those sound like weapons you might choose?"

I pinch my lips into a flat line, and my palms sweat beneath the staff.

"I'm surprised you've survived any challenges in the arena, honestly." Graeden returns his gaze to his own preparations. "You must be desperate to survive."

His words punch me in the stomach, and anger churns in my belly. "And what do you know of survival?" I spit. "Sitting safely outside the arena while others fight for their lives within."

Graeden's gaze flashes to mine. Forgetting his preparations, he strides toward me, closing the distance faster than I can blink. Gold veins weave through his irises, and his chest puffs with his anger. "Much more than you, Fallen. I doubt you will last long here," he growls. His eyes skim over my body as though assessing every weakness. "There's only one thing that will ensure your survival as a Marked Fallen, and clearly, you are incapable of doing it."

I tighten my jaw. I will not ask. My survival may depend on him right now, but that doesn't mean he controls me.

"You may want to escape Eida," Graeden hisses. "You may want to put us all to shame in this *fire-ridden* realm. You will fail."

I open my mouth to object, but Graeden throws his arm against my throat. He rams me into the weapon's wall. Pain splinters through my head, and I barely register gratitude for the lack of weapons on the wall. My staff clatters to the ground. Graeden presses harder. I scramble against his arm, my nails scratching, feet kicking. My efforts don't phase him.

"Do you think you are the first to have tried? The first Fallen who feels unjustly taken?" Graeden pauses as though waiting for a response. "You were all stolen! You. Them. Every Fallen was taken from their beds as they slept or exchanged as the price for another to get their wish."

My thoughts blur, his words spoken from behind a veil. Breath chokes against my throat, and I claw at his forearm. Darkness spots my vision—he's going to kill me. Graeden's eyes blaze with anger, but as the words leave his lips, his rage fizzles. He releases his hold. I collapse against the ground, air whooshing into my lungs.

"There is only one way anyone leaves Eida." Graeden's voice is calmer, and he steps away from me. "And it is through the beast's jaws. If you want to survive here, Fallen, fall into line. Releasing your monster is the only way you live."

I've made it this far without a wretched beast inside me. I don't need a monster to survive. My gaze slips through the training rings as the sounds of battle echo around us. Two years in Eida and I still don't have nearly enough kills to reach my pardon. If I ever return home, who knows how much time will have passed. Would Mother even be there for me to return to?

I swallow thickly. The breaths entering my lungs are frozen particles of despair. The ice shatters with each inhale and reforms with each exhale. I'm numb. I may not need a monster to live, but if I ever want to leave this realm, I must become the monster I've run from for so long.

I muster as much of my hatred as I can. My voice is ragged and raw, and glass shards climb their way up my throat as I speak. "Unfortunately, *Master*, I'd rather die."

A quiet tremor weakens my stomach at the thought. I don't want to die. I don't want to become a monster, either. An ache rips through my chest, because even though I hate it, I know he's right. If I want to survive—if I ever want to see my mother again—it will be as a monster.

The hair on my arms prickles, but I raise my chin.

"You may get your chance." Graeden clenches his fists at his sides. Instead of throwing one of them at me, he steps away and spins his staff in his hand. "It's not uncommon for some Fallen to shift by accident—a single occurrence they have no control over. A single shift they can't recreate on their own." Graeden narrows his eyes. "I have a feeling you offered the trolls more than you bargained for."

Worms burrow through my insides. He sees straight through me. Graeden nods to the staff lying at my feet. Gingerly, I lift the lightweight rod.

The resonant slap of wood against itself and the occasional clatter when my staff falls to the hard earth echo through the training yard. Dust swirls around our feet as we lunge and parry and dance through the ring. With only intermittent breaks to catch our breaths and wet our tongues, the day passes in a blur of sweat and weary muscles. As the hours fall, my focus slips, and my lungs can't suck in enough air. Yet, a subtle fire restores my waning strength, and my arms block Graeden's blows. The staff isn't much different from a sword, and I've practiced with them for years.

What I wouldn't give just to smack him in the side.

With no sun to rise or fall, it's impossible to track how long we fight. My arms tremble with each block, and my burned hand chafes against its bandage, as Graeden's staff collides with mine. More Fallen slip into the surrounding rings adding the clang of steel to the ever-growing melody.

More than once, Graeden forces me toward the ring's edge, his staff swinging in wide arcs between our bodies. I dodge his blows and duck, rolling over my shoulder and underneath his staff. He doesn't give me so much as a smirk.

"Think of his face." Graeden twirls his staff at his side before lifting it in the air and bringing it down above me.

Sweat clings to my body. My staff cracks against his as I hold it above my head. "Whose face?"

Graeden grunts and spins away from me before attacking again. "The man who sent you here."

"What makes you think it was a man?" I huff. My legs wobble as I lunge toward Graeden.

Graeden ignores my question. "You were taken. Forced to become one of Eida's Fallen. Who sent you here?"

Silence. In my mind's eye, Tib's colorless eyes lock onto mine as though he stands in front of me, trading me to the trolls again. Sacrificing my life for his. His gaze sears into my mind like its own branding.

"It wasn't Eida." Graeden answers his own question. "It wasn't me or any of those you kill in the arena. Only one person is to blame for you being here. You know who that person is."

A rift splinters through my heart as though I still care. Pain bleeds into the wounds I buried years ago. I promised Tib everything from me… and he threw it all away. Tib's face sharpens in my memory. Full-bodied, sandy hair that hung to his shoulders—hair every woman in our village lusted after. The small bulge of ripening muscles tracing his scrawny arms. The crooked smile that offered trust and protection. The lying, smug, traitorous coward.

Graeden's form arches and rolls around me in a haze, my own arms aching and trembling. But that small flame flares in my chest, warmth and strength radiating through my limbs. I don't question it. Instead, I catch each of his attacks, though my mind drifts to other times. And suddenly, both moments become one. Tib lifts the staff against me. It's Tib's boot against my back forcing me to my hands and knees. It's Tib slicing his staff through the air into my side. Pain. Pain. Pain.

All Tib brings me is pain. Anger pulses through my veins. Loathing blends with my sadness, and I growl as I wrap my hand around the end of Tib's staff at his next strike. His confidence slips from his face, and I tear the weapon from his hands.

Tib stumbles backward, and I swipe his legs out from underneath him with my staff. No time for air. Dropping my staff, I leap on top of him and pummel him deeper into the ground. Tib covers his face with his arms, my fists battering against his forearms. Tib thrusts me off him and pops to his feet. My hand curls around my abandoned staff as I leap to stand.

With a vicious roar, I swipe the staff through the air at Tib's head. Miss.

"There you are." Graeden's voice cuts through my rage like the crack of a whip, and I jolt back to the present. Blood streaks Graeden's cheek, but a smile curls over his lips. His fingertips blot the stickiness seeping from his wound.

My anger dwindles, the pain smothering to flickering embers. It doesn't matter what Tib did. I don't want to feel it.

Graeden's smile widens, showcasing his straight teeth. "Now we have something to work with."

"What are you talking about?" I mutter as the last few cinders of my rage die out.

Graeden folds his arms over his chest, corded muscle tracing his biceps, and walks in a slow circle around me. He purses his lips, and his eyes sweep over me from head to toe again and again.

"Stop staring at me like that."

"Like what?" Graeden mumbles without breaking his gaze. He strokes his beard.

Heat crawls up my cheeks as his eyes get lost around my middle, tracing my curves. "Like a stallion you plan to break."

His dark eyes flicker to mine, and his smirk returns. "Oh, that's exactly what you are. And once I break you, we will set your monster free." Graeden rests his weapon against the wall among a plethora of other reeds and staffs. "That's enough for today."

My shoulders wilt in relief as he excuses me from training. I drop my staff next to his and turn my back on him. Without the adrenaline of a looming fight, exhaustion swaths my body. I search for that flame that kept me on my feet all day, but it's disappeared, too. Now, I just feel tired.

"Fallen," Graeden calls. "Tomorrow at first light."

My head falls back, and I stare at the frothy violet clouds. Magic flashes behind their curtain where the trolls refill their supply of power each day. Fatigue seeps through my veins, desiccating every muscle in my body. Had I lost my pride along with my freedom, I would have collapsed straight to the ground. Instead, a groan builds behind my throat.

Before it can spill from my lips, Graeden speaks. "You are a Fallen. Called to protect the Troll King from granting undeserved wishes from those seeking miracles. No matter how you found yourself here, it's an honor to protect a magic as great as the trolls wield. So, start acting like it."

Contempt flares in my chest. How can he respect the creatures who pit us against each other for sport? He's as despotic as the rest of them.

I drag my head upright and sigh. I'm too tired to argue with him. I'd rather destroy the trolls' magic than have anything to do with those wielding it. Even still, if I'm going to survive long enough to leave this place, I need to release my monster, which means I need Graeden.

CHAPTER EIGHT

Days blur into a monotonous tapestry, each beginning and ending like the one before. Graeden and I meet at the rings before the clouds spark to life with their magic, and we put our weapons away as the clouds dim, their fine mist coating the land.

We train in speed, strength, and stamina. He tests my balance, my agility. I hang from branches until my grip falters. I climb ropes through the leafy treetops until my abs tremble. All the while holding fast to that strengthening warmth that burrows through my chest.

Each afternoon, Graeden hands me my wooden staff, a crack running cleanly through its center from overuse. And when my arms shake and scream that they can't take anymore, he finally switches my staff for steel.

Worse than the never-ending training is the incessant reminder of how I arrived in Eida. I spend every night tossing and turning in my sleep, lost to the nightmares of my past once more. And every morning, when all I wish to do is forget, Graeden tugs at the horrid memory of my best friend stabbing me in the back.

The grind of steel against steel reverberates in my head. No matter how far I roam from the training rings, the echo of battle shadows me. I stretch my sore muscles across my room's smooth stone floor. The cool granite is a welcoming balm against my skin.

As much as I hate to admit it, Graeden was right about one thing: training with a staff has made me more limber and fluid with my swords. I've never thrown my blades around me as effortlessly as I have the past few weeks.

With my muscles warm and aching to wield a short sword, I strap a clean girdle around my waist and my sandals over my calves. I tie my long, dark hair at the crown of my head in a thick braid.

A slow creak echoes through the empty hallway as I shut my door behind me. Most Fallen leave when the first sparks of magic flash through the sky. Graeden wants me to *be* at the training rings then. I grumble as I slip through the granite corridors. He says it's so we can have our pick of weapons, but I wouldn't be surprised if he drags us both out of bed early just to make me miserable.

I descend four staircases to the temple's ground floor. If Graeden was going to wake me at the crack of dawn, the least he could've done was secure me a room down here.

I skirt out of the temple with an eye locked on the clouds. I wonder how long until the first spark of magic will light them.

Iron screeches against stone, and my attention whips to the path ahead. I quiet my breathing, my body frozen to the shadows. Without a noise, I slink deeper into the darkness.

Quiet sniffles cut through the air as one of the Fallen shuffles toward our temple. Chains drape around her neck and adorn her wrists like baubles. Her dull, rose-dusted hair falls in lank, sinewy strands around her elbows, and dark circles sink into the skin around her eyes. Eyes that flicker to meet mine in the shadows.

I stumble backward and choke on my gasp. I hardly recognize the fairy from the bathing pools.

"Isla," I whisper.

Blood trickles in a meandering path against her pale cheek, matting her rose-colored hair to her skin. My stomach hardens.

"This is your own doing, Fallen." Her mistress seethes from behind her, the woman's hand locked around the end of the chain. A twisted smile crawls over the woman's lips. "How in Eida's fury did you think *you* could kill *me*?"

Dread pools in my chest. What has Isla done? She isn't a fighter. My thoughts dart back to her hollow—without it, she'll die in this realm. She has to get out. Biting the inside of my lip, I cling to the shadows but keep my eye on the pair. Pride softens the tension curling through my chest. Isla is a slight fairy, but with a pure heart. She isn't going to simply roll over and die.

The woman latches her hand around Isla's upper arm and whips her backward. She shakes the poor fairy, her cruel, venomous smile flashing. "Don't you want to defend yourself?"

I wish Isla would. She could rake those chains across the woman's face. Give her mistress a matching wound to hers. But then what? Isla has no weapon. Not that having one would save her. Isla's not a fighter.

Isla's gaze drifts over her mistress's shoulder—begging, pleading. *Help me,* she mouths.

My hand brushes my empty weapons belt, and my heart sinks. I want to help her. I do. No doubt I could bludgeon the woman and give her a nasty bruising, but I'm weaponless like Isla. The woman's blade would slit my throat before I could wrap my hands around hers.

Isla cocks her head ever so slightly, her pleading gaze a whisper of my darkest memory. My chest tightens, and my eyes burn. Smothering the tendrils of memory, I stumble back a step. Guilt gnaws at my belly as I stare at Isla's fear-stricken face.

Kill or be killed. Sooner or later, Isla needs to learn how to survive in Eida. If I step forward, it will be my blood staining the flagstone.

The woman squeezes Isla's arm tighter, her nails biting into the skin.

"What is it?" the woman spits. She catches Isla's gaze and pivots toward my cloaks of shadow. A scar slashes through her eye, marring a narrow brow and cutting through her cheek. A sinister smile crawls over her expression as her eyes lock onto me. She tugs on Isla's chain as though she steers a dog, her steps slow and methodical.

I grimace. Isla's fight has fled her, and she follows easily. She shouldn't have to follow at all. Closing my fist, I should, at least, help free her from her chains.

The woman slips closer, her eyes pinned to me. Suddenly, the shadows feel thin, less like a refuge and more like a cage.

Fight. The command echoes through my thoughts as it does in the arena. *Fight. Fight!* My feet are rooted to the ground. I could try to free Isla, but even if I succeed, she has nowhere to go. She'll have no choice but to return to her mistress.

Fight! A single thought cuts through my inner turmoil: *survive.*

I release my fist. My pulse is the calm of battle, my heart the breath before the fatal strike. Though I plan to do no such thing. Averting my gaze from Isla, I slip deeper into the shadows leaving the two behind.

The gnawing guilt chews through my core—sharp and painful—but I shove it deep inside. Isla will be fine—she's a seer. One of only a few I've seen in this realm. She might get a few bruises, but who of us here hasn't? The only thing I can control is my own survival, and by flaming nights, I'll do whatever I must to survive and, maybe one day, be free of this place.

As my footfalls press into the dry earth, blossoms stretch their petals to the sky, and magic sparks above, against the rolling clouds. It's already daylight.

Graeden is going to have my head for being late.

Picking up my pace, I jog into the rings only to find Graeden leaning against a bordering tree, his arms crossed firmly over his chest.

"You're late." His piercing voice is a mixture of nails and broken glass. "What? Did you sleep in?"

Rolling my eyes, I lift a staff from the wall.

"Was yesterday too draining?" Graeden's voice is clipped, baiting. "Feeling any real pain too uncomfortable that you couldn't drag yourself here on time?"

"You're unbelievable," I mutter. The suppressed guilt of abandoning Isla rears its head within my gut, and I raise my staff toward an unarmed Graeden. Better to hurt him than to feel anything. Isla must learn to survive on her own, or she's on a quick path to meeting Eida's beast.

Graeden catches my staff with his bare hands. The sudden slap unsteadies my arms. Tearing the rod from Graeden's grip, I sweep it at his feet as though I could level Isla's mistress instead of my master. Graeden skips over the strike and instead knocks me flat on my back. Catching my rod, Graeden forces it above my head, his legs straddling my waist.

"How can you live like this?" I growl. "How can you *be* like them?"

Graeden raises his brow.

The other Fallen already saunter into the training field and snatch their weapons from the wall. I tilt my head toward their masters. They bark orders and watch their Fallen like they'd sooner eat them than train them. My gaze catches as Isla's mistress arrives with another Fallen. Her gaze lingers on the boy's throat, her fingers brushing over bruised stripes curling around his wrists.

My chest tightens. I clench my jaw, my teeth digging into my lip. I could murder her.

"I'm *not* like them." Graeden speaks softly, his voice an icy crawl over my skin. "Masters? We are not all the same, just as no breeze carries the same air."

Graeden shoves me hard into the dirt before disentangling himself and standing.

I press myself to my feet and spit the sand coating my teeth onto the ground. "So, you don't bark orders at those you've marked? Break them down so they know they belong to you? Strip away their free will?"

"I never said anything about taking your free will, Fallen." Graeden snatches the rod from my hands and replaces it with a sickle. "We are all given so little here in Eida, I plan to take care of what belongs to me... even if that's an infuriating, selfish creature like you."

I open my mouth to retort but am caught off guard. His words sting. Isla's tear-stained face presses against my mind. Selfishness kept me from helping her. I pin Graeden beneath my glare as he strides toward the training ring.

For all his faults, Graeden has never once laid a hand on me outside of the rings or stolen passage into my room. My breath slips from my lungs in a rushed exhale. He may not be cruel, but he's selfish, too.

"Well, if you've had enough time accusing me of things I'm not at fault for," Graeden says. "You'll be sparring with the other Fallen today. I have duties elsewhere."

I choke on a gasp. Only now do I notice the wool tunic beneath the dull cloak he spreads over his shoulders. He didn't come prepared to fight. I narrow my eyes as Graeden glances over his shoulder toward the exit.

Graeden doesn't trust me farther than his sword's tip, so why would he allow me this freedom? Does it matter? My thoughts dart to the dozens of ways I could disappear. The mark on my wrist smarts, and I brush a thumb over the ridged scars. A stone sinks in my stomach, drowning my hope with it. He's not giving me freedom. Wherever I go, Graeden can find me.

"Don't look so shocked. It will be good for you to practice sparring with someone whose skills you haven't committed to memory. Besides, I'm not the only one watching you."

"Why?" My gaze wanders to Isla's mistress only a few rings over. Hair prickles along my neck. "Where are you going?"

"Despite what you might think, Fallen, I do have other things to attend to besides you." Graeden glances among the training rings. "I'm sure you can handle yourself for one afternoon. Don't make me regret this."

With his warning hanging in the air, Graeden spins on his heel and disappears into the growing crowd. My attention wafts to the another Fallen, cleaving his axe toward his opponent, no holding back. Bitter venom etches through each exhausted expression. My gaze falls to Graeden's brand. He could've been lying about tracking me through magic. A trick to force my compliance and stay in line. I could go right now, disappear into the wood…

Even if it were a lie, where would I go? Haven?

No matter where I flee, I'm still trapped in Eida. I will find myself in the arena again, and Graeden will claim me. Punish me. Maybe even kill me. A strained breath stretches against my lungs. The idea of escape is intoxicating but unrealistic. Rage-filled grunts surround me, the metallic clang of steel resonating through the air.

There's no point in running towards an execution.

The Marked lift their weapons, leaping, lunging, and parrying. The robust woman in the corner attacks her master blow after blow. The small boy to her right snarls as he cleaves an axe through the air. I could stay and fight. Be an obedient little Marked. In fact, I *should* be obedient.

My gaze drifts to where Graeden had disappeared. Why was he wearing wool in Araurteve? What need would he have to don a cloak in the temperate weather? I narrow my eyes. He's hiding something. I don't trust him as far as I can throw a troll. How can I obey someone I don't trust?

With a furtive glance at the other masters, I abandon the training rings. The fighters clash in a thick throng—no one will see me leave. I'll follow Graeden at a distance. At the first sign he can sense I follow him, I'll turn back.

Graeden's alabaster cloak soaks into the sand-colored temples, and he is near invisible—if it weren't for his dark hair and purposeful stride leading him straight for The Crossing.

I keep to the shadows as I trail Graeden through Araurteve. As he approaches the Crossing's Great Tree, I duck off the main path. Its braided trunk ascends toward the clouds above, and Graeden spares no time slipping through its opening. I stay among the shadows until Ghora's mist settles beyond the gateway. Then, I follow.

Graeden doesn't hesitate as he reaches Haven and slips into the long, street-like path flanked by our ill-attempted tents. The temperature drops as I step from the false sunshine into Haven's icy shadow. An unexpected barrage of nostalgia slams into my chest. The deception of safety I'd created among these shadows. The routine I'd come to expect. I lick my lips, my tongue dry as it often was in this fringe.

Whatever is to become of my life now, I wouldn't return to Haven.

Shaking my head, I sneak down the quiet street scanning the shadows for any sign of Graeden. The Fallen must be out scavenging along the edges of Haven. Ghora and Haven nearly bleed together, but no Fallen would be foolish enough to openly cross that line. There's not much food here, but an occasional vulture will fly by. And when you're starving, vulture is good enough.

My feet slow to a stop as I reach a tattered green cloak stretched between three obsidian turrets. I lift my hand, my fingertips caressing the dingy fabric that used to be mine. Time has eaten its way through the cloth, leaving it riddled like cheese. My thoughts grow hazy, and I close my eyes, my fingertips brushing the cloak's frayed edges.

I'd pulled out a thread each time I returned from the arena. My blade bloodied, my guilt thick, and another thread torn from its home. It became a sort of token to remember the dead. Not that they deserved to live but remembered.

Those frayed threads. All four hundred of them…

A whisper hisses over the otherwise quiet tents followed by the ruffle of canvas swooping through the air. I dart around my tent and hug the shadows. Graeden ducks out from beneath a nearby tent. His alabaster cloak is gone, replaced with a dark tunic and breeches as black as night. Graeden tips his head toward the tent he has just left and lifts a hood to shield his face. He stills for a moment, his form frozen except for the subtle rise of his chest. He's listening for spies. For me.

My gaze roams over his shaded clothes and lands on a woven satchel hanging heavy and full over his shoulder. Money? Is he purchasing another Fallen?

My stomach twists, and my jaw aches. I shouldn't care. I *don't* care. Unclenching my teeth, I squint into the darkness.

Ducking his head, Graeden slinks through Haven. I slip from hiding and follow, keeping my distance. He passes tent after tent before rapping a knuckle against a twisted turret. The canvas lifts, and Graeden crouches inside.

I keep an eye on the tent, carefully placing my feet on the smoothest parts of the ground. My breaths are silent as I tuck myself along the edge of a neighboring tent. I shut my eyes. My ears strain for a note of his voice, for some proof of why he has snuck into Haven.

At first, all I hear is a rustling of paper, a sigh, and maybe a hushed whimper. Whispers pelt the thick canvas, but I understand none of it.

My ears strain as I listen for a cry or a scream—something to show my master is as crooked as the rest of them—but I only hear the hushed whispers and then Graeden's feet stepping toward the door. Drawing myself deeper against the tent, I press myself into the shadows. Graeden straightens as he ducks out from the tent. He readjusts his hood before sneaking past me and entering another tent, his satchel lighter as it swings near his side.

With silent steps, I sneak toward the tent Graeden just exited. My hand hovers over the stiff canvas, and it scrapes against my skin. I hesitate, my gaze locked on the space where Graeden disappeared.

If he's recruiting more Fallen, I want to know. Swiping the material aside, I slip into the Unmarked Fallen's respite.

Leather scuffles against the hard earth as the Fallen pitches backward. A shimmering blanket tangles around his feet, a clean one—too clean. I narrow my eyes at the slight man. He's hiding something. Ignoring the Fallen's alarm, I crouch by the blanket's edge and run the fabric between my fingertips. Fairy Gossamer—silk as warm as wool yet as light as air. Trolls don't give Unmarked Fallen such gifts.

A savory scent fills the space in the small tent, and my mouth waters. My gaze flickers to a small bulge in the blanket strategically protected behind the Fallen.

"What are you hiding?" I ask on the barest of breaths.

The Fallen's eyes widen, and he shakes his head. Pushing past him, I lift the blanket. Broken pieces of aaerin, slabs of a hen plucked and cooked, food from Arautteve. My gaze flashes to the canvas barrier behind me.

Graeden is feeding the Unmarked. He's giving them bedding and keeping them warm? It makes no sense.

Returning my attention to the Unmarked Fallen, I whisper, "You tell no one I was here, I tell no one what I saw."

The Unmarked Fallen nods, and with his silent word, I leave his room. Mimicking Graeden's actions, I keep my face tucked toward the Fallen's tent as I slip out. My chin digs against my chest, and I glance along the streets toward my exit.

"What in the hell?" Graeden's hand fastens around my arm, his fingertips digging into the soft flesh above my elbow. A small whimper builds in my throat as his grip tightens, and my fingers tingle. Graeden drags me to the end of the makeshift street and throws me off the path.

I stumble over my own feet, and land hard on my rear.

"I ordered you to train in the rings." His voice is barely below a growl, the vein in his forehead pulsing. Graeden glances across the barren sky, his erratic gaze flitting from one corner to the next before it lands on mine again. His glare sears through me like a red-hot sword. "I thought you could follow a simple order." His eyes flick to my branded wrist. "I'll be paying more attention from now on. Unless you want to kill us both, leave this place. We will discuss your punishment later."

Without another word, he disappears into Haven's shadow.

Conflicting emotions wash through my chest. The rising tide of shame's icy touch swathed by the ebb of my confusion. What was he doing? The Graeden I know—the one I've sculpted in my head—would never help someone in Haven.

But he did.

My throat thickens. Pushing myself from the ground, I brush obsidian dust from my battle clothes. My gaze drifts skyward as I search for what Graeden saw. Rumor floats through every district that the Troll King has eyes in every shadow. Scouts to ensure the realm remains obedient. Their eyes are an extension of his.

I glare into the shadows, but all I see are the towering mountains of Ghora looming over Haven's courtyard.

Chapter Nine

MY MUSCLES WARM BENEATH my skin as I spin my staff through its regimen for the fourth time this morning. I arrived at the training rings long before light touched the clouds and armed myself from the weapon's wall.

Something rotten coils in my chest. It's been there all morning. It kept me awake all night. I spin the staff in front of my body before thrusting it against an invisible opponent. Stab. Retreat. Stab. Swipe. It isn't enough.

Gulping the air, I thrust my staff forward and attack harder. Anything to distract me from that tightening around my heart. My breath lances through my lungs, and the barest glimmer of light flickers through the clouds.

Any minute, Graeden will make his way to the training rings, ready to deliver his *punishment*. I grit my teeth and slash the staff in front of me as though fending off another opponent. My cheeks warm as I consider what his punishment will entail. Drawing a dagger from my belt, I throw it blade over handle toward the weapon's wall. It buries itself deep into the wood.

Sweat trickles down my cheek, and my chest rises with heavy breaths. I'm not afraid of him.

Besides, I may have disobeyed him, but he snuck into Haven. He isn't Unmarked, so he has no need to be in the fringe district. He isn't a Seeker, and neither does he wear the brand of a Marked Fallen. He is the Troll King's lapdog, training the Marked so we can fight instead of him.

As an Unmarked Fallen, I never saw him sneak through Haven's shadows. Why would he risk it now? Unmarked Fallen are criminals, disposable. We—they—sit only one rung higher in value than Seekers themselves. And it is strictly forbidden for Fallen and Seekers to mingle, forbidden for Graeden to visit Haven.

I lunge into the empty air as though skewering my enemy. Withdrawing my staff, I swing side to side as though aiming attacks against my opponents' nonexistent shield.

Light breaks through the darkness, and other Fallen meander into the training rings before I see Graeden. When I spy his dark, shaggy hair, my eyes fall to his hands. A set of shackles hang tight in his grip, and my heart steels. I clench my teeth to steady my nerves.

From the edge of the training rings, Graeden points to me and then points to the ground in front of him. I should have run from him when I had the chance. I shift backward a step through the dirt as steel clashes around me and the other Fallen begin their training. There's no way out.

Graeden's eyes widen, his mouth arcing into a frown, and he points to his feet again. Lifting my chin, I obey. I won't give him the satisfaction of my fear. He won't break me. Graeden's gaze drops to his fingers as he deftly secures one end of the shackles to a steel ring near the weapon's wall.

My jaw tightens, but I swallow my anger. I don't feel bad for what I did—I would do it again in a heartbeat. When I'm within speaking distance, I open my mouth to give him a tongue lashing, but he speaks first.

"Save it." Graeden doesn't lift his gaze as he unlatches one of the shackles and forces it onto my wrist. "How can I trust you if you won't trust me?"

I open my mouth, but he interjects.

"I can't." Graeden's gaze flickers to mine. "You won't be training today. If you plan to act like a *sulika*, then you will work like one."

I bristle at the derogatory name used for disobedient, untrustworthy Fallen. The second shackle locks into place over my free wrist. Graeden tosses a muddied rag at my chest, and I let it fall on the floor. Our glares burn into each other's.

"You will clean every weapon the Fallen throw at you. You will scrub the grime from their steel until they shine."

I leave the rag on the ground, not breaking his gaze.

"Get to work, Fallen. If the day ends with even one stained blade, I'll use it to rid our realm of you myself." Graeden turns his back on me. "When the sky darkens, your time is up."

I seethe beneath his command, my scowl following him as he weaves around the training rings. He will not break me so easily. A clatter of steel lands near my feet as a few Fallen toss their weapons in the dirt. Wrapping my hands around the steel chain attached to my shackles, I give a hard tug. The ring near the weapon's wall lifts, but it doesn't buckle. I jerk at it with more force. Nothing.

My gaze wanders to where Graeden speaks with another master. If I am to escape, I don't want him to watch, especially if I fail. I give another long wrench against the chain, leaning my entire bodyweight against it. It holds.

Fuming, I drop the chain. It's probably for the best. He'd only track me down using the marking on my wrist and dole out a punishment far worse than this.

More weapons splay over the ground near my feet, blood tinging their worn steel. There's no way these weapons could ever shine again. A growl rumbles in my throat, and I shoot a glare at Graeden. That dictator thinks he's better than everyone else. Thinks he can do whatever he pleases with a Fallen. My eyes trace the length of muscles stretching beneath his tunic as he points to something.

"That fire-ridden brute —" I cut off as Graeden's eyes flick to mine. He scowls.

Clapping a hand on the other master's shoulder, Graeden skirts around the edge of the ring, his eyes locked on me. My nostrils flare, and anger burns through my veins.

"Did you not hear me, *sulika?*" he barks. Graeden snatches the chain and crushes it beneath his boot, forcing the steel links and me to the ground. My knees land with a sharp thud against the dirt. "Clean."

I don't pick up the rag. Fire burns in my veins—I will not yield.

Graeden rolls his shoulders, tightening his foot against the chain. "Oh, you were bred wrong. With such insolence, I can only imagine how relieved your family must be to have you gone. It's a good thing they see nothing of you now."

My resolve cracks, and I know he sees the pain that flashes through my expression. A heavy ache presses against my chest carrying the sting of regret. Biting down against the locked memories, I shove them into the darkness where they belong.

"What would they think?" Graeden purrs.

A roar explodes from my throat, and I lunge toward Graeden. He doesn't flinch. The shackles catch my wrists inches before I can claw Graeden's eyes out. A cocky expression spreads over his face, and my blood boils.

"Clean up this mess," Graeden says. "You're causing a scene."

My gaze roams beyond Graeden, and, sure enough, dozens of eyes fall on me. Heat warms my cheeks, and I wilt onto my knees. My glare burns a hole in the ground right next to the soiled rag Graeden expects me to clean with.

What would they think? His cursed question repeats through my head as I lift the cloth and wipe a film of dried blood from the nearest dagger. One day, I will thrust a blade like this clean through Graeden's throat.

Smothering my anger, I focus on the other Fallen and let my hands work. At least Graeden doesn't require me to sharpen the weapons. With how often the warriors throw their blades to the ground, they dull quickly. That's another Fallen's work, though I'm not sure whose.

No one ever dies while training but scrapes and cuts are common. Most Fallen fight with their masters, but a few of them hover at the edges of rings. Their eyes dart over the fighters, watching. Learning. They track the fighters' every move: a punch here, a leg kick to the chest there. They memorize each fighter's tell, and when it's their turn to take up the ring with the champion, they demolish their opponents.

I should be out there training with them, not working like a *sulika*. Graeden thinks I can't be trusted. He's the one who can't be trusted.

Folding my arms over my chest, I watch as a well-built man steps into the ring. His black hair is slicked against his head, gathered in a small tail at the nape of his neck. His arms bulge with muscles that glisten in the warm daylight, and his steps are heavy and controlled. His sword scatters the daylight as he lifts it between him and his opponent.

"Swords, then?" the younger, smaller man squeaks.

"Swords."

Steel clangs like a roaring river as they lunge back and forth, swiping at each other. The larger man is slower, his steps clumsy, but his strength makes up for it. With every swing of his sword, the smaller man catches it with waning energy. Their swords meet, and the smaller man's arms vibrate like someone with the Plague. He clasps his hilt with both hands, but the larger man swings again. Clash. Clash. Clash. And the smaller man's sword cracks.

The larger man points his sword tip at the smaller man's nose.

"I concede," the smaller man says, scurrying out of the ring.

They all do. Not one Fallen stands up to the lout. Veins protrude from his arms, and a trickle of sweat runs down his cheek. He may have been the stronger fighter, but he's still just a man. He still sweats, which means he can still bleed.

By the time dusk settles over the training rings, I have scrubbed and buffed the weapons a dozen times over. Often, a freshly burnished weapon would cling to its hook on the wall only moments before a Fallen would come snatch it. My teeth ground together as the pile of blades at my feet grew faster than I could get them on the wall. Once, I bared my teeth when a slender brunette man reached for the sickle still in my grasp. He settled on a different weapon.

My gaze sweeps to Graeden, lounging on a wooden bench on the opposite side of the training yard. His hands lace behind his head, and he's kicked up his feet in front of him. Smug brute. I slip a rapier onto its hook, and someone tosses a set of battle axes toward me. The blades grate against each other and grind over the rough ground.

My stomach lodges in my chest, and I leap sideways moments before the axes would slam into my feet. "Watch your aim, you dolt!"

The brute with the slick black hair pivots to face me, a clock slowly winding backward. His expression contorts with bloodlust as he pins me with his stare. "A *sulika?*" His steps are heavy and thudding as he plows toward me.

Graeden is on his feet, the smug look wiped from his expression as he meanders through the other Fallen.

Abandoning the weapons at my feet, I straighten to meet the Fallen. He's large and strong, but that also makes him slow and clumsy. All one needs to do to beat him is ensure her speed and agility outweigh his strength. A smile crooks my lips, and the man's gaze burrows into mine. I don't look away.

"Want to try your crowing in a ring, *sulika?*" Ice laces his voice, and I expect my nerves to freeze, but they don't.

My gaze is locked on the man's, and my blood warms with his challenge. Graeden finally reaches my side, and I hold out my shackled wrists to him, not breaking my stare with the brute. "Love to."

Graeden narrows his eyes as though I had plotted this to get out of my shackles early. Unlocking them, Graeden leans toward my ear. "Of course you'd pick a fight with Ludvig. He's one of our strongest. Don't mess up."

Rolling my eyes, I rub the raw skin circling my wrists and pluck a short dagger from the wall. A crass guffaw explodes from Ludvig as he chooses a greatsword.

Ludvig trudges into the nearest training ring.

"And Fallen," Graeden says. "This punishment was a warning. Next time, I will take something of more value to you than your pride."

My jaw tenses, and I turn from Graeden and step into the training ring. As is a formality in beginning any sparring match, Ludvig places a hand over his heart to introduce himself. "Ludvig, Cortez's Marked Fallen." A proud smile stretches his wide lips.

Anger flames in my chest. None of us should be required to introduce ourselves this way. Glancing over my shoulder at Graeden, I say, "Ari. I am nobody's Fallen."

An even wider smile spreads over Ludvig's face as we retreat to our own edges of the ring.

Ludvig strikes first, aiming a heavy blow through the air. Darting to the side, I step out from his arm's reach. He stumbles against the missed collision, his heavy footfalls vibrating through the ground. Grasping both hands around his sword's hilt, he raises it above his head. It slices through the air, but I tuck my chin and roll over my shoulder. The blade carves a trench into the ground.

Ludvig tugs at the steel, and my muscles tighten ready for his next swing. He tears the sword from the ground with a guttural roar and doesn't hesitate before cleaving it through the air again. I dance out of the way focusing on my small frame and lithe agility rather than my skill with a blade.

Again and again, Ludvig strikes, and I pull away from him. That ember of heat flares in my chest, and I cleave to it as a slight sweat dampens my clothes. A subtle, metallic tang drifts through the air. My vision tunnels on Ludvig, and I focus on wearing him out.

Soon, fresh sweat trickles along his hairline, and his already slick hair sticks to his neck. I have eyes for no one else. Heavy breaths fill my chest, but Ludvig's chest rises and falls too fast. This is my chance.

Ludvig swings his sword again with his brute strength, and I dart to his side. Digging the toe of my sandal against his contoured calf, I leap onto his back and raise my dagger.

A chilled silence settles on the crowd. Stealing my attention for a heartbeat, I realize no one else fights. Instead, they gather facing the entrance to the training rings.

Ludvig's gigantic hand claps onto my shirt, robbing me of breath. I exhale in a sudden puff, and Ludvig throws me over his head into the ground. I skid through the dirt and slide out of the training ring.

My lungs burn, and I can't suck in enough air. The clouds dance with magic above me, ominous and breathtaking. Choking on the somber air, I push myself up, no longer interested in Ludvig. My gaze darts through the crowd until it settles on Graeden.

A quiet grinding echoes among the distant structures and floral-scapes. A chill tightens through my chest, and I stumble backward. Three trolls swagger into the training rings. Two servants by the looks of their own leather clothing, and the one troll I've never wanted to meet.

The Troll King.

CHAPTER TEN

A SHIVER RUNS DOWN my spine. I want to hurl my blade at him. I want to burn him with the fire that burns within me. I want to tighten my fist around my dagger. But I don't. I can't.

No matter how much pain I wish to see him in, an unsettling ease prickles over my arms. Ice coats my anger as I realize why.

Troll magic. A forced calm washes throughout the crowd.

Even still, panic thrums through my chest. *Why is he here?*

Lush, mulberry robes drape over the Troll King's shoulders, a small silver crown adorning his bald, liver-spotted head. He looks down his hooked nose toward the crowd. I hold my breath as he saunters a few steps forward. The light glints off the two gold circlets pierced along each of his pointed ears. His fingers uncurl toward the crowd, each adorned with precious gems.

No one moves.

The Troll King rules Eida and controls all troll magic. He is the only one who never needs to restore his powers. I've never seen him in Arautteve before. In fact, I thought he only mingled with Fallen when his visit was escorted by death. His dark, beady eyes glisten as magic strikes over us like a lightning storm. A cold void grows in my stomach.

"Graeden Thorne, Master of Marked Fallen." The Troll King's withered, rasping voice slices through the training rings.

My blood ices. Graeden said I'd get us killed.

He stands tall, his jaw firm, and he steps forward. "My King." Graeden bows, his arm tucked between his stomach and his legs. "What an honor—"

"Silence." One of the servant trolls hisses from the king's side. "You are not worthy to speak to the King."

Stomping to Graeden's side, the servant locks his fingers around Graeden's forearm. Graeden lifts his chin high, stoic, until the troll throws Graeden to the ground at the king's feet. Raising his foot, the troll slams it into Graeden's side. Graeden curls inward.

My entire body is frozen, the shout building in my throat turned to stone. The other troll servant flourishes his slender fingers. Magic sparks to life in his hand. With another flourish, the sparks disappear, and Graeden's body lifts into the air. Graeden raises his chin, his expression stoic except for the slightest twitch in his jaw. He knows what's coming. The troll snaps his fingers, and Graeden's body floats higher, leaving Graeden unable to do anything against the magic.

Not that he would. It would be a death sentence to raise a hand against a troll.

The magic beneath Graeden snuffs out, and his body freefalls straight into the hard ground.

The troll snaps its fingers, and Graeden rolls to kneel before the king. Blood trickles from his lips, a bruise already forming against his temple.

"I should probably thank you," the Troll King says, his voice like gravel crushed beneath a boot. "We've searched for the camp of Unmarked Fallen for years, and until yesterday, only added a handful to our ranks each turn of the moon. That's all changed. Our forces of Fallen have never been larger. Soon, we'll have drawn dozens of monsters forward. Fresh and raw."

My eyes widen as something sour curls in my stomach. Haven. I led the trolls to Haven. Sweat dews on my skin, and my gaze darts from the Troll King to Graeden. His head is bowed loosely before the king, but a muscle works in his jaw. Is he worried, too?

"So, Master Thorne, I should thank you." The Troll King's tone darkens, and a malicious smile curls over his lips. "But as it is, I can't have a traitor among my ranks. You delivered food and pleasantries to Unmarked Fallen. You betray our way of life. You betray me."

"Your majesty." Blood spatters across the stone with Graeden's words.

The Troll King raises a wrinkled hand. "You traveled to the Unmarked's camp, did you not?"

Graeden dips his head.

"It is forbidden for you to meet with Unmarked Fallen. They must survive themselves in the arena and out of it or join our ranks and unleash their monsters."

The Troll King snaps his fingers, and the servants crowd Graeden from both sides. Flowers drift toward them from the surrounding structures, weaving themselves into soft versions of our blades. The trolls grasp the hilts and blow the petals away revealing silver daggers beneath them.

Blinding panic flashes through my brain. Graeden must have seen a scout in Haven, and I drew it out by following him.

They will kill him. Breaking troll law is punishable by maiming or death. The higher your rank, the more severe your punishment. Graeden can die for all I care, but as much as I hate him, I hate the trolls more. And if he dies, his Marked Fallen must go somewhere.

The larger of the two trolls places a thick hand on Graeden's shoulder and rests his blade against the base of Graeden's neck. Graeden bows his head. My heart pounds against my ears, blood rushing through my vision.

My gaze flits through the rings at the various masters: paunches hanging over waistlines, sneers and scowls dripping with disdain, monsters. All of them. My gaze wanders back to Graeden's submissive form. There are worse monsters out there than him. If Graeden dies, the trolls will request another master to train me, perhaps even Isla's.

Guilt worms its way into my belly as I think of the girl I abandoned. Shushing the frothing anxiety, I separate myself from the frozen crowd. The troll raises his blade.

"He did not do it." My words echo through the quiet training center like a cannon.

Graeden tilts his head, his wide eyes meeting mine. His lips don't move, but his head drops a hair's breadth lower and swivels from side to side ever so slightly. The air hums with electricity as the trolls turn their darkened gazes onto me.

Shoving Graeden into the ground, the troll tromps through the dirt toward me. His thick, unwashed nails dig into my shoulder. A ferocious sneer spreads over his putrid skin.

"What did you say?" His breath smells like spoiled eggs among the bog. Acid roils in my stomach.

"My master did not do what you claim." My gaze drifts to meet Graeden's. His eyes flit between mine, but his expression is unreadable. "I did."

Graeden's gaze softens into understanding. His eyes slide closed, and his shoulders wilt. Instead of receiving his punishment, he will enforce mine.

A lump forms in my throat as the troll tightens his grip against my shoulder. "Why would one of the Troll King's masters risk everything to care for an Unmarked Fallen?" I ask. "He has no claim over them, and they'd return him nothing." I lower my head in false reverence. "A Marked Fallen recently stolen from her kin in Haven, though?"

I tuck my chin deeper against my chest, hiding the subtle quaver in my confidence. My heart thrums, and blood pulses through my ears.

"Why do you protect your master?" The Troll King's voice crawls over my skin like the brush of a feather.

"I do not protect him." I don't. They can kill him after I'm dead. In fact, I'd be happy if they did. But I refuse to be tied to one of these other masters. My throat dries, and the words stick against it. "Honestly. I traveled to Haven on my own to seek a friend." I force my eyes to meet the King's, so he cannot sense my lie. I have no friends. "My master hunted me down and forced me to return. He stole my satchel and everything within."

My glare falls on Graeden. His earlier words return to me: *What would they think?* My parents. My family. Pain crackles through my chest with the thought.

I should have let Graeden die, but I've already spoken the words.

Silence swells through the training yard. The troll holding me in place, tightens his grip as he watches the Troll King. Seconds tick by, and sweat dews on my skin. If they discover I lie, they'll kill us both. The Troll King dips his head, his chin disappearing into the folds of skin draped around his neck.

Graeden rises from the ground, the movement forced and unnatural. The Troll King's gaze bores into Graeden as he controls the master's actions. Graeden's sandals brush the dirt as he hovers over the ground.

"Fix his injuries," the king orders his servants. "I have a more suitable punishment for him, and I'll need him strong."

With another monotonous dip of the Troll King's head, Graeden crumbles to the earth in a heap. The blood fades from his skin, and the pain he's trying so hard to hide softens. Pushing himself to his feet, Graeden's hunched posture straightens. A sliver of relief threads through my chest. The Troll King healed him.

Magic crackles through the air, and a stone altar appears from nowhere. Another snap, and a multi-tailed whip lies coiled on top of it. I swallow against my dry throat. Small shards of bone are tied to each plaited tail.

"Punish her," the Troll King snarls.

Controlled breaths lift Graeden's shoulders as he stares at the leather weapon. His fingers curl around the whip's stock, and it uncoils at his side like a snake. His eyes bore into mine, and I can't tell if it's fury or pity that crosses his gaze. "Your hands, Fallen."

I clip my tongue between my teeth to keep my hands from trembling. He'll flog my hands so I can't wield a weapon, but at least I'll be alive. My steps are rigid as I approach the altar. Dried blood stains its surface, and I wonder how many Fallen have lost their lives here. I place my hands against the stone and fix my eyes onto them.

"You should look away," Graeden whispers at my side, too low for anyone else to hear.

"I'm not weak." The words float on a breath, the only sound I'm capable of making.

Graeden wraps a leather cord around my wrists, binding me to the altar. "I never said you were."

He steps back and raises his arm.

"Not her hands," the Troll King grunts. An edge has crawled into his voice. "Her back."

Graeden hesitates for a moment, the whip clamped in his fist, before retreating to the edge of my sight.

"Remove her armor," the Troll King orders.

Graeden's fingers brush against my neck as he moves my hair out of the way. He unstraps the buckles of my girdle, his fingers unsteady. It lands on the ground with a dull thud. Mercifully, he doesn't tear the clothing from my back.

"How many lashes?" Graeden asks.

The Troll King smiles. "Until I tell you to stop."

Graeden regrips the whip's stock. Clenching my teeth, I focus on my breaths, slow and controlled. The whip cracks through the air, and pain lances across my ribs and up my spine. I gasp, rolling forward, tears springing from my eyes.

White-hot pain crackles across my flesh, fast and angry. I breathe into the pain, pull it into myself until it fades. I roll my shoulders and straighten my posture. Another crack. Fire streaks across my back and curls around my ribcage. A cry lodges in my throat. I bite back the pain as it fades again. A piece of torn cloth flutters to the ground, streaked with blood.

Curse Graeden for taking his time. I set my gaze on my fingers, knotted in the cord around my wrists. Another crack. Another cry I choke on. Graeden lifts the whip again, and this time when it cracks against my flesh, I flinch. My breaths swell in my chest and press against my lungs. Deep inhales, slow exhales, and the whip's sharp crack grows distant as I center myself deep within my head.

A detached sting sears against my back, but my full exhales and heavy inhales hold the pain at bay. My back burns, and blood dribbles over my ribcage, painting the stones beneath me. My jaw aches, tight and stiff. Instead of releasing the tension, I clamp my teeth tighter, focusing on the ache in my jaw rather than the blinding pain spread over my back.

Black dots speckle my vision as Graeden cracks the whip for what feels like the twentieth time. My resolve wavers, and my balance does, too. I teeter against the altar, the leather bind tugging against my skin as I tip away from its firm foundation.

Graeden hurls the whip onto the altar, blood splattering the stained stone. Relief floods my mind that he's done, but my repose fades along with my consciousness. Darkness swarms the edges of my vision, and a fogginess floats through my head. The leather straps loosen around my wrists. I stumble away from the altar, and the darkness consumes me.

CHAPTER ELEVEN

Pain is everywhere.

I grit my teeth as lightning explodes across my back. My arms. My neck. I can't breathe, the pain... the pain. I gasp, and my eyes snap open to blinding light. I crush them closed. My chest rises with panicked wheezes, and my skin screams. I try to draw in a fresh breath, but it's metallic with the blood that drenches the air. So much blood. My blood.

I hear rushed, panicked words. His voice is familiar and commanding: Graeden. "Lay her down! Right here!"

I want to scream for him to help me. To beg him to save me. Light flashes against my vision, and the pain threatens to send me under again. Please take me. Let the darkness take me.

I suck in a sharp breath as my body lands roughly on a hard wooden plank. Hands fumble against my sides and gather my torn clothing. My lashes flutter as a blood-drenched hand drags a blade over the shredded clothes clinging to my shoulders and sides.

I suck in short, haggard breaths. It's not enough. I can't get enough. The pain drags me into the darkness of my subconscious.

"Stay with me, Ari," the familiar voice coaxes.

I don't want to. There's nothing for me with that voice except pain. I wilt into the darkness, letting the lack of everything wash over me. But there is nothing for me in death, either. A sharp breath lances through my lungs, and I choke against the copper-tinged air.

A haze covers my vision—I can't tell if it's tears or lack of oxygen, and I don't care. Graeden peels my clothes from my wounds with deft, precise fingers. No trembling, but his brow wrinkles and his arms stiffen as he works. His stern gaze never leaves my skin.

"Get me clean cloths," Graeden orders to someone I can't see. "We need to stitch and dress these wounds."

My eyes flutter closed, and I give into the darkness.

The darkness drums through my skull, a blanket weaved from Ghora's shadows itself. Life snuffed of stars. It doesn't last nearly long enough.

But when my eyes open, the cacophony around me has stilled. The energy subdued. I squint against the brilliant light splitting through my head, a sharp headache ravaging my brain to match the pain in my back. A groan escapes my lips.

My chest presses against a firm table or board. I can't tell which beneath the dark, coarse cloth covering it. I inhale softly, my head propped on a thin pillow. The air smells like overturned earth and rain. So, why do I feel like death?

My back throbs, and something weighs heavy across my waist. With a small turn of my head, I dare a glance over my shoulder. Pain lances across my back beneath a layer of blood-tinged gauze.

"Gah." I collapse against the makeshift bed. Bloodied gauze lies in a heap on the ground. I pray it isn't the same gauze that rolls over my naked back. Somewhere in the room, water drips onto the floor with an even, soothing tempo. I inhale the fresh scent of the rain and close my eyes.

My arm hangs over the edge of the bed, and my fingers twitch. Pain bolts through my arm. I inhale a sharp breath. This isn't good.

My gaze wanders over the small section I can see of a red rock cavern. An overcast light trickles through an opening near the roof to my left. I can barely see the sharp angle of stairs descending from the entrance. Rain splatters against the top step.

Rain. Finally. It doesn't rain in Ghora or Haven, but Arautteve... I listen to its quiet patter again. It's uncommon in Arautteve, but not unheard of.

A shuddering breath fills my lungs, and I wilt into the stiff board stretched beneath my body. A sheer, gauzy tunic covers my chest and stomach, but falls open at my sides, exposing the injuries on my back. Its white sleeves—now steeped with blood—cinch against my forearms. A heavy blanket is draped over my waist and shields my lower body.

Gooseflesh crawls over my bare skin. In another lifetime, I would have blushed at lying so revealed, but pain is everywhere, and I can barely hold onto reality let alone worry about my state of dress.

"What were you thinking?" Graeden's frigid voice cuts through the empty room.

Heat floods my cheeks, and races through my body—I'm not alone. Despite the pain and fatigue lacing its way over my back, anger careens through my heart. "I thought it was obvious." My voice rasps against the thin bedding pressed to my cheek. "Taking your beating." Fiery stripes sear over my skin, and I clench my teeth to drive the tears burning behind my eyes from brimming. "How long will this take to heal?"

"As long as it takes," Graeden snaps.

Scowling, my breaths sharpen. "Which is usually how long?" I gasp at the abrupt sting of my inhale. "Two weeks? Months?"

"It doesn't matter." Graeden's tone is clipped.

My brows raise as I realize he's mad at me. For what? Saving his life? Forcing a laugh, I spit, "Why are you upset? It's not like you're the one who's been beaten. A thank you would be nice."

"I didn't ask you to take my place."

"But I did. To save you."

"Or to save you," Graeden bites out. "I see the fear in your eyes when you look at the other masters." Silence follows his accusatory tone.

I clench my teeth and glare at the ground. He isn't wrong. Again.

"And now," Graeden's voice hitches, but I can't see his expression to understand it, "whatever your condition, you will fight when the trolls call you forward."

My brows furrow, and my cheek scrapes stiffly against the board-like bed. "They won't wait for me to heal?"

"Why would they?" Graeden steps into my line of sight. His nostrils flare, and he flashes me an incredulous glare. "You stood up to them in front of all Arautteve. Now my last Fallen might as well be dead."

My shock simmers, replaced by a cold void.

"Why would you do something so ludicrous?" Graeden sweeps his arms through the room.

Heat flushes through my body. "I could ask you the same thing," I hiss.

My eyes flicker to his, and he holds my gaze, waiting. Pain stipples through my back. It's the same pain that crackles through his stubborn glare. He never should have broken the Troll King's rules. He never should have snuck into Haven.

"Flaming nights, Haven," I whisper. For a moment, I'd forgotten. The Troll King ravaged their home. He stole them from their tents, and I'm sure left blood in his wake. "There must be something we can do to help them. Something we can—"

"There is nothing we can do." Graeden's voice is like stone, flat and unrelenting.

My chest tightens. I can't say the words aloud, but I know we both think them: I led the trolls there. I betrayed the Unmarked. "I don't believe that. I can't. He captured some, but not all. Those others—"

"Will be fine," Graeden finishes. "They're resourceful. We must trust them to be. If we go back now, the Troll King will kill us both and slaughter every Unmarked he finds."

My lungs constrict, and I shut my eyes against the strangled sensation. Instead, I cleave to the pattering sound of the rain.

"Train for them. Kill for them. Die for them," I whisper. "We're all pawns in this game, aren't we?"

Graeden exhales through his nose, and his dark, amber eyes bore into mine. His lip curls as though something rotten festers in his mouth. He says nothing.

Flames lick the edges of my wounds, and my raw skin screams against the stiff gauze. I clear my throat—I need his help. "You saved my life when you," the words sour on my tongue, "purchased me. Now, we're even."

His anger has dampened, and he frowns at me, a hint of sadness touching his eyes. "We will never be even, Fallen. What you did for me changes nothing."

Graeden gestures to the soiled gauze striping my back. "We need to redress your wounds and add a poultice. It won't heal the wound, but it might help. Brace yourself."

Graeden lifts the edge of a bandage, and flames spark against the wounds as they sear farther into my skin. My hands crush the narrow bed between my fists.

Graeden's fingers work deftly as he removes the gauze from my back. He presses a clean cloth against my skin and then spreads a poultice over my wounds. Its fibers stick to the clotted blood and tug at the stitches. Fire licks the lashes with his touch.

"It's going to hurt like the beast's jaws, but I need you to lift your chest from the bed," Graeden says.

"What?" I gasp. Pain spreads in fiery waves over my skin. "I can't."

"You must. I need to secure the gauze and compress your wounds." Graeden unrolls a fresh bundle of gauze. "Count to sixty."

Clenching my teeth, I squeeze my eyes shut. Panic thrums through my body. I can't do this. With a painful grunt, I press my forearms into the bed beneath me. Fire erupts over the lashes in an unquenchable rage.

Agony ripples through my back stronger than a thousand scorpion stings. I've never felt such pain—not when a Seeker skewered my hand during a match or when Graeden branded my wrist. No sword wound or melee within Badavaru has ever held this amount of pain.

"Thirty-six," I huff. Tears gather at the edges of my eyes and slip down my cheek. A scream builds in the back of my throat, but I try to swallow it. My body trembles, and darkness speckles my vision. My arms give out.

I land on the board with a thud long before I've counted to sixty.

Fire crackles through my back, a stabbing pain that dulls to a writhing ache. I tip my forehead against the soft pillow and choke on a sob. Tears trace the contours of my nose and gather in a small puddle beneath me.

I barely notice that in those agonizing moments, Graeden has succeeded in wrapping the gauze around my body and beneath the gauzy tunic. The pressure aches against my back, but I feel stabilized.

"Isn't there some way to relieve this pain?" I choke.

"No." Not a hint of remorse touches Graeden's voice. "The only thing that can do that aside from troll magic is the Jivanna—a healing flower in Vasa. But it's nearly impossible to find."

Graeden settles onto a small stool at my side.

"You act rash, Fallen. You are impulsive. You are going to get yourself killed." Resting his elbows on his knees, Graeden's laces his fingers beneath his chin. "But that day is not today. Not while I'm here."

My head lolls to the side, so I can see his eyes. Tears glisten on the bridge of my nose, but Graeden doesn't look at them. His gaze trails over the wounds on my back.

"We must keep your wounds clean," he says. His broken tone and sudden warm timbre surround me like a shield. I know it's not, but I curl into it anyway. "They will take time to heal. Time you unfortunately don't have."

My eyes widen, and a frost creeps along my veins. "We don't know that."

Graeden doesn't meet my gaze. "These wounds will take weeks to heal. Maybe months. You fight in the arena in five days, according to the king's messenger."

"What?" I twist toward Graeden, praying this is a cruel joke, and gasp. White-hot pain sears through my back. I clench my teeth and collapse onto the narrow bed. When I've caught my breath, I say, "That can't be. Marked Fallen only fight once their monsters are unleashed."

"Not for you." Graeden dips a soiled strip of gauze in a bucket of water near his feet. It sloshes as he rinses the blood from it.

No blood. No ili. I suppress a shudder thinking of the filthy rodents swarming me for a little taste. If Graeden weren't keeping this hovel as clean as he is, it'd be overflowing with the creatures.

"After your admission," Graeden continues, "the Troll King thought a better display of punishment would be sending you into the arena injured."

Hopelessness seeds within my chest and threatens to choke me. "Can't we just kill the Troll King?"

Tension rolls through Graeden as though he believes I'm serious. Even I know that's an impossible feat. With all the magic the Troll King possesses, no one could ever get close enough to do the job.

"I wouldn't joke of such things, if I were you, Fallen," Graeden says. "Eida must have a king, and if it isn't the Troll King, then who? There are many less worthy than him to claim that throne. Besides, you don't want that title and whoever kills the Troll King gets it."

"Really?" I ask.

Graeden nods, his hands dipping another soiled cloth into the water. "As the Troll King nears the end of his reign, he will select an heir and sacrifice himself to the heir's blade. Like everything here, succession requires a sacrifice."

I moan into the sheet. "Then why bother changing the dressings?"

"Would you prefer me to stop?" Graeden hesitates, a soaking strip of gauze held between his hands, trickling water back into the bucket.

I peek over my shoulder, careful not to move any muscles other than my neck. "That depends. How bad is it?"

Graeden's gaze traces over my bandaged back, his eyes weaving over it like a torn tapestry. "Do you really want to know?"

I've seen the results of a whip's lash before—black-red flesh torn, swollen, and raw. Even if it were irreparable, I couldn't give up. I have to fight. I owe that to myself and to Mother. "Actually, no."

"I changed your dressings because you are not going to die in that arena. Not like this." Graeden wrings out the last sodden cloth and hangs them all to dry on a root puncturing through the side of the cavern. "You're in no condition to train. But we can still work to unleash your monster again."

"How will that help if I can't even move?"

"You can't move, but your monster can." Graeden crouches near my side as though looking for the truth on my face. "How much do you know about monsters?"

"That we all hide them." My tentative gaze flicks to Graeden's. It's no secret that every person in every realm harbors a monster inside before they enter Eida. "That the troll realm has a way of tearing your monster out. How lost will I be when my monster is released?"

My eyes dart between Graeden's, a storm brewing in his gaze. He stifles a smile as though he's sharing one of Eida's greatest secrets. "Well, that's the thing," he says. "You won't be lost at all."

CHAPTER TWELVE

M Y BROWS PINCH TOGETHER, but before I open my mouth, Graeden responds to my unasked question.

"Your monster is a part of you. As mine is a part of me. One cannot exist without the other. When we unleash your monster, your form will shift into that of the monster you hide within, whether beast or fowl or some other fabled creature." Graeden's gaze roams over my face, absorbing every minute change in my expression and accounting for it by altering his answers to my silent questions. "You will be there, watching through the lens of your eyes, but it will be your monster who controls your body while you are in that form."

"What if I don't want to ever be in that form? How do I switch back?"

"I think you'll find your monster isn't as terrible as it may seem. After all, it is a part of you." Graeden rests his elbows on his knees. "At first, you won't be able to control the shifts. When your brain registers a threat, it triggers you to either fight or flee. Your monster won't let you flee. Instead, it will rear its head, and you'll shift. Your monster always chooses fight."

"Lovely," I mumble.

"Over time, you can learn to control it and even choose when to shift. The sooner you learn that, the better." Graeden shifts, tugging on his dark pants. "Until then, the trolls will activate inhibitors in the arena, so you can only shift during the third round."

"I've never noticed inhibitors before."

"You wouldn't have. They're cloaked from the natural eye." Graeden folds his arms over his chest. "Until you've proven you can shift, they'll stay off, too. It uses an immense amount of magic for the trolls to power the inhibitors."

"Perfect. So, they turn me into a monster, and I'm still trapped in prison."

Graeden's eyes trace the curves of my face smashed against the thin sheet. They wander over the arch of my nose and linger on my lips. His mouth tips into a subtle frown. Warmth crawls into my cheeks under the heat of his gaze.

"What is yours?"

Graeden leans back on his stool, extending his legs and crossing his ankles. He laces his fingers behind his head and rests against the curved wall. A subtle smile travels over his lips, but he keeps them closed.

"That bad, huh?"

Graeden closes his eyes, that smile still lingering on his lips. He's not going to tell me. Fine, but he at least owes me an explanation as to why I lie bleeding and broken.

"What were you doing in Haven?" I whisper. "You owe me that."

A grimace flutters over Graeden's still expression. His eyes slip open, and a chill replaces the warmth that had surrounded us only moments ago. Leaning forward, Graeden drops his head, his unkempt hair shielding his eyes from me. He drags his hand over his face, rubbing his eyes before stroking his jaw.

"The Fallen need help." Graeden's voice sounds tired. "How did you come to Eida?"

There's that question *again*. Tib's cowardly gaze settles on me in my mind's eye, and a growl rumbles in my chest. His warm voice spits the word "yes" in my memory, and I watch suspended from the sky as the trolls drag my body toward the Well of Eida. Anger floods my veins, betrayal shatters my already broken heart…

I could rip out Tib's throat.

Graeden must see the pain etched into my expression. "The Seekers come freely to Eida to kill us," he says. "The Marked have their monsters. The Unmarked are alone, left to fight the vultures they face in the arena with little skill, no protection, and a fool's form of nutrition. They aren't expected to survive."

"That doesn't explain what you were doing." The words grate over my dry throat.

"I was giving them a chance. Once upon a time, the Fallen could choose whether they released their monsters. The Unmarked and Marked fought side by side, and the realm cared for its own. It's not that way anymore." Graeden's words fade. He drops his head and rubs his brow, a quiet exhale. He shakes his head as though redirecting his thoughts. "The Troll King expects all Fallen to be Marked and to unleash their monsters. Those who hide from him are sentenced to survive on their own.

"When the Troll King abandoned the Unmarked, he condemned them all to death. With their living conditions—the filth and illness of Ghora at their fingertips—it's only a matter of time until they all die. More of them must make their way into Araütteve and be trained, rather than be slaughtered in the arena."

Graeden runs a hand through his hair, the midnight strands streaming through his fingers.

"We are warriors. All of us," he says. "The moment we pass through Eida's Well, we take on that title. Too many of us die needlessly from starvation or disease. Whatever I can do to protect them, I will."

So, he does care.

"If I can help even one Unmarked Fallen become strong enough to face what they'll need to survive, it would be worth any price. I feed and warm different Unmarked every time I travel to Haven, hoping they will seek me out when they find themselves in the market. I wait for them. I will claim them and coax their monsters forward, so they stand a fighting chance in the arena."

My gaze falters. Who is this man who buys and sells human beings like livestock but also gives a fire-ridden care? I tilt my head for a better view of Graeden's face. His eyes have wandered to the shelter's entrance, but he draws his attention back to me.

"Do you finally see it?" he asks. "I am nothing like the other masters you have met."

"No," I whisper, resting my cheek back on the bedding. A warmth spreads through my chest, as Graeden's gaze steels into mine. "You're not."

Graeden stays at my side, his elbows planted on his knees. His eyes occasionally wander over my bare back and tighten as though pained. Maybe it's a hint of the guilt he pretends he doesn't feel.

I watch the path his eyes take. He counts the stripes, his lips barely moving. He finds my waist, and his gaze trails up my side. A light flutter stirs in my chest. I wonder if he thinks of more than my pain tolerance when he looks at my skin.

"Where are your other Fallen?" I whisper.

Graeden's intense gaze fractures and falls to the floor. A hard line replaces the easy fill of his lips. Graeden buries his forehead in his hands. "A hellhound shifter is fairly rare." Graeden hesitates, lifting his face and interlacing his fingers in front of his chin. His jaw flexes. "You see, certain monsters can heal their hosts in battle. And the host can heal the monster. The hellhound, a wyvern, and the strongest of all being a dragon."

I open my mouth, but Graeden dismisses my question. "A dragon is even rarer than a hellhound. Not every monster can accomplish such a feat. When your troll buddies discovered the monster you hide, they *requested* I buy you. But I said no."

"No?" Rejection stings my lips, and the emotions I've stifled from Tib's betrayal gush to the surface as I feel Graeden's.

Graeden nods. "I had too many Marked already and expected at least half a dozen more to join my ranks before the end of the season. I had no capacity to train a hellhound—they are vile, unruly monsters." Graeden's eyes flicker to mine. "Gunther and Chorin, was it? They weren't too happy about my answer. Took it to the Troll King himself. A realm's most vicious monster should be trained by the realm's most experienced Trader. Though, they care little for how the Fallen fare. It's more about the coin for them, and, unfortunately, I've made a name for paying high."

My stomach twists. Then why was he so unwilling to pay any more than half what the trolls wanted for me? He would have let them take me rather than give up his coin. I inhale a tight breath—because Graeden is playing the game, too. My gaze flits between his eyes. But the pain that reflects in those darkened pools isn't a game. It's real.

"What happened?" A dread-filled shiver crawls up my spine.

Graeden's eyes stare into the distance as though re-watching that night. "I had left my Fallen in the training yard, and when I returned to their temples they were not in their rooms. Instead, I found their bodies strewn about in the courtyard, throats slit, blood pooling over the flagstone."

I gasp, the sudden movement sending a wave of pain down my side and grit my teeth.

"Empty capacity. Perfect to take on Eida's new hellhound—the girl with hellfire in her blood." Graeden grimaces, and a flicker of pain tightens near his eyes. He was their protector, and he lost them all. *I lost them all.*

Guilt burrows into my stomach, eviscerating any confidence that lying about my monster was the only way to save my life. Because of me, the trolls expect a rare, fearsome hellhound to fight for them; dozens of innocent Fallen were brutally murdered; and now, Graeden's fate rests on mine.

Because of my lie, we will both die.

I shrink against the board, wishing I could disappear within it. Perhaps Graeden was willing to let the trolls take me because he blames me for his Fallen. He should. He'd be better off had he refused to take me at all.

"Graeden." My voice flees, leaving me the barest of breaths with which to speak. "I have something to tell you." Shame floods my cheeks and muddles my thoughts. What have I done?

"What is it?" Ice crackles in his voice.

"The trolls were going to kill me," I whisper. "I couldn't—I had to—." My voice breaks again, my words faltering.

"Had to what?"

My brows crush together as I block the image of all those Fallen collapsing as their throats were slit from behind, their dead eyes reflecting the magic jolting through the dark clouds. Their pleas scream at me from their crimson blood, soaking the ground beneath them until they're empty shells.

Graeden's concern slips, his brows lifting, and his lips parting. "You aren't a hellhound."

I dig my teeth into my bottom lip and shake my head. "I don't know what I am."

Graeden's jaw tightens, and the vein crossing his temple pulses. His nostrils flare as angry breaths race in and out of his heaving chest. Standing, Graeden crosses the room out of my line of sight and then strides back into it.

"You are a greedy, reckless creature." The words tremble with barely controlled rage. Graeden's hands ball into fists, and the room swells with his pain. His Marked must have meant a great deal to him.

"I had no idea…" My words hang between us, void of comfort. It's no excuse.

A swollen silence settles around us and as Graeden's pacing slows, his fingers uncurl and his breaths ease, but his jaw is still tight. "I wondered. No one shifts into a hellhound. You are selfish and reckless, Fallen. But I see something else in you, too."

I dare let my eyes meet his. They swirl with a depth of Bridgewick's darkest ale, frothing and endless. Can he truly see beyond the broken beast I am?

"What you do with that possibility is up to you, though."

"I'm sorry," I whisper. I have nothing else I can say.

Graeden leans against a braided branch hanging through the doorway and folds his arms over his chest. "I won't lie; we are in a dangerous position."

My mouth dries, and pain stipples my back.

"It's my duty to keep you alive." Graeden presses himself away from the exit. A grim smile curls over his lips. "You are my last Fallen. By Eida's Well, I will not let the Troll King take you from me."

CHAPTER THIRTEEN

My breaths come easier today, but I can still hardly move my arms without eliciting a shockwave through my back.

Four days. Four days, and the trolls will throw me back into the arena. I can't stand, let alone wield a sword. Graeden might as well lay me at the Seeker's feet.

A short scrape echoes through the underground shelter as Graeden drags a clay pot from a nearby table.

"What is that?" I ask.

"Fresh water."

"Thank the stars," I sigh. Pain lances over my back, and I grit my teeth to keep the agony burrowed inside.

Graeden dips a ladle into the pot before pressing it against my mouth. I part my lips, and the water rushes over my dry tongue. I guzzle as much of it as I can. The water dribbles down my cheek onto the makeshift bedding, but I don't care.

"More," I rasp when the ladle is empty. Graeden obliges without question.

When my thirst is quenched, I relax against the board. Graeden eyes the stiffened gauze plastered around my body. "We'll leave it for a couple days. I want to be sure the bleeding has stopped, and we don't want to risk infection."

Today, Graeden has come to unleash my monster—whatever it is. Oh, flaming nights, I hope it isn't a unicorn.

Graeden drags his stool to my side. "Unleashing your monster is as much a mental game as it is physical. You are strong—the last two years surviving within Eida have proven that. Now, we just need to dissolve the barriers that bind your monster. Should we see what it is?"

My fingers tremble, and I'm grateful Graeden can't see them tucked against my sides. I imagine the process will be nothing short of excruciatingly painful, otherwise people would call upon their monsters all the time. And once I set it free, there's no going back. What if I'm a cockatrice and forever ugly? Or a selkie and totally helpless outside of the water?

I grimace. What would Mother think when I return as a monster? My hands are already stained in blood, but those lives were for my freedom. I fear that once I release this monster, the bloodshed will never stop. The creature may never be satisfied.

A slow inhale expands my lungs, and I exhale the anxiety. If I don't try, I'll never see my mother again. I either fight broken, or

I release my monster and hope it gives me the stamina I need to walk into that arena.

"Let's do it."

Graeden nods and settles onto his stool. "Close your eyes."

I shut my eyes without reservation, and my tension stills.

"Focus on your breath," Graeden says. "Control it. Calm it."

I inhale a soft breath and ignore the sparks of pain along my back. Instead, I wilt further against the wood as though I lie on a lush feather bed rather than a thin blanket.

Silence fills the small room, my steady heartbeat centering my conscience.

"Take inventory of your body," Graeden says. "Your wounds, your mental health, even the exhaustion from having lived in poverty in Haven."

My mind drifts through each muscle, tendon, and vein. A stiff ache crawls over my neck. Tension seizes the tops of my shoulders and cinches my shoulder blades together. The raw lashes on my back burn with a searing fire, angry and never ending.

"Who sent you here?" Graeden asks.

Tib's face dances into my mind's eye. A smirk spreads over his stubbled chin. He's furiously handsome, except for the wicked gleam in his eyes.

The stripes on my back sizzle as though my anger has ignited them fresh. A pain I now feel instead of Tib's mother. Gritting my teeth, I concentrate on Tib—a balance of holding on to his face and focusing on my pain so neither capsize me. When the betrayal that cuts through my heart grows too fierce, I focus on the embers crackling along my back. When their heat seems ready to burst into flame, I switch back to Tib.

If only I could thrust this pain into his body.

Gasping, my eyes launch open. Tib's face disappears from my mind, and all my pain barrels into me with unbearable force.

"Are you alright?" Graeden shifts to the edge of his stool.

I nod and adjust my weight against the wooden panel. Everything about my body hurts.

"What did you see?" Graeden's voice is soft and gentle but brims with excitement.

"Tib," I whisper. "The one who sent me here."

"Good." Graeden leans forward, planting a hand on his knee.

A cold sweat dampens my skin. "I don't want to hate him. I don't want to think of him. It's too painful. Why does he have to be a part of this?"

Graeden lifts his chin slightly as though he understands all too well. "It's the only way we can release your monster. Why do most people never meet the monsters they hide inside?"

I narrow my eyes. "Because they're smart?"

"Because they have no need for it." Graeden wets his lips and rests his elbows on his knees, bringing his face within arm's reach. "Monsters feed off pain. They draw strength from hatred. If you can bury your pain and shrug off your hatred, your monster will settle down for a wakeless sleep. But you? You need your monster if you have any hope of surviving. Which means you need your pain and your hatred. That's why we focus on the one who sent you here."

My gaze drifts to the ground. If I want to survive—and I do—I must fan the flame of my anger. Wiping my tongue over my teeth, I nod.

"Let's try again." Graeden settles back on his stool once more. "Think of your pain. What would you do to the one who is at fault?"

I hesitate, reining in every drop of courage I have to face the past, then let my eyes fall shut.

This time, I allow myself to drift deeper into the pain I have been drowning in since arriving in the troll realm. Blows I thought would kill me, wounds that should have bled me out. Bruises tinged my wrists and dressed my skin. I cleave to the pain as I remember how one Seeker's steel tore my flesh or the webbing agony that spread across my jaw as a troll gave me a blow without laying a hand on me. My stomach roils with the unfairness of magic.

What I wouldn't give to fight a troll with no magic. What I wouldn't give to fight Tib, show him the woman he's created.

Heat flares through my bones, and I grasp onto the sensation as, for a moment, it mutes the memory of my anguish. But Graeden said I need my pain, my agony, my hatred. A deep breath floods my lungs, and I release the warmth, falling back into the memories and anchoring each one to Tib's crooked smile.

Throughout the day, Graeden tugs at the strands of Tib's betrayal. Sometimes I wallow within my hatred for hours, other times for only minutes. By the time the lights outside the narrow entrance dims, exhaustion tears through my mind, and it begs me for rest.

Graeden must notice the dark circles forming under my eyes or my fatigued responses. He spreads a small blanket over my back before departing.

Heat warms my skin from the inside as dark shadows consume everything around me. I spin in a slow circle, a blade locked in my grasp. A deep growl rumbles through the darkness, and I whip toward the direction it comes from; but when I turn, the snarl rotates around me until I am surrounded by it.

Lightning crackles through the darkness, illuminating horned wings. Confusion rolls over me until the wings dip inward, and my feet lift into the air. Wind whips through my hair, and the darkness presses against my face as I soar through the overcast sky.

My eyes snap open, and blood pounds through my head. A dream. I grasp at the fading straws—darkness, a monster, and fire—and let the entire thing disappear. Graeden already sits at my side, his ankle crossed over his knee, his fingers laced behind his head.

"About time." Graeden uncrosses his legs and offers me a small bowl filled with pieces of meat.

I don't bother asking what it is—in fact, I'm better off not knowing—and shove the juicy things into my mouth. The savory meat is tender, and when the bowl is empty, my mouth salivates for more. Instead, I swallow the drool and pick stray fragments from my teeth with my tongue.

"Should we pick up where we left off? We've got three days until you're thrown back into the arena."

I stifle a groan. How long will I have to wade through memories of Tib's betrayal, allowing him to splinter my already scarred heart?

"You know," Graeden interrupts my thoughts, "life's not so bleak. Yes, however you came to find yourself in Eida is, but what better place to shine than in darkness?"

I tilt my head, still not wishing to return to my haunted memories. "So, now you believe in me?"

"If I don't, who will?" Graeden leans back on his stool.

"Gee, thanks," I mutter.

"You can do this," Graeden says. "Not only can you survive this darkness, you can thrive in it, Ari. You need only to believe in it yourself."

My heart skips a beat, and my lips lift into a tentative smile. My attention hangs on my name. Ari. He called me Ari. "You—? Why?"

He doesn't need me to explain further. "Because if this *is* the end, you should feel like a real person."

Comforting.

Flames ignite in my lungs, a slow burn at my center. "I trust you," I whisper. I wish I didn't have to say these words. I don't want to trust him. But how can I afford not to? My body aches, and if left on my own, I'm sure I wouldn't survive another night. I have no one else to put my trust in.

"Then close your eyes." Graeden's hand falls from my shoulder, and his presence disappears from my side. "Imagine *him*."

The wounds tracing my back ache and smolder, a pain less sharp than it had originally been. I hold to the thought that perhaps it's healing. My mind picks up where it left off, and Tib lies bloodied and dying on the troll's ragged altar instead of me. His wounds carve deep into his flesh, and I smile. He deserves it. He deserves everything that has happened to me.

Lightning bursts, and an onslaught of memories flash through my mind. My first kill and the anguish that nearly overcame me as I crumpled in a heap beside the woman's body. Ugly tears had poured from my eyes, a terrible, broken sound ripping from my throat. I'd torn my sword from her belly and placed my hands over the wound. Her blood had slicked my palms and stained my clothes.

A flash of light, and the memory shifts. I lie on Haven's cold stone, no blanket, no food. Tremors rocked my body either from the frigid air blowing south from Ghora or from the stark reality that I'd just slaughtered my tenth human. Maybe both. Vomit spewed and blanketed my floor. Illness set in, and I wanted to let it take me.

Then a strobe of images streak through my vision. My sunken cheeks and dark-rimmed eyes stare back at me, my tear-stained skin makes my heart sink, and the grotesque hatred that often filled my heart stirs within me again.

I snare that hatred as though I catch strands weaving the tapestry of my past. My hatred belongs to the trolls but more so to Tib. Anger ripples beneath my skin, and a tempered heat warms my flesh. It trickles over the burns I've nearly forgotten mar my hand from Gunther's magic, it streams through the wounds on my back absorbing all pain. I breathe easily into the warmth.

I open my eyes, refreshed rather than crushed by the pain. One day, I will pay Tib back for what he's done. Whether or not Graeden releases my monster, it's already reared its head inside.

Shifting to the side, I raise my hand to my eyes. New, soft flesh splotches over my olive-toned skin. The burned skin is gone. Healed. My brows pinch, and I stare at the impossibility, rolling my hand over in front of my eyes. The only thing marring it now is Graeden's brand.

There's only one way my wounds could heal on their own. My shocked gaze flashes to Graeden, and he cocks his eyebrow.

My monster.

CHAPTER FOURTEEN

"How can this be?" I ask, unable to break my gaze from the healed skin painting my hand. "We haven't released my monster."

Graeden offers me his hand, and I place mine in it. His hands are softer than I expect. Contoured and shaped to wield a weapon, but soft.

He lifts my hand, and his thumb swipes over the faint scars. A warm tingle races over my skin, raising the hair on my arms. I watch his movement, the short nail caked with my blood.

A pang stabs at my chest. Aside from a few brief moments, Graeden's hardly left my side since I took his beating.

Rotating my hand in front of his eyes, Graeden purses his lips. "If it's healing on its own this soon, you must hide a very strong monster inside. Hellhound or not."

Graeden releases my hand, and I offer him a weak smile. I shift on the bed, and pain crackles through my back. Sarcasm coats my tongue. "Of course, it couldn't have bothered healing any of my lashes, could it?"

Graeden lifts an amused brow but ignores my sarcasm. "We must be getting close. It's about time."

The days twist and morph into one another, a meld of darkness and pain each accompanied by my growing fire of hatred toward Tib. I wait for the crack of bone as my body shifts into a hellhound or to discover the healing was a fluke and for my head to split open as a banshee scream tears from my lips.

Heat spills through my body, it pulses through the marrow of my bones, yet I remain utterly human. And suddenly, I'm out of time.

Graeden presses his hand against my shoulder as he helps lift me from my bed. Fresh gauze is wrapped around my body and pasted to my wounds to protect them from infection during battle. Even still, I feel the tug of the stitches—the tightening around the scabbing—and plead they remain closed. It won't matter, though, if I can't lift my sword. My body's stiff and weak from days of uselessness.

"Just breathe," Graeden counsels.

My legs dangle over the bed's edge, and my body quavers as I put weight on my feet. A current surges through my back, and I collapse against the bed, catching myself against the sturdy board. I suck in a sharp breath between my teeth and gulp down a bolt of air. Closing my eyes, I concentrate on Tib. Fire sparks under my ribcage. It dances through my veins, igniting my body with its heat, and the pain subsides.

"The monster healed my hands," I say. "Why didn't it heal my back?"

"You haven't unleashed it yet." Graeden offers me his arm, and I take it. "Whatever you are, it's strong. It may be that it healed your hand trying to escape. A burst of energy and will. If you are one of the three monsters who can heal, you can't access its full power without releasing it."

Gripping the edge of the board, I stand upright. The gauzy linen tunic is stiff and plastered against my thighs. It's hem barely reaches my knees, its discolored fabric pinched together above my tailbone. Days of seeping blood have not done it well.

My gaze drifts beyond Graeden to a wall of the cave I haven't seen. A thin blanket is crumpled in a heap next to a flattened pillow. Graeden's been sleeping on the ground this whole time.

"You look like hell."

I glare at Graeden. "I feel like it, too."

Graeden sets a pile of leathers on the bed, and he grimaces. He can't expect me to change my clothes with these wounds. "Unfortunately, you look like easy game dressed as you are."

"What? You don't think the blood stains would strike fear into my enemy's heart?" I mean it as a joke, but cynicism soaks the question. We both know that without my monster I'm going to die.

My frantic heartbeat lurches in my chest. Since arriving in Eida, I've often thought of death, but it's never felt so in reach as it does today. In less than an hour, I walk to my execution. I'm not ready to die.

I inhale a shaky breath and release the bed. Sifting through my memories of Tib, I find strength as I obliterate him again and again. Sword through flesh, poison in his drink, a sacrifice to Eida's beast. Heat burns through my pain.

"Get changed if you can. I'll wait outside." Graeden climbs out of the concealed shelter.

Loosening the tie at my waist, my tunic slips from my shoulders and falls around my ankles. The gauze wrapped tightly around my body hugs my chest—a support and added protection I won't refuse. I look over my shoulder hoping to see healed patches of skin like my hands, but the gauze covers everything.

My gaze settles on the leathers mocking me from the rumpled bedding. I unfold the stack, the new sleeveless tunic, belt, and thick leggings tumbling into a pile next to my sandals. I recoil just imagining tugging the fitted tunic over myself. Stooping to lift my top from the ground, I gasp as pain bolts through my body.

"Graeden!" I cry and lean against the table for support. "I need your tunic."

"My what?"

"Tunic. I can't get into my own."

Leaves bristle above the cave's entrance. Graeden descends the first few steps into the cave, his close-fitting black pants and leather boots preceding his bare sculpted torso. Stopping with his head obscured aboveground, Graeden balls the tunic and tosses it onto the bed.

I finger the coarse black fabric. It's thicker than I'm used to fighting in. I lift the tunic over my head, breathing into the fire that snakes through my back, and grunt as it tugs against the gauze. I plant my hands on the edge of the bed, catching my breath and redrawing heat into every inch of my body. Rolling my shoulders, I cinch the belt at my waist, the fabric gathering in large swells. If anything, I hope his tunic will give my wounds some added protection.

"Are you decent?" Graeden's voice echoes from above.

"More so than I've been this past week."

Graeden climbs down the steps, his tanned skin darker with the sun at his back.

"Can you help me with the leggings?" Heat warms my cheeks, but I shove it away. I wouldn't be able to get them off the floor let alone pulled over my feet.

Graeden doesn't hesitate. He stoops to collect the clothing from the ground, and gently wraps his hand around my calf. Lifting my leg from the ground, he slides the cloth over my skin. A different type of fire trails his touch, and my cheeks warm again.

Graeden straps on my sandals once I'm dressed, and my blood runs cold. This is it.

My steps are pathetic shuffles toward the stone stairs that lead into Arautteve's outer border. By the time we reach Badavaru, the arena already pounds with the roar of trolls wagering on the fight waiting for a bloodbath. My blood.

My stomach churns.

Graeden grips my elbow before I step into the promenade hall. "You *can* do this, Ari."

I drop my gaze to my body. My hands tremble, and I clench them into fists. The clamor of voices fills my head, and spots speckle across my vision. Pain ripples down my back as I lose my focus and allow fear to cloud my hatred.

"Ari!" Graeden steps in front of me, his hands gripping my upper arms.

My eyes flick to his just as his drop to where his hands brush my skin. Ari. He still thinks I'm going to die. Graeden loosens his grip and slides his hand to my elbow, exposing my *ndoa*. Shame colors my cheeks as my eyes trace the design swirling around my bicep.

Graeden narrows his eyes at my reaction. Tipping his chin upward, he says, "What does this marking mean?"

My heart aches like someone has torn it from my chest, a gaping void filled with bitterness and heartbreak. Emotion closes my throat and chokes out my voice. Graeden has seen the mark before but has never asked.

Everyone in our village expected Tib to court me, not kill me. This mark was my vow to tie myself to him. The embers of my heart crumble into smoking ash. The village elders matched us as youths. We were paired for life, as all in Bridgewick are, to bring unity to our village and to strengthen our people. The village elders sought after nothing more than that unity and control.

I lift my hand to trace the mark, my thoughts far from Badavaru. "It reminds me that to survive, I can only rely on myself."

Flames burst in my vision as I sit around the matrimonial bonfire in the center of our village. An elder tattooed my skin to link me with Tib—his mark is an exact replica of mine. Shadows danced across Tib's face as he sat next to me, his crooked smile brighter than any flame.

Courting was archaic in Bridgewick. Men spoke to the village elders when they wanted to tie themselves to a woman. The elders decided whether the man and woman would make a good match, bear strong children, and strengthen our people. If the elders said no, then the suitor would abandon his feelings no matter how strong. But if the elders said yes…

It was meant to be a flawless system that benefited the greater good of our village. I guess they never expected someone's selfish heart to blacken to the point they would kill their own betrothed without cause.

"Ah," Graeden says, breaking through my reverie. "That is a true adage… to a point. But now?" Graeden unsheathes his sword and offers it to me. My fingers curl around the hilt, its weight lighter than any sword I've ever wielded. "You have me in your corner."

Warmth curls through my stomach. I raise the sword at my side and run my fingers over the reflective steel. My palm presses against the blade. It's lighter than any blade I've wielded. Yet, no weapon has ever felt more natural in my hand.

"Graphene infused with troll blood."

My gaze snaps to Graeden's. "Who did you get troll blood from?"

"That's a story for another time." Graeden rotates me to face the doors to the promenade hall. "Right now, you need to focus on your anger and hatred. Let your monster help you overlook your pain."

Questions burn at the edges of my lips. In this moment, teetering at the edge of my life, I don't care if they make me sound weak.

"Will my monster be able to help me with the inhibitors on?" My voice shakes, and I swallow against the tremor tightening my throat.

Graeden shakes his head. "They're not turned on, remember? Until you've unleashed your monster, there's no need for the trolls to use their magic to power them."

"Right."

Graeden plants his hands on my shoulders. "Ari, focus. You can do this."

"Stop saying my name." I close my eyes and turn my chin to my shoulder. "My name from your lips means you think I'm going to die."

Graeden's mouth falls into a hard line, and his shoulders relax. He lifts my chin with a single finger, drawing my gaze to him. "No. At first, maybe. But your name is the name of a warrior—stronger than any Seeker. You have a life to fight for, Ari. And a right to fight for it."

With a gentle prod, Graeden ushers me through the archway and into the promenade hall. Trolls line the open corridor, their raucous cheers swarm around me while others' blathering insults ricochet off my skin like arrows.

Tib. With each pain-ridden step, the trolls' chaos dampens. Pebbles scrape the packed dirt beneath my sandals, and I focus on the rough texture of stone scraping against stone. My lungs fill, and the warmth of my anger burns through my pain.

Before I realize it, I've reached the arena. Chains screech as they grind against the taut pressure lifting the portcullis. My enemy already stands inside. With a cautious glance over my shoulder at Graeden, I step into the arena.

The trolls stomp their feet against the stadium seats, and the ground rumbles with their lust for blood. My opponent shifts his weight from one foot to another as I take slow, careful steps toward him. Blood pounds in my ears, and I hope he sees my delay as confidence rather than caution.

A snug, bronze helmet twinkles on his head, the slit over his eyes too narrow for my sword's blade. Thick leather pads drape over his shoulders, dripping into an ornate chest plate hanging across his midsection. He wears armor along his shins, his forearms protected by bronze bracers. The man carries a large shield in his right hand, and a serrated scythe in his left.

A simple, spiraled emblem is emblazoned on his shield, one I've seen only a few times in the arena.

A weight falls heavy in my chest. He's a carver. A fighter who takes great satisfaction in a slow kill, the scythe used to disembowel his enemies. I've glimpsed them fight in the arena as I've come and gone from my battles, but never have I fought one myself.

Flaming nights! Why must he be my opponent today of all days?

My gaze roams over his armor—he's taken no chances. His vital organs lie protected beneath his heavy chest plate, and with my injuries there is no way in Eida's depths I will be able to deliver a blow powerful enough to bring him down.

Leather bracers wrap around my own forearms but are brittle scraps of parchment compared to his. He steps forward, and his chest plate clanks against his shield. Though he's protected, he will be slow. Hopefully, slower than me. That weakness is my only chance to survive.

I scan his armor again as the bronze assailant trudges forward, closing the distance between us. His thighs and his upper arms are exposed, and a subtle slit of skin is visible between his shoulder armor and his chest plate. That's how I'll have to kill him.

I swing my sword in a wide circle at my side. A shock surges through my back, and I gasp.

Tib. My monster's flame hardly flares. Slamming my eyes shut, I force Tib's traitorous smile to the forefront of my mind. His hand brushes my arm and instead of butterflies swarming in my stomach, a chill prickles the hair on my skin. Venom rushes over my tongue, and I imagine flipping his hand in mine and running my blade through him.

A subtle flame sparks in my belly. I grasp onto Tib's expression, the blood draining from his face as it has from so many others I've killed. Their blood screams from my hands because of him. The spark catches, and fire flows through my body, the jolt of pain smothered by my monster.

I open my eyes, and my heart lurches into my throat. The man slams his shield into my side, and I sprawl across the ground. The inner fire sputters as I lose my focus, but I draw it back to block the pain. The man thrusts his scythe toward my chest. I roll out from under its point. It slams into the ground with a deafening screech.

Pushing myself to my feet, I cleave to the fire burning against my chest. The flames leap through my body, erasing the pain as

I feel it. I draw myself to my full height, straightening my back. The man lunges, swiping his scythe through the air again, and I leap out of the way.

A bare tickle of pain ricochets through my scarcely healed back. My confidence grows with each dodge. The man edges closer, thrusting his shield between us as he approaches. I dart to the side and swipe my blade at his calves. The man stumbles forward, a trail of blood trickling down his pale leg.

Oh, if only I had my two swords.

The man growls. He lurches forward, his shield crushing into my arm and chest. I stumble backwards but keep my legs beneath me. His feet stir up the dust as he lunges again, his shield ramming into my side. Discomfort flickers over my ribs and stokes a fire across the wounds lacing my back.

I inhale slowly, regaining control over the pain. But the man slams his shield into my side again and again. My sandals slip against the dirt, and I scramble to remain on my feet.

The man roars and dives forward. His shield collides with my arm, and agony splinters through the bone. The ground meets my back, flat and unrelenting. My breath whooshes from my lungs, and I'm left gasping. The man straddles my waist and slashes his scythe toward me. Throwing my arms out, I barely catch the weapon between the Seeker's hands. The curved blade is inches from my face.

Blinding pain climbs through my arms as I push every ounce of my strength against the weapon. The blade moves an inch away, but I can't hold it.

My bones tremble and stabbing pain crackles through my back. Sweat trickles down my cheeks, and the scythe slips ever closer. I grasp for the fading image of Tib and shove it onto the man about to steal my life.

That stupid grin and idiotic smirk plaster onto Tib's face. He pinches his brows, and his lips dip into a frown just as they had done that night at the Well. Mocking me. Tib forces the blade toward me.

He's the one pinning me to the ground. He's the one drawing blood from my arms. It trickles over my skin and drips onto Graeden's tunic. He's the one trying to kill me.

No more.

Flames burst to life at my fingertips, and the heat that had warmed my skin quickly morphs into searing torment. Wood splinters as I tear the scythe from the carver's hands. Fire, thick and clouded, rages past my vision, and I scream. The sound is swallowed up in the growing fire. Pain surges through my spine, a loud crack and the sound of bone snapping echoes into the darkness.

The man's face shifts into an expression of horror, his eyes wide and his mouth open in a paralyzed scream. He stumbles away from me, abandoning his weapon altogether.

Heat blossoms in my chest and blazes through my body like I've never felt before. It consumes every other sensation—no pain, no heartache. Only rage. Expansive wings spread out at my sides like a monstrous bat, glistening in an ombre of berries and teal.

My body shifts, and my consciousness drifts inward as though taking a seat on the sidelines to watch the world from behind glass.

A large, scaled leg pounds into the dust, claws pawing at the earth. My head tips forward, and I glance a pale underbelly flanked by horned wings. Smoke billows from my maw with each step my monster takes toward the terrified Seeker.

I'm a dragon-shifter. Confidence obliterates my insecurities, and raw power tsunamis through my body.

Sweltering heat gathers inside my chest—I feel its warmth, I crave its eruption—but I don't control it. A deafening roar bursts from my monster's mouth, and the heat in my chest catapults toward the Seeker. Behind the glass of my monster's eye, the entire arena is caught up in the flames.

As it settles, the Seeker peeks out from behind his red-hot shield. The bronze armor droops, the metal oozing in large swells to the dusty floor. Throwing his armor to the side, the Seeker's panicked eyes snap toward me. The man retreats from my monster, but there is nowhere to run where she can't kill him.

Screams echo through the crowd, and the trolls' grotesque jeers and taunts for blood transform into a wave of manic cries. The inhibitors are off. I stare at the space between the arena and the stadium. There's no flicker of color rising into the air. The trolls are unprotected from the monsters within the arena. We could burn them all.

My dragon launches a tail studded with reflective spikes toward the man backing himself into a corner. He dodges the blow, a whimper escaping his lips. Fire burns against my chest again. The man is out of places to run.

The heat pours from my dragon's snout and drowns out the man's screams. When the flames die, all that's left is a pale silhouette against the stone.

Suddenly the raw power coursing through my veins stifles as though flooded with lead. My dragon can't move. Instead, our body teeters forward against our will. She fights it, snapping her jaws into the air. Heat builds against my chest again, but this time there's nowhere for it to go.

My dragon stumbles over her legs and her underbelly crashes against the ground, dust rising to consume the wayward flames. We are pinned against the ground, though no one touches us. I glance at the inhibitors now rich with magic. The barriers between me and the stadium pulse with the rare hues of this realm.

A dull ache spreads through my body growing in intensity as my dragon is stuffed back inside. I can't breathe. My fingers claw at the ground as the scales clinging to my body like feathers return to flesh. The remaining heat scalds my throat as it ejects in a sweltering cloud of steam.

Claiming my true form, the inhibitor towers release me. Full, easy breaths fill my lungs. Graeden's tunic hangs over my body, tattered and torn. Fire has singed its way through a good part of it. My leggings aren't much better.

I crawl to my feet. The crowd stares at me, their eyes full of curiosity. I doubt they've ever seen a Fallen release their monster for the first time. Or a dragon, for that matter.

I'm not sure what the trolls will do. Without waiting to find out, I march toward the portcullis. It doesn't budge. It doesn't matter.

Lifting Graeden's sword from the ground, I feel as though I walk on air.

CHAPTER FIFTEEN

"This is incredible." Graeden's hands hover over the smooth skin now blanketing my exposed shoulder blades.

I roll Graeden's tunic back over my shoulders and spin to face him. "I guess it wasn't hellfire in my blood after all."

Graeden's wide eyes linger on my bare arm as though trying to see the dragon scales beneath it. "You claimed to have fire in your blood, and here you are. Sometimes belief is the strongest power of all."

I pace along a wall of loculi in a vaulted stone room beneath Eida's surface. Every few steps, I pass another column of narrow graves carved horizontally into the hardened earth. They disappear into the shadows above. It's as if the grave-keepers built the catacomb and then dug out the floor as they needed space for more graves. The cold stone emanates a chill I imagine only the dead can truly feel the weight of.

After the battle, Graeden had ushered me to the farthest reach of Arautteve where the vibrant florals dissipate into a sea of crimson sand. The Blood Desert blazed beneath the unrelenting heat, and sweat had dewed across my skin.

Graeden had said the Blood Desert is rarely so calm. What I wouldn't have given for a slight breeze as we tromped through the sand. We kept to a strict path, weaving between vibrant sand dunes.

Graeden didn't tell me where we were headed until we had buried ourselves deep inside Eida's catacombs. Honestly, I'm not sure who they bury within these walls as most Marked are fed to Eida's beast. Regardless, I drew too much attention in the arena today, and Graeden would like to keep our trainings private moving forward.

My sandals scuff over the hard, stony floor, and the sound echoes toward the vaulted ceiling. There's enough room on this floor for not only my dragon to soar but at least another monster or two. As we descended through the catacombs' first few galleries, natural light poured into the shadows through carved apertures. On the fourth level down, however, we rely on oil lamps. Their flames flicker along the walls between each grave as Graeden lights them.

I settle onto an ornamentally carved bench resting between two columns of graves. "Are you sure we're deep enough?"

Graeden glances toward the shadowed staircase, setting down a small bag of provisions and the two staffs he'd brought. "We should be," he says. "No one travels into the Blood Desert. No one wants to risk meeting the Werebeast."

"The what?"

"The Werebeast. It's a vicious creature who protects the realm's life force." Graeden waves his hands. "It doesn't matter. The point is no one will come looking for you here."

"But you feel confident we can beat the creature, if it finds us?" I lift an amused brow, and a smile toys with my lips.

Graeden's eyes meet mine, and he smiles. "Well, you are a dragon-shifter."

"What does this mean?" My amusement slips.

"I think it means I'm going to need my tunic back." Graeden tosses me the new clothes from before my battle. "And that you have a real chance of making it home."

I roll my eyes. "I guess you'll be wanting your blade back, too."

Graeden inhales slowly, his eyes caught on mine. "That you can keep. For now."

A smile tugs at my lips. "Turn."

He does.

I shrug out of his ruined shirt, the edges singed and a large hole torn through its middle. The muscles along my back stretch as I raise my arms and slip the fitted top over my head. I tug on a new pair of thick leggings and almost sigh. A perfect fit.

"What do you mean I have a real chance?" The words spill over my lips, and I try to suppress the hope growing in my stomach.

"Your Pardon, Ari." Graeden turns to face me, his gaze raking over the new clothes. "Do you feel your dragon's strength?"

I don't even have to try. My dragon's raw power courses through my veins like nothing I've ever felt before. I clench my fists as though I can force the inner flames to my palms.

"Yes," I say.

Shadows cast from the small oil lamps' flames plunge Graeden's eyes into darkness. Even amidst the dead's chill, his body heat weaves its way between us.

"A dragon is stronger than perhaps any other monster." Lacing his fingers together, Graeden leans back against the crypts. "The trolls will throw you into the arena more often, but your dragon won't help you until the third round. Right now, she is primal and unrefined. She is strong, but she is like an infant thrashing about. When you learn to rein in your dragon's fire and to control your monster, then that strength can become your weapon. It's only when you accept both halves of yourself that you will be able to control her."

I flinch. Become one with my dragon? No one ever said anything about uniting with it. I imagine the monster's bloodlust overshadowing me, and my heart wars within itself. If I do this, will I truly become a monster?

"How many kills are you at?" Graeden asks.

I don't pause to count. The number drags me into my nightmares and glares at me each morning. I clear my throat. "Four hundred."

Graeden's eyes widen. "In how many years?"

I swallow my discomfort. "Two."

In truth, Tib's betrayal sowed the seeds of a monster before Graeden ever spoke of releasing my dragon. I stare at my worn sandals. Would uniting with another monster be so different?

"Then only thirty-six hundred kills to go until you reach your Pardon." Graeden lifts the two weathered staffs from the ground. I stretch my fingers before taking one from him. "You've been out of practice for too long. If you're going to reach your Pardon, you must make it through the first two rounds. Your monster can't do all the work for you."

A smile toys with my lips. I could reach my Pardon. I could be free of this wretched realm. I inhale a sobering breath, but it doesn't quelch my anticipation. This dragon could be my passage out of here. Forever.

Drawing a leather strap off my wrist, I tie my hair in a rough bundle on top of my head and then swing my staff at Graeden's legs. He lithely leaps over it, jabbing his own staff toward me, and we step into our dance.

The only way anyone gets out of Eida's realm is by reaching their Pardon—killing four thousand Seekers. It's an impossible feat, though maybe not quite as impossible as I'd originally thought. Maybe I can still reach the kills without ever uniting myself with my dragon. Instead, I could use it. A shimmer of hope soothes the knot tightening in my chest. In time, I might return home. See my mother again.

The nostalgia fades. See Tib.

Flames engulf my hope and burn it to a heap of ash. When I return home, Tib dies first. Emotion tightens my throat—what a villainous beast I've become in two short years. My four hundred kills were all done out of my need to survive—kill or be killed. But this last one...

Bloodlust sweeps through my heart, but this visceral craving for blood isn't mine. It's the monster's. Inexplicable rage barrels through my body. My vision tunnels, focusing on the coward who sent me here. Too long I suffered in the shadows of Haven, starving and buried with fear. Too long did others push me down paths I did not want to go.

My arms vibrate as our staffs collide. I swing. A crack splinters into the air. Faster. Harder. It's not my strength behind the advances. My arms arc through the air before I've given the command, and it's all Graeden can do to block the blows. Our feet scrape over the soft stone, and it's the monster inside who pushes me forward. Who sees Tib's face on Graeden's body.

I grind my teeth together and draw the rage inward. I focus on my advances—*mine*—and thrust my staff toward Graeden. He sidesteps, leaving an easy opening to crack my staff across his ribs. I don't. I'm not my monster. We end our spar in a stalemate, a few stray hairs clinging to my flushed cheeks.

My dragon's strength rushes through my veins. It's a constant rage, like an unstoppable river crashing in on itself. I step away from Graeden, away from the fight. The dragon's fury simmers with the distance between us, but not by much. I drop my staff and lean against the wall. My heart thunders in my chest. Closing my eyes, I will it to calm down.

"Again," Graeden orders. He slips the toe of his boot under my staff and kicks it into his open palm. Show off.

Rolling my shoulders, I push myself from the wall. I'm not afraid of this monster. It belongs to me. No one is safe from us. And Graeden and I dance.

Deep in the catacombs, I have no sense of time passing, but Graeden seems to know when the day has gone. After stashing our staffs in the shadows, Graeden leads the way out.

"There are a few things you need to understand about claiming your monster." Graeden's boots slap against the stairs spiraling to the surface. "You can shift on your own, but for a while, you will likely not be in full control. Not until you and your dragon become one. Until then, you obey me."

I bristle and open my mouth to object. Graeden shoots me a sharp look over his shoulder, and I press my lips together. The brand against my wrist burns as though I need reminding of why I belong to him.

"No other master or Fallen can force you to do anything by word alone. Magic, on the other hand…" Graeden pulls his attention back to the dark staircase ahead of us. A small pocket of light rounds the bend as we near the upper galleries. "We were quick enough slipping out of the arena, I think most of the trolls were still scratching their jaws wondering what in hell's fury happened. You can't be too careful, though. We will train with your dragon here from now on."

When we reach the second gallery, evening light dusts the walls.

"Even still," Graeden says. "Watch your back."

A laugh builds in my throat. I'm a dragon-shifter. I don't think I need to worry. At the first sign of magic, my dragon can reenact her arrival and incinerate the brute.

"Why are you smiling?" Graeden barks. He pulls up short in the first gallery of the catacomb. The walls separating us from the outer world feel paper thin.

I smother the humor and pinch my lips.

Graeden advances slowly, his cutting gaze never leaving mine. "Your dragon can heal any wound you receive in your human form. In its form, it can heal, but it is much slower. Whether you like it or not, your dragon is a part of you. There's nothing funny about controlling that type of power. You two will need to become one."

A groan tightens in my throat, but I swallow it. Instead, I answer him with a small nod.

Graeden leads me out of the catacombs' sole entrance. The light has darkened in the cloud-filled sky, a faint breeze blowing the sand around our ankles. It pricks my bare skin. We weave through the sandy terrain, our path blending into everything else.

When our feet find Arautteve's flagstone walkways, Graeden flashes me a stern gaze. "Figure out how to become one with it. Agreed?"

For a moment, I only stare at Graeden. He lifts an expectant brow. "Fine. Yes, I agree."

Graeden makes it sound so easy to become one. A spark of heat burns against my lungs. I think this will be anything but easy.

Graeden's eyes flick between mine, as though trying to decide if he believes me. "A monster needs a master, and if you won't master your dragon, then someone else will. Don't stall getting to your chamber. I'd hate for someone to try."

"Wouldn't dream of it," I sigh.

Graeden wanders down the path opposite from where all the Fallen live. My eyes trace the silhouette of his broad shoulders and roam over the corded muscles in his bare arms. Even in this dim light, his contours are easy to imagine. Heat rises unbidden into my cheeks. Averting my eyes, I shake the warmth from my skin.

Silence has fallen on Arautteve as I stroll through the emptying streets. Most Fallen have returned to their chambers for the night. I tip my face to the sky. Flames weave through my muscles, a simmering anger I can't quite smother.

"We're to become one," I whisper.

I don't know what I expect, but my dragon doesn't respond or even flicker her inner fire in agreement.

I scan the thick purple clouds. Maybe somewhere behind them hides a star? Something to encourage me that not all is lost. Some proof that someday I'll make my way out of this realm. I glance over my shoulder at the barren streets. I'll go straight to the temple… in a moment. Wilting onto a stone retaining wall, I exhale until my lungs are empty.

"A dragon-shifter." The words are a whisper, hardly a breath, but I need to hear them from my own lips.

All this time, who knew I carried such darkness? Such strength. For a moment, I imagine the look on the Bridgewick elders' faces when they see the wings at my side or the fire pouring from my mouth. A slight smile crooks my lips, but it doesn't last.

The elders would have called me what I am. A monster. Dangerous. A threat to our village. They would have been right. Shame crackles through my chest, and then I see those silver eyes.

I expect my mother to slip into my thoughts, but it isn't her. It's my father's eyes. That silver pair at war with the world, torn with sorrow as though the only light within them is my face in their reflection. And as my face shifts into my monster, even that light begins to die. The sorrow within that aged pair of eyes tugs the familiar gaze downward, and my heart aches. Shutting out the image, I force my own gaze to wander again among the starless sky.

"Well, what do we have here?"

CHAPTER SIXTEEN

I JOLT FORWARD. A troll stares down at me with a toothy smirk. His voice rumbles in his throat, and heat sparks beneath my skin. A small grouping of trolls surrounds me, three to one. The beasts. They think they can take me? I inhale a calming breath against the inner fire and force myself to concentrate.

My arms tense at my sides, and my hands clench into fists. One by one, I meet each of their beady, hungry eyes.

"This is the dragon-shifter?" Condescension pours from the second troll's voice. "She is a little one, isn't she?"

My muscles tense as the trolls circle me, a small ember crackling to life along my spine. I inhale through my nose—calm down.

"Do you think her dragon is small, too?" The third troll badgers, a thundering laugh nearly masquerading his question. "Should we poke it and find out?"

"I wouldn't if I were you," I warn.

My jaw tenses as my warning only brings smiles to their faces, alighting a challenge within their onyx eyes.

"Wouldn't you?" The first troll swipes a hand in my direction, but I leap out of his reach. His face twists with a mocking snarl. "You shouldn't be hard to tame. You're freshly changed. Undisciplined. Won't take much magic to bridle. I bet my little finger on it."

The other trolls tighten their circle around me, and the ember within me bursts into a small flame. *Control it.*

The air thins as they close in, the shrinking space between us feeling like a noose.

The first troll smacks his lips, and his expression settles into a smug sneer. He brandishes a blade, the steel glinting in the low light. "Would the dragon like to come out and play?"

Energy hums through our veins. My hand finds the hilt of my sword, and I draw the blade. I feel my dragon's defenses rise.

The small flame in my chest erupts into a bonfire, leaping from contained to uncontrollable in seconds. The dragon's heat scorches my veins. Dropping my blade, I fall to my knees. My hands claw at the air, and I tip my head to the sky. Her fire floods my bones and surges through my veins.

Everything is painted red, and I grit my teeth to keep from screaming. She wants to attack. To fight.

If I won't master my dragon, someone else will.

Horror battles for place next to my dragon's fire. Graeden had warned me. They want me to shift. My dragon's heat is too stifling, and it quickly snuffs out my understanding. Bone cracks through my body as my dragon's teal wings unfold into the dark night. She screeches into the air, a warning call before her attack.

The trolls gather—an easy kill. Magic cyclones from the stores above us, and bolts of power flash in the sky. My eyes trace its path, and though I watch it feed into the troll's palms, my dragon does not. The trolls whisper words I can't hear over my dragon's ferocious roar, her glistening teeth within striking distance.

Either strike or shift back! But my dragon does neither.

The ground quakes beneath her heavy footfalls, her claws digging into the hard earth. Magic collects around the trolls, a faint amethyst mist. My dragon roars again, and this time the sound wedges in her throat. I gasp. An invisible hand locks around her neck. Her body scrambles, panicked. My consciousness does the same. My dragon heaves small sips of oxygen, but it's not enough. Fire burns through her lungs, unquenchable. And I can feel all of it.

Stop.

My command is feeble. The trolls raise their hands, and my dragon's monstrous body rises into the air with the gesture.

You're killing us, I think, hoping my dragon can hear me.

Through the blood-red glass of my dragon's eyes, I watch her scramble against the air unable to hurt the trolls. She swipes her sharpened claws in their direction but is too far to do any damage. The more she fights, the tighter the trolls strangle her neck.

The tastes of fresh air disappear.

I choke, gasping against the enchanted noose. Darkness swarms through both our visions, bleeding into the red. My dragon's strength wanes, her attacks growing heavy and slow. We're going to die.

The fire raging in my chest vaporizes into steam, and I sense my dragon release her control.

Be still! My dragon's body falls limp at my command, dangling in the air.

The noose relaxes around her neck as she falls to the ground in a tangled heap. Air whooshes into her lungs, and my dragon gulps down heavy mouthfuls. The darkness invading our vision clears.

Pressure swells against my consciousness and against her organs. The sensation of the dragon trying to cram herself back inside my body is overwhelming. Something blocks her from shifting back.

"Don't try to hide now, beautiful." The first troll leers at my monster, his eyes hungry. "We have a job for you to do."

My dragon squirms, the pressure growing against our bones as she tries to force our shift. Magic sparkles at the second troll's fingertips—he's frozen our form, holding me hostage as my monster.

The first troll flicks his fingers toward himself, and a crushing weight grinds my dragon's neck to the ground. We stare upward at the troll's bulging belly and hairy chin. He squats next to my dragon's head and brushes a rough hand over her snout. His eyes flicker to the horns on top of her head, and he strokes them like he has any right to touch her.

Fire crackles to life inside of my chest again. *Be still,* I warn. *We can't win while under his magic.*

The troll waves a hand past our eyes, a violet shimmer trailing its path. The red overtone tinging my dragon's gaze fades into the same violet as the troll's magic. The weight disintegrates from her neck, and she rises to her full height.

"That's better," the troll sneers. "Let's go."

The trolls crawl onto my dragon's back, their sharp toenails digging between her scales and snagging the flesh beneath.

"Take us to Ghora."

Without a spare thought, my dragon unfurls her wings, and we're airborne. It won't be long before we reach the district where the Seekers' live, awaiting their battles in the arena. But why would the trolls want a dragon there?

Before long, thick obsidian rock blankets the land for miles in every direction. Every peak reflects the dull clouds above, every step slick and treacherous. Haven was only ever a shadow of despair compared to this. Darkness caresses my dragon's scales, and her mouth salivates with the promise of blood.

My gaze flickers over the rough strip of Haven. You can barely see the boulder line that separated the Unmarked Fallen from the Seekers. Not that it matters now. Shadows obscure the Unmarked's razed camp. No one's there anymore. My eyes wander through Ghora's darkness toward the mountains in the west. I wonder if those who survived settled elsewhere. My chest tightens.

The trolls guide my dragon away from Haven and toward the center of Ghora. Human men and women scurry across the blacktop as though they skate on ice. Air whooshes like a storm around my dragon's wings as we descend into the mountain. The ground trembles beneath my dragon's landing, and a fracture splits through its smooth surface.

The trolls leap from her back, drawing dull blades stained with blood. They retreat toward the twisted spires stretching to the blackened clouds like claws.

"Herd the humans," one troll bellows.

The trolls slink into the darkness. My dragon pounds her claws into the ground, roaring into the dark sky—a warning for humans to expose themselves. None do. She clamors to the nearest hill where a subtle tunnel weaves through its base. Bubbled air holes permeate the stone like pumice, some as large as a human.

My dragon lumbers to one of the larger holes and shoves her snout into the tunnel. Fire explodes in her chest and then tears from her throat, pouring into the tunnel. Humans scream as they scatter through the ends of the passageway and into the open.

Before they find another place to hide, a rivulet of magic weaves among them. Their terrified sprints halt, the frantic expressions plastered to their faces. The trolls slink out from hiding, magic flourishing at their fingertips. They slowly prowl from one unmoving Seeker to another and press a finger to each of their temples.

The first troll tips his head back, his mouth falling open, and his tongue salivating as though whatever he does satiates some part of him. Tendrils of light swirl beneath the Seeker's skin and then absorbs into the troll's finger. He lifts his hand, and the Seeker collapses as the troll moves onto the next.

What are they doing?

"More!" The troll commands as my dragon and I watch them rummage through the Seeker's minds.

"Stealing a Marked Fallen?" Graeden's voice cuts through the savagery. A torch blazes in his hand. "You trolls must have a death wish."

My resilience buckles, and relief slips through my veins. Thank the stars. The trolls' eyes fall on Graeden, their lips curving into twisted smiles. "Kill him."

Flames engulf my vision as we lunge at Graeden, out of control. Dropping his torch, Graeden rolls under my dragon's outstretched claw and darts beneath her belly, headed straight for the trolls. They stumble in retreat, taken aback by his deft avoidance of their enslaved monster.

Swords form in the trolls' grips traced with the light of their magic. Graeden swings his blade toward one, and embers of magic spray over the ground as the steel collides. Pushing off the troll, Graeden spins backward, catching another's magic-infused blade.

My dragon retreats from the clashing steel. Violence still fumes through her chest. We still want to kill Graeden, but the fight has distracted her enough to not advance.

The three trolls approach Graeden with their teeth bared. Graeden strides toward them and raises his sword. He doesn't hesitate. A quick swing at their necklines, and three dismembered heads bounce over the slick stone, blood pooling around their necks.

"Shift back," Graeden orders, picking up his torch.

The pressure collides with my body, and this time my dragon's form folds into my frame with ease. My clothes hang in shreds from my body. Graeden's blade is gone, left behind in Arautteve. Graeden sweeps a dark cloak over my shoulders and hands me a dagger. A rich musky scent floods the still air with his movement, and I breathe it in. There's a hint of sweetness like woodsmoke lightly touched by vanilla. As the scent settles with the cloak, my focus sharpens.

"We need to get out of here before others come." Graeden drops the lit torch near a charred corpse lying partly inside the tunnel where the Seekers had hidden. "This unlucky fellow is saving your life. Anyone who travels through here will think it was he who burned the others."

Cloaked in Ghora's darkness, we flee from the Seeker's district. Only when we slip through the Crossing does Graeden's grip ease around my wrist. As our gait slows, my legs wobble, but the tension in my muscles soften. It's over. My skin tingles as though the trolls still control me, as though their hands themselves wander across my skin. The hair raises on the back of my neck, and I push the thoughts away.

Graeden tramps toward Arautteve's temples. Breathing strength into my fatigued muscles, I follow. And with each step in his wake, my heart settles. Calm. Safe.

My eyes trace Graeden's form. The firm set of his shoulders, his tall posture, the anger that ripples from him in waves. I inhale, wrapping his cloak tighter around myself. Safe.

"What happened?" Graeden grunts.

"I have no idea," I whisper. "The trolls taunted me, and out of nowhere, my dragon took control. They enchanted her to take them to Ghora and flush out the Seekers. What were they doing?"

The veins running along Graeden's neck tauten, and his lips flatten into a hard line. "Nothing you need to concern yourself with."

"How did you find us so quickly?" I ask, making a mental note to press him later about the trolls.

"You belong to me, remember?" Graeden leads us east toward Badavaru. "Don't forget, your brand does more than mark your skin. Besides, a dragon soaring through the troll realm isn't something one can easily miss, especially when the only dragon here is you."

A light dusting of turquoise trails Graeden's triceps. I jerk my chin toward the color. It's the only sign I've ever seen that Graeden harbors some other creature inside. "Are you sure it has nothing to do with that?"

Graeden glances over his shoulder at the shimmering color. He swipes his hand across the back of his arm, and it disappears. "Positive."

A subtle wisp of amusement trickles into my chest before reality smothers it. "They could have destroyed everyone in Ghora." The thought makes my stomach churn.

"They could have." Graeden offers me a sidelong glance, and his anger cools. "They weren't always like this."

"How could you possibly know that?" I ask. "How long have you been here?"

Graeden lifts a brow, a sly smile curling over his lips.

"Five years? Six?"

"Long enough you should trust me when I say you don't want to know." Graeden breaks his gaze from mine and squints to the east as though he can see beyond something I cannot. "The trolls may be different now, but I don't believe they're lost. This realm began as a sanctuary. For some, it still is."

A sanctuary? Never have I heard of Eida referred to as a place of refuge. An insult tangles in my throat. Graeden's words carry a sincerity I haven't heard in years, though. I don't want to break whatever hope he's found in this hell.

My gaze flicks to Graeden's, and, despite the devastation of the night, he smiles.

"Now shake it off and go get some sleep. Tomorrow afternoon, you're in the arena."

CHAPTER SEVENTEEN

MY GLARE BURNS THROUGH the arena, a blazing ember compared to the rage bottled inside me.

Barely twenty-four hours. That's what the Troll King gave me between unleashing my dragon and executing his next Seeker. For the love of Eida, he could've given me a few nights to adjust.

The king's beady eyes flick to mine. I hold my glare as his head tips low, his pointed nose an arrow aimed at my heart. His thin mouth tugs into a deeper frown.

Though, I'm not sure he wished me to recover. Ever.

I grip and regrip my sword, but it hangs heavy in my grasp. A subtle tremor climbs through my veins, and exhaustion barrels through my limbs.

I tug against my stiff leather tunic—a new piece of battle wear I found at the bottom of the wicker basket in my room since my dragon shredded my other clothes.

You really must stop doing that, I chide her.

A flare of heat burns through my chest as though she says, *I will do no such thing.*

I grind my teeth and force the tremor in my arms to still. The Seeker dances lithely on the toes of his shoes, his narrow frame and soft face suggesting his adolescence. He must be younger than I, but only by a few years. I hate when they send youth into the arena. I'd much rather kill a warrior who's already stained his soul through murder and bloodshed. The ones who look at me like a woman they wish to conquer and a challenge they wish to vanquish.

Not those whose throats bob as they hold their weapons not nearly high enough. Or whose loose stances admit their inexperience in an arena.

The young man bares his teeth, and he swings his long sword high over his head before we're even in reach of one another. Wrong. I don't wait for him to miss with his blade. Sprinting toward the boy, I slide against the ground beneath his arm. He stumbles forward, trying to catch the momentum of his swing.

Popping to my feet, a new energy hums through my veins, and the weariness fades. My hand holds my blade stronger. More confident. The boy pivots to face me, and I swing my sword. A fireball collides against the inside of my ribcage, and my body sails away from the Seeker. I slam into the arena's wall.

Pain splinters through my middle. Breaths short, uneven, gasping. Rolling to my knees, I suck in a long, slow breath. The heat against my ribs sizzles to bare cinders.

What do you think you're doing? I growl at my dragon.

She remains silent.

Stretching my shoulders, I attack. The boy dodges. He raises his blade to get on the offensive, but I roll over my shoulder. The boy thrusts his blade into the earth, a hair's breadth from where my body just rolled.

I leap to my feet at his side. His eyes widen with panic, his blade anchored in the hard soil at his feet. He frantically tugs at the weapon. Locking my arm with his, I roll across his back and launch him through the air. He spins away, smashing into a heap against the ground.

Swinging my blade at my side, I step toward him. Pain ricochets through my abdomen, and I fall to a knee. Bolts of searing heat rip through my bones, a lightning storm of agony stabs the deepest recesses of my body.

The inhibitors should be restraining my dragon, but she's too strong. Too wild.

Flaming monster! You're going to kill us both.

The bolts settle, but not even long enough for my heartbeat to calm. The heat engulfs my body, and I collapse face first into the dirt. My lungs are on fire, the dry air kindling to feed her flames. I can't breathe. Can't think.

I barely register the boy reclaiming his lost sword and sauntering unsurely in my direction. The boy lifts the blade above my body.

Dragon! As fast as it came, the flames rein inward leaving behind a hollow chill.

I thrust my leg toward the boy and knock his feet out from beneath him. His sword clatters from his fingertips as he goes down. I snatch his steel, the hilt slick with his sweat. One step. One thrust. One body.

Blood crawls down the point of my blade and drips onto the dirt. My lip curls with the metallic scent I can never escape.

Riotous laughing and cheers bubble toward the sky. My shoulders relax, and the exhaustion returns to my body in full force. It's over. I toss the boy's blade next to his body and stomp from the arena.

What in the bloody sands were you thinking?

Warmth hums through my veins. My dragon didn't care about killing the boy. She cared about besting me. She cared about lording her strength and power over me. I frown.

Graeden meets me outside the portcullis, a faded rag in his hand. I snatch the cloth and scrub the drying blood from my skin.

"Four hundred and one." I ball the cloth in my fist. One step closer to reaching my pardon. I'm tempted to glance over my shoulder where the trolls gather my opponent's body but think better of it. He should've thought twice about entering Eida's realm.

Four hundred and one. By the time I reach four thousand, I'll be an old woman. Anger seethes in my stomach.

We are supposed to be one, I growl at my dragon. Fighting the beast I harbor inside will kill me before a Seeker ever does.

Graeden latches his hand around my upper arm and whips me back toward the arena.

"What the he—" I stammer.

"Hold your dagger tight," Graeden says. "And don't stop."

Graeden drags me back into the arena, my tired legs nearly buckling beneath his speed. I glance through the near empty stadium. The few trolls remaining shuffle toward the exits, their attention focused outside of the arena.

When we reach the Seeker's side, Graeden shoves me through the portcullis into Ghora. A quick glance over his shoulder, and he ducks into Ghora's shadows behind me.

"What are you doing?" The hairs on my arm stand on end. As dangerous as Ghora is for the Fallen, Graeden acts as though something more lethal waits for us through Arautteve's entrance.

"Trolls gathering in the promenade hall. If you see anyone as we pass through Ghora, keep your face to the shadows. It's better if they don't know who you are." Flicking his chin toward the darkness, Graeden whispers, "Let's go."

Darkness swallows us in an instant. My steps fall in line behind Graeden's like a child trailing after a parent. I scan the obsidian crags surrounding us like a prison. The cliffs blend into the black clouds churning at their peaks. A low, guttural hiss shatters the stillness, and I jerk back, nearly choking on a yelp.

Vultures perch on twisted rods of onyx, their unblinking eyes following our silent crawl through their lands. When we slip out of their sight, they take flight and perch on stone branches ahead. Waiting. Starving.

"You'll want to keep that dagger on your person," Graeden instructs as we tread deeper into Ghora. "Word has spread quickly among the trolls how you lack control over your monster. After that little display in the arena, there'll be no doubt. That makes them dangerous. I'd rather take our chances in Ghora against a bunch of inexperienced Seekers than face a crowd of magic-wielding trolls."

As though Graeden called the Seekers to life, a muffled groan crawls through the air. I tuck my chin, dipping my face deeper into the shadow blanketing Ghora, but my eyes leap through the darkness until they land on a mass of pale flesh.

The obsidian melts into mulched and rotted earth, our feet slipping onto a muddied trail. Crisp leaves spread beneath the man's thin body like a bed. He moans again, and the sound sends shivers up my spine. We keep walking.

I glance at the sky and am met with more thunderous clouds. Though the sky in Ghora always seems to be stomaching a storm, it never rains. I glance at the chalky dirt sticking to my sandals and cringe.

Splintered bones line the path, shallow indentations engraved on their edges. Whoever this was wasn't killed by a Fallen. This person died here in Ghora, and based on how bones sprinkle the path ahead, I'm sure it wasn't natural.

The deeper we travel along the path, the more starved faces find mine. The men and women cling to thin onyx trees or lie prostrate over the ground. Their eyes fill with hatred and envy at the same time. After all, Graeden and I haven't been forgotten.

The Troll King plays with the Seekers, leaving them for prolonged amounts of time in Ghora. They either starve to death or when they reach the arena, they're too weak to put up much of a fight.

My throat tightens. I've never fought a weak Seeker. Maybe if I ever let one slip past the first round to be forgotten here, I eventually would.

Despite sticking to the darkest parts of Ghora, the Seekers know exactly who we are. And, if they could, I'm sure they'd kill us faster than we could whisper a plea.

If only they could see. Out here in Eida, we're all prisoners. The thought makes my heart ache.

"Little Fallens lost your way?" A man crawls out from behind a stone. His fingers dig into the dirt, his arms bent at odd angles. He scurries over the ground like a broken animal. "We can help you. Come with me." The man offers a gap-toothed smile, his tongue stroking the corner of his lips.

His eyes linger on mine as my gait slows. His clothes are torn, holes exposing the waxen skin that stretches over his ribs. He starves just like the vultures. I take a step back. Perhaps, he's gone a little mad, too.

Kill or be killed.

He lives by the adage, too. Anger billows through my chest, and heat crackles through my heart. He chose to be here—they all did. They came knowing they'd fight me for a wish to make their world better. To kill me to make their own lives easier. All it takes is one kill.

They're sick.

With heat fuming in my chest, I spin on my heel and rush after Graeden. Though I try to ignore all the Seekers suffering—a few pleading for help—my eyes are drawn to them. Each set of eyes tells a tragic story. Betrayal's coal black gaze. Green's refreshing innocence. Violet shades of envy.

My eyes meet another pair veiled in shadow, a subtle sparkle dancing through the dismal ocean. It only takes a moment for the man's eyes to betray his secrets. Guilt and fury flood from his gaze, and—is that hope?

A laugh builds in my throat. Hope in Ghora of all places?

Familiarity twinges through my thoughts as a calm sky replaces the storm in his eyes. I drop my gaze. Was that—?

I glance over my shoulder, but the man is gone. Shaking my head, I stare at Graeden's back, resigned to tracing the sharp curve of muscle around his shoulders.

When we slip through the Crossing, indignation burns through my spine. How can humans – *my* people – have such contempt toward me simply for being a Fallen, a creature made through their desperate acts? The fire trickles through my bones and spreads through my veins; steam climbs up my throat and fogs my brain.

We climb the flagstone path toward the temple, other Fallen milling about, unphased by the injustice of our existence here. I gasp as the fire lances through my chest. It tears through my organs, and I fold in half, bracing myself against my knees.

"Ari?" Graeden asks, glancing over his shoulder. "Are you alright?"

I want to speak, but the fire scalds my throat, and I fear if I open my mouth, Graeden will receive my flames. Instead, I bite my tongue and shake my head. The anger sears through me, and my consciousness drifts into the back of my mind.

Graeden doesn't hesitate. Latching his hand around my upper arm, he races toward the outskirts of Arautteve with me in tow. Our feet slap against the earth, small plumes of dirt rising around each footfall. I concentrate on the rhythmic sound as Graeden weaves around the other Fallen.

The steam grows hotter within my body, and I swallow.

I do not release you, I think.

But my words lack tenacity, and her flames consume everything within. A narrow path winds into the distance, cliffs dropping into darkness on both sides. Jagged formations of red rock stretch skyward like a wave's crest caught in its spray. A soft breeze stirs up the Blood Desert's crimson sand.

Hold on, I think. Not for my dragon, but for me. Graeden steers us toward the catacombs. I need to hold on until we are within its safety.

Gritting my teeth, I let Graeden drag me through the sands. The dragon's fire sears through my bone's marrow, and just before I can no longer quell the heat, we slip into the catacombs and down the stairs. I collapse inward and give into my dragon.

Scalding heat blasts through my body in a heartbeat, and my dragon's wings unfurl at my side. She screeches into the air, and flames streak the empty space above us.

Graeden ducks out from the line of fire. "Control yourself!"

I'm trying!

My dragon whips her head and takes flight. Her anger surges through my body, and the only one we can punish is the only one here. Nausea rolls through me as my dragon circles Graeden like a bird of prey. He circles with her, never letting his eyes fall from hers.

Heat builds in my chest. I scream for Graeden to run, but no noise comes out, and he doesn't hear my silent pleas. My dragon's snout stretches open, fire streaming toward the sand. Graeden rolls over his shoulder and sprints out of the fire's path.

"That is not control, dragon!"

Surprise races through my veins, and my dragon's rage sputters. Of course, Graeden isn't coaching me. He knows better than anyone I'm not in control anymore.

A tingling sensation bristles down my dragon's spine, and she slaps her wings harder against the air. She climbs through the darkness toward the vaulted ceiling. Pivoting, she dives toward the ground.

Graeden tugs his tunic over his head and throws it to the side. He spreads his legs, as though prepared to catch our fall. My dragon roars, and a ball of flame rockets from her outstretched jaw.

Graeden frowns and dives to the side, curling his body inward. Before hitting the ground, Graeden shifts, sprouting his own wings and taking flight. A shimmer of gold trails his path, the white feathers tinged with turquoise. He swoops through the air in much smaller waves than my dragon as he approaches.

My heart catches. Graeden's monster is a phoenix. Beautiful. Strong. Venerated. He soars past my dragon's snout, and her head swivels to follow his path. Of course, he's a phoenix. They're among the strongest monsters. Warmth gathers within my chest, and if I had my own lips, I'd smile. An aura of ease spreads through our veins.

Dipping her head, my dragon swoops around Graeden's phoenix and falls into sync with his movements. My panic slips away. She likes him. I stare at the phoenix's illustrious coat of feathers as Graeden weaves in front of my dragon again. I do, too. A scornful laugh bubbles up in my nonexistent belly. He's my mentor—my master.

Shaking the thoughts from my head, I watch the two monsters sail through the darkness, Graeden shining like a beacon. A refreshing wave of peace washes through my veins. I shut my eyes against my dragon's vision. Silence. A faint scent of tender buds crawling from overturned soil. The sweet taste of hope in the air. It floods my dragon's veins—all of it—the scents, the sound, the independence. This is what true freedom feels like.

Though my dragon flies hidden in Eida's catacombs, she's never been freer. More complete. My gaze falls back on the glowing phoenix guiding my dragon toward the ground. Somehow, it's because of him. Graeden's feathers glisten beneath the gold sparkle clinging to his body.

What would it feel like to stroke those feathers beneath my fingertips? Silken like a newborn hare or coarse like the pelts Bridgewick men would bring home from their hunts? I imagine they would feel soft. The image in my mind morphs. Instead of fragile feathers, it's Graeden's tanned chest pressed against my palm. I jerk my mind from the illusion, and heat surges to my head.

My dragon and Graeden's phoenix glide together as though they've flown with one another for years. Graeden drifts lower, and soon, they both rest their talons on the ground.

Graeden slips into the shadows and shifts back into his human form, returning with only his trousers on. My eyes wander over his face and fall to his bare chest. If I had my own cheeks, they'd flush with the heat of a thousand suns, but I can't break my gaze.

My dragon stamps her talons into the ground, a sense of unease cutting a path through her peace. She flaps her wings and draws back a step from Graeden.

Graeden lifts his hands in a show of goodwill, and my dragon settles. "That's better." Graeden softens his words. "Your fire is your strongest ally against your enemy. Save it for your last blows when your opponent is unprepared to meet it."

I wait for my dragon's anger to spike at being told what to do, but it doesn't come. A strange serenity melts through her chest instead. She accepts his counsel. She respects him.

"So, then," Graeden says, his shoulders relaxing. "Aside from fire, let's see what you've got."

My dragon shoves off the ground and back into the air. With Graeden guiding her actions, my fear evaporates. I may not be in control, but he is, and my dragon has lost her rage. My dragon curls and weaves through the air, using every inch of space at her disposal. She lights our way with plumes of fire as she reaches the highest corner of the catacomb before spiraling downward, sending my nonexistent stomach into my throat. Even still, the stretch that races through her wings and warms her muscles brings me a sense of control, too.

Graeden guides my dragon landward, and she follows his gestures with ease. Her talons grind into the hard earth before Graeden, but he doesn't stagger. Instead, he spreads his legs and leans onto the balls of his feet. "Attack me," he says. "Without fire."

My dragon lunges toward him, swiping a claw through the air. Graeden is lithe on his feet and rolls underneath her attack as he had done in Ghora. She crawls toward him like a lioness, her tail batting the air. She lurches—testing her prey—and again, he dodges her blow.

Hours pass, the magic sparkling through the apertures dimming as night emerges. I have no idea how Graeden still stands, but he does. And when sweat glistens on his skin and fatigue slows his defenses, he raises his palm toward my dragon.

"Shift back, please."

She doesn't hesitate. Her mass condenses into mine, my consciousness strengthening in control. My warm skin wraps snug around my body after being in my dragon's form for so long. Graeden's gaze shifts, and his eyes travel over my jawline and follow the stream of dark hair cascading over my shoulder. His chest rises slowly with his deep breaths, and his lips part. He stands still for too long, and I wonder what thoughts cross his mind. He lifts his hands and offers me his tunic, averting his gaze to the catacomb's vaulted ceiling.

Heat floods my cheeks. At this rate, I'll be out of clothing in a fortnight. Tugging the rags, I slip the clothing from his grasp and pull the tunic over my head. Fidgeting with the hem, I mutter, "You can look."

Graeden tips his face to meet mine, his expression stoic and unreadable. "I'd tell you you'll get used to that, but you won't." Graeden's gaze flicks to mine, a heat smoldering within its darkness. "If you ever gain control of your dragon, you can teach her not to incinerate your clothing every time you shift. Until then, we'll get you a satchel and a spare set of clothing to keep at your side."

Nodding, I press my lips together and beg the heat frothing in my belly to stay there and away from my cheeks. I let my gaze roam from his. "I didn't know you were a phoenix."

Graeden's eyes linger on mine before he answers. "Few do."

The warmth I'd felt watching Graeden's graceful flight stokes again. A smile gathers at the corners of my lips, but I stifle it. "Well, it looks like you've got the dragon on your side."

His expression sobers. "I needed to know she was capable of allying with us. Most monsters only ever face their enemies—those they fight in the arena. Something's holding her back from considering you an ally." Graeden eyes me as if I know what he's talking about. "I've earned your dragon's respect. You need to, too."

"Yeah," I say. "I'm working on it."

"Have you let her in?"

My eyes widen before I gesture to his very flattering tunic now hanging around my body. "I don't know how I could possibly let her in any more."

"I don't mean like that," Graeden says. "I mean, have you welcomed her into your mind and your memories? Have you invited her to be a part of you?"

"I don't know." I refrain from the temptation to throw my hands in the air. "I told her we're supposed to become one."

"That's not the same," Graeden says. "It's not simply about controlling your monster; it's about uniting with it. Body, mind, and soul. Offering her every part of you so she can strengthen and refine you."

Body, mind, and soul. A barrage of memories batters against the barricade in my mind. I grit my teeth against their onslaught. I've locked those memories up for good. They don't exist.

Graeden rests his hand firmly on my shoulder. "Even those who choose never to release their creatures still harbor one. You've unleashed yours. Until you unite yourself with her, she will be your enemy in that arena. Whatever is keeping you from letting her in, you need to fix it." His eyes wander from the top of my head down my body. "You almost got yourself and countless others killed today. Had you shifted in Arautteve, she could have easily destroyed half the district."

My stomach tightens, and a tremor slips into my hands. He wants me to turn over every memory, unlock every door. He wants me to expose myself and my dragon to the darkest pieces of my past. The ones I'd rather burn than relive. I spent years crafting the vault in my mind, and now he wants me to tear it down. I swallow thickly. I don't think I can do that.

"I will," I whisper. There must be another way. "It's just taking time."

"You don't have time." Graeden crosses his arms over his broad chest. "If you cannot join with your monster, the next life you take *will* be innocent and it may be your own. I can't corral your dragon forever."

Anger stirs in my belly, and the raging heat has nothing to do with my dragon. Graeden is right—the only way I survive Eida is with my dragon at my side, but I can't let someone else in. Not the way he's asking me to. This is more than becoming a monster. This goes deeper.

Pain lances through my chest, and I fight the urge to crumple in on myself.

"Go to the seer first thing in the morning. She will help you unearth whatever this is," Graeden says. He gestures toward the exit, but I don't move.

"I don't need help."

"I'm not asking." A flare of the man I met in the market flashes through his gaze. "Go."

CHAPTER EIGHTEEN

AGAINST THE MORNING LIGHT, the temple looms over me like Ghora's cliffs, and anxiety gnaws at my stomach. After abandoning Isla with her master, I'd hoped never to see the Morrean fairy again. Fate isn't a kind creature.

Graeden prods his fist against my back, and I stumble toward the temple.

"You're not coming?" I ask.

Graeden folds his arms and leans back. His fresh tunic pulls taut with the motion. "Uniting with one's monster is a personal undertaking."

My stomach churns. I glance at Graeden over my shoulder and scowl when he smiles. Adrenaline buzzes through my nerves, and I want to bolt from this temple. Instead, I clench my teeth and duck beneath the arched entrance, disappearing into the temple's shadows alone. The temperature drops within the stone walls, and the hair raises on my arms despite my lightweight sweater. I'm quickly running out of clothes.

My dragon is out of control, bursting through my skin on her whims. Graeden is right, I need to control her, but I don't see how a seer can help.

I climb the stone staircase to the temple's highest floor. Graeden said all of Mistress Verean's property reside in the same place. I'm not sure which room is Isla's, though, until I step in front of it. Fairy symbols are carved into the doorframe—enchantments likely to ward off evil.

Oh, Nether Winds, I hope they've kept her safe from Verean. I shut my eyes, and my cheeks burn as I remember her plea for my help. And now I come, asking for *her* help. A slight quiver flits through my arms. Weak. With a steadying breath, I rap against the wooden door.

I have no idea what I'm going to say. Too soon, the door creaks open. Isla's slight build fills the small space. She wears a simple dress that falls to her calves. The sleeves are cut short at her shoulders, the skirt is baggy and stiff. My chest tightens. I should've at least tried to help her, but no matter what I did, Isla would have ended up at Verean's feet.

Isla stares at me with dull granite eyes. Her full rose-colored lips arc into a frown, matching the lackluster hair snarled against her head like a wild animal. Her sheer wings droop listlessly. Time itself is killing her. How long has she been away from her hollow?

"Come for help from the seer, have you?" Isla's eyes are as hard as stone. Her lips arc into a deep frown. She crosses her narrow arms over her chest.

My pulse ticks through my ears, and I restrain the urge to finger the hilt of my blade. This was a bad idea. I should turn. Run. "Believe me, I wouldn't be here if I had any other choice. Just tell me you're powerless to help, and I'll find another fairy."

I don't wait for Isla's answer. I give her my back, restraining the urge to run from her rooms and leave my guilt behind with her.

"But I'm not powerless to help." Isla's voice falters, the rough contempt crumbling with her words. "And you'll be hard pressed to find another fairy in this realm who can do what I can."

Dropping my head, I knead the space between my brows. I don't want *her* help. But I need help from someone. "You don't know what I need."

"I'm a seer," Isla bites out. "Your aura tells me more than your words ever will."

"You could have lied."

A glimmer of amusement flickers through Isla's eyes. "I didn't say I *will* help you. Only that I can."

"That's enough of an answer for me." Anything to get out of this place and bury my guilt. Graeden will have to find another fairy.

"Always so quick to judge a situation, aren't you?" Isla says. "You could save so many with your monster, yet you selfishly squander it."

"Selfishly?" My temper flares, and I try to rein it in. "You know nothing about me."

"Then you're afraid. Of what, though, I wonder," she taunts.

A shimmer of memory flits through my mind. Gritting my teeth, I swallow the rising pain that comes from thinking of my past.

"Are you afraid of Eida? Or is it the trolls?" Isla asks, toying with me. When I don't respond, she prods further. "Is it something you left behind in the human realm? Maybe someone?"

Father's silver eyes flash in my head, and I clamp my eyes shut to force them away.

"Ah, I've touched a soft spot, I see," Isla drawls. "Is it painful?"

Her eyes skim the empty space around me. "Darkness clings to you. It's growing fiercer, more disturbed with each passing day. Did that special someone see your darkness? Did they sacrifice you to the Well because of it?"

"Enough!" I shout. Before I realize it, I've pushed my way into Isla's room. I know darkness all too well. "You are a fairy of light. Don't pretend to know of real darkness."

Isla pins me with her granite eyes. "Everything I've known in this realm is darkness."

Isla's gaze flicks over my shoulder, and her arrogant façade disintegrates. Her eyes widen as she traces the fairy symbols carved on the inside of the doorframe. She presses her fingertips to her lips and whispers softly against them. "It's not possible."

Turning her back on me, she wanders deeper into her chamber. Tattered drapes dangle from the ceiling as torn and weathered as Isla's own tunic. Stains stretch over the walls like beasts clawing their way to the light. A single cot is shoved against one wall, a pot in the other for the privy. A prison would be more welcoming.

"What are you doing?" I ask. Some of my anger deflates with Isla's distraction.

"No one should have been able to cross into my room," Isla mutters, her anger lost with the revelation. "The fairy runes should have ensured it."

An air of relief eases some of my tension. She's been able to keep Verean out.

Isla whips around to face me. Her previously lifeless eyes sparkle with an excitement I've never seen in anyone's before. She closes the distance between us, her pointed nose inches from mine. "But you did," she whispers, her knuckles brushing her lips. "You are destined for great things."

Stepping back, I scoff. They say fairies can see into the future. I swallow the huff in my throat. No one knows a person's destiny.

Isla's eyes pan over the doorframe behind me as though she reads a book. "If I turn my back on you—with fate's threads hanging over you as they are—I'd be turning my back on *Idrium*, my hollow."

The tension loosens across my shoulders, but coils in my stomach. I need Isla's help, as much as I wish I didn't. "Thank you."

"Don't thank me." Isla's voice hardens, a bitter wasteland void of light. "I do this for the realms and my hollow. Not for you. Besides, I do nothing without a price."

Shame warms my cheeks. A price. The last person in this fire-ridden realm I want to owe a debt to is Isla. And yet, I know of no other way. The memory of my dragon attacking me in the arena still curls through my mind. I feel the scorching heat, the relentless barrage of fire. I can't win. If my dragon is against me, I'll surely die, by another's hand or my own.

"She's getting too strong," I admit, my eyes cast to the corner of her room. "I need to control my monster. Unite with her."

Isla's stare bores into me, and my gaze flickers to meet hers.

"I'll do anything," I whisper. I don't mean to speak the words aloud, but they're true. I would give anything to escape this realm, and if this dragon can help me reach my pardon, then Isla can have whatever she wants.

A feral grin spreads over Isla's face, lifting her sunken cheeks. Her eyes don't move from mine. "You have yourself a deal. One day, I will call in my favor. I never forget a price unpaid."

A shiver races down my spine, and the hairs on my arms prickle. I inhale to settle my nerves.

Isla gestures for me to kneel in front of her. Ripples of icy air drift upward from the stone floor, a climate more akin to Ghora's than what I've ever felt in Arautteve. Cautiously, I roll onto my knees.

Isla lifts her delicate hands and presses two fingers against each of my temples. Closing her eyes, Isla lifts her chin and says nothing. Her fingers trace the edges of my face from my temple to my chin like a river's meandering crawl. When she reaches my chin, she presses a thumb gently against my forehead. A silver glow spreads beneath her thumb, and I squint as it pulses brighter and brighter in my vision. Isla's eyes slam open, the grey-stone color eclipsing into a brilliant white.

"Shall we see what holds you back?" Her voice is far away.

I say nothing as Isla's nostrils flare, and her consciousness sinks deeper into my head. Without other instruction, I close my eyes. Fractures of memories pulse behind my eyelids. Distant memories I've nearly forgotten. Others I wish I could forget, like Tib abandoning me at the Well.

"You are angry," Isla whispers.

"Of course, I'm angry." I scowl. "I'm in Eida."

"No," Isla says. "This goes much deeper, etched with grave pain."

My hands grow clammy, and I tighten my jaw. I know the memory she seeks—Father. Atarah. It's the only one I've truly locked away and vowed to forget. Living it once was pure torture. I can't sift through it again.

"There is a door," Isla whispers. "It won't open."

Her fingers press deeper against my temples, and I can feel her trying to pry open the door I've worked so hard to seal. I wet my lips with no intention of reopening my past.

"There is so much darkness in your mind. It leaks around this door."

I bear down deeper on my mind to keep the door bolted, but Isla doesn't give up. Her ethereal fingers brush the door's edge. She skims over every inch of the barrier, searching for a chink in my prison cell. I don't leave one.

"Ah, there we are," Isla says.

My eyes flick to Isla, and all at once the room feels too small.

"There is a keyhole."

The strong fortification shudders in my mind as Isla approaches the door we shouldn't be entering. Sweat dews on my palms, and I interlace my hands together.

Isla's consciousness kneels before the door, pressing her eye to the keyhole. And I see it, too.

Darkness. Flames. Blood-curdling screams of the innocent echoing into the chilled air. The inferno surges beyond the doorway, devouring everything in its sight. Devouring *them*…

Grief crashes onto my shoulders, tearing through my heart. In a burst of pain, I shove Isla away from me. "Get your hands off me!"

Quickly, I rebuild the barrier in my mind, ensuring to meld the keyhole closed. Air fills my lungs, but I can't breathe.

I told Isla I'd give her anything, but not this. Never this. I can't reopen that door. Tears burn behind my eyes, and I tilt my face away from Isla. Even if my monster did help me reach my pardon, who's to say the trolls would honor my release? I'm their only dragon shifter.

I can't shove a blade into the wounds of my past for only a possibility of escape. I won't do that.

I leap from the floor and sprint from Isla's room. I haven't made it to the end of the corridor, when she calls after me, standing in the hallway in her rags. "There's darkness inside your mind. You must wade through your grief and clear it before anyone else can enter your heart."

Her words die with the echoes, and I launch myself down the stairs.

I crash past Graeden as I race around him into Arautteve's courtyard. Graeden raises a brow, his shaped arms folded over his chest.

"So?"

"She couldn't help," I spit.

CHAPTER NINETEEN

"You're shackling me?"

Graeden's fingers graze my wrist, and a flutter darts through my chest. My gaze flits to his. His fingers linger, soft and warm on my skin. Such a difference from the last time he held my arm like this and branded me.

The moment we left Isla's, Graeden had steered me toward my temple. He snaps a gold cuff around my wrist. The warmth from Graeden's hand is gone.

"It isn't a shackle."

"What would my dragon think?"

Graeden rolls his eyes. "Your dragon will think nothing of it. I'm not *shackling* her."

I tuck my chin and raise my brows. "It's me then, is it? Well, I do think something of it."

"Of course, you do. Fortunately for us," The usual storm in Graeden's eyes sparkles, like a crack in the clouds unveiling a starry sky. "It doesn't matter what you think."

Light magic pulses beneath the cuff, misting over my skin. No warmth. No chill.

My smile falters as I scrutinize the gold. "How did you get access to troll magic?"

"You aren't the only Marked who is struggling adjusting to their monster. We masters have a small collection of cuffs." Graeden lifts a brow when my eyes widen. "They're very well-guarded so as not to fall into the wrong hands, I might add. We're only using this while you're learning. This cuff will keep you in control of shifting."

"You mean, keep my dragon locked inside where she should be."

Graeden busies himself with his satchel resting on my bed. He glances over his shoulder. "The *shackle* is not for her, remember? She's only out of control when you are."

Candles burn along my room's stone walls. Their small flames flicker in the evening's darkness, and flash against the cuff's smooth exterior. Shadows dance over Graeden, shielding his expression.

"As long as you wear this, you won't shift. When you want to shift, simply remove the bracelet." Graeden returns to his place in front of me. "Try it. Shift."

Closing my eyes, I concentrate on the darkness. Not that I'd know how to call to my dragon anyway, but I try. Nothing. No spark in my chest nor fury in my veins. She's still.

"Let me see your hand."

I lift my hand between our bodies, and Graeden's fingertips brush along the underside of my forearm as he meddles with the cuff. My throat dries. Warmth curls over my arm, and my gaze rises to his.

My hand has his complete attention. As his fingers work with the metal cuff, lines etch into its surface. They bend and twist, intricately swooping around each other until they spread across the entire piece.

Graeden's scent curls around me in the small space between us. I close my eyes and breathe it in. Tension seeps from my veins and evaporates from my body. He buries my anger, dresses my pain. Everything stills except for the quiver in my chest. My thoughts sharpen, and I'm very aware of his skin against mine.

Never has anyone calmed me in such a way. Not Tib. Not Mother. I open my eyes, and they land on Graeden's lips, his attention focused on the cuff. I'm not sure why he can calm me so. Graeden releases my wrist, and gooseflesh crawls over my skin where the warmth of his hand had been.

A quiet click echoes around us, and the gold cuff falls to the floor. Reality settles over the room, sopping up the warmth like a mop. Graeden is my trainer—my master. We could never—I could never...I'm supposed to hate him.

Shaking the haze from my head, I stoop and lift the glistening band.

I should hate him, but I don't. Not as I once did.

Graeden taps the cuff in my grip. "You need to be careful, though. The cuff suppresses your monster, but it also inhibits other magic in your system, including the mark I gave you. If you get into trouble, I'll have a hell of a time trying to find you."

A soft smile plays at the corner of my lips. With the cuff on, Graeden won't be able to track me. *Freedom.* Or as close as I'll get in this realm.

"Just make sure you don't announce you're wearing one of these," Graeden finishes. "So long as the trolls don't magic it off you—which they will if they discover it's the reason you can't shift—then they can't force your dragon to do anything." Graeden's gaze flicks to mine. "It's the best I can do under the circumstances."

A sad smile tugs at my lips. "It's enough. Thank you."

"Get some rest," Graeden says. His expression is trained, his amber eyes dark and indifferent. "You're in the arena again tomorrow."

"Can't they give me a break for once?" I groan. Exhaustion pulls at my limbs, and the lightness from Graeden's touch dampens.

"You're a monster now." Graeden loops his satchel over his shoulder. His eyes wander down my arm to the gold cuff, and I wish he held it in his hands again. His gaze flicks back to mine. "One of the best. The rules are all different."

Graeden slips out of my room and into the temple's dark hallway. Silence hangs around me like a swollen rain cloud.

Outside my balcony, the sky flickers with violet remnants of magic. My feet barely scuff the floor as I wander to the balcony's edge. I lean over the marbled balustrade, my hands dangling over its rail.

The magic is beautiful in its own right. Turning my palm skyward, I imagine tendrils of power drizzling into my hand. What would it feel like to wield such power? Who could I hurt? Who could I save?

"You should sleep, Fallen." I jolt and then lean farther over the balustrade. A dark smile toys with Graeden's lips from where he stands far below me. "A woman waiting at the edge of her balcony may give some men the wrong idea."

My stomach lightens, and my cheeks burn. "Good night."

Heat roils in my stomach, and a smile presses against my cheeks. I bite the inside of my lip to keep it under control. I may be the only Fallen who has been marked by a master she doesn't loathe. But it's best if he doesn't outright know it.

With a nod in my direction, Graeden ducks his head and disappears into the night. A tingle meanders through my chest, and I swallow my smile.

Inhaling, I leave the enchanted view and return to my room's shadows. I spread a blanket over the floor and fold my legs beneath me.

"Alright, dragon," I whisper. "We can do this the easy way or not at all. Graeden says we must become one if either of us wants to survive."

Heat stirs through my veins and sifts through my head. She's toying with the lock I've welded shut on the barrier separating me from my memory.

"It won't open," I say. "The barrier is a protection. I won't unlock it. We'll need to figure this out without that."

Resting my hands on my knees, I close my eyes. Arautteve's thick air fills my lungs—the heady scent of sweat and the metallic taste of blood ride the air. I rub my fingers over my palms, the blood smells so strong I worry my hands are still drenched with it. The warm citrus of cedar wafts through my window from somewhere in the distance. My thoughts dissolve as the scent swirls through my brain and then fades.

Another smell curls through the air. The sweet tang of anticipation laced with a gentle spark of wonder. They're softer than the others, near indistinguishable, but there. They're definitely there. My nose twitches, and my eyes flutter open. Magic. Magic has a scent?

"Is this you?" I whisper. Never on my own would I have discovered such a scent.

Heat warms my chest. My dragon has caught the scent of magic. As the smell fades, my excitement does, too. Stretching my arms over my head, I curl towards the floor. My muscles groan as I extend the worn ligaments. My dragon's heat healed my lashes, why doesn't she heal my growing bruises and bleeding grazes?

"How about it?" I ask.

The heat in my chest fizzles. Figures. Refocusing my thoughts, I return to the memory of fighting in the arena, broken and sure I was going to die. Pain crackles through my side as my opponent's shield forces me to the ground. I grimace, the pain shattering inside my arms, the agony searing through my back. But nothing came close to the terrifying reality that everyone would see my monster. Everyone would know what darkness I hide.

I grind my teeth, forcing myself to stay within the memory. Every death at my hands has been well-deserved. Fire sparks in my belly—at least there's something both my dragon and I can agree on. I'm not afraid to kill them. Blade cuts through flesh in my memory, but I don't flinch.

My dragon's fire sizzles, steam inflaming my lungs. Opening my eyes, I shove myself from the floor.

Swollen masses of flesh pound the stone seats lining the promenade hall, shouting for blood. As an Unmarked, slinking down the path toward the arena had been terrible enough. Now, the trolls chant *Dragon! Dragon! Dragon!* as I step into the dusty corridor.

The air electrifies with their energy, tinted with the faint scent of overripe sweat. Anger cuts through my chest. These creatures have no right to ask this from any of us.

Badavaru's sweltering heat presses around me, almost as suffocating as my dragon's heat within. I tighten the bracers on my forearms and cinch my weapon's belt tighter to my waist. Blades brandish my thighs.

Round one. I fight without my dragon.

My sword rings against its sheath as I draw it into the air. I block out the crowd's banter and raucous cheering until the noise fades to a muffled hum. Slicing my blade through the air, I attack it as though the empty path ahead of me is my enemy. My practice swings are effortless and smooth.

Whoever waits inside the arena doesn't stand a chance, even without my dragon. I could incapacitate him or her to face again another day, but I won't. Why delay the inevitable? In the end, only one of us is walking away, and I will be one step closer to my pardon.

The portcullis creaks as it rises into the air. My opponent stands at the arena's center. He isn't a tall man, though taller than me. His broad shoulders are framed by lean muscles, and his fingers grip and regrip his war hammer. Spikes trail down the weapon's head like a mane. He doesn't carry a shield like so many others, but leather bracers cleave to his arms, a full girdle shields his torso, and a bronze helmet sits atop his head. A quick swipe, and I could take his head clean off. A small pouch hangs from his waist, and I tilt my head, wondering what he carries inside.

I step into the arena, the sand stirring at my feet. Badavaru's heat clings to my skin.

Let's get this over with.

The dirt is packed beneath my sandals, small pebbles moving beneath my soles as I circle the arena. My steps are precise and controlled, and my Seeker matches each one. Being smaller, it's usually to my advantage to let my opponents use their energy in attacking, but this one doesn't seem to be in any hurry.

Is he afraid?

The crowd's chatter quiets as we size each other up. I angle my steps to close the circle as we rotate around each other like two dance partners waiting for the other to lead. A roar tears from my throat. I brandish a dagger from my triple sheath and hurl it at him. The knife cuts through the air hilt over blade, closing the short distance between us in a second.

Without waiting for the blade to hit its target, I dart behind it, thrusting my sword toward his chest. The man dodges the dagger, as I expect, and ducks beneath my sword. His shoulder rams into my torso, and he lifts my feet from the ground.

My fist tightens around my sword, and I swipe it at the man's back. Before it can cut through his leathers, the man throws me over his head onto the ground. The small pebbles bite into my back, but I roll over my shoulder and pop to my feet.

Heat flares against my shoulder bone, the nerves tingling into my hand. I readjust my grip along the hilt of my blade and leap back as the man swipes his war hammer between us. He swings again. This time our weapons clash. My arms shake beneath the blow, but I shove my weight into it. The man's footing slips and, thank the stars, his weapon gives, arcing to the side.

He retreats, and I stay on him, giving him no room to breathe. I dodge each of his strikes, all the while pressing him toward the outer edge of the arena.

Liver-spotted hands claw over the ledge of the wall, grasping for the Seeker or me. What I wouldn't give to cut just one of them off. Shaking the thought from my head, I draw my second short sword from its sheath and focus on the Seeker. If I can get his back against the wall, I can plunge my blade straight through his leathers.

Ten feet. Eight. His hammer slams into my sword again, and a sharp ache clamors through my arms. Fatigue begs me to quit, my weariness offering a welcome rest from his weapon. I tighten my grip on my sword. The man twists his hammer, and I slip. He throws one of my blades in an arc to the ground. Lifting a foot, he slams his sole into my stomach. I stumble backwards, struggling to keep my balance. He gives me his back and races toward the wall.

I dart for my fallen sword. When the Seeker reaches the wall, he slashes his blade into the hard ground. Again and again. His gaze finds mine as he slices a shallow cut on his forearm. Blood trickles from the wound. It falls to the ground. And he disappears. My feet skid to a halt, and my gaze tears through the arena searching for him. He rematerializes thirty feet above me on the wall's narrow ledge.

"What in the--?" I pant.

The trolls leap back, a chorus of gasps echoing around him. He dashes along the wall, his balance not wavering for a second. The trolls lunge at the Seeker. Their hands swat at his feet. With any luck, they'll snag his leg, and he'll fall.

But the trolls are too slow, and the man is too stable. Drawing my last dagger, I toy with its hilt as I track the Seeker's path. I inhale slowly, centering myself. His movements over the ledge are smooth, but he's running out of track. When he reaches where the edge drops into a cliff face, I launch my weapon. It whistles through the air and slams into the wall inches behind his head.

The man bends his knees and leaps. His feet land square on a thin vine of iron jutting out from the arena wall before he leaps to the ground and rolls over his shoulder.

The Seeker tosses his war hammer into his other hand, and flames fume in my chest. I sprint across the arena toward him, and he to me. I raise my sword, and the man's feet give out as I reach him. I expect his dodge, however, and cut my blade low, toward his exposed throat. The steel lances off his helmet, catching the armor right above his chin.

Flaming Nights! Why won't he die?

The man rolls to his feet, tearing the dented armor from his head. Short-cropped sandy hair covers his head, traces of a thin beard framing a strong jawline. Slender nose. Piercing blue eyes.

Those eyes flash in a thousand memories. Eyes as calm as an untouched ocean that stood out among the dark-haired, dark-eyed people of Bridgewick.

My heart hammers in my chest—relief, confusion, excitement, fear, all the emotions the man has ever evoked in me roil together into one mass of rage.

Tib.

His shoulders are broader than I remember, and his face carries the lines of experience. Stubble traces his once youthful face. He looks older, but it's him. I'm sure of it. I would recognize his eyes anywhere. Though, they're no longer colorless.

A guttural roar tears from my throat, my dragon's fire exploding in my chest. Thanks to the inhibitors and my cuff, though, she stays bound beneath my skin. I launch myself at Tib, swinging my sword through the air. He rolls backward, the tip of my blade severing the small pouch from his waist.

The corded leather falls to the ground as though time suspends around it. A dusting of crystalline sparkles wafts from its opening. The sack smashes against the ground, and the magic plumes into the air with a subtle sheen.

I scramble to slow my momentum, but I skid straight into the cloud. Gasping, I inhale a mouthful of magic.

Fire flares in my chest, spreading like wings over my heart. Something is wrong.

I step toward Tib, and the arena tilts to the side. I stumble over my feet, pressure building in my lungs. Blinking, I glare at the goading faces in the stadium, and a thick haze blankets the arena. I stagger toward Tib again, and a shocking pain radiates through my lungs and into my legs.

The fire in my chest lances through my body behind the pain. Flames engulf the magic's strain. I collapse to my knees, the magic strangling the breath from my lungs. My dragon's fire isn't enough.

My breathing morphs into a high-pitched wheeze, the magic leeching the life from my airways. My dragon rams into my body, trying to escape, but there's no exit for her.

I will not die. Not at your hands. The thought burns hotter than any fire.

Anchoring my foot into the ground, I push myself to stand. The arena still tilts, and Tib wavers back and forth at the edge of my vision. If I can only get myself out of the magic's vicinity, then it should clear my head... right?

Tightening my grip, I lunge away from where Tib's form hovers. The sandy ground scratches my bare legs as I fall. I press my body from the dirt, baring my teeth at the man who failed to kill me years ago and has come to finish the job.

My hazy vision trails across the muscles rippling over his arms, the stubble that dots his strong jaw. His sculpted chest rises and falls beneath the fitted leathers. The years have done him well. But he still wears his lopsided smile, the one that used to paint a matching smile on my cheeks.

How can he smile at me like that?

Rage grinds out the memories. Screaming, I spring from the ground and launch myself at him. Our bodies collide, and we roll across the ground in a heap of flesh and sweat. We skid to a stop with his body pinned beneath mine. I don't hesitate to aim my elbow at his head.

Tib's eyes roll back for a moment before he wrestles me to the side. Lifting my short sword, I thrust it toward his abdomen. Miss. Tib locks his hand around mine and tears the sword from my grip. It clatters across the ground.

Tib forces me to my back, pinning me beneath him. I wrestle against his weight, snaring his injured arm. Digging my fingers into the wound he'd given himself, I squeeze. Blood paints my fingertips and dribbles over my hand. Tib shouts and pulls back before wrestling my arms against my sides. His posture slackens, and he grimaces. I thrash against his hold, but he's stronger than I remember. Raising his arm, he hesitates for a single breath before slamming his fist down.

CHAPTER TWENTY

TIB'S BLOOD STICKS BENEATH my fingernails.

A dull ache throbs through my head. Graeden had dragged me out from the arena and, when I awoke, brought me home. He'd laid a damp cloth against my brow, and then took his leave. Emotions flood my body, leaving me haggard and exhausted. The skin around my eyes is swollen, color blotching my cheeks.

Tears morphed to anger which shattered into heartbreak. Again and again and again. Night settled beyond my balcony, and I finally stilled with unshed sobs held hostage in my chest.

I never thought I'd see Tib again. He betrayed me. He abandoned me. But he *had* loved me. At least for a time, it was real.

Forcing the barely reined-in hurt into a bottomless pit of my mind, I inhale slowly. My feet are tucked beneath me, my hands resting on my knees. Magic bolts through the violet clouds as morning stirs in Araútteve. Exhale. Tib may have sent me here, but everything I have done since has been my own choice. Every defense. Every kill.

Tib may have sent me here, but I unleashed my monster.

A subdued flame warms my chest, and a small smile buoys against my lips. I bet Tib never expected me to be a dragon-shifter of all things. Pride surges through my chest, bolstering the tiny flame. Tib never could have expected to face me in the arena. My smile grows. He never would have guessed how I would kill him.

He should have died yesterday. Seekers rarely make it to the second round with me. Next time I face Tib, I'll have the strength of my monster, but I'll still fight in my human form.

The fire ripples through my chest. Powerful. Capable. I shut my eyes, absorbing the strength that courses through my veins with my dragon's heat.

A blood-stained vision flashes behind my closed eyes, marring the refreshing swell of power. Bodies lie in heaps throughout the arena. Four-hundred and one of them. Their lifeless eyes bore into my soul. Their slack mouths scream, *Murderer!* My chest tightens, and my dragon's fire sputters. I gasp as pain crackles through my chest. Crushing guilt boils beneath my skin, and I abandon my attempt to connect with my dragon.

Snapping my eyes open, I stare at the dried blood speckled over my hands. It depicts patterns so familiar yet so grotesque. I trace my fingertips over Tib's blood and clench my teeth against the betrayal sparking to life in my chest again. The blood burns against my skin like its own kind of branding iron.

Snatching my cloak from the bedpost, I slip through Arautteve to the bathing pool.

I stand at the water's edge, my gaze roaming the pool's glassy surface. Dried sweat clings to my hair, and a dark bruise forms on my temple. Fatigue tugs at my eyes...

A spark flashes against their hazel depths in my reflection, a sudden sizzle of energy. My exhaustion lifts—there's fire in my eyes. The excitement doesn't last long, and when it dissipates, I'm left with a sense of unease. The hairs on my neck stand on end. I glance over my shoulder, but the pool's bank is empty.

Oh, to the Nether Winds with Tib! One look at him, and he has me completely high strung.

Slipping the satin cloak from my shoulders, I disrobe and lower myself into the pool. The clear water brushes my neck, and warmth encircles my naked body. Knotted tension melts. I scrub the blood from my knuckles, and it disperses through the water, trickling over a nearby waterfall.

Tipping my head back, I soak my hair. Iridescent pixies flit overhead, zipping between the few trees as though they expect to find something there. I wonder if Isla might fly among the smaller of her kind, though she's more human size. Feathered foxes the size of my palm dart among the foliage, sneaking to the pool to drink.

The water's warm caress eases my anxiety. I shut my eyes and drift, the water carrying me wherever it would. I float towards a bank, and my unease returns. With my eyes shut, I lean into my other senses. The air wreaks of hydrangeas and daisies with... a hint of cinnamon.

My pulse quickens, and my muscles tighten as if for battle.

A snap splinters through the foliage hugging the edge of the pool. I slip on a mask of indifference and swim towards the bank. When my toes dig into the pool's sandy bottom, I drag my long hair from the water.

Tib's scent is all over the place.

But how? No Unmarked I've ever known has made it this deep into Arautteve unnoticed. How would a Seeker? This shouldn't be possible. I inhale deeply. Yet I'd recognize this scent anywhere.

I stare into the distance. The pixies' quiet hums fall like a backdrop over the pool, muffling the sounds of other Fallen. Small feet pad over the moist soil as critters scurry to and fro. A near silent inhale followed by an even quieter exhale. Without moving my head, my gaze wanders to the bush at my left. It roots at the edge of the bank, a good amount of thick foliage sweeping over the water. The leaves tremble ever so slightly.

Standing until the water brushes my shoulder blades, I thrust my hand into the bush while using my other to unsheathe the dagger still anchored to my thigh. Graeden did say to keep it on my person. Tib stumbles forward from the foliage, nearly falling into the pool himself. Instead, he lands hard on his hands and knees at the pool's edge. Snatching his brown, sleeveless tunic in my fist, I wrench him toward me as I stand in the water and press my blade against his throat.

A thick leather hood falls back from his face. "Ari!"

Tib's smile is light and charming, and a flutter rises in my traitorous heart. I stamp out the memory of a past time. A growl rumbles in my chest, and my dragon's fire spits like a volcano.

"Tell me why I shouldn't kill you right here!"

Tib's crooked smile deepens. "Because then you'd have to admit you were afraid of defeat. I still remember our last match in Bridgewick. You did *not* win despite what you told everyone." Tib's amusement softens, and his eyes dart between mine. "By the stars, you look the same as the day you left."

Left? A snarl pours from my lips, and I press the blade deeper. "And you've only aged."

Tib's smile falters, and his brow furrows. My heart thumps wildly. *Flaming nights,* I should've killed him in the arena, and I didn't. Now's my second chance.

"How's the family, Tib?" I sneer, the rancor in my voice masking the raw emotion that still finds its place when I speak of my old life. "All better?"

"My family?" Tib asks. "They're fine. Always have been."

My fingers falter over the dagger, and I choke on my words. "What?"

"My family's fine." Tib's brows draw close together, and his gaze sweeps over me. "Are you?"

"Am I?" A deranged laugh escapes my lips. "Of course, I'm not fine. You sent me to this hell-hole to save your mother! You traded my life for hers." I tighten my grip on the blade and growl. "I've been waiting a long time to meet you again."

Tib's expression sobers as though my words finally sink in. "Ari, I would never have sent you here."

"Your words can't save you now, Tib." My arm aches to drag the blade across his throat, to let his blood spill down his front.

Tib raises his hands in surrender, and I pause. Why do I pause?

My lip curls with disgust at my weakness. For all the time I've wanted to kill him, now I hesitate.

"I swear to you," Tib says, his gaze unwavering. "I didn't send you to Eida."

Tib rests a hand against mine and pushes the blade away from his throat. A tingle spreads through my fingers where his soft touch warms my skin. An easiness I had forgotten swirls through me with his touch. Cleaving to my anger, I shove the emotions away and glare at Tib.

Kill him. Kill him! The thought echoes through my mind just as it has a thousand times before. Tib offers me a tentative smile, his head tipped to the side, concerned. Clenching my jaw, I lower my blade.

I want to believe him, but how can I? I saw him turn his back on me at the Well.

I stare at Tib for too long, and I can't help but wonder how long he's been in Eida. My thoughts are a frenzied, harried mess. I drop my gaze to the steaming water. Droplets gather against my collarbone and trickle over my bare skin. My cheeks warm. I've never stood naked in front of a man before.

Shutting my eyes, I gather my anger and place it near my heart for safe keeping. This isn't over. If I find out Tib's lying, I'll kill him in the arena. Right now, though, I just want to get out of here.

Leaving him with a withering glare, I sink beneath the water's surface and glide to the other end of the pool where I left my belongings. I snatch my clothes from the bank and tug them on beneath the water, soaking them through. A small puddle gathers around my feet as I climb out of the pool and drape my dry cloak around my shoulders.

I try to ignore Tib, but as I focus on my cloak's clasp, the hairs on my neck prickle. He still watches me. I bristle. How dare he think he has any right to. My fingertips brush my blade now strapped in its sheath against my leg.

Before heading down the path toward the temple, I glance over my shoulder. Tib's gaze is locked on the bank near his feet, an amused smile curling his lips.

I clench my teeth as the heat gathers against my cheeks again. He's smiling because of *me*. The thought sours and turns my stomach.

My sandals rap against the stone ground as I weave through the colonnades toward Arautteve's courtyard and my temple. It doesn't take long for Tib to skirt around the pool and trail my steps. His eyes trace the tall columns stretching skyward. They linger on the keystones of every arch we walk beneath, but they lock onto the magic rolling through the late morning clouds above us.

My gaze wanders to where he stares, and I try to remember the first time I saw it. The sight was both fearsome and filled me with awe. The crackling magic was wondrous, but the trolls' use of it snuffed my curiosity and replaced it with dread.

"Ari." Tib softly touches my elbow and tugs me to face him. I flinch, and my hand goes to my blade. Tib's shoulders sink. "Don't you think I could've killed you in that arena if I'd wanted to?"

Resentment cuts through me, and I see him sacrificing me at the Well all over again. He still thinks he's better than me. That he's the one in control of my life.

"What about when you cut through my satchel? Magic debilitates mortals who ingest it. You were an easy target."

Flames lick my temper. I turn my back on Tib and keep moving. If he knew what was good for him, he'd leave me alone before I change my mind and stab him in the street. Tib keeps up easily, though.

"I had you pinned." Tib snags my arm again, more forceful this time. He roots me in front of him, giving me no choice but to listen. "There's no reason you should be alive, Ari, unless I wanted it so."

"You are so arrogant!" I thrust my forearm against his, breaking his grip. "I'm only alive because you wished it so? Oh, Tib, you have no idea what I've become."

"Then why don't you take half a heartbeat to tell me?"

"Because I owe you nothing!" I spit. "Except maybe a swift sword to your throat."

The idea sounds better and better, and my hand itches to palm my blade.

Tib pulls back as if I'd slapped him. He said he didn't send me here. He could be lying. My chest rises as I rein in my anger. He is lying. I saw him there.

"I told you," Tib's voice breaks. "I didn't send you here. I would never have asked something so dangerous of you."

"But you did!"

My anger burns as hot as dragons fire. I've waited for so long to face Tib and show him what he's made me. To show him how sharp my blade is and how greatly he failed in killing me. But standing in front of him now face to face is too much. I want to scream, to cry, to make him hurt like he hurt me. And suddenly it's just too much.

My anger peters, and I'm just tired. "You did."

I stare at the man who reflects so much of my childhood best friend yet has grown into something so much more. I gaze between his eyes searching for the boy who sacrificed me to Eida. I search for the hate, the greed, the apathy, but I don't see it.

Tib shakes his head. "I remember the morning you disappeared. Caelum came blustering out of the Enchanted Wood spluttering about how you'd snuck off to the Well. He said he followed you—tried to stop you." Pain etches the skin around Tib's eyes, adding years to his face. "It was his fault, he said. He stepped on a branch, and when your attention went to him, the trolls grabbed you."

My brows sink low over my eyes, and my lip curls. A hopeless, sickening feeling settles in my belly.

"Caelum has carried his guilt all this time," Tib says. "Ari, why would you ever risk sneaking to the Well of Eida?"

My stomach knots, wringing with nausea. "You didn't betray me," I whisper. "Caelum did. Caelum sent me here."

CHAPTER TWENTY-ONE

That no good, fire-ridden filth. Tib's brother. His twin.

Fire flares in my chest matching the crimson shame that colors my cheeks. How could I have been so blind? How did I not notice the difference between them? I rub my eyes. That night, he'd kept his face cast in the shadows on purpose. Something roils in my gut. I was blinded by my own infatuation with love to truly notice anything amiss. I didn't want to see it.

Caelum lied to me. A chill snakes around my arms. He pretended to be my best friend. To be Tib. He let me think Tib was the one who sacrificed my life for his mother's. I always knew he envied Tib's and my pairing. I knew he harbored resentment after I rejected a pairing with him, but never to this extent. Never to tear us apart for it.

Caelum tried to kill me and then returned to our village and lied about what he'd done. My dragon's heat rages through my spine, and her warmth gathers around the cuff against my wrist. Thank the stars Graeden had the foresight to protect us all from her.

"Caelum?" Tib growls, breaking my reverie. "What do you mean Caelum sent you here?"

My attention flicks to Tib, and the pain of his betrayal—Caelum's betrayal—splinters through my heart.

"I thought he was you," I whisper. The shame tingles against my cheeks again as I admit overlooking the difference. "He pretended to need my help at the Well. The coward used me. He knew I'd never say no to you."

Tears brim against my eyes. Tib may not believe me—not that I care, but he needs to know.

I inhale a shaky breath. Not all matches in Bridgewick were happy, I knew that. But at least I got to choose between two suitors. I chose Tib, and though I was angry at having to choose anyone at twelve years old, I was grateful for the choice.

"It wasn't until we arrived at the Well that I realized something was wrong, but I didn't think for a moment it wasn't you." Disgust rises in my throat. How could I not have known? Tib spent four years proving I'd made the right choice and taking my heart. "Caelum called the troll forward and offered me as his price."

An onslaught of memories surge through my mind as though I relive that night. Fear, shock, pain. All competed for space within my body as I tried to run. The troll's rough skin grated against mine as he dragged me through the creek. The utter hopelessness as they shoved me into the Well. I squeeze my eyes shut, and darkness cuts through the memories.

When I open my eyes, I find Tib's hands balled into fists at his side. Tension ripples through his strong shoulders. His body trembles, his expression twisted. "How could he have done this?"

My frown deepens. I don't answer Tib. I can't.

"He's my brother. We didn't always get along, but we trusted each other." Tib's shell of rage splinters, pain seeping through. "Or I thought we did. I can't believe Caelum did this to you. Of all people. I lov—" Tib's words cut off with his rising anger.

"I knew Caelum resented our match. I knew he harbored a grudge that you chose my offer for your hand." Tib grinds his teeth, anger fuming beneath the surface. But the Well? I never thought he'd cross that line."

My jaw tightens, and I grumble. "I guess you never know what someone is capable of."

My mind flits through the past two years, the countless lives I've taken, the monster I unleashed. That night when Caelum stole into my window, I never would have imagined I'd be standing here now. My gaze flicks to Tib's. Or that *he'd* be standing here in front of me.

My pulse races, and I inhale a tight breath. It's not enough, and my chest aches for more. Tib's going to die. The Seekers may have monsters buried deep inside, but they're never released in Eida. How's he supposed to stand up against a dragon?

"Why would you risk coming to Eida, Tib?" The question sticks in my throat. "No wish is worth the risk."

"Mine was."

I plant my hands on my hips and raise a brow. "What?"

"I thought it was obvious. I've come for you, Ari."

My arms fall slack to my sides.

"I thought you were—" Tib's expression softens, mournful. He can't bring himself to say the word dead. "Everyone told me to move on after you left."

"Why didn't you?" Warmth thrums through my veins, and a sadness settles against my heart. I've missed him.

"Because I gave my heart to you a long time ago, Ari. I will not leave you behind."

"Tib," I whisper. "You need to leave Arautteve. Now."

"I won't. Not without you."

"I belong to Eida until the day I die." I slip my arm out from beneath my cloak and thrust it toward him. Graeden's brand glows pale against my wrist. "You see? I'm Marked. There's no escape for me. You can't take me from the troll realm. They'll always come for me, find me. I either reach my pardon or die."

I tighten the cloak around me, and my hands tremble. Tib could never save me from this hell. Now, he won't be able to save himself, either. I ball my hands into fists, straining to regain some semblance of control. A muscle works in my jaw, and my throat tightens. He and I must fight each other. For one to win, the other must die.

Tib's stance relaxes. "Your pardon?"

"It doesn't matter," I say. "The point is, I've got it handled. You must leave me. Forget about your wish."

Tib crosses his arms over his chest, immoveable. "I can't. You don't know what it did to your mother when you disappeared. What it did to me. Since the day you were taken, I have trained for this moment."

"Everyone here has *trained for this moment*."

"Not like me." Tib lifts his chin, and an unwavering confidence flits through his gaze. "I will rescue you."

"Don't you understand?" I step toward Tib, and my voice falters. Only a pocket of space separates us. His scent curls around me, and the past punches me in the stomach. The broken rules. The stolen nights. The gentle pressure of Tib's arms wrapped around mine. "Only one of us will walk out of the arena alive."

Tib tilts his head down to meet my eyes as he stands a good foot taller than me. "Then I expect it will be you. This is not the life you deserve."

My stomach churns, the acid clawing its way up my dry throat. He doesn't deserve to die, either.

I glance over my shoulder at the barren street. Very few Fallen walk the flagstone paths, likely already sparring at the training rings. If he hurries, Tib can slip away from Arautteve unnoticed. He could abandon the arena and make some façade of a life for himself. He's resourceful. He could do it.

"Leave," I order, "before the trolls catch you here. Before they sacrifice you to Eida's beast for trespassing and conspiring with their Fallen."

Tib lifts his hands and presses his warm palms against my cheeks. "I'm not leaving you again."

The warmth from Tib's touch reaches my heart and calms the tremble in my arms. I ache to nuzzle my cheek into Tib's hand and forget these past few years. But I don't.

Tib won't abandon me, and it's only a matter of time until I kill him. Once we reach the third round, my dragon will be the one fighting the man from my past. And I have no control over her.

"You sure have grown stubborn," I say.

Stepping back, Arautteve's stuffed air presses between us. My lips arch into a deep frown, and I can't tear my eyes from Tib. He's walked into his grave, and I'm going to escort him there myself. Sorrow tugs at the corners of my eyes.

Leaving Tib alone deep in the heart of Arautteve, I turn my back on him and stalk away. Tib chose to come to Eida on his own—a poor, miserable, naive choice, but still a choice. He'll have to find his own way back out. But I'll do everything I can to not kill him.

I dart inside my temple like it's a respite from the world rather than the prison I call a room. Shirking the damp cloak from my shoulders, I slip into dry leathers. I should relax. I should let my body recover from the near constant battles. I can't. I won't.

There's no way in Eida's depths I can rest with my mind so torn as it is. My stomach twists into a knot as Tib's words parrot through my head. He didn't sacrifice me to Eida. He came to save me from it. I sheathe my weapons and sneak out of the temple.

Anger churns through my stomach, but I don't know who to be angriest with. Me, for not recognizing Caelum led me to the Well instead of Tib? Tib, for foolishly coming here? Caelum, for deceiving me in the first place? Or the trolls, for having a kingdom where this killing is acceptable?

Maybe we all deserve some of my rage.

My dragon's heat engulfs my temper, exploding it through my veins. Pressure builds inside my fingers, and my arms crave a sword to thrust. I won't rest until I've cut through this confusion.

The distant sound of scraping steel echoes through the tall flowers stretching upward like trees. I dart along the path toward the training rings. Shoving my thoughts of Tib and Caelum to the deepest recesses of my mind, I step onto the open field.

Fallen dance around each other, weapons clashing, masters chanting instructions. My fingers curl around the hilt of my sword. A large man fights in the corner, corded muscles wrapping around his arms and through his neck. His opponent barely reaches his full pecs, his stone torso absorbing each blow.

I want to fight him. He can take my anger and, hopefully, distract my mind.

Skirting around the other full rings, I stand on the sidelines of the brute's. As soon as he crushes his opponent to the ground, I step forward. A hand snags my shoulder, and I stumble back. Isla aims a sharpened spear at my chest, its tip brushing the bone between my breasts. White feathers hang around the spearhead, and her arms firmly hold the weapon's weight.

"Isla." I grimace, my bottom lip catching between my teeth as the spearhead pokes my breastbone.

Isla stands tall behind her weapon, a confidence aiming her blade. Dark circles frame her soft eyes, and a savage look churns within her gaze, but she doesn't look a step out of control.

I frown. My hands twitch at my sides to raise in surrender, but I don't lift them. Isla is a prisoner here like me. It's kill or be killed inside and outside the arena. We may have a deal, but I don't plan on surrendering to her anytime soon.

"What do you want?" I ask, my voice flat and emotionless.

Isla withdraws her spear and rests it against her shoulder. She tucks a lock of hair behind her ear, exposing an angry slash over her flushed cheek. "To fight."

The tension in my shoulders eases. She isn't a fighter. She's a seer, a psychic who has never even stepped into the arena. I raise my chin and wet my lips. She's hurting. Like me. Like we all are.

It doesn't mean I won't kill her if I think she risks my life, though.

Isla circles me, her steps even, her pale eyes predatory. Her wings flutter at her back, and she floats into the air and drifts into an empty training ring. Sweat coats my palms. I follow.

Isla swings her spear through the air, and it crashes against my blade. I parry, throwing her weapon to her side. She barely keeps it in her hand. Locking both hands around the now splintered wood, Isla whips it toward my legs. Wrong. I leap over it effortlessly and launch my knee into her side.

Isla splays against the dirt. She crawls to her knees, wiping the back of her hand over her chin. Baring her teeth, Isla charges. Her shoulder rams into my stomach, but she can't upset my footing. We slide across the packed dirt a few paces until I break her grip and shove her off me.

Isla leads me through our training ring, and I pull back my blows. Her arms lack the toned curve of mine, her legs soft and thin. She may have the spirit of a fighter, but she's not built like one. Flaming nights, she's a fairy!

Isla's chest expands with uncontrolled anger. Sweat dampens the flyaway strands along her hairline, her cheeks have grown a deep crimson. She has lost her weapon but raises her fists and plants her feet.

Isla scowls. Pain bleeds from her glare. I should have tried to protect her from her mistress that night in Arautteve's courtyard. There are many things I should have done throughout my life.

Lowering my sword, I retreat from the training ring. "I won't fight you anymore, Isla."

Isla races to the edge of the ring. "Because I'm not worthy, Fallen?"

I flinch. She uses our shared title as though she means to cut me with it.

"Because you're not a fighter," I say softly. "Be grateful for that. The world needs less people willing to kill."

"You will kill us all," she hisses.

I ignore her baiting and slip into the growing mass of Fallen coming to train. But I can't shake her last well-aimed attack. I am a dragon shifter who has no control over her monster. Could I really be the end of us all?

A giddy shout rips through my thoughts and silences the surrounding melody of clashing swords.

"Eida's beast!" a man yells, his voice high-pitched with his excitement. A twisted smile curls over his thin lips. "Eida's beast is feasting on a thief. Come, and see." A slight giggle leaves his lips as he tries to stifle his merriment. Turning from the crowd, the man darts down the path leading away from the training rings.

A silent chill crawls through the crowd, icing the thin sheen of sweat on my skin. For a moment, no one moves. Then like a herd of cattle, every Fallen sheathes their weapons and clambers down the path after the man.

Bodies bump into mine, dragging me along with the rest of them. It's morbid for someone to be excited to watch such a thing. The trolls likely sent him to fetch us all to come to see what happens to the Troll King's Fallen who refuse to fight. Or for Seekers who need to learn their place. That doesn't mean he needs to be happy about it.

My thoughts flit to Tib, and anxiety worms its way beneath my skin as we cross through Arautteve. He's safe. It can't be him. The trolls feed the beast regular sacrifices—anything with magic in its veins. Most often, it's a Marked who fell in the arena. Rarely, it's a troll who found their way to death. I swallow the lump growing in my throat.

That doesn't mean they won't throw a Seeker or an Unmarked on the beast's altar. With so little magic in their veins, it may not eat the sacrifice, but it will still kill it.

If this sacrifice is a thief, I doubt it's a troll, and I doubt it's dead. Oh, stars, please don't let it be Tib.

Blood pounds in my ears, and it's no longer the crowd that ushers me toward the outer edge of Arautteve. I run.

When the lush flowers begin to wither and thorns sprout in their place, my feet skid to a stop. A troll stands in the center of the grove, flanked by needle-like plants that twist in unnatural positions. He folds his thick arms over his chest and grunts.

The man leading the crowd rounds a bend behind me and nearly squeals and claps his hands together like a child. "We've come to see the sacrifice."

My blood pounds through my ears. The troll places his open palm against the soil. Magic glows beneath his hand, and the ground shudders. I stumble back, knocking into a few other Fallen. The earth splits open ahead of us, and an arched doorway rises from the ground.

Unease settles on my shoulders and heightens my senses.

What am I doing? If the trolls caught Tib, it's not like I can rescue him. They'd feed me to the beast next, just for trying. My fingers brush the gold cuff strapped around my wrist. Graeden would never know what happened either. Tucking my wrist against my side, I push the thought from my head and refocus on Tib. What's the point of coming after him only to stand before him in the arena again?

Anxiety hums through my nerves, but none of my questions matter. I need to know.

In a rushed clamor, a dozen or so Fallen stampede toward the doorway, leaving the bulk of the crowd behind. I'm caught in the swell and shoved inside its darkness. Feet slap against stone. Bodies knock into mine as we tumble down a narrow staircase.

I wish I hadn't run. I wish I hadn't let Tib into my head. Had I cautioned myself, I wouldn't be plummeting toward Eida's beast.

A subtle veil of decay clings to the stone walls. My nose twitches, and my eyes burn.

Darkness swallows the distant light from the surface as we descend ever deeper, and the comforting warmth from Arautteve shifts to a fear-inducing chill.

Gooseflesh crawls over my skin, and I bite my tongue to keep my teeth from chattering. Only when we feel death's familiar cloak does the chaos still.

As we round a bend, the darkness gives way to a dim ambience of white light. Small flecks of light dot the darkness above us like stars in the night sky. I knead the growing knot coiled through my chest, and a sense of loss washes over me. What I wouldn't give to see the stars again. They don't belong in such an ugly place.

We step from the staircase onto a wide plateau. The other Fallen scatter across its surface, finally giving me space to breathe. But instead of fresh air, I swallow a violent barrage of putrid rot. I gag and cover my mouth.

My gaze sweeps past my burning tears and through the darkness. I search for his sandy hair, his blue eyes, anything to confirm my fear that Tib is the thief. I don't see him, and my throat tightens. I pick my way through the crowd, searching for more trolls. Surely, they would be guarding their prisoner.

The plateau is engulfed in shadows, and my feet skid to a halt a few paces from its end. My breath seizes, and I step back from the sheer drop ahead of me. My gaze wanders to three trolls bowing low across the cold floor.

I scan the darkness ahead of them, and my heart drops so fast I'm surprised it doesn't knock me off the edge. A human hovers in the air over the endless chasm. Her salt and pepper curls fall haphazardly from the tie at her neck, and fear widens her dark eyes.

Relief softens the tension lacing up my spine. It's not Tib. The relief is short lived as my gaze wanders over the woman, her eyes staring into the dark abyss beneath her. Small lacerations mar her bare arms. Blood drips into the chasm.

Then, a vicious roar cuts through the chamber.

CHAPTER TWENTY-TWO

Conversations die, leaving only an echo of the beast's ear-splitting cry.

A warning. The beast is coming.

The magic-bound woman doesn't flinch, and I wonder which of the trolls bowed before her holds the key to her release. Adrenaline thrums in my chest. The beast is here. It's only a matter of time until it feeds.

The plateau shudders. I stumble to my knees and brace myself against the uneven stone. A clattering of rocks echoes through the cavern. The ground trembles again. Something scrapes across the stone, screeching through the darkness. Like a dropped axe… or claws. My breath hitches, and I retreat from the edge of the plateau. I fasten my gaze where rock meets shadow. Something is climbing the cliff face.

A deafening cry erupts from the chasm, and the blood crackles in my vessels. Shoving my hands over my ears, I collapse against the flat rock top. Bodies drop around me, and we all try to block out the screech. The beast can paralyze victims with the sound of its cry. A sharp rock presses into my cheek, but I pay it no attention. Pressure swells in my brain. It's going to explode.

Mouth gaping, I dare a glance at the woman suspended above us. Her expression is twisted by pain with her hands bound by her sides. Blood trickles from her eyes and streams down her cheeks.

A massive claw snatches the edge of the stone, and the beast drags itself onto the plateau. I stifle my gasp. It's not one creature, but a mutant of three. A lush, fire-like mane travels down the beast's neck and billows off its chest. Part lion. Scaled feet and a thick, whip-like tail. Part dragon. Furred hind legs with sharp, jagged claws. Part wolf. It's an alphyn.

The beast snarls, and its steel canines catch the artificial light. I scramble backward, but it doesn't approach. Instead, it spins in a wide arc. It only has eyes for the woman. For the blood.

Opening its jaw, the beast releases another paralyzing cry. My skull hurts from how hard I push my hands against my ears, but I don't relent. The woman's face contorts once more before all expression melts from her face.

The beast must like them dead.

With a single bound, the beast snatches his sacrifice from the air and disappears into the chasm.

In the creature's wake, we are left with silence's mournful tune. A melody of life and loss that doesn't exist. Although the beast is gone, I remain crouched against the floor, my gaze locked on the shadows.

"Foolish," a Fallen whispers as the crowd slowly rises and returns to the staircase. "Why anyone thinks they can steal from the trolls is pure idiocy. Seeker or Fallen, once in Eida, we're all prisoners."

My feet are planted against the stone floor as the others meander around me. In my mind's eye, Tib scoops a handful of water from the bathing pool. It dribbles down his chin. If his life is anything like mine was in Haven, he must be parched. Starving, too, I'm sure.

He's never been one afraid to take what he needs. But if he's caught stealing from Arautteve, there's more at risk than an Unmarked releasing its monster. He'll find himself suspended above this chasm next.

Whipping around, I dart past the other Fallen and spring up the staircase. I shouldn't care. If the trolls kill him, then I don't have to. A pang pierces my chest. I don't know what I'm going to do, but I can't let him become Eida's next sacrifice.

My spine stiffens, and I run faster.

I reach the surface and dart through the doorway into the daylight. My stomach tightens as the grotesque execution replays in my mind, the woman's wide eyes, her tied tongue strangling a scream. Her panic beats an echoing cry in my heart.

Before the rest of the Fallen arrive, I race back to my temple. I scramble through the small pile of clothing tossed haphazardly in the wicker basket at the end of my bed. Tugging on a pair of fur-lined leggings and a wool-knit sweater, I throw my cloak around my shoulders and shove a few pieces of aaerin into my cloak's pockets. My gaze catches on the untouched bed, the blankets spread neatly across it. My weary body begs me to rest even for an hour. I hesitate, my palm resting on my door's handle. The stars know I could use the sleep.

Pinching my lips, I turn the handle. Not now. Not yet. The courtyard is near-empty as I duck back into the daylight and head north to the Crossing.

I fix my gaze ahead of me, but every other sense scans the grounds for a threat. Graeden expected to meet me at the training rings hours ago. Surely, he's heard of the sacrifice by now. All the Fallen will be speaking of it for days. But when the last Fallen trickles out of from the beast's den, and I'm nowhere to be found, he'll come looking.

The panicked roiling in my stomach hardens as I approach the gateway to Ghora. Aside from Haven's fringe, I've never wandered into the district on my own before. I stand at the Crossing's entrance, shadows roiling like clouds of kohl beyond its threshold.

Seekers hate the Fallen. My gaze roams through the shadows. If they get the drop on me, they'll take it now rather than wait for the arena. Most Seekers who've waded through Ghora's unrelenting darkness for some time have learned the trolls don't play fair, and they've heard tales of our monsters. I fist my hand, wiping the sheen of sweat from my palms.

I'm Eida's dragon. There's nothing the Seekers can do to me. A seed of doubt flickers in my chest... I hope. My short, cuffed boots scrape against Ghora's hard earth as I pass through the Crossing. How I wish my dragon and I were united already. That she would come if I called her.

A harsh wind whips through the land, cutting through my leggings and whistling through my ears. I strain to hear beyond the wind's roar—a quiet step or a vulture's disturbing hiss. But the growing storm masks all sound. My eyes lift to the churning cloud of shadow. I'd better make my journey quick.

My steps are silent beneath the wind's howl as I dart into Ghora. The closest I've ever made it into Ghora in my human form was when Graeden dragged me along its border. Not exactly an all-inclusive tour. Obsidian climbs the tallest peaks and hangs from the stone trees. I weave through the shadowed haze, darting wherever the paths lead and completely losing myself in the maze.

I hush the thought of what could happen if I get lost in this district. My fingers brush over the cuff clasped at my wrist. If I remove it, would my dragon save us? Would she shift and fly us home?

I'm not sure she would do anything for *me*, but maybe she would if her life was in danger, too. Still, I'd better not chance it. Ghora's landscape rises and falls, twisting in knotted spirals. At first, I see no one as I slip in and out of the darkest parts of the district. But soon, Seekers strew over the ground. A few staunch bloody wounds, their pale faces glistening with sweat. Crimson dyes their fingertips, deep shudders rocking their bodies.

I skirt past without an offer to help. They may be weak and dying, but there's no telling what energy they'll find if they know a Fallen has crossed into their lands.

Others cling to the stone trees like lifelines. Loose skin drapes from their starved bodies. Bloody stumps dot their fingers where the nails have been gnawed to their nailbeds. Olive green secretions crust the rims of their bloodshot eyes. Sunken cheeks and drooping eyelids deepen with the shadows.

The Plague.

I press my nose and mouth against the crook of my elbow and distance myself farther from the Seekers. One wrong inhale, and I'll find a blade in my heart just like Erom did outside of Haven. My throat dries as the memory of his sacrifice slips into my mind.

My gaze sifts through the shadows, searching for Tib. If only my dragon could help me find him with her sharp sense of smell.

Shutting my eyes, I search for my dragon. Her strength. Her heat. But all I feel is cold.

I sigh. I'm on my own.

I march through the chilled wasteland. What am I thinking, wandering through Ghora? I'm nowhere near Tib, and I have no idea how to find him. Why would he risk settling around a community of plagued Seekers? It'd be a death sentence for him.

My blades hang heavy at my waist. It won't be long until I'm his executioner. He either dies in the arena at my hand or dies waiting in Ghora.

My mood sours, and I frown. Tib knew what he was getting into when he chose to come here. I can't protect him. My stomach tightens. But I want to. My fingers brush the small lump in my cloak bumping into my hands with each stride.

The broken aaerin may not look appetizing, but at least it's edible. Maybe it can keep him from stealing. Maybe I could bring him more.

Perhaps boiled sausages or sugar-dusted pastries. Anything would be better than what he now has.

My thoughts are so wrapped around getting it to him, I don't realize when the trees begin to thicken along the path or how they curve around me like a coffin.

A branch crackles at my side like breaking glass, and my full attention snaps to the present. The terrain has shifted into a narrow valley, flanked by hundreds of stone trees. I can barely see the flickering sky through the tightly woven branches overhead. My gait slows, and I spin in a slow circle, scanning the shadows.

The sounds of cracking glass surround me, and the trees moan. Any minute they could shatter, collapsing onto any passersby. I keep a wary eye on the stone trees. Perhaps that's what keeps Tib and the other Seekers safe.

My heart thunders like the roiling clouds above. The breeze whistles in my ears. A silent mist curls through the darkness ahead of me, shimmering with the sky's weak light.

I toss a nervous glance over my shoulder. I should turn back.

The quiet scuff of leather against stone rustles through the air. I can't tell from which direction it comes. My palm toys with the hilt of my blade, and I glance from one direction to the next.

I turn, and tension cramps through every facet of my body. A sharp silhouette sprints through the trees toward me. I lunge from their path, but not fast enough. The dark shadow collides with me. We roll to the jagged ground. I scramble to my feet, but the Seeker grabs at my arms to keep me low. A scream builds in my throat, and I shove my chin in the air to release it. A calloused hand smothers my voice, the man's shadowed face leaning into my ear.

"I wouldn't do that if I were you." I inhale the warm, peppery scent of cinnamon. Tib.

My body wilts beneath his touch, and relief floods the flames crackling inside me. Tib's grip relaxes as my defense does. Throwing my hands against his chest, I shove him and hiss, "Get off me."

Tib rolls to the side, but his eyes are locked in the distance. His gaze darts from one corner of darkness to another. "It isn't safe for you here."

"Nor you. This is Eida."

Tib's eyes wander to mine, a dark haze settling over them. "I'm not a child anymore, Ari. I knew what I was getting into when I came here."

He's certainly right about one thing. He's not a child any longer. My eyes linger on his strong jawline. The edges of his eyes crinkle as he squints into the darkness. There's an age to them I hadn't noticed. Ever since the man returned to Bridgewick from Eida without having aged a day, I've considered if time passed differently in the troll realm. Now watching Tib, I can't help but wonder just how long I've been gone.

The question rolls over my tongue, but before I can ask, Tib lifts me to my feet. His hands are warm and steady, but our path together only leads to one end. I swallow against the tightening in my throat and release him. Tib's hood shields his eyes, and he's dressed for battle. Blades hang from his waist, and his war hammer is strapped to his back.

He purses his lips in a silent plea to stay quiet and jerks his head toward the thickening darkness. I don't want to traverse even deeper into Ghora, and my dragon's fire sparks the embers in my stomach.

"Why?" I whisper.

Tib tenses, and his gaze darts through the stone forest. "Trolls," he whispers against my ear. Tib extends a hand. "Trust me."

Fire burns through my veins as my dragon awakens. Tensed and uneased. My cuff warms with her agitation. I may not be able to shift while wearing the cuff, but I can still feel my dragon's power when she wants me to. She purrs, and an edge crawls through my veins.

Tib has never led me into danger before—not the real Tib. It's just like him to walk with me, hand-in-hand, the whole way. Ignoring my dragon's flames, I place my palm against his. Tib's slender fingers curl around my hand, cocooning it in warmth.

My dragon bristles, her heat growing, but she wasn't here as I searched for Tib. She doesn't get a say now.

As we travel deeper between the valley's steep walls, the harsh winds die, and the metallic tang of blood tinges the air. I wrinkle my nose, catching a whiff of decay amongst the blood. Crumbling structures pockmark the narrow floor, their roofs disintegrating, their entrails gutted and left in smoldering heaps throughout the valley.

Before long, Tib's rushed gait slows. Firelight cuts through the veil of darkness, the amber flames fanning out through the valley. Their fires are small but plentiful. Quiet moans permeate the still air. My eyes widen as my gaze darts through the Seekers' camp. I tear my hand from Tib's and step back.

Flaming nights, Tib led me straight to them.

CHAPTER TWENTY-THREE

I DRAW A DAGGER from my belt. The faint light glints off its steel between mine and Tib's bodies.

I curse under my breath. Tib could have been lying all along. Fire licks the underside of my skin. My dragon thinks so, too. Tib *did* sacrifice me to the Well, and now he's brought me here for the Seekers to finish the job.

Tib lifts his hands in front of his chest as though he approaches a wild animal. "No one's going to hurt you here."

"You're lying," I hiss. "Seekers hate the Fallen. They'll slash my throat before I ever speak a word. I came to warn you—to protect you—and you walked me into the heart of Ghora."

"No." Tib's voice is strong, the single word echoing around us. "I would never do that to you."

"How long have you been here?" I ask. I'd assumed Tib had only just arrived before our battle, but the trolls always make their Seekers suffer first.

Tib hesitates.

"How long, Tib?" I snap.

Vultures scatter from the tallest branches with my voice, their guttural hisses a beacon to where we hide.

Tib's jaw tightens. "Four months."

Reality washes over me, its chill icing the fire in my veins. I brush my hair from my face. "Four months? How?"

"The only way any of us survive in Ghora. Here. In the solace of others." Tib sweeps his arm toward the valley. "This is where we survive—those of us not yet affected by the Plague. They won't hurt you. They won't even know you're a Fallen—it's too dark to differentiate that here."

I shake my head and step back. "I'm only here to pass along a warning."

"You'll have to pass it along and walk at the same time." Tib strolls past me and heads deeper into the valley. "There are people waiting for me."

I tighten my grip around my blade and tune my ears for any sound in the surrounding wood.

Shriveled bodies curl around the gentle heat, the blazes near embers. It's as though they are more concerned about dying from a chill than catching fire. I tilt my head away from them, but it doesn't matter. They don't see me, and if they do, they are much too burdened to care. Some of the Seekers huddle around their flames, roasting creatures with spindly tails or sagging ears.

How has Tib survived here for so long? No one can survive on the mutated creatures of this land.

Tib wanders to a young woman's side. She's hunched forward, her legs tucked against her chest. As Tib drops to his knees, the woman lifts a ghostly face to meet him.

"Broth and aaerin." Tib unwraps Arautteve's delicate pastry and crumples the dried leaf wrapping. The sweet buttery scent perfumes into the air.

My fingers play with the edge of my pocket, where the aaerin now resembles a fine powder rather than food. I leave it.

Tib is stealing from Arautteve. But he's getting away with it. Pride wars with panic in my chest. What he does is dangerous, but so is surviving in Ghora without real food or water.

Tib presses the soft crust against the woman's lips, and a whimper of pleasure whistles through her nose.

"You stole this." It isn't a question, and Tib doesn't answer.

My mind flashes to the woman suspended above the chasm. Even now, the crack of bone echoes through my ears as the beast's teeth had latched onto her body and it swept her away. All because she stole from the trolls. My warning hangs on the tip of my tongue, but I swallow it.

Stealing from trolls is dangerous. But Tib is, too. He's been in Eida for four months. He steals from our gardens; he spies on our bathing chambers… seeing me in Arautteve wasn't Tib's first time crossing over. He knows what's at stake. He knows how to survive here.

Tib presses the edge of a clay bowl to the woman's lips, and broth trickles down her chin.

"Where are your strong?" I ask, my gaze sliding among the Seekers. Every one of them is battered and broken, teetering on the brink of death.

Tib glances up. "Not here. This is where the abandoned Seekers end up."

"I've never heard of abandoned Seekers."

"You wouldn't have." Tib rocks back on his heels, giving the Seeker a moment to catch her breath. "The trolls are in no rush to grant our wishes. The longer we wait between battles—with no resources—the weaker we become." Tib spreads his arms wide, gesturing toward the derelict valley. "Most of the Seekers in this place have been waiting for months for their next round in the arena. Forgotten."

My gaze sweeps through the Seekers. Most are sick. Many appear near death.

"They'll hardly be able to stand in the arena when they're called," Tib says. "That's if they're called at all before they die."

Something rotten stews in my stomach. I don't want the Seekers entering the arena any more than the next Fallen, but to be abandoned in a strange world without necessities... It feels wrong.

"Why would he do that?" I challenge in a hushed tone. "He has us—his Fallen—to keep the Seekers from gaining their wishes. Besides, that's part of the arrangement. Seekers enter the Well *to* fight for their wish."

"Oh, we all get to fight for our wish. *When* exactly we get to do that isn't as clear." Tib sets the bowl next to the woman and gives her shoulder a comforting squeeze before standing. "Many of these Seekers have fought at least once, but they weren't killed. Neither was their opponent. So, they're just waiting for another chance. Seems to me that even with all these forgotten, there are still plenty of Seekers entering that arena. Guess it doesn't matter what corner of the world you're from, we're all a little selfish that way."

Tib moves away from the woman and weaves through the other Seekers. He props listless bodies against the cold trees, applies a sticky salve to wounds, and bandages those who have seen the worst of the arena.

"How do you know how to do all this?" I whisper.

Tib shoots a playful glare at me, his lips twisting to hide his smile. "What? Do you think I've been sitting in Ghora eating berries and fanning myself with a reed and just happened to decide one day I should come get you?"

Tib brushes the crumbs from his hands and pivots to face me. His expression sobers.

"I've been searching for you for a long time. Ever since Caelum told me you'd been taken, I've never reconsidered coming for you." Sadness touches Tib's eyes, but only for a moment. His playful smile crawls over his lips and smothers the pain flickering in his gaze. His eyes roam over my body, lingering on my legs. "Though, I didn't expect to find you so…" Tib mulls over the word. "adept."

Heat floods my cheeks, and I clench my jaw willing the warmth to disappear. Same old Tib.

His eyes jump to mine again, and a spark catches within my chest, raw and hungry. I inhale, my breath pressing against the swelling excitement. The spark consumes my pain and anger, dissolving my anxiety and fears and growing into something I almost lost: hope.

The flames pockmarking the dark valley reflect in Tib's bright eyes, and the fire in my chest blazes. I haven't felt this free since I was a youth with dreams of a beautiful future. A Seeker's soft moan cuts through the hope of my past.

Tearing the desire from my chest, I shove it deep away from my heart, and my dragon's flames engulf it. I step away from Tib, his brows furrowing. That child who had once hoped for a bright future doesn't exist anymore.

No matter what future I find when I leave this realm, it won't be the same as what I once wished.

"Be careful, Tib." Groans stretch into the dark night and drift away like smoke. No one will remember these dead. No one will remember us, either. "Whatever you're doing here to survive is dangerous. Just... be careful."

"Always am." Tib's light-hearted smile never falters.

"Tib—" I open my mouth to object, but Tib's air of ease disappears. His gaze darts into the distance south through the valley. "What are you doi—?"

"Trolls!" Tib shouts through the valley.

A wave of panic surges through the camp. The Seekers' fatigued moans disappear, and they stagger to their feet. Their contorted bodies curl inward, and they shuffle on swollen feet toward hiding.

Tib locks his hand around my bicep and drags me with him into shadow. We crouch near the base of an obsidian tree. Releasing his vice around my arm, Tib presses a finger against his lips before pointing to the main path. Blankets lie in forgotten heaps, tin bowls still wobble where dropped, and the fires still smolder.

Slow, heavy footfalls crunch through the broken obsidian scattered across the ground. I draw deeper into the tree's shadow until Tib's chest presses against my back. His heart beats in frantic swells.

An acrid stench curls off the trolls and rides the air. Even at this distance, it stings my eyes. I wait, my chest barely rising as their thundering steps pass by our hiding place. Peeling myself from Tib, I peek out from behind the tree.

Three brutes stomp through the camp, their clubs dragging across the ground. The sound of tinkling glass dances through the air as the kohl shards clink together. One of the trolls lifts his large nose into the air. He sniffs.

"Come out, come out little Seekers," he says in a singsong voice unfitting of his brusque demeanor. He inhales again, and his head swivels toward where Tib and I hide.

My hands tremble, and I bury them between my knees. This is no different than stepping into the arena. Hot air flushes beneath my skin as though my dragon agrees.

Oh, these trolls will wish they hadn't trailed into these parts. Whatever they seek they won't find from me.

My fingers brush the edge of my gold cuff. The trolls can't force me to shift, but if I release my dragon, I could protect us all. Doubt creeps along my veins, snuffing out my confidence. I can't guarantee my dragon will emerge—I'm not in control. And there's no telling what the trolls could do with my dragon form if they catch me within their spell again.

I drop my hand from the cuff. The chance to protect them isn't worth the risk. Besides, every Seeker in Ghora chose to come to Eida. They don't deserve to live. The words twist together in my head. Words I've said many times over the years somehow feel marred and wrong now.

I shake the thoughts from my head. The troll lingers behind, staring into the shadows. As slow as night's foreboding ascent, I draw my gaze back behind the tree again. My legs burn from crouching, and I silently lower myself to sit between Tib's legs.

I clutch my legs against my chest, my back pressed against Tib again. One of his arms wraps around mine. The other hand rests against the back of my thigh, his fingers pressing against the underside of my knee. Together we attempt to disappear into the shadows.

The troll's thundering steps shake the earth as he approaches our hiding place. Tib's fingers flex against my skin, and his body tenses behind me. My gaze turns upward as the troll looms over us, his broad frame extending around the tree's exterior. He thrusts his hand into the brittle treetop, shattering obsidian branches and sending a cascade of splintered glass around us.

Tib presses my forehead to my knees, wrapping his arms over my head and burying his face against my back. The glass pricks my skin as it rains down around us. My fingers find my dagger concealed against my thigh. Tib's fingers dig into my leg, and I lock eyes with him over my shoulder.

His jaw flexes, and he shakes his head so subtly I almost don't see the movement in the shadow. A scream tears through the darkness, and my gaze whips toward the main path. A petite woman dangles from the troll's grasp as he trudges into the center of camp.

The woman kicks and scratches with energy I doubt she's had in a long while, but the troll doesn't release her. When the three trolls gather around her, magic sparks at their fingertips. The troll who still holds her presses his finger to her temple.

"What are they doing?" I breathe.

Tib gulps, his jaw pressed against my head as we both watch the display. "Siphoning her memories."

Magic burns beneath the woman's skin, her entire skull lighting up. Her mouth opens as though to release her agonizing screams. There's only silence. She gnashes her teeth and her body wretches, fighting to expel the magic creeping through her mind.

Soon, glowing strings of memory slip from the Seeker's temple into the troll's touch. The troll tips his head to the sky and shuts his eyes. A brilliant blue light courses through his veins. The scene makes my stomach curl.

"They steal our happier memories and leave behind empty shells. Can you imagine surviving this place without any recollection of a happier time?" Tib's breath stirs my hair against my ear. He smells like home, and his scent calms the bile in my stomach.

"Why would they do that?" I ask.

"As far as I know, it has something to do with their magic," Tib whispers. "I've seen them bottle it, too. I assume to trade."

So, that's what they barter before each game. "That's awful."

My fingers play with my dagger's hilt. Fallen or not, I doubt the trolls will hesitate to strip my memories away, too. And by Eida's beast, I will not let them steal what little belongs to me.

The troll drops his finger from the woman's temple, staggering backward as though drunk. A leering smile slathers over his face. The woman writhes on the ground between the other two trolls as they each take a turn slogging through her memories in search for ones they'd like to keep. When they've finished, they stumble out of the camp leaving her still form in a heap on the ground.

An eternity seems to pass, and no one moves. Silence steals throughout the camp, the occasional fire crackling against rotted wood. Tib is the first to move. Slipping out from behind me, he approaches the woman, keeping a wary eye in the direction the trolls departed.

I peek out after Tib. He cups the woman's head, pressing two fingers against her neck. Swiping the listless hair from her face, he returns her head to the ground and stands. She doesn't move.

The other Seekers emerge from their hiding places. Instead of hobbling on their feet, they crawl against the cold earth. Their languid bodies drag behind them as they slither towards the flames for heat.

No one speaks of what happened.

Drawing my dagger, I slip out of the valley unnoticed. I keep a sharp eye out for the trolls as I dart through the shadows back to Arautteve.

If Tib knew what was good for him, he'd worry less about the abandoned Seekers and me, and more about how he plans to win in the arena. My chest tightens, and a quiet slew of panic stirs in my stomach. I can't kill Tib, and yet, I know of no other way to survive.

CHAPTER TWENTY-FOUR

"Where have you been? I was to meet you at the training rings." Graeden rises from a wrought iron bench. A stained cloth rests on the seat, and he sheathes his blade. Cleaning it. Is that worry flickering in his eyes?

Sweat trickles down my back, and I try to control my nerves. My gait wavered often as I sprinted through Ghora's shadows, only losing my way once or twice. My dragon must have sensed my failing stamina. Her fire strengthened my muscles as we ran. Thank the stars she did, otherwise, I'm not sure I'd have had the energy to make it back.

As the sky's light faded, I passed through the Crossing and stumbled upon Graeden.

I lick my dry lips and raise my brows. My muscles burn, and I need sleep. "Hmm?"

Ghora's chill clings to my bones, and I try not to shiver. Graeden has never given me a reason not to trust him—I should tell him of Tib, he'd know what to do. My confession lies behind my lips, but they remain closed. Once I tell Graeden of the boy from my past, Tib has no chance of survival.

Graeden's brow wrinkles. "Why are you acting strange?"

"Strange?" I force myself to meet his gaze.

"Were you visiting Haven?" No judgment seeps through with Graeden's words. "It can be hard to let go."

"I've let go." I roll my shoulders. "I wouldn't risk returning to Haven again. No one is worth that risk even if they were still there."

Tib's crooked smile flashes in front of my eyes, and I tuck my arms around my waist. I risked traveling through Ghora, though. I suck in a deep inhale. What was I thinking?

"Good." Graeden's stare bores into me. "So, where were you?"

I swallow and force my gaze to remain fixed to his. "There was a sacrifice."

"So, I heard."

My breaths are shallow. Weak. He knows. There's only one place this path we're on leads: The Crossing. My eyes beg to abandon his unrelenting gaze. Instead, I tell him the truth. The best lies are those shrouded in truth.

"I've never seen it before," I whisper. The memory of the woman slips to the front of my mind. I shiver. "It was awful. I needed to take a walk. Think through some things. I'm sorry, I should have come straight back to the training rings."

The suspicion slips from Graeden's expression. "The first time I saw a sacrifice, I couldn't sleep for days. It has a way of sticking with you."

Silence settles around us. My heartbeat is a quick, uneasy tune, waiting for Graeden to catch my lie.

Rubbing his neck, Graeden jerks his head toward Araurteve. "Can I walk with you?"

I open my mouth to say no, but it lodges in my throat. After tonight, I wouldn't mind the company. Instead, I nod.

Graeden dips his head, a subtle, respectful gesture. "I want to discuss your new Seeker."

Ghora's chill laces up my spine, and my posture stiffens. I swallow against my dry throat. "What about him?"

"He disappeared."

"What? When?"

"During your fight. One moment he was on the ground, the next he was gone and slipped onto the barrier's ledge. That's dozens of feet above you both," Graeden says. "He's been trained in Taiatum."

"The City of Gold?" I blurt.

"You know of it? Good," Graeden says.

I shake my head. "Only the legends."

Some said Taiatum was a village of ghosts, lost souls trapped on the earth until the end of time. They poisoned dreams, turning them into nightmares. They were to blame for the loss of crops or the storms that ravaged the lands.

"But they were only tales," I say.

"Taiatum is very real and very powerful. Only a handful of Seekers from Taiatum have entered Eida, but all have returned with their wishes granted. He is no ordinary Seeker."

"Ghosts came into Eida?"

Graeden screws his brows. "You believe in ghosts?"

"No." Heat floods my cheeks. "That's what the stories told us as children."

Graeden nods. He takes a step closer to Arautteve, and a step closer to me. His cloak brushes my arm as we walk, and the heat from his body curls against mine. The warmth in my cheeks deepens. Dropping my gaze, I stare at the path ahead of us.

"They're not ghosts," he says. "They're the vapor of death itself."

"And the difference?" My tone grows cautious, and I glance at Graeden's shadowed expression.

"Ghosts are dead," Graeden says. "Those from Taiatum are alive but capable of vaporizing their corporeal bodies to sift through the air. They become untouchable."

Tib. What price did he have to pay to train in Taiatum? Exhaustion pours through my limbs. I can't believe it was only yesterday that I fought Tib in the arena.

"If your Seeker is from Taiatum, it's only a matter of time until he disappears in the arena and shoves his blade into your back."

I shift uncomfortably at his side, but Graeden doesn't notice.

We round the bend as a mangled cry splits through the air. My stomach twists with the feral sound.

"Keep walking," Graeden mutters at my side. His gait grows rigid, and he slows his pace to match mine better—a barrier between me and whatever had cried out.

I stretch my head around Graeden. Beneath the night's dim light, a woman stands over a cowering pile of curls. Her sharp nose flares, and she bares her pointed teeth. "You miserable, worthless mutt!" The woman stabs a flaming rod toward the creature, and it roils on the ground. Another miserable cry escapes its lips. The creature rolls over, its hands covering its face.

I can still see him, though. A human torso, human hands, a human face except for the horns sprouting from his head. Fur covers his lower half, and his hooves kick wildly. This man's inner monster is a faun.

My dragon's fire sparks in my belly. Her heat burns into anger. The woman thrusts the hot rod toward the faun, and he covers his face and coils into a ball. She's going to kill the creature before he ever has a chance to step in the arena.

"Leave it alone." A grating hum carries Graeden's voice into my ear. "That monster belongs to Tarvea. Each master will train his or her own Fallen. It's not our place to intervene."

Gritting my teeth, I smother the blaze in my core, willing me to fight. This isn't our battle. But the creature squeals terribly. Fire builds in my throat. In this form, it'll come out as nothing but aching, painful steam. I shove the heat away.

"Fauns aren't violent creatures," I hiss. I don't know that, but my dragon does. "How is a faun someone's monster?"

Graeden guides me around the cruelty, his eyes set on the far end of the courtyard. "Some harbor tamer beasts inside. I'd bet my sword she thought he was something fiercer. If it doesn't learn violence, though, it'll never survive in Eida."

A splinter fractures through my chest. Graeden says it so matter-of-factly like no *monster* with any semblance of humanity can survive this realm. I shake my head, willing my dragon to stifle her feelings. Graeden's right. They can't.

Even still, the words slip between my lips. "You don't know that."

Graeden gives me a sidelong glance, his gaze lingering. His nose flares as though he understands what I'm about to do before I do.

The faun cries out again, a wretched, broken sound. Dragonsfire surges through my core, and her emotions overtake mine. The unjust brutality writhes like acid, the crisp taste of freedom on the tip of my tongue.

We can give it to the faun. The thought's not mine, and neither are my actions. Despite the cuff, I'm no longer in control, though I don't shift.

We lunge toward the bird-like woman with her cruel features and violent hands. A roar rips through the air—and I'm gone. Lost to my dragon's fiery rage and determined will to free the weakest creature of us all. It's still my legs that thud against the ground, my arms that pummel into soft flesh, but all I see is red.

My dragon's bloodthirst engulfs everything. Her thoughts fixated on one thing: *Set the creature free. Set the creature free.*

Heat sears against my eyes in the crimson prison my dragon has forced me into. Flames lick every part of my body. And there's nothing I can do to stop it.

"Restrain yourself." Graeden barks in my ear. Sweet relief floods my dragon's heat. If anyone can get through to her, it's him. His voice softens as though his words are only for my dragon and me. "Trust me."

His rough hands latch around my arms, and he drags me through the dirt. My dragon thrashes for another single moment before conceding to his command. The rage vanishes, leaving me exhausted. My body slackens against Graeden.

The woman lies in a heap on the ground, snarling. Her face is already swollen, a red splotch spreading over her temple where she's going to have a nasty bruise.

"You better get a muzzle for that dog, Thorne!" she screeches.

Graeden hooks his thumb in the crook of my elbow to steer me away. "It wouldn't hurt to fit in a few more trainings for yourself, Tarvea."

She shrieks, every curse I've ever heard in this realm trailing behind us.

I expect a reprimand, a lecture, something, but we don't speak as Graeden steers me toward the catacombs. I don't know what I'd even say.

Instead, I allow my thoughts to wander back to Ghora. I should tell Graeden about Tib. Knowing my Seeker didn't come to hurt me could change everything… and yet change nothing. I pinch my lips shut. I'm not sure why I don't tell him. Maybe because if it comes down to my survival or Tib's, I'll choose mine.

My cheeks warm. Not that I care what Graeden thinks of me. When the third round comes, my dragon won't hesitate to kill Tib. It will be him beneath her anger just like Tarvea.

Before we enter the catacombs, I anchor my feet at its entrance. Red sand blows in calm swells around my ankles. Graeden has thoughts about what happened, and I want to hear them. My defense churns behind my lips.

"Say it."

Graeden glances over his shoulder, his face partially cast in the tomb's shadow. "Say what?"

"That I'm incapable of listening. That there's no place in Eida for a disobedient Fallen. That I should've left Tarvea alone. That I'm out of control."

Graeden offers me an amused smile. "Are you?"

I clench my jaw. Graeden sweeps his arm toward the catacombs' welcoming darkness. Lifting my chin, I stroll past him into the tomb.

Graeden, for once, lets me lead the way. I don't stop until we reach the lowest level.

"Have you been practicing uniting with your dragon?" Graeden's voice cuts through the darkness stronger than any lamp.

"I've been trying," I admit, "but I don't think it's working."

Graeden lights an oil lamp. Then another. "I didn't think so."

"You're not mad about Tarvea?"

Graeden shoots me a sidelong glance. "How can I be mad at you for defending the very thing I've taught you? You didn't choose this life. Neither did that faun. Honestly, if your dragon hadn't stepped in, I may have."

"But you said—"

"I know what I said." Graeden finishes lighting the last lamp. Shadows flicker over his face, and my chest lightens. A smile toys with my lips. Are we on the same side for once? Graeden's gaze pins me to the wall, and I don't dare break it. "Let's go."

Lifting a lamp from the wall, Graeden leads me toward a corner cast in shadow. He presses into the darkness and slips into an obscured tunnel. A subtle unease rolls in my stomach. Someone could have easily hidden in this tunnel and watched us train.

I slip into the shadows behind Graeden. My gaze anchors to the oil lamp he holds.

"Where are we going?" I ask.

Graeden disappears around a corner, and I'm swallowed by the darkness. I stiffen as I tiptoe forward. Everything ahead of me is silent. I see nothing. Hear nothing.

My fingers stroke the smooth stone wall as I round the bend. Graeden stands at the edge of a wide pool, the oil lamp capped and set next to his feet. Light pours through the vents in the vaulted ceiling.

"To the only place you can truly feel alone in Eida," Graeden whispers.

Midnight water reflects the flickering lights overhead. They look like stars. I inhale, and the tension eases in my chest. A smooth stone bank surrounds the glass-like pool.

"You and your dragon are out of control," Graeden says. "And it's going to get you killed."

I open my mouth to defend myself, but I have nothing to say. He's right. I can't fight my dragon and a Seeker at the same time.

"Your dragon pushes its boundaries against the cuff, and she is strong," Graeden says. "You're stumbling during battles and making critical errors. I think your anger is too strong."

"What do you mean?" I ask. "I thought you said my anger fueled my monster."

Graeden turns to face the pool. "It does. But your anger is all over the place. You are scattered, and your dragon can feel it. That makes her scattered, too." Graeden fingers the hem of his shirt and pulls it over his head.

My heart skips, and a slow heat burns through my stomach. Even in the faint light, I can see the contoured muscles framing his back. The strong shape of his arms. And the scars he bears from his own journey in Eida.

"We wielded your anger to unleash your dragon, but I think you have stowed more anger than you realize." Graeden speaks over his shoulder, his body still facing the pool. "Is it the boy who sent you here? Or the trolls who took you? Are you angry with yourself?"

Flames lick the edges of my memory behind the sealed door. Tightening the restraint, I smother the fire, and my lips part. How can he see all that?

"It doesn't matter," Graeden waves the questions away. "If your anger is causing too much instability, we need to dampen that anger. We need to ground you. Center you."

Graeden steps from his trousers, knee-length breeches beneath. I tighten an arm around my waist and press my fingers to my lips. Heat floods my cheeks. I lift my gaze to the apertures overhead. Thank Eida's beast the darkness hides my flushed cheeks. Graeden lowers himself into the pool. He swims in a small circle and lifts his arms toward me.

I shake my head, but I'm not sure he can see me. My voice is dry and rasps as I speak. "No, thanks. You enjoy."

"Get in the water," he orders. His tone has lost his usual edge, though. Instead, a hint of amusement buoys his words.

A flutter takes flight in my stomach, and I'm not sure what he expects swimming in a pool surrounded by the dead will do. I step out of my boots and pull the wool sweater over my head. A short, lightweight chemise hangs loosely over my chest. I slide, clothed, to the edge of the water. It brushes my toes and climbs over my calves like a summer sun. I dip my fingers into the warmth. The water trickles from my fingertips.

Graeden's hands find my waist, and he lowers me into the pool with him. I swallow against the dryness in my throat and try to ignore the flutter swarming in my stomach.

"You're not going to drown," Graeden says, the tease easy to hear in his voice.

I swallow again, my hands resting lightly over his. The water laps against my chest, and my toes brush the rocky bottom. Graeden doesn't let go of my waist as we stand in the water, and his gaze holds mine. Graeden draws me farther into the pool.

"You're not going to drown," he says again. "But you might feel like it."

CHAPTER TWENTY-FIVE

"What?" I stiffen beneath Graeden's hands. "What do you mean it's going to feel like it?"

"We're going to deprive your senses of everything," Graeden says. "Set your inner self back to zero. Help you get grounded once more."

"And you have to drown me to do that?"

"Do you trust me?" Graeden asks.

I study him through the fading light. The way it silhouettes his strong, defined jaw. The way shadows seem to cling to his thick lashes. The way his full lips are perfectly balanced as they curve into a smile. And I'm staring.

Dropping my gaze, I know the answer. I do.

Graeden has never given me a reason not to trust him. I nod and let my body close the distance between us.

Lifting his hands from my waist, Graeden says, "Float on your back."

With a steady inhale, I lie back. The warm water bleeds into my hair and draws the ache from my muscles. I could sleep for a thousand years down here. Graeden presses a palm against my back, supporting my body, while he places his other hand on the frontside of my hip.

"Don't fight me, understand?"

The swarm hums in my stomach again, and my nerves stand on end. "Understood," I whisper.

Graeden applies a soft pressure against my hip. The water embraces my body. It blankets my shoulders, and veins of water seep farther into my hair. I clench my jaw as the warmth kisses my cheeks and covers my chin. A single wisp of air touches my lips before I submerge.

It's quiet. Serene. I hear nothing, smell nothing, feel nothing except for the gentle pressure against my hip. I imagine myself alone, free from all expectations. For a moment, I abandon my fears, my worries, my purpose. I give it all up to float here, present in this void.

Too soon, pressure swells against my lungs, and I wish for another breath. Graeden holds me firm beneath the surface. How long will he keep me under, I wonder? Long enough to warrant his warning to not fight him.

My throat dries, a quiet flame building against my lungs. I snare the fading serenity I'd felt to douse the growing heat. It doesn't last long enough. The flame sparks in my lungs, and fire licks my throat. My body jerks, but I rein in my control. I bite down as my lungs shudder. Graeden said I won't drown. I can trust him. My body jolts, and the fire surges through my chest. Don't fight him. Don't fight him.

I lose control.

My body panics. A taste, a breath, even a whisper of air would do. I lurch beneath the water, kicking at everything, clawing at anything. Whatever it takes to get away. My nails find Graeden's arm. I can't help it. I curl my hands into fists, trying to find that controlled part of myself. My fingernails dig into his skin, but he doesn't loosen his hold.

In my mind, a warm face flickers into shape. Her fading curls bounce as she tilts her head, her soft smile a welcoming balm. Her skin is etched with lines of laughter but also carries the weight of sorrow. Mother.

My thrashing slows as I focus on the woman's expression. For a moment, I imagine stepping into her embrace again. She'd hold me tight and stroke my hair. In my reverie, I release my mother and a wave of heat washes over us. Fire flickers in her eyes as she watches me, and her smile slips…

I can't even imagine how she'll react when she discovers I harbor a dragon, but I do. I don't want to lose myself to a monster. Graeden has said I don't need to. But if I can't control my dragon, then she'll control me, and I am lost.

If we become one, maybe I could find a way to my mother and face her without shame. Maybe her smile wouldn't slip.

Gritting my teeth, I force my thoughts away from this pool, away from the catacombs, away from Eida. I guide my memory to the glade near my parents' home. The soft summer grass that tickled my bare skin. The light breeze that rustled the leafy canopy. A shadow blocks out the noonday sun, but in my memory, it's not Tib's face as it was in reality. It's Graeden's.

Trust him.

I do.

Forcing the tension from my arms, I release Graeden. With my calm, Graeden eases the pressure against the front of my hip, and I drift toward the surface. Water trails over my cheeks, and the cavern's chilled air sifts into my lungs.

I listen for Graeden's instruction, but all sound has died as stiffly as those buried around us. The water laps in a slow beat against my cheek. Its slap is hushed and muted. Darkness blankets my vision, and, for once, I think I could abandon the world around me. No more battles, no carnage nor death. I could leave the chaos and desert the hatred. I could be happy. Free even.

A quiet river of dragonsfire floods my veins. Free. I can hardly remember what that's like. The warmth gathers around my heart, an ember of change.

Battle cannot exist where there is no hatred or greed. Chaos is destroyed through peace. And freedom is found when you abandon your anger. I don't want to be angry anymore.

I drift in the waters for longer than I care to track, allowing my mind to wander.

It's time to abandon some of my anger. Not all of it, but some. Tib doesn't deserve my anger. Caelum does. And if anyone will pay for it, it'll be him. My mind sifts through the pain that unleashed my dragon, and I try to fix Caelum to it all instead of

Tib. If I can leave behind my hatred, maybe I can make room for my dragon.

I grasp at the fading straws of my thoughts as the trance disintegrates. Graeden's hands still support my body. I'd almost forgotten he held me. I cling to his lifeline and pull myself back to the present.

"How do you feel?" Graeden's grip softens, and he releases me.

I pull myself upright, losing most of the distance between Graeden and me. "Refreshed."

Standing in the water, Graeden doesn't tower over me. His eyes are level with mine. His lips inches away.

The flutter I'd felt in my stomach strengthens, great wings now beating through my chest. Something I've never seen rolls through Graeden's gaze. He stares at me as though it's the first time he's seen me. My cheeks warm beneath his lingering gaze, but I don't break it. The small space between us shrinks.

The woodsmoke clinging to Graeden's skin permeates the air around us. I catch the subtle sweetness that's his, and my entire body is electrified.

"Do you want to know what I was thinking when we arrived?" he whispers.

My throat is as dry as the Blood Desert. Not trusting my voice, I nod.

Graeden hesitates, his hand hovering near my cheek. His breath is as quiet as mine, his movements just as slow. Releasing a breath, Graeden folds his fingers to his palm and brushes his knuckles against my cheek. Tentatively. As though he doesn't dare. My heart stills. My breath stolen. I ache to turn into his touch.

"No immortal fate stands a chance against you. No man, either." Graeden's gaze flickers to my lips, and I wonder if he speaks of the men in the arena or himself.

Graeden opens his fingers and threads them through my hair. His hand curls around my ear before sweeping over my jawline. The focus his scent brought to me has disintegrated. I can't remember how to breathe or speak. Graeden's thumb brushes over my top lip, and his eyes linger on them.

I tip my chin upward. His lips nearly graze mine.

A slew of rocks clatter from the wall and splash into the pool. I jerk away from Graeden, and the cave's musty, cool air slithers between us.

Graeden's gaze sweeps through the cavern. He clears his throat and pulls farther away from me. "We better go."

He draws himself through the water and climbs over the pool's edge. A stone sinks into the pit of my stomach, stealing the heat that had swarmed every cell of my body with Graeden's touch. I swim behind Graeden, reaching the edge too soon. Graeden pulls his tunic over his head and shakes his wet hair. Water sprinkles over the pool like raindrops.

Offering me his hand, Graeden tugs me from the water. He wraps a thin blanket I didn't know he had around my shoulders, and he tucks it near my chin.

Graeden steps back, and his welcoming warmth disappears with the shadows. A soft breeze floats through the cavern. Gooseflesh crawls over my skin, and I wish I'd taken my leggings off before soaking them through. Tightening the blanket around my form, I snatch my sweater and follow Graeden up through the chambers.

"As a Marked Fallen, you now get the grand honor of participating in the Kelasa." Graeden's voice slips back into his formal, detached tone. "A competition in your monster's form against all of Eida's other Marked Fallen."

"The Kelasa," I mutter. "Right." I glance at the shadows clinging to the stairwell's wall. My thoughts are far from the arena. The Troll King not only stole my mortal life, but he had to steal this moment, too. My body still buzzes with the energy that had stirred between us. In the feeble light, I barely make out tension coiling through Graeden's arms. His gait is stiff, controlled. I release a quiet sigh. It's for the best, I suppose.

"There's no risk of death, of course." Graeden speaks as though he recites a memorized text. "It's a show for the Troll King at the start of each new year. Plus, the prize isn't too terrible."

His words trail off, and the stifled smile in his voice is hard to miss. "What prize?"

"Five hundred kills removed from your total pardon."

A confident smile tugs at the corners of my lips. "Five hundred?"

Graeden glances over his shoulder. "Enough to make every Fallen fight their hardest. The location of the Kelasa changes every year. Right before the event, the king's servants will let all the masters know. We're responsible for getting you there."

I hardly listen to the details. Five hundred souls removed from my pardon. Five hundred. It's not an exorbitant number in the grand scheme of things, but it couldn't hurt. Although, nothing can help if I can't kill Tib.

I grind my teeth and press my lips into a firm line. "I don't think he can dematerialize."

"Who can't?" Graeden reaches the top level of the catacombs.

"My Seeker." It would be impossible. He's not from Taiatum. He's Tib. "Something else must have happened in the arena."

Graeden shifts his weight to face me. "What would make you think that?"

My gaze flicks over Graeden's shoulder. Despite Tib's sudden appearance, Graeden's still the only one I know is on my side. "I can trust you, can't I?"

Graeden narrows his eyes. "What is it?"

"The Seeker isn't from Taiatum. He's from my village, Bridgewick. It's Tib." My voice cracks. It wasn't Tib who sacrificed me at the Well, but admitting he's here in front of Graeden, the cutting betrayal still burrows deep.

"He's here?" Anger flashes in Graeden's dark eyes. A vein protrudes from his neck, pulsing wildly. "The coward who thought his life better than yours decided to come and try to kill for himself?"

"But, Graeden—"

"Oh, he is in your realm now, Ari," Graeden growls as though the revenge is his own. "Your Seeker will meet his death at your hands as it should be."

"Tib didn't send me here," I say. "He didn't come to fight me. I was wrong. He came to save me."

My words fall on deaf ears. "There is no *saving* in Eida. It's kill or be killed. You know that."

My chest tightens. I do know that. Regardless of what Tib's intentions were, he'll find himself on the other side of that arena. Kill or be killed.

The most I can do is keep him alive until the third round. What my dragon does to him then is out of my control, and one of us will die.

I swallow the lump forming in my throat. "Isn't there something…?" I say in a thick voice.

Graeden paces ahead of me, his hands planted against his sides. "There's nothing you can do—not for any of them. You've been given a gift, Ari. A chance at justice. Don't let him get inside your head."

CHAPTER TWENTY-SIX

Hooves clatter along the flagstone path in front of my temple, and horses made of midnight draw a line of carriages toward where Graeden and I—and a hoard of other Fallen—wait. No coachmen. No guards. Just the beasts and their carriages, come to take us to the Kelasa. Froth foams from the horses' mouths, their gaits disjointed and angular, as though they bear the forms of their inner monsters.

"Wear your confidence as your shield—whether or not you feel it." Graeden's breath warms my neck as he whispers against my ear. His sweet, calming scent cuts through the cacophony of my thoughts.

I close my eyes and let it wash over me, stripping away my anxieties and insecurities.

"Show them you fear nothing, and the other Marked will destroy themselves." Graeden straightens his posture, a subtle chill creeping over my neck where his breath had warmed.

"I do fear nothing." My gaze slides to Graeden's, and I wink. The thing I fear losing most is the one thing most at risk here in Eida: my life. Unconsciously, I rub my hand over my throat and return my gaze to the approaching carriages. No one is supposed to die today, though.

As the creatures halt, the surrounding Marked don't hesitate to swing the doors open and climb in. They wedge their bodies into the small coaches, followed by their masters.

A single window is cut from the carriage in front of me, a dull mulberry curtain swaying slightly behind it. I stare at my reflection in the carriage's sleek shell. Kohl lines my eyes, accentuating their natural hazel and giving me an air of superiority. A dusting of Eida's unique hues shimmer against my cheeks, disguising the softer parts of my face and leaving a ferocity I don't feel. I roll my head from side to side, stretching the exhaustion from my shoulders. The woman within me is tired, but the woman everyone will see is ready for the Kelasa.

Graeden tugs on the door's latch, and it swings wide. Weathered steel coats the carriage's four walls. Dark stains are splattered across them and spot the matching seat. The stale, sickly sweet scent of stewed fruit rolls out of the carriage. The odor curls around me and hits the back of my throat. I gag, coughing and spluttering.

"Flaming nights, it's like a hearse," I wheeze, turning to Graeden. "Only worse because I'm still alive. Can't we walk?"

Graeden rolls his eyes. "Get in. The Troll King deems it an honor—these carriages are only used once a year for the Kelasa."

I plug my nose, letting my palm filter the air to my mouth. "You get in."

"Ari, we don't have time for this." Graeden's words fall flat as his eyes flash with amusement. "Be an adult and climb into the carriage."

I cross my arms over my chest. "I won't. You ride ahead and tell them I'm coming by foot."

"By the time you reach Vasa, the Kelasa will have ended."

My shoulders brush my ears, and I look to the north as though if I try hard enough, I can see through the landscape toward the troll's district.

"Wrong direction." Graeden juts his chin to the east.

Pursing my lips, I tighten my arms over my chest. The creatures pulling the contraption stamp their hooves impatiently against the flagstone, and carriage doors slam shut around us. "Go ahead and climb in if you like. I won't risk catching whatever disease the last corpse that rode in this thing carried."

"It's not a hearse!" Graeden's shoulders slacken. "Last chance."

Hope flares in my chest. Is he really going to let me choose? For once, let me have a say in anything that happens to me? I tilt my head to the side, a satisfied smile crawling over my lips. "I fear nothing, remember? Last chance gone. I'll see you there."

Turning my back on Graeden, I move to the edge of the path. I wonder how I'll find my way to Vasa—not that I'm all that concerned. The five hundred souls would be nice, but I wouldn't regret never fighting in a Kelasa.

Suddenly, Graeden's hands grip my waist and tug me back toward him and the carriage. He wraps an arm around my back and sweeps my legs out from beneath me. A small yelp escapes my lips. Graeden cradles me against his chest like a newborn child, his fingers pressing against my thigh and gripping my waist. Heat warms my belly and rises to my cheeks. I shove against Graeden's armored torso, and his arms flex around me. His chest presses against my arm, his gait calm and assured.

Woodsmoke swirls around me again, strengthening the warmth in my belly and spreading it throughout my body. My thrashing slows, calming. My gaze drifts to Graeden's face—a faded scar cleaves over his neck, disappearing behind his ear.

He is not untouched by this world. Like me. Yet that amused smile still plays on his lips, and that heart of his simmers behind his eyes.

"What are you looking at?"

I jolt at his words and drop my gaze to his sculpted chest. Heat floods my cheeks and blurs my thoughts. Shutting my eyes, I give my head a subtle shake.

Graeden dumps me onto the cold, hard seat inside the carriage. The odor swallows me whole, and I'm stolen by another wave of retching.

"Scoot over unless you want to ride to Vasa alone."

Smothering the gag coating my tongue, I slide to the far end of the carriage where there's no respite of fresh air. "You're the worst."

"I told you, we don't have time for this." Graeden tries to hide his smug grin, but he doesn't do it well.

The carriage jerks as the creatures break into a trot toward Vasa. I brace myself against the rough steel seat, my fingers curling around its edge. My gaze traces the scars that weave over my own skin.

He and I aren't so different, trapped in this hell. Graeden braces himself as the carriage lurches, his eyes roaming the scenery that passes through the carriage's sole window. The carriage jostles again, and the edge of Graeden's hand brushes mine.

I roll my shoulders uncomfortably, still able to feel the pressure of Graeden's hands on my skin. A soft tingle trails across my waist and behind my thighs. I swallow the dryness forming in my throat and hold my gaze in my lap. I can feel Graeden's eyes lingering on my face.

The carriage bumps along Arautteve's cobbled streets for a time before slipping onto Badavaru's sandy roads. I welcome the smoother path, my stomach still churning from the carriage's rotten smell. Much too soon, we cross onto the winding trails that cut through Vasa.

"Whoa," Graeden says as the carriage lurches forward. He thrusts his arm in front of me, catching me before I tumble from the seat.

The horse-like creatures whinny, their rumbling cries more like snarls. Graeden cracks open the carriage door to peer around the skeletal creatures. A chorus of shouts from the other carriages float through the woods. Sitting back in his seat, Graeden draws his blade. "You've got your cuff on, right?"

I lift my arm, the gold bracelet glinting in the slanted ray of light peeking through the door. "What's wrong?"

"Debris in the road." Graeden rotates his dagger, so he holds the steel and offers me the handle.

I wrap my fingers around its intricate carvings. "Why do I need this? I can help you clear it."

"You're a dragon shifter on your way to the Kelasa." Graeden closes the door, a breeze wisping through the open window. "Don't underestimate how much the other Marked want a few hundred souls removed from their pardon. The others can help clear it. You stay put." Graeden's gaze meets mine, his warm amber eyes pinning me in place. He jerks his head toward his blade firmly in my grasp. "Use that if anyone approaches."

I nod, bringing the blade to my lap.

My gaze is trained on the window, the ragged violet curtains peeled back to the sides, but my attention is on the heavy thud of steel against wood. It could be a long while until they've cleared it. My stomach rolls with the thought, and something bitter crawls up my throat. I rest my head on the back of the seat and inhale a thin breath to calm my nausea. Graeden said to stay put. My thumbs mindlessly trace the hilt of his blade. I will.

A light breeze dances through the window, lifting a strand of my hair. It tickles my skin, and I yearn to step away from the foul carriage.

Peeking out the window, I'm met with towering trees whose canopies spread above us like an umbrella. Skylight streams between the leaves, pockmarking the forest floor. I inhale the refreshing vitality of life that grows only in the troll district. I haven't seen a real forest since I left Bridgewick. And never have I seen a forest so vibrant and green as this one. Well, except for the bold colors of the Enchanted Wood.

Up ahead, at least a dozen or so men and women hack away at a pile of debris blocking our path. I lean back against the seat and am immediately encompassed in the carriage's sickly-sweet scent. If Graeden doesn't hurry, I'm going to lose my breakfast in the carriage before we ever reach the Kelasa. Heat flushes over the back of my neck with the thought.

How fearsome for Eida's dragon to arrive covered in vomit.

The soft breeze toys with me again, ruffling the drab curtain. I peek outside the window again. Aside from those clearing the road, Vasa's forest looks empty. I bet the other masters told their Marked the same thing Graeden told me.

Tightening my grip on the dagger, I slip the carriage door open. I won't go far. I step away from the hearse and stretch my legs. Unlike the others, I won't sit surrounded by someone else's decay any longer.

The breeze rustles the leaves, the scent of damp moss and softwood swirls around me, and a branch snaps in the distance.

Spinning on my heel, I scan the foliage. Ripples swell over the ground cover with the stirring wind. Branches scrape against each other, their leaves abandoning their perches and floating to the ground. A heavy hand latches around my wrist, forcing my arm with the dagger behind my back and another hand presses over my lips. My scream builds in my throat until his voice whispers against my ear.

"Well, hey."

Twisting in Tib's arms, I shove him. His crooked smile lifts his thin lips, and he keeps a wary eye on the front of the carriage where Graeden and the others work.

"Are you insane?" I hiss. "I could've run you through."

"Ah, but you didn't."

"I'm still deciding." Peeking over my shoulder, I scan the line of carriages. Most of them have their curtains drawn, but still. "You shouldn't be here. Anyone could see you."

"I'm blending in."

Tib wears a fitted tunic with his leathers. Honestly, there's not much difference between him and me except for my dragon. I glare at him.

"Come with me." Excitement bleeds through Tib's eyes.

"I can't come with you," I scoff, stepping toward the carriage. "I'm headed to the Kelasa—where all…" I hesitate, unable to say the word *monster*, "Marked Fallen are expected to be today."

Where I want to be, right? Especially if it can get me five hundred kills closer to leaving this realm… The dull thud of steel striking the fallen tree echoes through the grove. My palms warm, and I wipe them against my skirt.

"You need to get out of here," I say.

"Alright, I will," Tib says. "As soon as you say you'll come with me."

My stomach twists as I imagine Graeden circling back around to our carriage only to find it empty.

"I can't." I shake my head. "I won't do that."

Tib grabs my hand, and I tear it from his grasp. One way or another only one of us is going to walk out of that arena alive. I don't like it, but why pretend anything different can happen in the end?

"You can't go around doing this," I hiss. "If you want to survive, there are rules you must follow."

"Maybe I'm not here to survive…"

"Stop it." I shift my weight and pull my gaze from Tib's. I refuse to feel guilty for what I must do to survive. I didn't ask Tib to come here for me. My throat tightens, and I shove the thought away.

"Kill or be killed, right?" Tib lifts a brow and jerks his head toward the dense forest. "Why not have some fun while we're at it? Just in case we're the latter."

Tib closes the distance between us, his sweet scent of cinnamon and cloves swamping the forest's crisp life. "You've been in Eida for years."

Silence. I don't know where he's going with this, but I don't want to play.

He doesn't wait for a response. "And how much of it have you actually seen?"

Silence again. I glance over my shoulder toward the front of our company. More of the masters hack their weapons into the debris. We're going to be here for a while.

"That's what I thought. If you're going to die in Eida, don't you want to have at least seen more than the bloodshed?" he asks.

"I've seen more than bloodshed." Not that I can remember much else.

Tib opens his arms to the sky and spins in a slow circle. "Have you ever seen this?"

My gaze wanders to the leafy foliage above us. I admit, it's amazing, and it's been too long since I've seen anything other than Badavaru's stifling desert, Ghora's endless chill, and Arautteve's stuffy extravagance.

"Come with me, Ari. I promise I'll have you back in time for the Kelasa."

My eyes wander toward the sounds of Graeden's endless efforts to clear the road. "How can you promise that? You don't even know where it is."

Tib's face lights up, his smile creeping back into place. "I guess you'll have to trust me."

CHAPTER TWENTY-SEVEN

TIB EXTENDS HIS HAND, and I hesitate.

I should see Tib as my enemy. He and I *will* fight in the arena again. We get two more rounds until one of us is killed or defeated and then sacrificed to Eida's beast. My gaze flicks to Tib's crooked smile. It's too reminiscent of our past. There's a carefree feel to their slight curve, a feeling I haven't felt for a long time. Tib should be my enemy, but all I see in his eyes is the best friend I lost.

My heart aches for him, for me. For the girl I was two years ago. For the girl I had to leave behind to survive. I'll never be that girl again, but if I close my eyes and run, maybe for a moment I can pretend. Tib's eyes sparkle with the same anticipation they used to when we'd sneak out from Bridgewick.

With a quiet groan, I rub the back of my neck. If I stay here with Graeden, I'm choosing this cursed realm and life over the one I lost. Bridgewick wasn't much better than Eida, but at least it was mine to choose to live in or to leave. Staying now would be betraying my declaration that Eida doesn't control me.

Tib outstretches his hand a few more inches. I glance over my shoulder to where the carriages wait. I'm not leaving—not really. I'll return before long, but for the first time in two years, I need to run free. Shutting out the warnings in my head, I place my hand in Tib's.

An air of nostalgia curls through my veins, and Tib's smile widens. This isn't the first time Tib and I have snuck off together. Though, it is the first time in this realm.

The sky's light glints off the gold cuff on my wrist. Graeden won't be able to track me while I wear it, but he won't need to. I'll come back. With a final peek towards the front of the carriages, I duck into the foliage behind Tib.

Graeden is loyal to the people of Eida. He always will be. This isn't my home.

The sky flashes overhead, writhing with magic. The Kelasa doesn't begin until late afternoon. I may miss out on some warm-up training, but so long as I reach it before then, I can still enter the competition.

Our feet crush the underbrush, the sodden soil masking the slap of our sandals. My lungs burn with giddy freedom, however short and fabled it may be. Tib weaves between the trees as though we're children darting through the Enchanted Wood. My hair sails behind me caught up in the wind's excited rush.

I let myself run full speed at Tib's back, keeping a mental point fixed on where we left the carriages. We dodge branches and leap over roots. Before long, my lungs gasp for air, and my feet slow in the thicket. My breasts rise and fall with my laden breaths, and a wide smile plasters across my face. I tip my head to the sky and pretend we stop in the Wood near our home, free from the carnage of this realm.

When my head falls forward, Tib stands only a pace away. The corners of his eyes pull upward, his grin ever larger. "Worth it, right?"

Unable to catch my breath, I nod and try to gulp down more air. "I've never seen anything like it."

"Ari!" Graeden's faint voice carries through the treetops, and the childlike thrill flattens in my chest.

My smile fades as I glance over my shoulder toward the line of carriages I can no longer see. It didn't take long for Graeden to notice I was missing. A warm ache spreads through my chest. Of course, he noticed. It's Graeden. This is exactly what he was afraid would happen.

I rub the golden cuff absentmindedly before planting my hands on my waist. As my breaths ease, I step away from Tib. "I have to go back. This is beautiful, but—"

"This isn't what I want to show you." Tib slips his hand into mine again and tugs me toward him. His fingers brush my forearm, and he cups my elbow. My gaze wanders over Tib's bare shoulder, the shaped muscles of his arm disappearing beneath his sleeveless tunic.

Neither a Fallen nor a Seeker should be wandering through Vasa's wood, but especially not together. I pull my arm out of Tib's grasp. This was foolish.

"We're risking our lives. It's not worth it," I whisper. Graeden's voice echoes somewhere behind us again, and I take another step away from Tib. I shouldn't have left the carriage. I shouldn't have made Graeden worry. "Once we're dead, that's it. We disintegrate into dust—no memories, no experiences. Just nothing. I don't want to die. I won't."

"Who says we become nothing?" Tib challenges.

My brows knit together. "Everyone. That's the way it is. The Bridgewick elders have passed that knowledge down since the very beginning."

"But where did they get that knowledge?" Tib waits for the answer he knows I can't give him. "Ari, there's more out there. We die, but we don't end."

"Do you think there's a god?" I lift a skeptical brow.

"I don't know," Tib admits. "But something. What is the point of just surviving? Without our experiences, we're no better than that shroom over there or the mud on your sandal. Only ever going where you're told is a quick way to never get anywhere or see anything."

I shrink a little farther from Tib, and he sighs.

"We've already made it this far. Can I show you?"

I stare into the forest beyond Tib—the streaming sunlight and open freedom. I've missed that simpler time when Tib and I ran carefree through our Wood. I'd give anything to return to the human realm. Somber reality deflates my yearning. It's not possible.

But, if I can never return, maybe I can hold onto that freedom a little longer here. With Tib.

Graeden's voice splits through the forest, and my eyes flash to Tib's. He's closer. Much closer. "You'll return me to the Kelasa before it begins?"

"Only if you decide you want to." Tib's eyes twinkle, and he jerks his chin toward Graeden's shouts. "You've never been one to enjoy a warden."

Anticipation weaves through my chest. He's right, I've never done well with an overseer. Even back home, the only one who ever had any sway over my actions was Tib or my father. My heart aches, but my father, too, drew caution at times. My gaze flickers to where I imagine Graeden races through the forest.

Graeden isn't exactly a warden. My mind slips back to the catacombs. The caution in Graeden's eyes as he cupped my cheek, the tension in his movements as the distance between us shrank. My lip still tingles from the soft brush of his thumb. Heat blooms into my cheeks, and a thrill takes flight in my veins. He almost kissed me. He's not a warden at all.

I bite the inside of my cheek. Even still, I'm tired of living a life that isn't my own. I'll return to Graeden and the Kelasa in time. Right now, I need this moment, for me. Shaking off the rising shame, I slip my hand into Tib's and nod. "Let's go."

Tib's fingers lattice between mine, and he tows me through the towering trees. The deeper we travel, the thicker the vegetation grows until trunks are nearly smashed against each other and the treetops block out all light. My momentum slows, my hand tugging back on Tib as shadows replace daylight within the wood.

"Are you sure this is the right way?"

A sly smile spreads over Tib's face, and he holds a finger to his lips. Keeping his hand tied to mine, Tib leads me quietly through the underbrush. He points to a muddied wall in the distance as he tiptoes us around it.

I squint through the darkness. Crumbling stones pattern the wall's base. Above, dried mud swoops toward the forest floor as though the structure was melting before it hardened. Cracks spiderweb over its face, and a dark hole is carved into the upper region. I stare at the composition when a light flickers on in the window. My eyes widen, and I shrink back into the shadows.

It's one of their homes! We're on a troll's property. I tug against Tib's arm to draw us deeper into the tree cover, but he holds firm. Peeking over his shoulder, he jerks his head toward the house and squeezes my hand.

My brows furrow. Is he mad? If a troll catches us, they'll steal our memories and leave us empty shells, or worse. My gaze drops to the gold cuff on my wrist. Tib doesn't know what I am—and I plan to keep it that way—but every troll does.

"Trust me," Tib whispers.

I sigh. I've trusted him this far… Without my confirmation, Tib creeps toward the troll's hut, his shoulder brushing the crumbling wall's stones.

"Tib," I warn under my breath, keeping my eye locked on the window above us. I'd rather not have to fight our way out of Vasa, of all places.

Tib slips around the hut and ducks under an arched trellis. I follow, slipping inside the leafy tunnel with him. My jaw drops. Leaves drape over us in a delicate arch, sweeping the floor at our sides. Slender strands of cherry blossoms hang above us, and golden orbs of light float among them in meandering paths.

"What is this place?" I whisper.

"That troll out there is the guardian as far as I can tell," Tib says, circling my question. "Though he doesn't seem to do much guarding."

I'd glare at Tib for ignoring my question if I wasn't so transfixed on the magic swirling around us. "And what is he guarding?"

"That's what I want you to see."

My gaze drops from the small suns above, and I follow Tib deeper into the passageway until it just ends. The glowing orbs float beyond us, leaving us in the arch's shadow. I glance at Tib, his eyes twinkling and a smothered smile pressed over his lips.

"What are you grinning about?"

Tib jerks his chin upward, and my eyes wander to the leafy roof. My own smile fades as utter awe spreads through my chest. The leaves no longer hang above our heads. Instead, a smattering of stars twinkle against the night sky—a *real* night sky. I exhale slowly, tears gathering at the corners of my eyes.

I never thought I'd see the sky again, complete with her vastness of stars and stories. "What is this?"

"It's the night sky."

I ignore his obvious answer. My eyes dart from star to star, tracing the designs I've gazed at with Tib since childhood. The creatures and warriors who I thought were so far from me while trapped in Eida. It's a window into the human world.

"Oh, how I've longed for the stars," I whisper. Settling onto the soft soil, I stare at the small lights winking in the darkness as though this moment is a secret I will share with them forever.

Tib settles at my side, and his gaze burns against my face. "Worth it?"

I have thirsted for this moment for years and never expected to quench it. I can't draw my eyes from the light that pierces through the darkness. No matter how small the light, it shines beyond the darkest sky. My lashes flutter as Eida becomes that darkness. And I the light.

No matter how small my light, I can shine beyond any darkness.

"I stared at the stars every night thinking of you," Tib whispers. "Remember before the trolls, we used to sneak into the Enchanted Wood…"

A small smile crawls onto my lips, and I lean back into the leaves climbing up the arch. "Yes, and you always got us lost to the clearing."

"Uh, no. I always took the scenic route."

"A *new* scenic route because you could never remember the last one," I chide.

Tib leans back next to me, his arm pressing against mine. It took years for me to come around to Tib, even after we were betrothed. But once I did, we were inseparable. We used to hold hands as we watched the stars twinkle above us. Tib's knuckles brush mine. The memory eases the tension I've grown used to in Eida, and for a moment, I indulge the tingles that climb up my arm.

But this isn't the Enchanted Wood, and we aren't at home watching the stars. Drawing my hand away from his, I tuck it next to my side.

A comfortable silence settles over us, and I sink into the ground, pretending for a moment I'm not worlds away from my home.

"I came to bring you back." The words slip from Tib's mouth and rise into the darkness above us. "I thought you were dead. We all did."

"But I'm not dead." Pride fills my chest—no one expected me to live in Eida. Not Caelum, not my family, not Tib. I proved them all wrong. I'm stronger than anyone ever thought I could be. My dragon's fire sparks against my ribs as though reminding me just how strong I've become.

I could destroy villages or kingdoms, if I wanted. I imagine Caelum's expression when he sees me rise from the ashes he's buried me in. How he'll tremble beneath my fury. How he'll plead for forgiveness, cry for mercy. And when he's finished begging, he'll finally join me in my hell.

"Guess my plan to come rescue you wasn't as foolproof as I thought." Tib lies back on the ground and interlaces his fingers behind his head as though he couldn't be more relaxed.

A laugh escapes through my nose. Of course, it's not. Why would the universe ever bend to the whims of mortals and allow something to happen in my favor? I'm as much a prisoner of fate as I am to the trolls.

Tib had to make his wish when he entered the Well of Eida. If he defeats the Fallen, the trolls will grant his wish and bring me back to life, except if I'm not dead, the bargain is null. There is no one for them to return to life.

Tib rolls onto his side and props his head up in his hand. "What if I kill you?"

CHAPTER TWENTY-EIGHT

I PEEK AT TIB from the corner of my eye, and he grimaces.

"The trolls must honor my wish," Tib says. "You would be dead, and I'd wish to bring you back to life. The thing is," Tib hesitates, "you'd have to let me."

"And put my trust in the trolls?" I face the sky again. "Not in this lifetime. Their word means nothing. The moment they discover I'm whom you want to save, they'll slit your throat and offer you to Eida's beast."

"Why would they do that?"

"I'm not that little girl from Bridgewick, Tib." I drag my hands over my face. "The trolls have waited for me for a very long time. They won't give me up."

Ever. I don't say it aloud, but there's no way out for me. No wish, no pardon that will set their precious dragon free into an unsuspecting world. I swallow the despair creeping through my chest. I've clung to my hope that one day I could return to Mother for so long. But the truth is, there is barely a thread of hope left.

"We're going to die here." My words hold no emotion, the feelings strangled in a web at the back of my throat. They ring true. "The both of us. Sooner or later, we will all die in this realm."

Tib's nostrils flare. He brushes a finger across my upper arm and lies back to face the tear in the realm. "Is it enough for you to just survive?"

My jaw twinges. A sinking depression sweeps through me. "It's the only thing I can do."

Tib's shoulder presses against mine, and my body aches for the life I was promised. A life as Tib's wife. A life of simplicity. My life.

I never thought I'd wish for simplicity. But lying here in Vasa beneath the stars, I'd rather claim simplicity than bloodshed.

Tib and I had plans to leave Bridgewick and settle elsewhere. They were simple plans. Mundane in every aspect, but there'd be no rules. No expectations or constraints put upon us by the village elders. It was simple, but it would be an undertaking like we'd never had. Just me and him and one grand adventure. I don't want to survive. I want to live a real, full life.

I blink and return to the shadows of Eida. It doesn't really matter what I want anymore. It hasn't mattered for a long time. This realm may be a prison, but Bridgewick wasn't a refuge. My cheeks warm, my darkest memory emblazoned onto my heart. It wasn't the first time Bridgewick tightened like a noose around my throat. I was suffocating there.

Tib reaches over me and presses his hand to my cheek, his calloused fingers stroking my jaw. I close my eyes against his touch, tears burning behind them.

"There are so many places I never got to see in our world," I say. "How I would've loved to have visited our bordering kingdoms and, one day, Eifelgard. I've heard it's beautiful with snow-capped mountains."

"It is," Tib says. "Or so Caelum tells me. He traveled there a year ago and saw it from a distance. Got lost in the Dark Forest and had to return home."

A smirk toys with my lips, and I don't bother hiding my pettiness. If I can't see the human kingdom, I'm glad Caelum never made it there, either.

"I don't want to die a prisoner," I whisper more to myself than Tib. The stars twinkle as though they press the desire through me.

"You're not going to." Tib's gaze lingers on my face, his words spoken with such confidence. His slender nose is less than a foot from mine, and I'm wrapped in the scent of cinnamon and clove.

"And you know that, how?"

Tib drops his hand. "I have a way to get you out."

I smirk and roll my eyes in the low light. "A way out? Such a thing doesn't exist in Eida."

"Ari," Tib's tone has tightened, his voice low. "I can get you out."

Propping my elbow beneath me, I narrow my eyes at Tib. I search the soft planes of his face—or what I can see of them—for a hint of teasing, but his brow is furrowed and his gaze intent.

"What?" I ask. "Why haven't you said anything?"

Tib rubs his fingers and thumb across his eyes and pinches the bridge of his nose. "It's not easy. Or safe. In fact, it may be one of the most painful things you ever do."

The sound of bone cracking echoes through my memory. I doubt much is more painful than shifting into a dragon.

"I'll do it."

"You don't know what *it* is." Tib straightens, so we meet eye to eye. "There's a reason I hoped to try every other option before telling you this."

"I don't care. If you can free me from this hell, I'll do it," I say.

Magic crackles across the stars, faint and wispy, but still reaching this far corner of the realm. For a moment, my attention is drawn skyward. "What's happening?"

"Don't worry." Tib looks up under his brows at the faint strips of color marring my beautiful sky. "It's always here if you need it. The darkness may touch the stars, but nothing can destroy true light. Not completely."

The faint strands of magic flash above us, but my gaze returns to Tib. What would it be like to have wandered along a different path? What would it have been like to have left Bridgewick for an ethereal world? A spark kindles the anticipation in my chest.

"You found Taiatum." It isn't a question. That's how he's going to free us.

Tib stiffens. "I did."

"Why would you dare?" I ask. I'm grateful he did, but he could've been killed.

Tib stares at the stars as though he hasn't heard me, but I wait for his answer. No one just travels to Taiatum. The ghost village.

It simply isn't done. And if it is, those who travel there don't come out.

"The same reason I dared come to Eida." Tib's gaze warms as he meets mine, though tension still seizes his body.

"What if they didn't let you leave? What if they turned you into a ghost?"

Tib's lips curl into a smile. "Into a ghost? Who's been telling you the legends?"

My concern fades and is replaced by confusion. "The elders, same as you."

Tib shook his head. "I never listened to their tales about Taiatum. My mother taught me about the City of Gold."

"Sounds like you've been bewitched by it," I say.

Tib shakes his head. "Hardly, and it's not filled with ghosts either."

"Vapor of death?" I ask, trying out Graeden's words.

Tib presses his lips together, stifling a smile. "Sort of." Sweeping his gaze through the darkness to ensure we're alone, Tib leans closer and whispers. "The warriors of Taiatum use blood magic to turn into shadow."

My mouth drops open, my brows furrowed. "Truly? Into shadow?"

Tib presses his finger against my lips. "No one knows. And you can't tell anyone. The Taiatum protect themselves with our fearsome legends of death and disembodiment and, apparently, ghosts. They're a peaceful people, though."

"Why do they need warriors, then?" I ask.

"To ensure that peace, I guess." Tib's expression softens as though he cares greatly for the people in Taiatum. "I didn't only train in swordsmanship and human weaponry to save you, Ari. I knew what I was getting into when I went to the Well of Eida. I knew what I'd face here, and I'm prepared for this."

"Will you teach me?" The words escape my lips before I can stop them.

Tib raises a brow. "How else do you think we're going to escape Eida?"

A smile crawls over my lips. I've dreamed of a day when I could return home. To breathe the smoke-filled air in Bridgewick, and to listen to the crackling fires. To wrap my arms around Mother.

My chest tightens. I left her in Bridgewick. Alone. The elders will care for her. They've always preached unity. I must believe they'll watch over her as she ages. As her contributions to the village weaken. She has no children and no husband to offer, but they would still protect her. They must.

Father should be there. My sister, Atarah, too.

I squeeze my eyes shut against the memory of my father's kind face. Silver has begun to weave its way through the roots of his dark hair. Age wrinkles his face in the many places he smiled and deepens the lines of worry near his brow. I grind my teeth until his face melts into the back of my mind, the memory no longer locked behind the barrier I had once erected, thanks to that fairy.

I quietly exhale my buried grief. When I shift into shadow, I'll find my mother, and together we'll run.

Tib climbs to his feet and offers me his hand. I stare at his long fingers, and my vision tunnels as though I stand on the precipice of a great cliff. If my palm touches his, we walk off the cliff together. Away from safety and protection, and we will risk everything.

"The stars have no war with us, but if they did, we will not fall. Hand in hand. In light or darkness. Together." Warmth tangles through my chest as Tib recites our vow, and a bitter ache splinters through my chest. The last time I heard those words, they were a lie. A disguise Caelum wore to deceive me. "I won't abandon you. Not again."

I look to the stars for an answer. Light dances through them as though waving me on. A refreshing breath fills my lungs and blankets the mild panic splintering my nerves. This is Tib, not Caelum. His vow to me has never been anything but true. I place my palm against Tib's, the heat of his touch crackling over my skin and through my arm. "How does it work?"

Tib's crooked smile cuts across his face, and he pulls me to my feet. He opens his mouth to speak, but it's not his voice that says my name.

My heart leaps into my throat, and I drop Tib's hand. Graeden shouts my name through the clearing.

How did he find me? I lift my wrist level with my eyes and inspect the cuff still snapped around my arm. He can't track me through his branding. My gaze flits through the darkness toward the exit. He didn't need to. Graeden probably has never needed to, instead tracking whatever wreckage we caused on the vegetation and the depressions we no doubt left in the soft soil.

"I think I should take my leave." Tib lifts my hands and presses his lips to my knuckles. I wait for the flutter in my stomach, but it only churns as Graeden shouts my name again. "I'll come for you. Good luck in the Kelasa."

Tib retreats into the forest's shadows and disappears. Standing alone beneath the stars, I press my lips together. How am I going to explain this to Graeden? Claim I was lost? Stolen? My mind scrambles through a dozen excuses, but each one falls flat. He's never going to believe me no matter what I say.

I glance over my shoulder to where Tib disappeared, and my chest tightens. Fear prickles the back of my neck that Tib may slip through those trees and disappear forever.

The leaves rustle in the quiet breeze, and I wait until the forest grows empty at my back. With a silent inhale, I weave out from beneath the ivy tunnel. Graeden searches through the surrounding foliage, his lips turned into a deep frown. Ducking underneath the arched gate, I tiptoe around one of the mud homes.

No one can know about the stars. I want there to be one thing in this realm they can't take away.

When I'm far enough away from the hidden tunnel, I pick up my pace and jog into the clearing. "Graeden!"

Graeden's attention snaps to me, and he sprints out from the tree cover. The tension rippling through his neck relaxes, and his stern eyes widen. "Ari! What happened? Let me look at you."

"I'm okay," I say.

Graeden lifts my chin, his touch softer than I expect, his fingers leaving a trail of heat against my jaw as he turns my face. His fingers linger for a moment against my skin, worry painting the space between his brows. Graeden steps back, his gaze flitting over my body. His expression softens, and his earlier panic washes from his shoulders in waves.

"You're alright?" His eyes roam over my body once again as though to make sure.

Heat rises to my cheeks and coils through my stomach. "I am."

"Was it the trolls?" Graeden's voice leaps from worried to vicious in a single breath. His gaze snaps to the cuff secured snugly against my wrist, and some of the tension in his shoulders seems to ease. At the very least, they wouldn't have been able to control my dragon. "Or was it the other Marked?"

"It was nothing I couldn't handle."

Graeden's shoulders relax, and his gaze meets mine. "You're sure? Are there any bodies I need to clean up?"

Flames roar to life in my chest. Graeden doesn't question how many I faced or how I ended up here. He trusts me, believes I could do it on my own. A smile plays on my lips. "You think I'd leave a trail?"

"Even the best Fallen might." Something sparks in Graeden's eyes, and his own smile gathers at his lips. "But if you had, I would take care of it for you."

For *me*.

I smile, my eyes tethered to my *master*. He's not the same man I hated weeks ago. He's walked with me through this hell. He's the only person over the last two years who has bothered to care about how I fare inside or outside the arena. I drop my gaze to my feet, shame pricking at the back of my neck. He's been traipsing through the woods while I lied beneath the stars with Tib. I swallow against the tightness in my throat.

"Okay, if you're good." Graeden tips my chin, so I must meet his eyes again. "Let's go show them who you truly are."

CHAPTER TWENTY-NINE

Sweat beads along my brow and clings to my skin. After throwing a robe over my shredded clothes, I smile as I jog out of the arena, my muscles warm and strong. My sprint slows as the crowd weaves into Vasa's forest and thins. Warmth swirls through my chest, and my lips lift into another smile.

Never have I felt this way in Eida before.

Trolls roared from the stadium seats, and we Fallen cheered with them. Magic sparkled along the seats' edges, down the monstrous columns, and it rippled through everything—a stadium completely made from magic.

Unlike any other battle I've fought in, the Kelasa was *fun*. I ignore the fact we still fought to entertain the trolls, but no one was going to die. No hatred bloodied the ground. It was Marked Fallen challenging Marked Fallen—basilisks wrestling werewolves, gryphons warring against harpies. And I destroyed them all.

Graeden claps a hand on my shoulder and gives a little shake. "Nice work, Fallen!"

His fingers spread over my neck until they brush the base of my skull, and his body is nearly pressed against mine. My chest flutters as I remember his closeness in the catacomb's pool. My eyes slip shut, and I lean into his sweet, wooded scent, allowing it to focus and muddle my mind at the same time.

"Have I lost you?" Graeden asks.

I open my eyes, and Graeden's face is inches from mine, both his hands resting on my shoulders. A wry smile lifts the corners of his parted lips.

"Could you use a drink?" he asks.

My teeth catch my bottom lip, and my cheeks flush. Not trusting my voice, I nod.

"Come on, then." Graeden jerks his head toward where the carriages line the forest trail. "After you."

Graeden swings the carriage door open, and I'm assaulted by the scent of stewed fruit. Stepping back, I cross my arms over my chest and offer him a smug smile. "You're speaking with a champion. After *you*."

Graeden's gaze roams over my face for a moment, his lip twitching with a smile. "Only this once."

With a bounce in my step, I climb into the carriage behind Graeden. We weave through Vasa's lush forest with the other carriages. Resting my elbow on the carriage door, I keep my face turned toward the forest. A twitter of birds descends on us from the treetops, and a distant river babbles over the moist ground. Vasa teems with life outside the window, from the new buds sprouting in the soil to the dew coating their leaves. The air hangs heavy on my tongue, crisp and full.

"Where are we headed?" I ask.

"Vasa's tavern." Graeden runs a hand through the dark strands of his hair. The humidity sticks to his skin, flushing his tanned cheeks and brightening his sunlit eyes. "This is the only time of year any Fallen are allowed inside Vasa. You fight, and then you drink."

"Sounds like a good day to be a Fallen," I say.

"It is." Graeden's eyes ignite with something almost playful. "Look up ahead."

I peer around the line of Fallen scrambling through the thick foliage. Trees stretch skyward, and as we round a bend, a small cobblestone hut rises into the clearing looking much like the last troll home I saw. Though, this structure is taller than it is wide, with a patchwork roof made from dried grass and reeds twined together. It doesn't look nearly large enough to hold a dozen people, let alone the hundreds that file in through the entrance.

Graeden climbs the steps, and I follow him in. My vision tunnels, and the room rocks like a ship tossed at sea. Nausea crawls up my throat, and my head feels faint. I grip the doorframe for support, but I think I'm going to be sick. The room rolls and stretches in every direction. I close my eyes and press my forehead against the wall's rough wood.

A chilled hand presses against my cheek, and I peek through my lashes. "I should've warned you."

I give him a dry smile. "The tavern's enchanted."

"Only for the Kelasa. Your head will come back to you in a few moments." Graeden's fingers find my hand, and he rests it in the crook of his arm. "I see a free table in the corner."

Graeden weaves through the growing crowd with ease. I cling to his arm and close my eyes to calm the pounding in my head. When we reach our table, Graeden unwinds my hand, and I drop into my seat.

"I'll grab our drinks. Take a rest," Graeden says. "After your victories today, you deserve it."

He disappears through the crowd, and I lean back against the thin, wooden chair. Torches flicker along the tavern's walls casting shadows over the other patrons. Atop each table are candlesticks nestled within frosted vases. Their glow sprinkles light across the tabletop like stars.

My thoughts drift back to the tear in the realm. To the real stars. To Tib. I roll my shoulders, and I feel the flex of my dragon's wings. She flew free and unrestrained by me or the trolls' inhibitors. Her gigantic wings took her to the peak of the stadium shrouded in the magic barrier, and she soared. It wasn't just a fight for her. This was more. This was her taste of freedom.

Her fire rumbles contentedly in my stomach. She needed that fight as much as I did.

"It feels good to be free, doesn't it?" I whisper.

My dragon's warmth spreads into my arms, and a smile tugs at my lips.

We could find more of it, I think. Tib's face drifts into my mind, the starlight twinkling against his hope-churned eyes. *With shadow magic, we could be free. Soar when we want to soar. Go where we please. Never fight again.*

The warmth banks in my veins, and a chill creeps under my skin as my dragon withdraws her heat.

I peek between my lashes as though I can see my dragon's expression to know what she's thinking. The warmth dissolves in my belly. My shoulders slump with my resignation—she wants to fight.

Freedom. Freedom to me is abandoning Eida, leaving the monsters and trolls here to rot. Shame colors my cheeks for the second time today. Leaving the monsters includes mine. If I returned to the human realm, can I honestly say I'd ever free her again?

The answer isn't an obvious yes.

Graeden returns with a female troll in tow. A long, blonde braid curls over her shoulder, and a dull floral apron hangs over her full skirts. Graeden sits on the edge of his chair, his eyes anchored on me. The troll sets two clay mugs on the table with a heavy thunk. Amber liquid swirls inside.

"Here you go, Master Thorne." The barmaid leans toward Graeden, her voice rich and silky. A smile curls her full lips, and her eyes twinkle as they meet Graeden's. But when her gaze rakes over me, the light snuffs out from her eyes, and her lip curls. She nearly spits as she says, "And with your Mighty Fallen."

I shift in my chair, and it screeches loudly as it scrapes against the floor away from the barmaid. Graeden doesn't seem to notice the barmaid's hostility.

"We've got a first-timer here." Graeden nods his head toward me and rests his elbows on the table.

"Oh, love, you are in for a treat." Her lips curve back into her attempt at a sultry smile, and she bats her lashes at Graeden.

I glance between the two. Is she flirting with him? A troll and a human?

Graeden's gaze finds mine, a well churning with passion. I drop my stare to the troll's slender hand. Is he passionate for the drink or the troll? Graeden's eyes still fall on my face, and he nods at the barmaid.

The troll snaps her fingers, and crimson flames spark at their tips. She spreads the fire on the drinks' surfaces. The amber liquid sizzles and swallows the flames. "Your drinks. Enjoy. I'll return with your meat."

Graeden slides a mug across the table before wrapping his hands around his own. The troll's gaze darts between Graeden and me before she disappears among the crowd.

"Exciting party trick." I drop my gaze to the steaming mug. Violet-tinged foam churns on the surface. I sip from the cup, the foam brushing my upper lip. The drink coats my tongue, a thick syrup of sweet cream laced with a subtle bitter edge. Lowering the cup, I swallow. The taste lingers on my tongue. "It's good."

Graeden's gaze doesn't waver, but his smile deepens, his eyes anchored to my lips. He brushes his thumb over the corner of his mouth. "You've got a little—"

Heat flushes through my cheeks. "For the love of Eida." I swipe my hand over my lips, moist foam smearing against my fingers.

"They're *balists*," Graeden nods toward the drink, gracefully saying nothing else of it. "You'll get the sense of ease without the alcohol."

"Of course. The Troll King would never give us a true escape from our realities, would he?" I take another sip, parting my lips farther.

"The trolls aren't all terrible," Graeden says.

"Right," I mutter. The barmaid seemed friendly. I smother the itch to roll my eyes.

Graeden lifts his own mug and empties the contents in a single swallow. "In fact, there was a time when none of them were."

How could he know that? I shift in my seat and rest my arms on the table. "How do I know so little of you?"

Graeden raises his mug to someone in the crowd before setting it in front of him. "It doesn't suit a master to share the privacies of his life with his Fallen."

"Why not?"

Graeden lifts his shoulders. "It blurs the line between the roles of master and Fallen. Not to mention, failures in the arena are hard enough to handle without personal connections."

"So, you'll tell me nothing of yourself because I might die?" I raise my brow in a challenge. My hands rest one on top of the other near the center of the table as I lean forward, my drink forgotten between my arms. "Even if I ask nicely?"

Graeden's gaze drops to my hands, and my palms warm. His hands sit inches from mine, his fingers intertwined with each other. Would he dare cross the line he's trying so clearly to draw between us?

"I shouldn't," he says.

"Do something you shouldn't," I whisper, testing the strength of the wall he's built between us. "Just once."

His eyes remain locked on my hands. "I've already done a lot of things that I never meant to do with you."

The lightheadedness brought on by the non-fermented ale fades. My heart stills, frozen with his words. I fear I may drift through a dream where I'm no longer facing this hell completely alone. I feel each heartbeat like an anchor in my chest, count each pulse like a lifeline.

"How long have you been here?" I ask.

A strained smile brushes Graeden's lips. "Time works differently in Eida."

I lean back, a playful grin on my lips. I've had my suspicions about the time ever since Tib arrived. "I know. How long?"

Graeden rubs a hand over his eyes. "By the human realm's standard? Best I can guess, just over fifty years. Here though, I've only aged about a decade and a half."

"Fifty years?" My mouth falls open. I knew something was odd with the time, but fifty years and Graeden is still a young man. I can't imagine being stuck here that long. Grimacing, I take a long pull from my mug. If I ever get out of this realm, everyone I know will be dead. "Were you a child when you were taken?"

Graeden nods, his thumbs circle each other. "I was a child, but I was not taken."

My brows furrow. "Then how did you find yourself in Eida?"

"I was born a wanderer in Fayhost."

The tavern's sweet scent is suddenly stifling. I've heard of Fayhost—a traveling village that never spends more than a fortnight in a single area. The people are prone to hunger during the dry season and frostbite during the wet and cold. Their villagers are often ill and die.

A travel-worn face flashes in my vision. Frost clung to the woman's blue-tinged cheeks, her expressionless eyes staring into a void I couldn't see, her body stiff in my father's arms. She was a lucky passerby, the Bridgewick elders had told me as they dug her grave. Most of the abandoned bodies in Fayhost are used to feed their people. The corpses left on the side of the road were those infected with disease or too frozen to serve the rest of the village.

I settle back in my chair. I can't imagine Graeden living in Fayhost, gnashing his teeth against human bone like a wild animal.

"I've heard of it," I say, softly.

Graeden nods, a grimace replacing the smile that had smoothed his lips only a few moments ago. "Then you've heard the tales, I'm sure. It is a life I would not wish on my worst enemy. One winter season when I was a child, we traveled through the Enchanted Wood. Pitched our tents as night fell, and when I awoke at sunrise, the village had moved on. Left me behind, forgotten.

"It was the best thing that could have happened to me, but at the time I was left to wander the forest. Winter was beginning to frost the treetops, and the ground iced each night. It didn't take long before I knew I wouldn't live through the season."

"Sorry for the wait, love." The barmaid bustles through the ever-growing crowd and pours more ale into Graeden's mug and sets down a steaming plate of meat. She doesn't spare me a second glance. "No matter how much extra space we cast into this pub, it never seems enough come Kelasa."

The barmaid winks at Graeden and shimmies between the backs of two chairs nearly pressed together.

"It was dawn when I saw her. Though she looked different then." Graeden's eyes follow the troll as she serves the other tables. "Citali. She was a child as I was. And she was a Starfallen."

I gasp and splutter my drink. "A Starfallen?"

Graeden nods. "They all were. Every single troll. You have heard of Starfall, no?"

"Yes." I stiffen. "Their people went extinct a long time ago."

"Not extinct. Transformed. Cursed." Graeden stares at his fingers motionless on the tabletop. "Only a century ago, the Starfallen were the only immortals in the human realm. Spellcasters. Witches and devils, some called them. The Dark Queen of Eifelgard, at the height of her reign, cursed all those who had a claim to magic. Their power threatened her rule. She cursed them to become trolls, and they were hunted. Slaughtered by her Shade Warriors."

My lips part as I absorb his words—details so different from anything the Elders ever spoke of to us. I'd heard of Starfall in legends and stories. Nothing real. Nothing concrete.

"What you see in this realm is a people who've started over from the scraps the Dark Queen left behind. The Starfallen are tethered to this realm. They may leave it for short periods of time but can't travel far from the Well. Most only ever leave to bring someone back." Graeden raises his brows and gives me a poignant look.

Like the trolls who were guarding the Well. They who dragged me through the river and forced me into Eida. My gaze slips through the tavern, crossing every troll. They're Starfallen. All of them.

CHAPTER THIRTY

For once I look at the trolls through a new lens, but it changes nothing. They're still the vindictive, bloodthirsty creatures who stole me from my home.

"The Dark Queen shackled the Starfallen—or trolls as you know them—to this realm with her curse," Graeden says. "It wasn't long before the Starfallen were sought after to grant wishes, treated like slaves to any who ventured into their realm and wanted their power. They wouldn't have that. So, the original Starfallen king erected the arena for those worthy of seeking wishes to earn them."

I swallow against my dry throat. Opening my mouth, I consider asking a question, but where to begin? My eyes scan the table in front of me, and Graeden continues.

"When I saw Citali in the woods, I wondered what she was doing in the human realm. She played with magic. It leapt from her fingers like flames, and my own were tinged with frostbite. Citali kept me from losing them, and when hunger twisted my stomach more than I could bear, she lifted me from the frozen ground and brought me to her home. Her people were kind, albeit disfigured. She was kind.

"A year later, Citali bore the curse's token, and her own form changed. When a young Starfallen reaches adolescence, only then does the curse take hold of them. This has been my refuge ever since from the death and bitterness of the human realm."

"How did she bring you here? The Well is the only portal into Eida, and it didn't arrive in the Enchanted Wood until I'd reached adolescence."

A smile tugs at the corner of Graeden's lips. "The Well moves. I don't know what triggers it to do so, but we've had enough Seekers finding their way through it from every corner of the human realm to make me believe it does."

I glance at my hands, nestled around my mug. There's so much we never knew.

"Why would your parents leave you?" My voice cracks with the words. My childhood hasn't exactly been a bright spot in my memory, but I never doubted my parents loved me.

Graeden lifts a half-hearted shrug and picks at the meat between us. "I don't know for sure. Typically, the villagers in Fayhost only left someone behind if they were diseased. The rest of us offered our bodies when we died to strengthen the village, but," Graeden pauses, and a near imperceptible shudder crawls over his skin. "I like to think it's because my parents knew I was going to starve first, and they wanted a better burial for me. Even no burial would be better than what waits for the dead within Fayhost."

My heart aches for the boy abandoned on the side of the road, left alone in the maze of the Enchanted Wood. His parents didn't expect him to survive. They only wanted him to die in peace. "Did you have to fight in the arena? As a child?"

"The young don't fight in the arena." Graeden tips his now empty mug toward himself. "I lived with Citali's family for a time and among the Starfallen. It was unheard of, but Eida was also a different place back then.

"When I was ten, the late Troll King sent me to live among the Marked Fallen to begin training, even though I was still a few years away from fighting. But I was always welcome among the Starfallen."

"Would you ever leave?" A little too much hope is etched through my question.

"No," Graeden doesn't hesitate. "There's nothing left for me in the human realm. And the Starfallen are like family. Their past has hardened them towards those without magic, but they weren't always this way. They were groomed to be. Eida began as a type of refuge. Do you remember how I said time works differently—more slowly—in Eida?"

My eyes find his, and I nod.

"Just over five years ago," Graeden says, "many Starfallen grew vicious, earning their names as trolls."

"Many of the Starfallen?" I ask. "They're *all* vicious and bloodthirsty."

Graeden shakes his head. "There are many who live in the depths of Vasa who never gather at the arena to watch the fights. They remember life not long ago under our late king when it wasn't all about blood.

"When a Troll King is ready to move on to the heavens and abandon his immortal frame, he will choose from among his Starfallen to kill him and take his power. Our king did not do that. Under this curse, he would not return to the heavens. But his heir took the throne from him, regardless, and then changed the rules in the arena. He was vicious for blood.

"For those Starfallen who let it, spilled blood spiked their ferocity, it fed their craving for revenge. They began kidnapping and forcing mortals to become the monsters the Dark Queen once forced upon them. The Troll King has encouraged his people's bloodlust, and the Fallen have had to adapt to survive, playing the brutal game. There are still good Starfallen here, and I will forever protect and remain loyal to their kind in this realm. They are my people."

Graeden sips from his mug, casting his eyes around the room. I wonder how many Fallen he has seen arrive in Eida, and how many others he has had to send to Eida's beast after their deaths. To live a lifetime in Eida, I can't even imagine. Graeden swipes a hand through the dark locks of his hair. His lips rest slightly pursed, his jaw tight.

Now, I know why he is loyal to this death-seeking realm.

"When I came of age, it was my rite to step up in the arena," Graeden says. "The Fallen drew my monster out."

"A phoenix," I whisper.

Graeden's eyes raise to meet mine, and my breath is stolen by the depths swirling within his. Passion. Darkness. Secrets.

I peel a strip of meat from the platter and pop it in my mouth. I haven't eaten much today, but somehow, I don't feel hungry. "How did you survive so long in the arena?" I ask.

A subtle smile cuts into Graeden's stoic expression as though reliving a distant memory. Instead of answering, he finishes his drink and stands. Jerking his head toward the door, he says, "I think we've had enough distraction for a day."

My lips curve into a pout, and I glare at him. "Had I known asking my questions would have cut our drinking short, I would've kept my mouth shut."

Graeden's eyes twinkle. "Next time, you'll think twice. Let's go."

I pour the rest of the ale down my throat before following him out. Contemplative silence fills the carriage as we travel through Vasa back to Arautteve. Graeden's past is so different from my own yet so similar. He was a child abandoned by those who should have cared for him. Nowhere near a man when he had to determine his own fate. To live or to die with what was given to him.

My eyes trace the taut muscles curving over his shoulders and disappearing into his tunic. He rests his palm on his long sword, his fingers drumming against the sheath as he stares out the window. He isn't the frail child on the brink of starvation anymore. I wonder what his family would think if they saw him now. Saw the man he's become. Pride fills my chest, and a warm smile settles on my lips.

And somehow, he now sits on the safe side of Eida. No longer fighting within the arena but training others to do so.

"Did you reach your pardon?" My voice cuts through the silence like the crack of a whip, but Graeden doesn't falter in his answer.

"Are you sure you wish to ask more questions?"

I purse my lips and scowl. We've got nothing but time as we bump along to Arautteve. Shifting his weight away from the window, Graeden glances at me from the corner of his eye.

"No."

"So, how'd you get out of fighting?"

Graeden smiles. "Until you came along, I was one of the strongest creatures in the realm. I've always been one with my phoenix—it's a very difficult creature to kill. I didn't need a pardon. Besides, the better question is, how will you get out of fighting?"

My jaw stiffens, and I steel myself for where this conversation is headed.

"Your only path is with your dragon," he says.

"I know," I mutter. We may have bested every other creature during the Kelasa, but it's different. We were fighting for fun, not for blood. Blood changes things.

"Have you made any progress?"

I drop my gaze to the shadows cast throughout the carriage. "Not much."

"Maybe we should try Isla again."

"No," I snap. Memories flash through my mind—flames and that ear-splitting scream that for years soaked my nightmares. I shut my eyes against the crack Isla made in the barrier of my memory. He never should have died. Not for me.

A sobering breath numbs the flames in my chest.

"Why are you so resistant to letting Isla help you?" Graeden shifts and turns to face me. The question rattles the chains draped across the barricade in my mind.

"I'm not resistant." I fold my arms across my midsection and stare into the distance. "I already told you she couldn't help."

"Yes, you did." His jaw tightens, and his warm eyes cool.

I try not to squirm beneath his hardened gaze. "What?"

Graeden lifts his shoulders. "I just find it odd there's absolutely nothing the strongest fairy in Eida can do."

I pin my own unwavering glare against his. "Well, there's a first for everything. I'll find another way."

"You better do it quick," Graeden unfolds his arms. "The Troll King will throw you back in that arena sooner rather than later. Without your dragon reined in, you're walking to your own ruin."

I frown, my mood growing sourer with each passing moment. "Thanks for the vote of confidence."

"Hey!" Graeden grabs my knee, the ease lost from his voice. "Unleashing your dragon has changed everything. You rein it in, or it will kill you. This isn't a game."

"Everything here is a game." And we're the pawns.

"The Troll King expects each of his Marked to fight *with* their monsters." Graeden's touch softens. "Including you. It's the only thing that keeps him from granting wishes and the only thing that makes you valuable."

"Gee, thanks."

Graeden releases my knee. "That's not what I mean."

"No," I interrupt. "It's fine. My value is determined by how many I kill in the arena. Makes perfect sense."

Graeden's shoulders slump, and he rakes a hand through his hair.

"Just answer me this," I say. "Why do you care so much? Aren't you tired of fighting for the trolls?"

"We aren't fighting for them," Graeden says. "When you step into that arena, you are fighting for *you*. For *your* life. Not the Starfallens'. You are fighting the Seekers so you can get the hell out of here. As you should."

"But we shouldn't be fighting the Seekers." Heat rises in my cheeks, and my neck warms. "We should be fighting the ones forcing us into that arena."

"And go up against magic? Not even your dragon succeeded in such a feat." Graeden rests his elbows atop his knees. "This is Eida. It's kill or be killed."

"And you're okay with that?"

"We have to be." Graeden says. "The Troll King's predecessor deserved our protection and loyalty. I was honored to serve under him. We are in a different season now, but I won't abandon the Starfallen under the Troll King's reign. This is not who they are. I must believe Eida and its people can become the stalwart race they once were."

"How can you?" I don't mean the words to sting the way they do, but Graeden flinches. "These aren't your peaceful Starfallen anymore. They never will be. They steal memories and kidnap dragons. They push and they shove until someone's blood spills over the ground, and then they laugh."

Graeden's jaw clenches, and his gaze hardens. Without answering my question, Graeden settles back into his seat. A cloak of contempt passes over his expression, and he turns to stare out the window. My anger deflates against his back, but it still sizzles through my veins.

I cringe as I remember the way Graeden looked at Citali. The fact he can look at any of the trolls with empathy stirs my distrust. He's always claimed to be on my side, but I'm not so sure. If he stands with the trolls, how can he stand with me?

Vasa's soft soil shifts to slick stone as we enter the outskirts of Arautteve. I pinch my lips, knowing I won't talk my way out of this with Graeden.

Flames lick the edges of my memory, and heat warms the back of my throat. The wall barricading the darkness in my past shudders. It's buckling. According to Isla, these memories are the only way to unite with my dragon. I press the barriers back in place as best I can. I refuse to relive that agony.

As the carriage slows near the border of Vasa and Arautteve, Graeden straightens and places his hand on the door's latch. "Until you're willing to do whatever it takes to unite with your dragon, we might as well cancel training for the amount of good it'll do you." He barely looks over his shoulder. "Come find me when you're serious about reaching your pardon."

Opening the door, he slips out of the carriage without waiting for it to come to a stop. He slams the door behind him. I resist the urge to stick out my tongue and slump into my seat. My pardon? I scoff. Thanks to the Kelasa I'm five hundred kills closer to reaching it, but my best chance to truly survive here is becoming a master like Graeden. It's not the freedom I'd hoped for.

Maybe my dragon is not a monster, but to make room for her I'll have to face one. I'm not ready to do that.

To Eida's depths with Graeden. I'll find another way to unite with my dragon, and I'll do it without him. My anger simmers, and my throat dries. But even if I don't find a way, I'm going to figure out how to leave this realm.

Night is upon us by the time the carriage stops in front of my temple. I slip into the drafty room and close my eyes for a few hours. It doesn't take long, though, for my warring thoughts to wake me. Tib told me to leave it to him. I can't wait that long. Every passing day is a day closer to our next battle and one of our imminent deaths. Eventually, my dragon will kill him. Unless I become shadow and we disappear.

The mediocre rest will have to do. I can't linger here. After donning my warmer clothes, I drape a navy cloak over my shoulders and slip into the courtyard. I peek over my shoulder, half expecting to find Graeden waiting for me. My lips arc into a frown, and my brows pinch together. I shouldn't care. I don't care.

Maybe Graeden's only escape from the arena was turning himself over completely to his monster, but it's not mine. As soon as I shift into shadow, Tib and I are leaving this realm and everyone in it.

CHAPTER THIRTY-ONE

Tib is easy to find. He crouches next to a dying fire in Ghora's valley, his hand propping up a listless head. Broth slips between the abandoned Seeker's lips and dribbles down his cheek.

I stick to the shadows, watching Tib care for his own—our own—even as death caresses their sunken cheeks. Moans rise into the darkness, a symphony of pleading cries for death to take them.

My hand rests against the woven satchel hanging against my hip. Why I thought my meager offering of food from Arautteve would be enough to do any good is beyond me. I tuck the bag behind my back. Inhaling, ice coats my throat and lungs. I step from the shadows, and Ghora's chill bites against my cheeks. Shaded eyes follow my steps, and I stop in front of Tib.

Tib's gaze flickers to me, and he does a double take, nearly dropping the earthenware bowl he holds. Amusement flashes in his eyes. "Didn't I say I would find you?"

"You expect me to wait on you?" I plant my hands on my hips. "We battle again in twelve hours…"

"Same old Ari," Tib smiles. Setting down the bowl, Tib gives the Seeker's shoulder a gentle squeeze before standing. "This way."

Tib slips off the main path and weaves a trail among the trees. My pulse quickens, but I follow him as he climbs a steep hill.

Tib is the same as I remember, and yet so different. There's an age to him—a maturity—I never saw in Bridgewick. My mind flits to a faded memory from years ago. The sole warrior to return to Bridgewick from the Well. My gaze roves over the youthfulness of his face in my mind. He returned so young. I pin my gaze to Tib as the incline deepens. My sandals dig against the solid ground, and I use my hands to brace myself against the growing incline.

"How old are you?" I ask.

"Twenty-three." Tib doesn't hesitate.

Heat swarms my head, and I blink hard. When we were betrothed, we were the same age. He's now five years older. I swallow against the dryness in my throat. Time truly does work differently in Eida.

Tib offers me his hand when he reaches the top, and I grasp it. He lifts me to his side. An emerald-green river flows past us, the bank at our feet narrow and soggy. Mud clings to its edges – I've never seen soil in Ghora. Nor water.

"You have water?" I thought Ghora had nothing.

Tib squints, his mouth puckering. "It's not really water. Not drinkable anyway." Crouching, Tib scoops a handful of sludge from the bank. "But it has its uses."

"What's wrong with it?"

Tib rises and tucks a stray hair behind my ear. His fingers stroke my cheek with feather-like gentleness, and he smears the mud across my skin. "Enchanted. It doesn't quench thirst, but that doesn't stop many from trying."

"What does it do?" I draw my hair into a knot at the base of my neck and lift my chin. Tib wipes the mud across my throat.

"The same thing as everything else in Eida." Tib's tone is matter-of-fact. "It kills you."

"How thoughtful of the trolls to remind you of what you lack." Sarcasm bleeds from my tone, but my words are tinged with pity.

The Starfallen. I shove the sympathy away. Whoever they *were*, they aren't so anymore.

How terrible to be so close to water, but unable to drink it. My tongue dries, and I wish I'd brought more than two waterskins.

Tib brushes a hand across my forehead, moving the wisps of hair plastered against my hairline. My skin tingles from his touch. The warmth of a steaming mug on a snowy night. His fingers comb through my hair, and his hands lock behind my neck.

We share the same breath, his hands no longer working at my disguise. Instead, they're still. Hesitant. Questions burn in Tib's eyes. Questions I don't want to answer.

Clearing my throat, I pull away. So much is said with the small gesture, and Tib flattens his lips into a firm line.

Guilt draws my chin to my chest. It shouldn't be this way. We were supposed to be together in another time. Another world. A lump throbs in my throat. Tib is my betrothed. I should want him to kiss me. To touch me. But the warmth of Graeden's hands still burns against my skin.

I don't know what I want except to be free of this place.

Stepping back, Tib drops his hands. He offers me his crooked smile, but it's stilted and wrong. "There. Now, you'll blend in. Those in the abandoned valley have no strength to fight you, but everyone else in Ghora would slit your throat before asking questions."

I raise my fingers to touch my dirt-encrusted cheek.

"Shall we?" Tib slips down the fractured stone extending one hand for balance and the other to brace himself against the hill.

I follow suit, small obsidian shards raining into the valley beneath each of my footfalls. I leap over the last bit of the incline and land hard on the valley floor. My satchel slips from my shoulder and hits the ground with a thud. The contents spill out from its flap, the waterskins skidding toward Tib.

Tib lifts the waterskins and tests their weight. "What's this?"

I quickly gather the spilled food—an apple, some aaerin, even a few pieces of dried meat—and shove it into the bag. Avoiding Tib's eyes, I hand the satchel to him. It's not enough, but maybe it can sustain him for another day.

"Food. Water," I say. "It's not much, but maybe it can help."

The satchel's strap wraps around Tib's fist and hangs in front of his chest. His eyes narrow the tiniest amount, his lips curving up. "You're full of surprises, aren't you?" He doesn't wait for my response. "It's more than enough. Thank you."

I rub my neck and change the subject. After all, I came to Ghora for one reason: to shift into shadow. "If we're going to do this, we must be so careful," I warn. "If the trolls find out what we're doing, we risk more than just you and me."

Tib leads the way through the hardened trees. "You mean your warden?"

"For one," I say. Though perhaps they'd have a little mercy on him seeing as how they're *family*.

"He would be so lucky for the trolls to kill him before I do," Tib growls.

My train of thought evaporates. I've never felt such sudden anger wash over Tib.

"We've all heard the rumors," he continues. "How slaves are treated in Eida—sold to the highest bidder, beaten into submission, coerced to the whims of taskmasters who claim their women to their beds and force their men to brutal labor. And all before pitting you to kill for them."

Tib's steps slow as he reaches the clearing. He pivots to face me, his eyes somber and filled with pain. His gaze roams over my face and trails over my filth-covered body. "I can barely stand to imagine what that *master* of yours has done to you. He will pay for everything, Ari."

"Tib," I breathe.

"What has he said to you?" Tib challenges, his voice fierce. "Has he said you're helpless? That you need him? How about that he's the only one here willing to help you? How many times has he had you enter his bed, Ari?"

Anger flashes through my veins, and my chest rises with great fury. I can't tell if the sudden rage is mine or my dragon's, but the fire snaps beneath both our skins. These are not questions he has any right to ask. Fiery breath huffs from my nostrils, and the cuff against my wrist warms. If I weren't wearing it, I wonder if my dragon would slaughter Tib right here.

"You know nothing of what I've gone through," I spit. "How dare you pretend otherwise?"

Stepping around Tib, I stomp into the clearing. I thought Tib was going to teach me of nightmares and shadows, not slander my virtue. Tib is wrong about Graeden just like I was. He can be absolutely terrifying, but he's loyal and kind and protective. He trusts me and treats me like I'm strong. He's gained my trust. Fully.

My jaw ticks as I remember our argument. I'm such a fool. I don't have to trust the trolls to trust Graeden. He's the only person in Eida who's ever earned my trust. That should be enough.

I have no time for this. The low-lit fires burn against the earth, and I slip around them with ease. No one stops me or gives me a second glance. Doesn't Tib realize how much I risk by coming here?

Tib grabs my shoulder softly. I spin on my heel ready to engulf him in flames, but his shoulders slump and his head bows. "I'm sorry. I shouldn't have said any of that."

I shake him off. "It's been a long time since you've known me. A lot has changed. I've changed."

"I don't believe that."

"It doesn't matter what you believe. I've been here for years—alone." My own anger simmers, my dragon calming beneath my skin as Graeden's face drifts into my mind's eye. Tears brim at the edges of my vision as the memories flood my head. "That *master* is the only one who *has* ever been willing to help me."

Tib nods, though I'm not sure he agrees with me. "I wish I could've been here for you sooner."

I shake my head, a pained smile crossing my face. Had Tib arrived sooner, I would still be Ari, daughter of a Bridgewick elder, a simple human warrior without a monster. Somehow, it feels like a piece of me would be stolen without my dragon.

"That's not how the fates designed it." My anger dies leaving a somber calm in its wake.

"I understand," Tib says. "You've done what you've had to survive with what little help you've been able to find."

Resignation settles on my shoulders. He still doesn't understand. Graeden isn't my only option. If I had to face the arena with anyone in this world, I would *choose* him.

"Do you still want to go home?" Tib asks.

My longing to see my mother tightens through my chest, snuffing out everything else. Loss. Regret. Desire. All folded into a shred of hope that I can find her again one day. I don't have to answer.

"I still want to help you get there."

My throat tightens, and I can't speak so I offer him a hard nod.

Tib leads me deeper into the abandoned valley where the dying thin out, leaving the obsidian trees untouched. A lone crumbling structure juts out from the ground. The roof has long since been torn away, and rebar protrudes from its skeleton like broken bones. We duck inside where there's some respite from Ghora's climate.

"Is it safe here?" I ask.

"As safe as any training court, I suppose," Tib says. "Don't worry. You look like one of us. No one will be any wiser about who you truly are."

"So, how do I do it?" I scoot to the edge of a stone jutting out from the deteriorating wall like a chair.

"What we're doing is dangerous, and I have no actual proof it'll get us out of Eida." Tib rests his elbows on his knees and interlaces his fingers. "It wouldn't be right if I didn't ask you to reconsider."

"And if I don't?"

"I would pull the stars from the heavens for you, if it is what you wished." Tib holds my gaze as though he can burn his will into mine. As though his silent plea alone can change my mind.

I know he has good reason to hesitate in teaching me—he's spent years learning his craft in Taiatum. I glance away from his stare to the holes eating their way through the structure's roof. Faded strands of magic brush the dawn-lit sky. No stars. No hope.

Tib and I fight again in less than twelve hours, this time with the strength of my dragon. One of us will likely die. What could I possibly learn in so little time? But I can't not try. I may find Tib on the wrong end of my sword tomorrow, but to what end? To fight another day? To kill another person? That's no life. If Tib teaches me to become shadow, no one could control me. No man. No monster. We could be free.

"Then do it," I order.

Tib smiles, an electric energy sifting through his shoulders. He's always been one willing to play with fire. "The only way to become shadow is with blood magic."

A nervous thrum vibrates through my veins. Blood magic. The words are pungent and sweet, thin and yet they burst with possibility. Rumors in Bridgewick spoke of such insidious darkness. To use blood magic, you must always offer a blood sacrifice. A way to weaken yourself before searching for more strength. I swallow the sudden dryness in my throat. There's a reason it was banned throughout the human realm.

Although, clearly, it being illegal didn't stop those in the City of Gold.

"How much blood?"

"It's not that bad. Just enough to fill the rune."

My brow wrinkles, but I watch quietly as Tib draws his dagger. He thrusts his blade into the stone, and I cringe each time it screeches against its mark. Soon, a shallow well appears at our feet in a swooping design.

"The Winter rune." Tib wipes the black dust from his blade. "If one knows the right rune, one can access its magic. But you add a little magicked blood to the rune, and its power changes."

Tib tips the point of his blade to my forearm and gestures a quick slice over my flesh.

"The Taiatum have magic in their blood. We don't." Tib unlaces one of the small satchels at his waist and holds it between us like a precious stone.

"Is that--?"

Tib opens the satchel and dips two of his fingers inside. "Without blood, it's only dyed powder."

An air of burnt pine circles my head, and the powder's subtle scent throws me back into the arena. Choking, gagging, stumbling around like an idiot.

"Why did it affect me in the arena then?" I ask.

Tib grimaces. "You inhaled it. It must have found some of your blood."

My thoughts dart uncharted through my head. Tib's drawn the symbol. He's brought the magic. I just need to supply the blood. Laughter bubbles in my throat, my gaze locked onto the shimmering ivory powder in Tib's hand.

I wonder how Tib came by the magic, let alone smuggled it into Eida, but I don't ask. Something so powerful could absolutely overthrow this realm—if he had enough of it. But even with the little he holds, he could do some damage.

I strangle the thought. This small satchel of magic is our ticket to freedom. The cost will be high, though. I'm sure of it.

"Once we become shadow, how do we get back to the human realm?"

Tib raises a brow, a sly smile spreading over his lips. "A person is never without their shadow. I figure we hitch a ride with the next Seeker who wins in the arena."

It's so simple.

"The only one I know of who can send someone out of this realm is the Troll King," Tib continues. "So, we'll have to wait for him unless you know of another way."

I shake my head. "Magic runs naturally through the Troll King's veins. He has a never ending well of it. All the other trolls simply borrow power from his stores in the sky."

I lean forward and peek inside the satchel. I'm new to Blood Magic, but the powder only fills about half the bag. There isn't much there.

"How much of this will it take before I shift?" I ask.

"It depends," Tib says. "We'll add the magic to your blood and your blood to the rune. A Winter rune made from your magicked blood will force you into your darkest memory."

My throat tightens. Flames crackle against my ears, and I listen to the snapping wind from my past.

"I told you this wouldn't be easy," Tib warns. "That it may be the most painful thing you ever do."

I swallow thickly. Perhaps I could shift into shadow with another's sacrifice.

"What if I used someone else's blood?" I ask.

"Then it'd force you into their darkest memory." Tib rests his elbows on his knees, closing the gap between us. "To become shadow, you must visit the darkness within *you*. You must embrace the pain, the fear. And then let it transform you. Another's blood would only force you into *their* darkest memories. Nothing more."

Tib grimaces. He knows very well what he's asking me to do. He stood with me as I lived through it all the first time. Flames and screaming drift through the forefront of my mind. I squeeze my eyes shut, and a frown tugs at my lips.

Tib's knuckles brush mine. "You can still change your mind."

For a moment, I wish to. I want to bolt from Ghora and leave my own darkness behind with its shadows. But there's nowhere to run in Eida. I don't want to face my past, but it's better than nailing my future in its coffin.

A whisper tickles the back of my mind, and guilt stirs in my stomach. My dragon. This very memory I refused to unlock for her, yet I'll walk into it with open arms to escape this realm as shadow. My stomach curls, and I tuck my arms around my waist.

Shadows will help me flee this prison. A stronger monster is only more of me for the trolls to rule.

"No," I whisper. "I can't."

"Then let's get started."

My breath is heavy as Tib lifts my arm between us and rolls the sleeve of my wool sweater up to my elbow. I swallow as the faded rivulets of magic in the sky glint off his blade. Tib presses its point against my forearm.

The blade bites into my skin. I gasp as hot blood pools against my arm.

Tib lifts his satchel and sprinkles the ivory powder across my wound. The magic sizzles as it soaks into my blood. Tib's gaze roams over my face. Tension tugs at the edges of his eyes, and the same energy buzzes through my stomach.

Moving my arm between us, Tib guides the dripping blood into the roughly carved rune. It glints with raging embers. Before I know it, Tib wraps a thin gauze around my wound. I place my arm against my chest to stunt the blood flow. With any luck, my dragon will heal it, and Graeden will never know.

The rune pulses with a low blue light. Apprehension lines my stomach, but the flames of my memory lick the back of my eyes. I can do this. Just a peek beyond the wall.

Tib raises a narrow brow, his usual charm sobered.

His fingers curl around my hand, a warm embrace strengthening my determination.

Tib was there with the fire and the screams. I barely recall his face flickering beyond the heat waves.

My throat tightens, and tears burn behind my eyes.

Tib's grip tightens around mine. "No matter what you do, cleave to those memories. Make this worth it. Prove you are strong enough to embrace your darkness. Show yourself you aren't afraid of it."

But I am afraid of it. My words lodge in my throat. I don't think I can speak without whimpering.

"I'm right here with you," Tib whispers, his voice too far away.

My mind grows hazy with my panic, that wall in my mind trembling with barely any resistance left. The light strengthens, the pale blue intensifying into a torrent of silver teals that I can't help but shield my eyes. Then, darkness.

My grip slackens against Tib's, but he holds tight. The darkness caresses my skin, an old friend welcoming me home. Cutting through the shadows, images race past in a flurry. Burnt trees. Clashing steel. Blood drenching my hands, splattered over armor, sprayed across the sandy floor.

A pearly skull in a pile of ash.

CHAPTER THIRTY-TWO

"*Bravery, Aribelle.*" *My father's unshaven face prickles my cheek as he whispers against my ear.* "*You're built for more than this world. I won't choose a suitor for you or make your choices as the elders would have me do. Your future is in your hands.*"

"*And I choose to help Atarah.*"

Father presses his lips against my temple, the soft touch lingering. I close my eyes as his arm tightens around my shoulders. I've wandered the outskirts of Bridgewick many times with Tib, though rarely at night. I wouldn't dream of sending Father and Atarah out there alone.

Father releases me and shuffles into his bedroom to bid farewell to Mother. My gaze locks onto the candlelight flickering beyond the arched doorway. His limp is more pronounced tonight. His step more haggard.

He will never make it through the forest with my sister alone. And the penalty for what they do tonight is their lives. The elders of Bridgewick stand for nothing that threatens the unity of our people. We give to one another, united and collected in all our endeavors. We are each a thread in the grand tapestry of our strength. Disobedience, such as we plan to do tonight, snaps a thread, weakening and dishonoring the entire village. Not only that but abandoning your husband and your village is among the worst you could do.

I swallow against the words so often drilled into my mind. The elders keep our people strong and united so we may stand safe against any outsiders. But they do nothing to protect us from those within our own borders. Nothing to protect Atarah.

Father needs me out there.

I tear my gaze from my parents' silhouettes and slip toward our hut's entrance. Father shouldn't have to do this to protect our family. Drawing my cloak from its post, I don its hood over my long hair and disappear inside its folds.

The thatch door barely creaks as I slip into the moonlight with Father to where Atarah already waits. The moon's glow paints my sister in its light, paling her skin. A dark bruise already forms across her cheek. Atarah wears her own mulberry hood.

My gaze burrows into hers, grief written all over her face. None of us speak as we turn into the sparse forest. It's not much for cover, but in Bridgewick, it's the best course to mask us from Atarah's husband. Ever since the elders matched and wed Atarah to the filthy man, she has been at the back of his hand.

We've tried to prove his offenses, many times. But he's the son of an Elder, preferred and admired even if he does often return at night with his head swimming from ale. Atarah's always been too fearful to cry against her husband in public, but tonight we take a stand. This goes on no longer.

Family first. Always. In a few hours, we'll reach the outskirts of Bridgewick, and Atarah can escape her marriage. I glance at Atarah beneath her hood. She has full lips I imagine any man would dream of kissing and piercing eyes that swarm like a hurricane. She's only in her seventeenth year—five years my elder. I can't imagine her being on her own in the wild, yet she stands a better chance of surviving an unknown world than this one where men rule their women as slaves.

The night's chill whips around us, and time doesn't pass near quickly enough. Father falls farther behind with each unsteady step. I slow my pace to match his. The only sound besides my shallow breaths is my heart ramming into my ribs. *It's taking too long. If we're caught outdoors after curfew…*

A shuffle of steps skitters through the leaves behind my back followed by a loud thud. I whip around. Father lies on his side, a moan clinging to his lips. I lurch into a sprint before kneeling at his side. My fingers fuss over the edges of his face, but I don't speak. I can't.

Bridgewick's forest has eyes and ears. There's always someone watching, always someone listening. I press my hand to Father's heart and point home. He shakes his head and rolls to his knees. He has hardly any energy left. He may make it to the border, but I doubt he'll make it home.

Placing one hand on his shoulder and the other on his heart, I shake my head. *He has nothing left to give Atarah.* Father's shoulders bow. He knows it, too. When he lifts his head, a fire of determination settles in his eyes. With his hands between us, he forms Bridgewick's sign for path. Another sign: light.

When it comes time to choose a path, he wants us to stick to the light.

I give him a curt nod. Father places his hand over my heart, his watery eyes charged with a shield of victory. Wrapping his free hand behind my neck, Father pulls me into his side and kisses my temple. He does the same with Atarah and drapes his own cloak over her shoulders.

This is the last time they'll see each other.

With Father's back to us, we race swiftly through the thinning trees. It doesn't take near as long for us to reach the border. My feet slow in front of the two paths. One wanders in a straight line bathed in moonlight. The other is swathed in shadow.

Father said for Atarah to follow the light. I glance at the two paths I've often traveled along with Tib. The darker path is much shorter. Atarah will have a better chance of slipping unnoticed through the shadows and will find safety among our neighbors in Norgrave much sooner.

Sorrow beats into my chest, but it isn't as strong as the relief I feel that we made it. The tension in my chest loosens, and I gesture to the darkness. My sister kisses my tear-stained cheeks before cleaving to the shadows and walking away from Bridgewick forever.

The chill enters my bone as I return alone to our house. Somehow the world seems quieter—emptier—without Atarah. Our thatch door nestles into its lock, and I tie the door closed. My lips brush both my parents' brows before I collapse onto my blankets next to them.

Atarah will be safe now.

My throat dries with the thought, and tension crawls up my spine. I fall into a fitful sleep. Moments could not have passed when I jolt from my bed. A cacophony of snarling voices rises through the night. Mother and Father already stand at the windows, peering through the tattered curtains. I race to their sides.

Father rests a calming hand on my shoulder and drops a forlorn gaze at me. He says nothing, though his mouth curves into a worried frown. Father helps Mother drape her cloak around her shoulders, and I wrap a small blanket around mine. We step into the dirt streets, loose pebbles digging through the soles of my leather-wrapped shoes.

A scream curdles through the air, and I whip my head in the direction of the Gathering. We rush through the streets toward Bridgewick's central area, Mother's cloak flapping behind her. Rough voices bark orders while others wail and plead in pitches almost too painful to hear.

My feet skid as I slide around the corner into the Gathering. The empty round has been filled with branches and twigs and kindling, piled into one massive heap. A rotted tree stands at its center and tied to it is Atarah. Tears streak her cheeks as sobs burst from her mouth. Snot runs over her lips, and a fresh cut divides their symmetry. She splutters her pleas, but her husband won't hear of it. He stumbles around and throws more wood onto the pyre.

He's drunk. Her husband's black eyes wander to mine. A chill runs up my spine as a sneer crosses the man's face. He points a bloodied hand at me and slurs, "The accomplice."

The blood drains from my face, and my legs tremble. I try to find my voice, but it has vanished. Four brutes trudge forward, and I stumble backward into my parents. One of the men throws a rumpled cloak at my father's chest. It falls into a heap at our feet.

The tremor in my arms seizes. My heart's frantic pounding softens to the quiet patter of raindrops. The world seems to crackle, a glacier melting beneath the summer heat. It's Father's cloak. The one Atarah wore as she traveled down the shadowed path. The path I sent her on against Father's wishes.

I should have listened to him. She should have stuck to the light. She should never have gone into the shadows even though it was the shorter path. Bridgewick's forest has eyes and ears, and they found Atarah while lying in wait among the shadows.

The man curls a fist around my father's arm, and he throws Father onto his knees. Raising his boot, the man lands a well-aimed kick against Father's ribs.

"No!" My voice tears through the night, shrill and animal-like. They're going to kill him. Launching myself to my father's side, I find his hands in mine. "Father..."

"Go, Aribelle."

"It's all my fault," I whisper. Tears pool between our fingers laced together under my chin. I press my wet lips against his knuckles. "You don't deserve this."

"No one does."

Lightning splinters across my side as the man's boot finds my body. I gasp at the sudden pain.

"I failed Atarah. Let me save you," Father whispers.

The man throws me to the side like a sack of barley. I land at Mother's feet in a disgraceful heap. She falls to her knees and wraps me in her arms. Her body shakes violently, but she holds us firmly away from the pyre. There's nothing stopping Atarah's husband from strapping us next to her and Father.

Across the Gathering, villagers watch the execution. Atarah's husband has every right to punish her based on Bridgewick's laws. She broke the cardinal rule of unity. Father, too. Tears slip down my cheeks. I should be up there with them. Tib stands beyond the burning pyre, his eyes fixated on me the entire time.

The wood snaps as flames consume the kindling and then leap onto Father and Atarah. Father holds his tongue longer than any man should be able. In the end, though, he cries out, too. Their screams echo into the night long after their bodies have turned to ash. And I just lie there at Mother's feet. Watching. Selfish. And when they're gone, every good part of me has been destroyed, too.

The crowd thins, and a pain-filled silence settles over Bridgewick. Even Atarah's widower has turned his back on the empty Gathering, disgust twisting his sobering features.

The memory shifts from a nightmarish reality to watching the smoking embers through a film. Tears had burned behind my eyes as I watched my father and sister's execution, but I'd smothered them as I had wished to smother the flames that stole them from me.

The guilt boils against my chest as it had done years ago. I had buried it then, but I can't bury it now. Their deaths are my fault—through my recklessness. And I never even bothered to say goodbye. Hot tears roll down my cheeks as I embrace the pain, and I choke on a sob. It swelters beneath my skin, and I can barely breathe. My heart constricts. Tight. Suffocating. The air pungent and bitter with remorse. I gasp and press a hand against my chest, and my heart continues to mangle itself until only skeletal remains are left. Broken and hollow.

The burning pyre still smokes in my vision, leaving me devoid of emotion. But then, something bubbles within my chest. I pitch forward as thick regret flows through the barren cavities of my heart. Sorrow tinges the edges, and my sob tumbles from my lips.

"I'm sorry," I whisper. I crumple in half, and slick stone presses against my forehead. "I'm sorry for everything."

My father died so I could live. Not cry. Not bemoan. Not survive. Live. I will live for him. For Atarah.

The ashen pyre fades, and Ghora's darkness replaces the vision. Blood pulses through my head, and the darkness suffocates me as I slip from the nightmare.

"Ari." Tib's grip tightens in mine. "Just breathe."

I cleave to his voice. Breathe. Breathe. My body curls forward over my knees. The air burns my lungs as I draw shallow breaths. My muscles are stiff, and my joints creak as I shift to press my cheek against the chilled obsidian.

Tib doesn't seem surprised that I lie on the frosted ground, tears streaking the dirt on my cheeks.

You're built for more than this world.

Sweat threads through my hair, and my father's words loop through my mind. My gaze flutters to Tib. Four days after my father's execution, the elders presented me with two suitors. And it was up to me to decide. Caelum or Tib?

I would have chosen neither, but Atarah's screams still rang in my ears, and I couldn't walk into hers and Father's same fate, not with my father's sacrifice pressing against my shoulders. So, I chose Tib.

"Give it a few days." Tib loops his hands beneath my arms and helps me into a seated position. "It's very taxing on the mind and body, isn't it?"

I suck in a strangled breath, and it scrapes over my raw throat. Did I scream in this reality, too? Instead of answering Tib, I nod.

My grief weaves through my chest, but it's lighter, buoyed by a strength that isn't my own. Dragonsfire warms the agony of that night so long ago, a deep crawl of heat aging the pain until it's the distant memory it should be.

Her heart beats softly within my chest. Her strength flows through my veins—the warmth of a growing sunrise burning my skin. Peace smothers the anxiety that has plagued me since arriving in Eida. And a sweet confidence melts over my tongue, softening the ache in my throat.

Hello, I think. The greeting feels foreign, but my dragon is here. She returns the greeting with a rush of warmth as though we sit at the fireside. A name whispers through my head.

Hello, Inaara. Savior. Deliverer. I smile as Bridgewick's translations of her name follow. Graeden was right. We are strong.

Could my father ever have known how true his last words would become? How I'd find myself a dragon shifter in the forsaken troll realm?

With renewed strength pulsing through my muscles, I climb to my feet.

"Take it easy." Tib says.

"It didn't work," I say. "Why didn't it work?"

Tib's brows knit together. "Did you make it to the end of the memory?"

I nod, my throat tightening. The raw and ragged emotions stir near the surface. Inaara lights a fire in my chest, ushering away the pain.

Tib scratches his cheek and stares at the Winter rune. "You should've shifted, then." Tib runs his fingers along the edge of the rune and stands. "The rune's drawn correctly, and we added magicked blood. It should've been enough."

A heaviness settles on my chest. The thin strands of escape slip through my fingertips.

"Maybe you need more. We'll add extra magic to your blood next time." Tib's eyes travel over my face and narrow. He tucks my hair behind my ear, his thumb trailing along my cheek. "What's this?"

My fingers brush my cheek, and I straighten. Scales bleed along the edge of my hairline and contour my left cheek. Her scales. Our scales.

I've never seen anything like this. No feathers or webbed fingers or wings. No other Marked carries traits of their monsters while in their human forms. My lips curve into a smile. Except for me. Somehow, this is the first time I've ever felt whole. And it's with her—my dragon. Inaara. No more hiding.

"Who I am." Who we are.

Magic grows against the dawn sky. Morning is on the horizon.

Tib's gaze wanders to the sky, too. "We should get you back before your *master* notices you're gone."

Tib ducks out from the crumbling structure that reminds me too much of the ashen debris in Bridgewick. A pang lances against my heart, no longer barricaded in my memory, but the dragonsfire swaths it. I pinch my eyes shut, happy to leave the memory behind.

I tie my hair into a knot at my neck. Graeden won't miss my absence. He told me himself to only find him when I'm ready to unite with my dragon. I just did. My gaze wanders to the gold cuff strapped against my wrist. A smile curls the edges of my lips as I loosen it and drop it against the hard earth. I won't need this anymore. Besides, I don't want to return to Arautteve yet. We have time.

Tugging my sweater over my head, I readjust the fitted camisole beneath it. I draw my sword from its sheath, a quiet peel echoing through the wastelands. Tib raises a brow as I back away from the crumbling structure. I jerk my head, gesturing for Tib to follow.

"You said this is a training court, right?" I ask. My sandals glide over the glass-like ground as though it's water. I pay attention to the way the rock meets my soles, how its silken waves barely impede my movements. It'll take less exertion to fight in Ghora than Badavaru.

I huff. Even if the Seekers train here, they would never gain enough stamina to fight in Badavaru, let alone enough to beat those of us used to fighting in difficult terrain. Figures. Everything about this wasteland is to keep the Seekers in the most vulnerable state possible.

"It is," Tib says. He pulls his war hammer from its place against his back and grips its handle. "Let's take the edge off."

Spinning my arm toward him, I swipe my sword in a wide arc, and Tib leaps back. His lips twist into his crooked smile, a challenge resting in his gaze. I swipe again, thrusting the sword toward his center, but he dodges the blow. Another attack, another sidestep.

Steel screeches as my blade meets his hammer in a chaotic melody. I ease into the movements, my muscles warming and stretching with each swing of my blade.

"Does it get easier?" I ask, breaking up the flow of our lunges and parries. "Entering your own mind prison?"

Tib stumbles, and I take advantage of his distraction. I sweep his legs out from beneath him, and he falls flat on his back. Lunging toward him, I tip my blade's edge against his neck, drawing short a hair's breadth from his flesh.

Tib's chest rises to meet the flat of my blade, but I put no force behind it. Tib releases his hammer, his palms facing the sky by his head. His lips arc into an amused smile. "Mind prison?"

"That's what it feels like. Does it get easier?"

"Not always, but for most people."

I withdraw my sword and retreat a few paces. Tightening my grip around my sword's hilt, I wait for Tib to rise.

"Was it your father?" Tib grabs his weapon and pushes himself to his feet. He already knows, but he asks anyway.

My throat dries. I don't want to speak the words aloud.

Tib understands and steps forward, anchoring his stance. "I saw when Caelum returned from the Enchanted Forest without you." Tib swings his war hammer at his side in controlled rotations. "You may watch it again, but it'll be like observing it as a third party instead of reliving it."

Tib lunges, throwing his hammer with the momentum of his swing into me. I barely dodge the blow, rolling over my shoulder out of his way.

The sky grows as bright as it ever gets in Ghora as sweat soaks my clothes. Our second battle in Badavaru is only hours away. And when the magic stores pulse their strongest at midday, he will fight against the strength of a dragon. Exhaustion rolls through my shoulders, and my eyes droop. I force a hard blink to evade the blur threatening my vision. If I close them and rest, too soon I will face the inevitable.

I don't want to die. But I don't want to destroy him, either.

No, it's better to push through. To cling to these last moments I may have with the only piece of my past I've found.

When we both gasp for air, Tib lifts a hand in surrender. "I think it's time," Tib says. "I don't know about you, but I need at least a few hours' sleep if I'm going to give you hell today."

Anxiety builds in my stomach, and I fear the same thing. Only that he'll be the one beneath my blade and me without the power to stop Inaara from using it.

Inaara will be repressed with the inhibitors, but only barely. When Tib threatens us, her strength will ripple through that arena. I'm sure of it. I may not look like my dragon, but I'll most certainly fight like her.

Tib places his hands on my waist, his shoulders heaving with his labored breaths. He steps forward and draws me toward him. His scent curls around me like cinnamon sticks roasting over the open fires in Bridgewick. Tib presses his forehead against mine, and I nearly wilt into him at the gesture.

Bridgewick's custom for men to bid farewell to their women before heading into war. Tib's hand wraps behind my neck, anchoring me to him. My eyes slip shut, and I inhale the familiar scents of home.

He knows the risks we face today.

"What is this?" A snarl cuts through the reverence of mine and Tib's farewell.

I jerk away from Tib, and dread smothers my calm. Graeden.

CHAPTER THIRTY-THREE

Rage pours over Graeden's features, twisting his expression into something visceral. His eyes flash between Tib and me, lingering where Tib's hand still presses against my waist. Graeden's gaze darkens.

"Release her, Seeker," Graeden spits.

Tib's hand tightens, and the tension thickens the air around us. "Why? So, you can use her?" Tib shakes his head. "Not on my life."

"So be it." Graeden slips a curved sword from its sheath, the steel blade as dark as kohl.

Tib releases his grip and slides a dagger from my waist. He elbows me to the side, both my blade and his war hammer drawn.

The growing friction coats my tongue, bitter and pungent. Leaping between the two men, I hold a hand up to each of them. "What do you think you're doing?"

How did Graeden even find us? My gaze falls to the disassembled cuff lying on the midnight ground. Dread pools in my stomach. I removed the cuff, and Graeden could suddenly track me again. I lick my dry lips.

"I could ask you the same thing," Graeden growls. His gaze flashes to mine, and betrayal is etched within his.

"We're not at battle. This isn't Badavaru."

"These are our enemies," Graeden snarls. He aims his blade toward Tib.

"No," I hiss. "They aren't our enemies. Our enemy sits in the stadium. Our enemy hides behind their magic, forcing the rest of us to play this cruel game for their twisted pleasure."

Graeden's shoulders rise with his controlled rage. His gaze drifts beyond me, and his jaw tightens. He isn't attacking. He's deliberating, plotting. Suddenly, Tib shoves past me, and I stumble from between the two.

Tib's dagger is right against Graeden's neck. "One more move, and I'll slit your throat."

"You see," Graeden barks. "Each Seeker you save is a Fallen you condemn to death."

"Or a human I rescue." Placing my hand on Tib's forearm, I press his arm away from Graeden. I don't know where the words come from—I haven't tried to save any of them, and they aren't all human. But isn't that the truth? We're all the same—Seeker or Fallen. "Why should there be a difference?"

"You of all people know why." Graeden's nostrils flare, and his demeanor grows distant and cold.

I do. Seekers chose to come here. To kill us. Fallen didn't. I didn't.

The moment Tib's blade is no longer at Graeden's neck, Graeden swings his own. I leap out of the way mere inches from his sword's reach.

Tib widens his stance, and Graeden swings again. Steel clashes, splitting the swollen silence.

"Stop!" I shout.

They don't. Graeden advances, and Tib matches his blows. His feet slip over the slick rock, but he holds his balance even as he withdraws from Graeden.

A dark smile crosses Graeden's lips. Taiatum trained or not, Tib doesn't want to fight a master who only has one Fallen left.

"I said stop!" I thrust my own blade between theirs and catch Graeden's next swing.

The momentum reverberates through my arm, and an ache settles into my shoulder. Graeden stumbles forward but catches himself before he falls. His scowl deepens, and he draws a second blade.

Fire fumes through my chest. I tighten my grip on my weapon, but I won't attack him.

Snarling, Graeden bares his teeth. "Now's your chance, Ari. You desire to abandon the Fallen. Go ahead. Prove how much you hate being *owned*."

Embers stir in my stomach, but I smother them. He doesn't mean it. He's baiting me.

When I don't attack, Graeden sweeps his leg low and takes mine out from beneath me. I land gracelessly on my back against the ground's sharp stone.

Graeden's gaze flickers against mine for a heartbeat before he steps over my body toward Tib. "You still have much to learn, Fallen."

In a blur, Tib slams into Graeden. The two sail through the air before crashing in a heap against the stone earth. I pull myself to my feet, a patchwork of bruises already aching over my skin. Tib lunges forward, raising his war hammer against Graeden.

"Don't!" I order.

Graeden throws his blade against Tib's weapon, and the steel locks above their heads.

"This fight is between Graeden and me," I pant.

Rubbing my aching hip, I approach their stalemate. The subtle glint of steel glimmers against Graeden's boot. Throwing knives. Graeden only needs to abandon his weapon and roll to the side for Tib to get three blades in his back.

"This is between us," I huff again. This isn't the first time Graeden and I have fought—though, this is the first time lightning has crackled through his eyes. A growing storm of malevolence and pain.

Their steel hisses as they both shove off each other. Graeden doesn't miss a beat. He pops to his feet, and a throwing blade arcs through the air toward Tib and me. Warmth trickles down my cheek before I feel the bite of his steel. I suck in a sharp breath and stumble back a step. A haze hovers around the edges of my vision.

I touch my fingers to the gash seeping blood down my face. Its thick warmth coats my fingers.

Graeden's expression falls. His gaze traces the blood's trail to my chin, and he looks broken. The trivial scrape has obliterated his rage but done nothing to staunch his betrayal. Graeden lowers his blade. He's done.

Tib roars and lunges, tearing Graeden's sword from his limp grasp. Graeden rounds an arm aimed at Tib's jaw, but Tib gets a blow in first.

"I said don't!" I shout, but it's too late. Their bodies slam into each other like giant boulders, blades abandoned. It's personal.

My gaze skims the horizon, and terror settles in my stomach. Dozens of dirt-stained bodies camouflage against the obsidian, their forms growing ever closer to our small gathering.

Racing to where Graeden and Tib fight with their fists, I hiss. "Stop it! Stop it!"

They ignore me, Graeden aiming a swift knee to Tib's unprotected side and leaping back to his feet. The Seekers creep like shadows themselves, the whites of their eyes reflecting the growing light overhead. Tib finds my dagger against the ground and thrusts it toward Graeden's heart. Graeden catches Tib's wrist and twists, forcing Tib to release the blade.

"We aren't alone!" I grab both of their shoulders and shove them away from each other.

Their attention snaps to the dark shadows where I stare. Tib recovers before Graeden and plows a deft fist into Graeden's cheek. Graeden doesn't have time to respond before he falls. And the Seekers rush us.

Raising my sword, I step back, and Tib angles his body in front of me. But they don't come for me. It all happens so fast. They throw their bodies—both the weak and the strong Seekers—on top of Graeden. He fights, tossing their bodies to the sides with ease.

Sweat gleams on Graeden's brow, and my chest tightens with anxiety. He'd told me his loyalty was to the realm. He'd told me he'd never turn against the trolls. He'd never cross that line even for me. The thought stings. I clench my teeth and bury the feeling.

This is where his loyalty has brought him.

The Seekers will never defeat a trained master, but they're enough of a distraction to lure Graeden's ire away from Tib and me. It's all the distraction I need. I'll do no good facing Graeden while at Tib's side.

"Let's go," I whisper to Tib. "Graeden will be fine, and we have a fight to get to."

Maybe some space before the competition will help him cool down. I follow Tib through the wasteland with only a glance over my shoulder at Graeden. There's a flash of gold in the distance, and then it's gone. I furrow my brow, and my stomach twists. He'll be fine. I just hope he and I will be.

Dragon fire surges through my veins. I try to smother the heat and focus on the wooden portcullis in the distance.

"C'mon, Fallen!" the crowd jeers. "Be a good slave, and spill blood!"

I clench my jaw. They have no idea how much self-control it takes not to launch my sword into their throng.

"She's so thin!" another troll sneers. "My bet is on the Seeker. A quick slice through her throat—"

I drown out the troll's call for my death with my own anger. Inaara shudders beneath my skin.

"Why so worried, slave?" "We own you!" "Give us blood!"

These are the creatures Graeden wants to protect? I glance over my shoulder, but there's no sign of him. My stomach tightens, and I turn back toward the promenade hall. The trolls' cries for carnage grate against me until I'm ready to engulf them all in my dragon's flames. They want blood? A show?

My gaze reaches the crowd, and I raise my steel into the air. The trolls pound their feet against the dusty floor. Their mouths twist with bloodlust, and they scream for the blood to rain.

I should've warned Tib about what he'd face in the arena today. But I didn't.

Our second battle means he'll face a Fallen with the strength of her monster. My monster. A dragon.

My gut wrenches. The trolls' hellish praise fills my ears, but all I can think of is Graeden. I know why he defends them. They're his family. Flames lick the edges of my vision. How I wish I'd done more to protect mine when I had the chance.

A heavy breath fills my lungs. I shouldn't have left Graeden alone with the Seekers. Shifting my weight, I glance over my shoulder again. I need to apologize to Graeden and help him understand. The trolls may be his family, but they aren't mine. Guilt gnaws against my spine. I shove the unwelcome emotion to the darkest corners of my soul.

The place where I let a man and his daughter burn.

Shaking my head, I slip back into the present, bombarded by the trolls' applause. First, I need to finish this. Had I not shown to face Tib in our second battle, the trolls would have scoured the realm for their precious dragon.

Inaara's fire erupts in my belly, molten lava pouring through my veins slow and steady. Her strength courses through my muscles, tightens my joints, eases the bruises from last night's confrontation. Her smile crawls over my lips.

I may fight as a human today, but Inaara is only bound in form not power. May whatever gods exist help Tib.

The trolls barter, trading vials of sparkling fluid up and down their rows. My gaze lingers on the incandescent silver and blue hues that glitter between the trolls' overgrown nails. A heavy stone rolls through my stomach.

The memories they stole from the Seekers. Disgusting, vindictive creatures. Tearing my gaze from their trifles, I focus on the walk toward my portcullis. Tib waits for me behind it.

Strength ripples through my muscles, Inaara begging for release. The trolls already cheer in near hysterics. The cacophony funnels into a chant I can barely understand.

"Dragon! Dragon! Dragon!"

My gaze flits to the prominent pillars towering over the arena. Four of them are nestled along its walls. The inhibitors. Outside the arena, the inhibitors have no power to restrain Inaara.

I brush my fingertips over my bare wrist where I'd worn the cuff. The trolls want a *real* show? I'll give them something real, so they'll never doubt that no one owns me. Ever.

Graeden would tell me to brush it off, the real battle is inside. I'm not so sure anymore, and Graeden isn't here. A flutter erupts in my stomach. This is the first time I'll release Inaara, united with her as one.

"If I let you out, you better come back," I mutter.

Inaara's heat engulfs every part of me. My skin sizzles but doesn't burn; her pressure inflates against my body from the inside. I reach the portcullis and catch a glimpse of Tib waiting at the other end, leaning against his war hammer.

At the last moment, I step up onto the portcullis and throw my body backward through the air. I arch over the ground and before my feet hit the dust, scales rip through my skin. I clamp my jaw against the searing pain of my body shifting forms. Illustrious wings catch me midair, and we soar.

The crowd silences. Their faces are painted with a mix of awe and reverence. Inaara climbs as high as she can before swooping toward the trolls, pulling up her descent inches above their heads. A few duck or throw their hands above their heads, and I can't help but laugh.

When she rises again, they erupt with uncontrollable excitement. *Flaming Nights!*

Inaara's talons snag the hard earth, and I only briefly register she's returning to form as I had warned. I hold my chin high as she returns into my body leaving me fully clothed. A frown smears against my face—I'd expected the trolls to cower with fear.

Not heighten their thrill. Ignoring their praise, I dart toward the creaking portcullis.

Tib wears another bronze helmet. He holds his weapon in a defensive position, but there's a slackness to his posture. As though he doesn't plan to really fight. Placing his steps with caution, Tib closes the distance between us. I leave my weapons sheathed and strut toward him.

Here, in the arena, Tib is just another Seeker. A crest is carved into the front of his girdle unlike any I've ever seen. Could this be a gift from Taiatum? My eyes narrow as I stare at Tib through the tiny slit in his helmet. Would he dematerialize into shadow to kill me? When my blade rests against his neck, would he let me kill him?

Ten feet. The closer we become, the more relaxed Tib's arms grow. When we're within arms distance, Tib has almost released his weapons. I draw my dagger and brush it over the soft flesh beneath his arm. A flesh wound.

Tib gasps, his head cocking to the side, and I imagine his shocked expression beneath his helmet. Spinning to his other side, I carve my dagger through the air.

"You didn't think I would surrender, did you?" My words slip between us on a breath. Words only for our ears.

Tib doesn't respond. Instead, he jerks his elbow up into my chin and throws his sword's hilt into the small of my back. I double over. Pain radiates into my ribs, but my dragon absorbs it within moments leaving behind only a disquieting ache.

Inaara bristles beneath my skin. I don't need her to fight this battle. Her strength burns through my arms, but I rein it in. I don't want to kill him. Tib sweeps toward me, throwing his knee into my core. His bronze bracer swinging through the air toward my face.

I thrust my blade toward his hand, nicking the soft flesh between his thumb and forefinger. Miss. Tib backhands me, and I spin backwards, landing in a heap on the ground. Blood trickles down my cheek and into my mouth. Red speckles my vision. I shake my head to force Inaara's fury away. But my chest rises and falls, steam burning the space behind my nose.

The speckles turn splotchy. I squeeze my eyes shut and shake my head again, but when they reopen everything is bathed in blood. My body raises to its feet, but I don't tell it to. I feel the sword's worn steel beneath my palm, but I don't order it to raise. And Badavaru's heat streams through my hair as Tib's form grows larger, but I never thought about charging him.

I've lost control.

Before Tib can swipe his weapon, I slide parallel against the ground. The sand bites into my skin, but I barely feel it beyond Inaara's rage. Dust sifts into the air and hits the back of my throat. Killing the space between Tib and me, I hook my arm around Tib's thigh and wrap the other around his waist. Arching my back, I lift Tib into the air and throw him into the dirt with me.

Steel clatters as his hammer and my sword slide through the growing dust.

Rage floods my veins, and all Inaara wants is blood. My mouth salivates, and I can't block the thought of Tib's gore coating my tongue. The tang of copper. The warmth of it fresh.

Stop! I order. The words cut through the savagery. *We will not harm him.*

I'm vaguely aware I stepped into this arena to do that very thing, yet I still must try to get us both out of here alive.

Restrain yourself. I command through the gritted teeth of my consciousness.

A powerful urge to defend and protect rushes through my veins. She sees him as a threat. Inaara is trying to protect us. I rein in her fire wherever I can, trying to draw her back.

Inaara rolls my body over its shoulder and grapples with Tib. Blood streaks his helmet and seeps down his arms, but he still stands. Both our weapons have long become obsolete. She can kill him with my bare hands.

We are one! I said, restrain yourself. Her heat is suffocating, but I pull the fiery strands inward. The heat sears my core and blisters my consciousness, but I don't release. I have no idea what I'm doing, but it seems to work.

A cool rush flushes through the flames, and Inaara submits to my commands. My body's movements slow, and our attacks grow tame compared to the ferocity we entered the arena with. The threads of Inaara's ire hitch in my veins, and a wave of respect smothers the rest of her flames. This isn't over, though.

Leaping against the stadium wall, I land on Tib's shoulders, and my dragon disappears. Tib's hand locks around the back of my neck, and he throws me over his head. His body somersaults over mine, and my sword scrapes the earth as he snatches it from where it lay abandoned.

Tib shoves the tip of his sword at my neck and pauses. Sweat trickles down my temples as my vision resets itself, and the crimson veil leeches inward. Sparks catch in my chest— Inaara wants to attack, to defend. Tib's head swivels to the throne where the Troll King sits. The king's elbow rests on his throne's bone-covered arm, his palm shoved into his cheek hiding a bored eye.

The riotous crowd simmers as Tib waits.

"Well," the Troll King booms. "Finish her!"

Before Tib can move, I press my palms against the flat edges of my sword and twist it from his grip. My leg catches him between his in a cheap shot, and Tib crumples. I stand, taking my time to catch my breath and gather my sword. An ache crawls through my body, and I wonder if Inaara doesn't heal it based on principle.

I approach Tib who has pressed himself to his knees. I hope he sees the apology in my eyes. Drawing back, I thrust my sword into Tib's shoulder. Not his heart.

Tib collapses forward into the dirt. It was close enough to his heart that the Troll King will call the round. Tib won't die, though. I'll make sure of it.

CHAPTER THIRTY-FOUR

I UNWRAP THE BLOOD-STAINED cloths from around my fists and duck beneath the portcullis. Drying blood splatters across my forearms. I rub my fingers against it, trying to hide the reality that I stabbed Tib.

But I didn't kill him, I remind myself. Didn't kill him, as if that should be something to be proud of.

The trolls dragged Tib's body from the stadium before his wound had even begun to clot. They'll dump him near the arena's entrance—an omen for the other Seekers to stumble upon when they come to fight for their own wishes.

I'll get to him before the vultures do and clean up his wound.

The Troll King announces our final battle in a few days' time, and the trolls pull themselves from their seats and saunter away from the stadium. No one's eyes fall on me. No one cheers anymore. They couldn't care less who won so long as someone draws blood.

Inaara's anger diffuses, and I relish the calmer breaths filling my lungs.

I scan the promenade hall for Graeden, sure he would still have come to the fight, but aside from me, it's empty. I frown and glare at the path ahead. Something shifts through my chest—a pang I don't understand. Who cares if he's here or not? I don't need him to win my battles.

"Did you hear?" a high-pitched voice trills from one of the lower stadium seats.

My ears perk up, and my gaze wanders to the woman. She grabs onto another troll's shoulder and shakes him.

"What, woman?" The troll man huffs.

"The Seekers found a renowned Trader."

I stop walking.

"They caught him in Ghora."

Ice splinters through my veins. *What?*

Turning on my heel, I sprint towards the troll. The woman curls her lip as I approach and retreats a few steps. The man shifts his stance so he stands in front of the woman, but only barely. He, too, leans far enough away one would think I have the Plague.

"What did you say?" My voice is frantic, and I grip the rail that separates me from them. *Flaming nights, Graeden.*

The trolls' brows scrunch together simultaneously.

"Where in Eida's fury did the Seekers take him?"

The woman scowls, her expression twisted by anger or fear, I can't tell. I don't care.

"I don't know," she spits. "But if I did, I wouldn't tell the likes of you."

Whipping around, the two trolls race up the stairs to exit the stadium. A sour tang crawls up my throat. Graeden didn't get away. The Seekers caught him. They're going to kill him. I bolt back into the arena and through the Seekers' portcullis.

A rush of gratitude slips through my chest. No one saunters near the Seekers' entrance. I don't want to explain to any troll or the Troll King himself what I'm doing in Ghora.

Darkness enshrouds the land like always. A chill weaves around my bare forearms and blankets the skin on my undressed legs. I'm not afraid.

Scanning the shadows, I gather my courage and step farther into Ghora. The lone river's sulfuric edge curls through the air. The pungent scent of their dying and decomposed carrying a subtle note beneath it.

"Tib," I hiss. "Where are you?"

My gaze flits through the shadows as I cling to the wall that separates Ghora from Araurteve. I follow it all the way to where the darkness meets the arena.

"Tib," I hiss again. This time a quiet moan floats through the air.

My gaze flashes to the bend in the arena wall. Tib's shoved against the obsidian cloaked wall where they left him to die. He clutches his arm.

"Tib!" I fall at his side and immediately tug his tunic from his shoulder. "Are you okay?"

"You stabbed me," he mumbles.

Blood seeps from the wound, but it isn't deep. "It's not the first time."

His lips quirk in a strained smile, and an air of ease surrounds him. I wonder if he thought I wouldn't come.

"The Seekers have Graeden." I tear a strip of cloth from Tib's tunic and ball it against his wound. "I must do something. They'll kill him."

"*You* must do nothing." Tib hisses as I put pressure against his shoulder. "You're better off without him. Besides, if they don't kill him, I would have."

"Honestly?" My fingers falter against his bandage for a moment. "You don't even know him."

"I don't need to." Tib's gaze hardens, and he sets his jaw. "Besides, it doesn't matter. There's nothing you can do. Prisoners don't return from where the Seekers have taken him."

Tears brim along my eyes, and shame colors my cheeks. I choke on a sob. Graeden doesn't deserve this.

Silence fills the acrid air around us. I tear another length of fabric from Tib's tunic and busy myself with his shoulder. The fabric is coarse in my fingers as I wrap it around his shoulder and back, tightening it across his chest.

"Where did they take him?" I whisper.

Tib drops his head. "The Seekers are ravenous for blood. If you step in, they'll kill you, too."

I tuck the edge of the fabric into itself and secure Tib's bandage. "I asked where."

Grunting, Tib rolls to his knees and pushes himself to his feet.

"What are you doing?"

"Coming with you."

"No," I say. "You need to rest. You need to give that shoulder time to heal."

Tib flexes his chest and grimaces. "What? And watch you die trying to save a Trader? I didn't come here for you to die."

Blood seeps through Tib's bandage. It's not going to last long.

"I can't protect you and rescue Graeden." I jut my chin toward his shoulder. "Go home."

A pained smile flickers over Tib's lips. "You forget, this is my home."

Tension ripples through the darkness as we both think what neither of us speak. It won't be our home much longer.

"You said you know where they have Graeden," I say. "I'll traipse through every inch of Ghora to find him."

Tib places a wearied hand on my shoulder, but his grip is firm. "That's a fight you don't want to walk into. Only something truly ferocious can save him now."

My gaze drifts to the silhouettes of Ghora's looming mountains. "I think I can handle it."

Tib opens his mouth to respond and then closes it again. His eyes flicker between mine for a moment.

Turning my back on Tib, I make a straight course towards the mountains. If I harbored a Fallen Trader, I'd tuck him away in the farthest reaches of my district. So, that's where I'll look first and work my way back to Arautteve.

Tib doesn't follow. For a moment, I think he'll stay behind where he can heal and be safe. But I know Tib better than that.

"You're going the wrong way," Tib says.

"Then by Eida's depths tell me the right way." My voice raises, and I swallow my growing frustration.

The barest hint of Tib's crooked smile passes his lips, but his gaze is serious, fraught with an intensity I haven't seen in them before.

Tib's gaze wanders from mine, and he rubs the back of his neck. "I'll lead you there," Tib drops his hand, "but I can't help him. If you free your master, you and he can return to the Crossing. I can't. If the Seekers find out I'm helping you, they'll kill me before I ever reach the arena again."

Gravity of the risk Tib takes presses down around us like a thundercloud. I should tell Tib to go back to the abandoned valley. I should push him to hole up safely somewhere. But he's the only one who can help me find Graeden. I can't risk not finding him in time. I won't.

I swallow the lump forming in my throat. "Thank you."

Without a word, Tib turns west and slinks into the shadows. The obsidian shifts beneath our feet, its moaning barely above the whisper of Ghora's wind.

Last time, the Seekers mistook me for one of them. This time there'll be no confusion. One look at my face, and they'll draw their weapons. Heat warms my chest. Both Inaara and I would like to see them try.

My fingers trace the silky scales contouring my cheek. They're a shield, a scar of what Eida has done to me, but they're more than that. They're a reminder of what I'll do to Eida one day. What *we* will do.

Inaara's fire blazes. From here on out, we're in this together.

Darkness thickens around me as day turns to night. My ears perk for the slightest sound of pursuit, and my eyes scan the darkness for any Seekers. I rest my hand on my dagger's hilt. It'd be much easier to soar above this wasteland. Inaara's fire churns in my stomach. She agrees. If the Seekers saw me, though, I'd lose the element of surprise. Inaara may be my only hope of getting Graeden out of here alive.

"Tell me he's going to be all right," I whisper as we traipse between two wide turrets.

Tib peeks over his injured shoulder and grimaces. "They all look at it as revenge, though I don't think they realize the trolls care just as little for the Fallen as the Seekers."

"Revenge?" I ask. "For what? Every Seeker here in Ghora *chose* to be here. None of the Fallen made that choice. Graeden didn't make that choice."

Tib shakes his head and massages his eyes. "Your words will fall on deaf ears here. Many of the Seekers aren't just seeking wishes anymore. They're bloodthirsty."

Bloodthirsty? My chest tightens. "Hurry, Tib."

The wind whistles around us, tugging at my hair as though trying to press me farther from Graeden. The loose obsidian shards shift into slick blankets of midnight stone as we travel deeper into Ghora.

"What was that?" Tib asks, nearly having to shout to be heard above the growing winds. "In the arena? I've never seen you fight like that before."

I cringe, hoping he hadn't noticed. Of course, he did. "It doesn't happen often. I'm sorry, I thought I was in control."

"In control?" Tib asks. "Of what?"

"We all hide monsters within, Tib." I pause. "All of us. Mine is not buried quite so deep anymore."

Tib presses his hand against a stone at his side and leaps over a wide crevasse splitting the trail. I jump over it behind him, my lungs warming with the exertion.

When our feet shuffle over more stable ground, Tib says, "The monster?"

My gaze locks onto my feet as I climb over boulders rooted in place. It's as though someone poured hot tar over the landscape and waited for it to harden. My cheeks burn, and I wrap my arms around my waist.

Inaara warms the unease and guilt. I'm not ashamed of my dragon—she has helped me survive this long, but my shame comes because of my inability to face the troll's malice without agreeing to let them unleash her.

I was weak. Afraid of dying. I gave myself over willingly to the trolls.

"The trolls don't play fair. Anyone who thinks otherwise is a fool," I say. "The monster inside of me is like nothing you're equipped to face. It took everything I had to keep her from killing you today."

"I didn't fight a monster—"

"You did," I interrupt. "She may have looked like me, but you fought my monster. And she would have torn you apart."

Now that Inaara and I are united, and she knows how I feel about killing Tib, I wonder if she'd still feel inclined to do so in the arena. I'm not sure I want to test it.

"What's your monster?" Tib asks.

"What's my monster?" I repeat. Does Tib not fear that there's a terrible creature waiting to kill him?

"Yeah. Are you a troll like the rest of them?"

I shake my head. "If only you could be so lucky. You have to understand, you're the reason I have a monster… Or I thought you were. You fueled her escape, satisfied her appetite. She was unleashed with the anger I centered on you. You were the key to unleashing her."

I slow my steps and listen for a change in Tib's breath. Any sign of his heart pounding or of growing fear. Nothing. He's not afraid.

"She may understand you're a friend," I say, "but when you stand opposite of me in that arena with your sword raised, I don't think it'll matter much to her. Kill or be killed."

"So, I'm essentially walking around with a target on my back?"

"Essentially."

"I won't abandon you. Not again." Tib climbs with more ferocity ahead of me as though to prove his point.

"It's not abandoning. It's survival. If you enter that arena you risk—"

"I would risk everything to be with you again," Tib shouts.

"One of us *will* die in this arena!" Fire surges through my chest. Why won't he listen? Regret flashes through Tib's eyes, and he turns his head from me. He won't listen because he's too busy trying to save me. But I'm unsavable. My determination deflates. I can't be around him right now.

After Caelum sacrificed me to Eida, anger and sorrow had battled within me for nearly a year before settling. Finally, I gave myself over to my anger, but the pain of my sorrow never healed. I've already lost Tib once—or thought I had—and I can't do it again, not if he dies at my hand.

Tib pulls up short and points into the distance. "We have to get to that mountain. The Seekers have him restrained at its peak."

Turning to me, he tenderly wraps a hand around my shoulder. His scent curls around us, and I inhale the warm cinnamon aroma that returns me to the night we were betrothed. My eyes slip closed, and my heart aches.

Home. Tib is home. His slender fingers sweep over my shoulder and move to my neck. My head yearns to lean into his touch. His thumb traces intricate designs on my collarbone, a tingle of excitement trailing his caress. My breath catches, and the ache for what could have been spreads into my lungs.

"Nothing you say will change my mind," Tib whispers.

My eyes slip open. Tib closes the distance between us, and my heart batters into my sternum. I'm sure he can feel its thunderous beating. Warmth coils in my stomach and rises to my cheeks. The air is thick with his sweet scent.

My gaze drops to his lips. In Bridgewick, women were only ever to kiss one man and not until their wedding night. I've imagined for years what Tib's lips would taste like. Sweet like glazed rolls turned over the fire, or fresh and cleansing like the moments following a rainstorm? My lips burn as I stare at his. For so long, I've imagined how one day his lips would be all mine, how it would feel for his lips to press against every inch of my skin. The heat rises in my stomach, and the small distance between us is swallowed up.

Tib brushes my lips with his, soft and light. Heat warms my cheeks, and I want to melt into his arms. But something roots me to the ground. I always imagined our first kiss would be at our wedding surrounded by friends and loved ones, not at the base of a precipice biding our time until one of us dies.

I draw back, breaking the nostalgic energy that hums between us. Instead of lace draping my body and hand-carved beads tied in my hair, I wear Tib's blood under my nails and dragonsfire in my veins. This isn't the same. This isn't home.

Pressing my lips together, I stare at my feet. I wipe the back of my hand over my nose, and a tear rolls down my cheek. Caelum stole everything from Tib and me. We live in a different world—I can't think about love.

Tib's shoulders bow inward, and a muscle in his jaw ticks, his gaze downcast. He takes a steady inhale before forcing his eyes to meet mine. Uncertainty swirls within their cerulean depths. His eyes are touched by sadness and a glint of resignation. Deep down he, too, knows things will never be the same between us.

My gaze roams over Tib. His arms hang heavy at his sides, and exhaustion rolls from him in waves. "We've traveled far enough."

"What do you mean?"

I recognize the haggard lilt to Tib's steps, and the stiffness in his arm. He needs rest. Stars, we all need rest. "I can make the rest of the way on my own."

My gaze lifts to the black sky overhead. Graeden needs my help. I'll rescue him and then, by the Well itself, find an escape out of this nightmare for Tib and me.

"There's a narrow trail on the north side of the cliff." Tib points to where the cliff face rounds to the north. "Watch the winds—they're brutal as you reach the peak."

Tib's shoulders sit lower than normal, and his easy smile is lost within the tension.

"Be safe up there," he says. "You essentially betrayed the man, and I won't be there to protect you from him."

"I don't need protection." Graeden would never hurt me. The pain that had flashed through his gaze when his blade accidentally nicked my cheek is all the confirmation I need.

Tib cocks his head to the side with a shrug as he backs away from me. "People can change after suffering. I'll see you again."

CHAPTER THIRTY-FIVE

I watch Tib head southeast until he disappears into the darkness. My eyes wander back to the precipice ahead of me. It would take at least two more hours to walk the rest of the way. I don't plan to take another step.

Are you ready for this? I ask in my thoughts.

Inaara's heat sparks in my chest and floods through my veins.

I roll my shoulders and close my eyes, trying to move myself as much out of the way for her as possible. *Ready whenever you are.*

Fire blazes through my bones, and their grotesque cracking fills my ears as my body shifts, her full wings unfurling at my sides. Thank the Nether Winds my dragon at least absorbs the pain as it comes. Without hesitation, Inaara launches us into the air. The wind catches beneath her wings, and she soars through Ghora's shadows and closes the distance to the mountain in minutes.

Careful, I warn. *We don't know what waits for us up there.*

Inaara shifts her wings, and our momentum slows. From this height, the whole of Ghora spreads beneath us like a map. I can even see Arautteve's countless temples in the distance. Soon, we're tucked within Ghora's thick, dark clouds. Inaara's wings beat in slow, steady folds as though she swims instead of flies.

Get above the peak, I order.

Wind whips over Inaara's scales as she climbs higher, and I close my eyes imagining the feel of its caress against my skin.

As we near the cliff's edge, the clouds turn wispy, and I realize the peak is more of a small plateau. Inaara circles the mountaintop like a vulture circling her prey.

At least a dozen Seekers are sprinkled across the plateau. They arm themselves with rock fragments and broken obsidian branches. A few of them hold torches.

My gaze flicks from person to person through Inaara's crimson vision. The Seekers are ripe with tension, their weight tipped to the balls of their feet. Some keep their eyes on the cliff's edge, others on the sky. It's like they know I'm coming.

A lump forms in my throat as my eyes settle on Graeden. He kneels at the plateau's edge, his hands bound to an obsidian post buried in the mountaintop only inches from empty space. His body falls limp to the side, his binds stretching against his wrists.

Thin out the perimeter. My eyes dart through the Seekers. *Get rid of at least nine but be careful not to hit Graeden or make the mountain crumble.*

Graeden sits on the plateau's edge, his eyes shut. One wrong move, and he could careen to the base of the mountain.

Inaara tucks her chin and dives. A growl builds in our throat, but I swallow the sensation.

Keep it in, I think.

The burning embers in our throat cool, and Inaara spreads her wings to catch our fall.

Those two, there. I mentally point to two Seekers with their eyes tipped toward the ground.

Inaara swoops toward them and digs her claws into their shoulders. Their heads snap up to stare into our blood-red eyes, and their mouths twist open in silent shrieks. Before a sound spills from their lips, we launch back into the dark mists above. Pebbles crumble from the cliff, and air tears around us.

The other Seekers whip their faces to the sky and jostle around uncertainly.

Release, I say.

Inaara's claws open as though I relaxed our grip myself. Screams tear from the two Seekers' lips as they freefall through the clouds and into the darkness below.

Rescue, I order.

Slipping farther from the plateau, Inaara dives again, swooping beneath the two Seekers. They land against our back with a hard thud. Despite having something to grip beneath their bodies, they don't stop screaming. Only a dozen or so feet from the ground, Inaara bucks her riders and sails back to the plateau.

We won't kill unless we must. Graeden is our priority.

Keeping to the shadows, we reduce the Seekers from over a dozen to four, picking them off a few at a time. In all honesty, what are a few measly stones and torches going to do to a fire-breathing dragon?

The mountain shudders beneath Inaara's weight as she crashes onto its top. The Seekers' expressions drip with fear, and two abandon their posts, bolting down the narrow path. I stare at the two remaining, one on either side of the plateau. They skirt around the edge, and I can feel Inaara's confusion. Who should she attack?

Inaara whips her head back and forth, hissing at the men who circle her. She paws at the ground with a clawed foot snapping at one before jerking toward the other. I watch the men's faces, their fear turning bloodthirsty and vicious.

The man on the farthest corner of the plateau's eyes flicker toward Graeden for just a moment, and he nods.

The other, I shout. *Kill him.*

Inaara whips her head toward the Seeker closest to Graeden and snaps without a second thought. Blood pools between her jaws, and his mangled body slips to the ground. A knife clatters next to Graeden's leg. The Seeker almost killed Graeden.

Launching our heavy body across the small plateau, Inaara snaps her jaws for the last man, but he's already gone. I wonder if he jumped. The mountain shudders again beneath our weight, slabs of rock crumbling to the ground far below.

Shift back before the whole mountain disintegrates.

Pressure suffocates my lungs as Inaara obeys and pulls herself back into my frame. I gasp as my body is returned to me, the air thin and stale this high in the realm. A chill sprinkles over my skin, and I wish I'd brought my wool sweater. Graeden had said when

I united with my monster, she'd stop incinerating my clothes. I'm glad he was right.

"I promise it won't be for long," I whisper.

I race to Graeden's side, lifting a fallen blade from the ground. Graeden's head rests slack against his shoulder. Blood streaks his pale skin, and his hair is soaked with it. I press my hands against his jaw and lift his face to mine, brushing his drenched hair from his cheeks. A deep gash cuts through his temple, and blood coats my fingers. My eyes flit over his body, and I lower his head.

A coarse rope chafes against his wrists, the skin mottled and swollen. I catch a sharp breath as a faint glint of gold peeks out beneath the rope. His cuff is thinner than mine was, but it's the same shape and woven with the same intricate light. He'd had no chance to shift and escape.

Apparently, the other masters don't keep the cuffs as well-guarded as he thought.

My fingers fumble over his tunic, and nausea curls in my stomach. There's more blood. It soaks the cloth below his ribs. *Flaming nights*, he's been stabbed.

"Please don't let it have hit something important." I swallow and force my gaze to Graeden's face.

"Graeden?" I whisper, my voice trembling. "You need to wake up."

I glance over my shoulder and strain to hear if other Seekers approach. Against my dragon, they stand no chance. But alone in my human form, it would just take one Seeker to slit my throat from behind.

Reaching behind Graeden, I swipe the blade through the leather cord of his binds. He slumps forward but doesn't crumble into a heap as I expect.

"Why are you doing this?" The words slip from his lips, colorless and flat.

"You've watched my back," I say. "I'm watching yours."

Graeden tucks a foot beneath his body, and I brace his arm as he stands. He grunts and presses a hand against his abdomen. His eyes flash with pain, and my chest tightens. I'm not sure his agony is because of the stab wound or my betrayal. I'm not sure I want to know.

"Tib is a good man," I say. "Please don't hate me."

Graeden steps forward and curses. His legs give out beneath him. I swoop under his arm and catch him before he falls. His gaze locks on the ground as though ashamed of needing the help, but his weight leans into mine.

"You're injured," I say. My eyes wander to his core where blood seeps through his tunic. "Let me help you."

I reach for his shirt, but Graeden pushes my hands away and gasps. A shudder ripples through his body as he forces himself to stand upright. "It's not deep enough to kill me," he grunts.

"And you thought I was stubborn. At least let me try and get that cuff off." I reach for Graeden's wrist, and he flinches as if I stung him.

Setting his jaw, Graeden offers me his arm. I curl my fingers around the smooth gold. It's warm despite Ghora's chill. I search for the right pattern to unlock the cuff, but I can't figure it out. My gaze flashes to Graeden's quickly staining tunic.

"I can't get it off, and your wound is deep enough to worry," I say. "Keep pressure on it."

I brush the fallen hair from my face, and the warmth of Graeden's blood smears across my forehead. A phoenix doesn't heal their human like a dragon does. Eida has no healers, either.

"There must be something in this cursed realm that can heal your wounds," I say. "A spell or a plant? Or something?"

Despite himself, Graeden's lip twitches. "Like the Jivanna?" He sucks in a withered breath. "They're near impossible to find."

I frown. So, he's told me. Long ago, before Graeden ever found himself in Eida, the trolls squandered them and never bothered to grow more of the healing blossom. My gaze falls to his blood-soaked tunic. I'm not a healer; I don't know how to help Graeden as he did for me before I shifted. But I can find his flower. If nothing else, I can bring him that.

"I will find it, Graeden," I whisper into the wind. "I will scour the fields of Vasa until I have it."

Graeden shakes his head, and his chin sinks deeper toward his chest. His haggard steps pause while he speaks, the words raspy and torn. "Ari, I'll figure it out. No one makes it to Vasa and lives. Not Seeker nor Fallen. Only trolls can cross through unless for the Kelasa."

Stars sparkle above me in my memory. Tib and I did.

"No one shifts into a dragon, either," I say.

Graeden glares at me, pain seeping from his eyes rather than anger. He blames me, and he's right for doing so. If I hadn't slinked off with Tib and removed my cuff, Graeden never would have followed. Inaara's warmth curls through my chest. I don't regret the decision. It's how I connected with Inaara. However, I do wish I'd been more careful.

If Graeden dies from this, his blood is on my hands.

Graeden stumbles again, nearly collapsing at the edge of the cliff. If his blood loss doesn't kill him, the tumble from the narrow pathway will.

"Let me take you home," I say.

Graeden's expression looks like he'd rather do anything but accept help from me, but I'm the only one offering.

Tucking my chin, I whisper. "Shift."

My dragon ripples through my skin and tips a wing to Graeden. I won't let him die from this.

CHAPTER THIRTY-SIX

My feet stick to Vasa's moist soil. The air smells like fresh rain, a morning dew clinging to every branch and leaf. Vasa's rich vibrancy refreshes my soul even as I place careful steps through the forest.

Coral in color. Small blossoms with long, curling filaments. Likely surrounded by dust fairies. Between brazen curses, I'd dragged the descriptions out from Graeden as he stood on his porch fussing over the cuff. He wouldn't even let me help him inside to stitch his wounds.

With nothing else to do, I returned to my temple and drifted into a light sleep. If the Jivanna was as small as Graeden said, I was going to have a hard enough time finding it in daylight let alone in the middle of the night.

I creep through the foliage, lifting heavy fronds from the ground and kneeling on all fours to peer inside decaying logs. The Jivanna should stand out among Vasa's greenery, but it doesn't.

By the time the sky sparkles bright as noon day, my sandals chafe, and my back aches. I sigh. I still have a lot of ground to cover. The Jivanna is small with intricate blossoms no larger than my fingernail. At first, I thought Graeden had been teasing. I stare into the distance. Vasa goes on for miles. I look to the east. More miles. If the Jivanna exists at all, it could be near impossible to find.

"What are you searching for?"

I jump and whip around to face Tib, leaning against a tree with his arm in a tightly strung sling. "What are you doing here?" I hiss. "You don't want to get caught in Vasa."

Tib's smug smile has returned as though our kiss yesterday never happened. His eyes don't lift with his smile as they normally do, though. "You don't, either."

I glare at Tib for a moment. Shaking my head, I slink past him through the vegetation back the direction I'd come from. "The trolls won't kill me." Inaara's wings flare through my back. They can't afford to. "They'd use any excuse to kill you outside Badavaru, though."

Tib ignores me. "You forget, this isn't my first time in Vasa. And you look like you could use some help."

I cross my arms over my chest and raise a brow at him. "And what's your help going to cost me? A week of boasting?"

Tib plants his free hand on his waist, his cocky grin widening. "Maybe. Or maybe this one's on me."

My gaze wanders through the thick trees. The Jivanna could be nestled beneath a single leaf, and I could tiptoe right past it and never know. A second set of eyes would be helpful. My shoulders slacken and I spin to face Tib.

"You have to be careful."

"Always am," he says.

"You're infuriating."

"You love it."

We stare at one another for a moment, and my eyes flick to his lips as I remember his kiss. Any other realm, and I would have relished in that kiss. Instead, my thoughts wander to Graeden.

He'll be fine. I've told myself the same thing for hours. He knows how to stitch and dress a wound, and though he's weak, he's stable.

"What are we searching for?" Tib asks.

"The Jivanna." I rub a hand over my eyes. The past few days of built-up fatigue weigh heavy on my body. My muscles cramp, and I settle myself on the edge of a fallen tree.

I left Graeden early last night. After only a few hours of sleep and grabbing some supplies, I'd made my way straight for Vasa. Though I'd slept, it wasn't well or long enough, and the fatigue tugs at my arms. I'm in desperate need of a day off. With a deep inhale, I repeat everything Graeden told me, which isn't much. When I finish, Tib's brows hang low over his eyes.

"So, we're chasing a myth."

"I hope not." I rub my forehead. "I need a break, though. I've been wandering this forest all morning."

"Would you like to try shadow shifting again?" Tib offers. His cheeks pale, and the color seems to drain further from his face. Despite the sling, his injury's taking more of a toll on him than I expected. "It'll give your body at least an hour to relax. Let your brain do the work for a little bit."

I grimace and glance over my shoulder at nothing. Graeden needs the Jivanna. We shouldn't stop, but I need a break. Rubbing my hands over my eyes, I sink deeper against the trunk. Tib and I, also, need to figure a way out of this realm before it's too late.

Dropping my gaze to the ground, I adjust my posture. A thread of insecurity tugs at my courage. What if watching Father and Atarah die is just as terrible as it was last time? What if I still don't shift? How many times can I swim through my own nightmares unscathed?

I jerk my head in a quick nod. "Will it be the same memory?"

"It could be." Tib quickly carves the Winter rune into the soft earth before offering me his free hand.

I place my hand in his.

"We all carry a lot of darkness. Chances are you'll pass through some others before you relive the pyre." Tib's thumb brushes over the faint scar on my wrist. Graeden's brand. "I want you to use my blood with yours."

My eyes widen, and I frown. "Why?"

"I once met a paired shifter in Taiatum." Tib's fingers fumble with the cloth against his arm as he rolls his sleeve up. "Pair shifters can't turn to shadow without a mate. Their blood needs a little extra strength. We could pour the rest of the troll magic into your blood," Tib glances at my bare arm. "But, if it doesn't work, then we won't have enough to try again. Your blood isn't strong enough to shift into shadow on your own. Perhaps combined with mine, it will be."

A pair. Tib and me. It makes sense, but I'm not sure I'm ready to share all my darkness with anyone. I swallow the thought. "I don't like this. Will you see my memories, too?"

Tib grimaces. "I'm not sure. I've never done this before." Tib's eyes catch mine beneath his furrowed brow. "One way or another, I'm going to see you through this even if it kills me."

Tib lifts his blade with his restricted hand, but his grip is unsteady. Softly, I take the blade from him. "Here, I'll do it."

Tib sinks backward but holds out his uninjured arm. In a single swipe, I draw the blade over Tib's forearm. The blood barely begins to seep from the wound before he sprinkles the ivory powder into it. I clean the blade before carving an identical gash into my own arm.

Once he's added the magic to my blood, we tip our arms above the rune dug into Vasa's soft earth. The blood soaks into the ground. My head swims, and Inaara's fire burns through my veins.

I help Tib tie a strip of fabric around his wound, and he pulls it tight with his teeth. A tingle ripples through my arm as Inaara stitches my skin back together. I tuck my arm against the inside of my knee. Placing his hand in mine, Tib grips onto me tightly. "Find me. I won't let go."

"We leave after a few memories," I say. My brain fogs, and my vision tunnels. "We must find the Jivanna."

I resist disappearing into my mind prison to finish my thought, but it's too late. Tib presses a hand gently against my head and coaxes me to the ground.

Tib's voice floats around me, but I don't hear his words. I stand in my mind's darkness, alone. I know exactly where I am.

The trolls stomp their feet against the stadium seats. My blood pounds in my ears. My blade trembles in my slick grasp. My first Seeker stands less than a dozen paces away. I swallow the lump lodged in my throat. I'm not a killer.

The girl isn't much older than me, her full blonde hair tied at the crown of her head. Her lips twist in a vicious smile. I'm going to die.

Steel clashes. My arms shake beneath the girl's blows. She darts around me faster than the wind, and I barely keep up. Strike. Deflect. Dodge. My heart roars, a drum counting the moments until her blade will cut through my body.

This is nothing like sparring in Bridgewick.

My memory is sparse, muddled.

Each strike of the blade echoes through my head. The pressure of fear building in my chest threatens to suffocate me. Before I realize it, the warm spray of blood splatters across my front.

I killed her. And then I threw up everywhere.

Wiping the bile from my mouth, I glance at the fading straws of memory. The trolls disappear. The blood pooling around my feet vanishes. I sweep my gaze through the darkness.

Tib should be here. Step after step, I wander through the abyss of memory. I can't find him, though. I can't feel him. Panic ripples through my stomach, and my determined stride crumbles. I run.

I race past memory after memory, refusing to relive any of them. I search for Tib, nothing else.

Everything is dark and empty. A shell of a life I can barely remember. Cinnamon weaves through my senses, and my sprint falters. A wisp of light flickers in the darkness.

"Tib," I whisper. I approach his fading form. He's weak, sickly. His eyes droop, his smile a forced, ailed little thing. I press my palm against his temple and am bombarded by his darkness.

I cry out, his memories whipping past me like lightning. I snag glimpses—Tib collapsing against the earth, pain lancing through his chest. Caelum stands in front of him, my name hanging on his lips. Hunger rumbling through Tib's stomach so strong I think it may digest itself. Tib's fatigued hands feeding the sick in Ghora. An eternal dread settling into Tib's stomach. His future lost.

It's too much. I can't follow it. I can't hold on. Removing my hand from Tib, I bolt from the memory.

I lurch from the ground, gasping. Sweat coats my hair, and my chest rises and falls as though I've run the length of Eida. My erratic gaze sweeps around me—lush foliage, soft earth, Tib.

My labored breaths soften, and the tension rolls out of me. I curl over my knees and press my forehead into the damp soil. I'm a dragon warrior. I'm with Tib. I'm not alone.

When my raging heart has softened to an even, tranquil tempo, I tip my head toward Tib. He leans against a tree, a sheen of sweat covering his sallow forehead. A dark undercurrent races along the veins in his arm like the early stages of bruising.

"Are you alright?" I gesture to Tib's arm.

He glances at his hand and then tucks it behind his back. "Fine. Just tired. What did you see?" he says, changing the subject.

I stare at Tib, my words caught in my throat. When I speak, my voice is raspy and sore as though I had screamed outside the memory. "Didn't you see?"

Tib shakes his head and shuts his eyes. "I stayed right here, holding your hand. The rune didn't send me anywhere. If one sacrifices another's blood, they'll enter that person's darkest memories instead of their own. Together, though, our blood should've been enough to help you shift." Tib's chest rises slowly, and he whispers, "What did you see?"

"Nothing." My voice is a hollow, empty sea. A lie. I saw everything.

I shouldn't have pushed away from Tib. If only I'd embraced his darkness, maybe we would have both shifted. We could've left this realm right now. My stomach tightens. Escape right now would mean leaving Graeden to die. I can't do that to him.

Pushing myself from the ground, I scan the forest. I need to find the Jivanna. Now.

Following suit, Tib leans east and sort of rolls his body in that direction. "Let's try this way."

"Any particular reason as to why?" I scan the forest to the north where I'd been headed.

"C'mon, Fallen," Tib teases. "Any direction is better than standing still."

He's right about that. Stepping in line, I weave through the vegetation behind him. We wander through Vasa without speaking, the sky growing brighter with the passing hours.

The richness of the forest swirls around my head, and with every inhale, I'm flooded with its scents. Decaying bark and moist soil. I inhale a slow and steady breath to reach beyond the surface. The newness of life seeding beneath the tree's flaking bark. The scent of moss growing across the surface of a small rock near the river's edge. I even detect a pinch of fear from some hidden animal. A squirrel, maybe. I sniff again. No, a hare. My nose twitches and releases the scents back into the open air. I wonder if I'll ever get used to my dragon's sense of smell.

"You care a lot for him," Tib says, interrupting the feast I'm having with Vasa's forest. "Don't you?"

The scents completely evade me as Graeden's face returns to the forefront of my thoughts. He'd been so relieved when he found me before the Kelasa. So determined to have my back and clean up any trouble that may have followed me. Would it be so odd for me to return the concern?

I nod, but Tib marches in front of me so instead I clear my throat. "I do. He's been my only ally in this hell. Graeden made me strong enough to survive."

Tib weaves between the thick trees ahead, and I wonder if he's heard me. "I'm glad you weren't completely alone in here."

"I was for a while." Memories crash through my mind, untethered. All blades and blood and fear. I've only ever locked away the memory of the pyre; even still, there are others I'll never return to unless forced. "In Haven. But I barely remember that time."

"If he's important to you, then he's important to me."

My steps falter, and I narrow my eyes at Tib's back. I keep my voice low so as not to attract unwanted attention. Not that anyone is nearby. "Why the sudden change of heart?"

Tib slips between two oversized trunks and crawls gingerly over a fallen tree. He glances over his shoulder. "I don't understand it, and I don't trust him. But I do trust you. I have to. As the stars fall from the heavens, your master will live."

Tib pivots and takes our path straight south. He picks up his pace, and his stride lengthens with confidence.

"Where are you going?" I ask.

"To get you your Jivanna."

My jaw drops, and my heart picks up to beat in time with Tib's steps. "You've seen one?"

"It's not easy to get to, but I think I have." Tib jogs toward a tree trunk and plants his foot against its bark, leaping over a towering pile of debris. His leg trembles against the trunk, and he barely clears the obstacle.

I scramble after him, my clambering much more childlike than his graceful, albeit fatigued, leap.

"How many times have you been to Vasa?" I ask.

"As often as we've needed water to drink in Ghora."

Pride rises in my chest. He isn't the carefree, fun boy from Bridgewick anymore. He's a caretaker. A survivor like me. He said *we*. He takes care of the other Seekers, and he's not afraid of the risk to get what he needs.

Tib weaves between the towering trees with ease, as though he's already a part of their shadows. His soft voice rustles the leaves as he speaks of the past, of what could have been. We trek through the dense foliage for what feels like hours and the magic slips from the sky.

As the night wears on, Tib's steps grow more wearied. He stumbles on small stones and trips over exposed roots. He can barely keep his feet beneath him. Pulling up short, Tib leans against a wide tree trunk covered in thick moss.

"We should be getting close," he pants. "The last time I saw the flower you seek, it clung to a cliff face in this area."

Tib slides to the ground. He looks haggard, and he rests his head against the soft trunk. "I just need a moment."

Tib's eyes slip shut, and his breaths soften. He clutches his injured arm, supporting it where his sling has loosened. He's hardly stopped to nurse his injury since yesterday. It's taking a toll on him.

My gaze roves over his face, his expression relaxing. His reminiscent words as we journeyed were everything I've held in my mind lately. His hopes for a future are what I once wished for, but it's an unreachable dream now. Tib has seen me in Eida, fought with me in the arena, but he still wants me as the Bridgewick girl.

I can never be her again.

With a silent farewell, I slip away from Tib while he rests. He said the Jivanna was nearby. I'm going to find it. I can't wait any longer to return it to Graeden.

CHAPTER THIRTY-SEVEN

Picking my way through the trees, I place a mental note of where I left Tib and round a bend. The dense foliage grows sparse, and I wander to a cliff's edge. Tib was right. We were close.

I lean over the edge and stare at the chasm opening beneath me. The mountain plummets into a Ghora-like darkness, thick smoke churning against the rock. The blood rushes to my head, and a strange sense of vertigo tips me off balance.

Leaning backward, I stumble away from the edge and shake my head. I've never been afraid of heights, but a sudden ache builds in my head, and unease tightens in my chest.

I sweep my gaze across the chasm to another cliff face mirroring our own. The smallest fleck of coral peeks out from a stone on the middle of the cliff. I squint but still can't make out the shape.

Inaara? I ask. In a single moment, my vision tunnels, and the smudge of coral forms into the smallest Jivanna bud. A smile curls over my lips.

"We did it," I whisper.

My gaze wanders to the tree cover where Tib rests against the forest's soft earth. He gave this to me. Without him, I would never have found the Jivanna. I consider returning for Tib and waking him, but a part of me doesn't want to shatter his illusion of me. I'm afraid to show him what I've become.

Turning away from the forest, I tiptoe through the brush toward the edge again. "Are you ready?" I whisper. "The Jivanna is straight ahead. Pluck it from the cliff face and return here. Understand?"

Inaara's fire sparks in my chest, and an amicable warmth follows. I savor the heat and sift my consciousness to the farthest corner of my mind.

"It's all yours," I whisper.

Inaara erupts from within, and my body contorts to form hers. Within seconds, we nosedive straight into the chasm, Inaara's draping wings catching our fall and buoying us up toward the sky. She takes a detour on our way to the Jivanna, spiraling into the fog.

Her thrill rises in me. It feels good to be free. She swoops over the churning smoke, the thick clouds rolling over her wings like water. A harsh roar cuts through the air, and ice crackles through our veins.

The beast of Eida.

Up! I order.

Inaara pivots toward the sky, but she isn't fast enough. From the smoke, Eida's beast launches off a ledge, the razor-sharp steel teeth grazing Inaara's wing.

Inaara screeches a high-pitched, deafening cry. The beast howls, drowning Inaara's warning. The breeze against our back sends a chill through our bones.

We slam into the cliff side, our talons scrambling to find a hold among the small outcroppings of rock. Inaara fans her wings wide as a warning against our predator, blood seeping from the wound. The cliff shudders as the monster rams into its base. Once. Twice. Like footsteps crawling up the cliff face. My heart drops. Climbing just like I'd seen the beast do to devour its sacrifice beneath ground.

I swallow hard. We're the sacrifice now. I wish we could see through this smoke!

I swivel my gaze through my dragon's for the beast, but my eye catches on the Jivanna. It grows from beneath a small stone just out of reach. *Quick! The flower!*

Inaara launches herself a dozen feet over the rock wall toward the flower. Her talon closes around the delicate blossom, and pain bolts through our spine. The alphyn slams onto our body, digging its claws deeper into Inaara's back. A terrifying roar tears from our throat as Inaara's talons scramble against the rock, and we tip away from the cliff. The pain ribbons through our body, our muscles spasming. And we fall.

The wind slows our descent, caught against the back of our body, but we spiral out of control. Pain is everywhere, and my lungs—our lungs—struggle for breath. I imagine the monster's thick canines waiting for us beneath the smoke. How long will the pain last before we die?

I know it hurts, I cry. *But fly!*

Inaara obeys, a whimper caught in our throat as she attempts to beat her wings. The pain triples, lancing through the muscles connecting her wings to our body. She releases a long hiss between her teeth. Flipping over so our belly faces the smoke, Inaara swoops her wings again, and the air catches beneath them.

Pain ripples through our shoulders, but Inaara doesn't stop. She flaps her wings, pushes through the pain, and we ascend. The beast roars, but we don't look back. Inaara beats her wings until we reach the opposite cliff and slam into the earth.

I don't have to order Inaara to shift. Her wing is wounded, and gashes pattern her back. As her body absorbs into mine, I stare into the dark chasm beneath us.

As my body returns to me, my leathers chafe the raw wounds streaking my back. I stumble backward and catch myself against a thick tree trunk. My frantic breaths slow, and I press my forehead against the smooth wood.

Already I feel the familiar sting of Inaara stitching up the wounds along my back, but it'll take longer because Inaara was wounded in her form not mine.

"Well, that was new."

I jerk and spin to face Tib. "How long have you been awake?"

"Long enough to know you haven't told me everything." Dark circles frame his eyes, his cheeks slightly sunken beneath the bone. His posture is slack beneath his leathers, and each of his breaths rise in his chest with great effort. It's been a long night for us both. Even still, his eyes fill with wonder.

I sigh. "You might want to sit down."

Tib purses his lips and frowns. "I think I can handle it."

"Dragon shifters are rare." I cinch my weapons belt against my waist. I won't apologize for what I am.

"I know," Tib says. "So, this is your monster?"

I nod.

"What happened out there?"

The tension slips from my shoulders—he doesn't even question her existence. That she's now a part of me. My gaze wanders to the ground at my feet, and a small coral blossom is stamped into the soil. I peel it from the earth and hold it in my palm.

"We got the Jivanna." A wide smile covers my face. "We can save Graeden."

Tib tilts his head sideways and looks at me through narrowed eyes. "You're a dragon," he whispers. "And you still want to save him? You don't need anyone's protection."

I step around Tib, tucking the blossom into my leathers. "I never did. And this isn't about survival anymore."

Though night surrounds us, Tib and I hurry through the forest toward Arautteve. Silence weaves through the trees as we both lean into our own thoughts. I can't pretend to know the first thing Tib thinks, and I'm not sure I want to know.

Our steps crush the lush foliage beneath our feet. We fight again in a few days. After I get this to Graeden, I won't rest until I shift into shadow. Otherwise, when we enter that arena, only one of us will walk back out.

Tib's labored breaths fall into a rhythmic wheezing. My ears prickle, taking in his uneven steps and the soft brush of his hand supported against a tree's bark. A hint of decay wafts through the air.

My eyes burn with the scent, and my nose twitches. It's familiar—a scent I've come across before, but never in Vasa. I can't quite place it. When we return, he needs a salve for his shoulder wound.

Picking up our pace, we race through the forest until Arautteve's stones meet our soles. Tib stays at my back all the way to Graeden's quarters. I draw the blossom from my leathers and finger its delicate stem. Graeden's face flashes against my vision—the betrayal, the rage, the damage I can never undo.

Unlike regular Marked, crammed into their temples, Graeden lives in a stone cottage alone. The wood door is scratched, and the stones are weathered, but it looks sturdy.

Inhaling, I climb the steps to his door. The Jivanna weighs heavy in my hands. I'm not sure Graeden will even accept my help. I wouldn't. My fingers play with the blossom's stem, and I peek over my shoulder. Tib's already slipped into a nearby alley without so much as a reassuring glance in my direction.

I empty my lungs and rap my knuckles against the solid door. My ears strain to hear his footsteps or a shuffle or any tell that he's okay. Instead, I hear nothing.

"Graeden?" I ask through the door.

No answer. Honestly, I didn't expect him to, but that doesn't change the worry pinching my throat. My mouth dries, and I consider knocking again. If he didn't answer the first time, he won't a second.

Grasping the latch, I shove the door open and drop the Jivanna. Graeden kneels on the floor, his gaunt face bowed, and his cuffed arm stretched across his bed. His spare hand holds a cleaver inches away from his wrist, desperate to remove the gold piece.

Every thought in my head disintegrates. Rushing forward, I snatch the cleaver from his grasp and throw the blade into the corner of the room. It clatters with a wild echo.

"What are you doing?"

Graeden rolls off his knees and falls against the legs of his bed. Dried blood smears over his sheets. He clutches his abdomen where a blood-soaked bandage is pressed against his wound. His head drops back against his mattress. He looks much worse than when I left him here.

"What are *you* doing?" he rasps.

"Saving your life." I snatch the Jivanna from the floor and slam the door shut. "I told you I would get it for you and what, you're just going to remove your hand? You'd bleed out faster than you already are."

"It's not like that," Graeden wheezes. His eyes fall onto the cleaver, and he slumps. "If I can't get this cuff off, I can't release my monster."

Monster. He's knocking at death's window, and he's concerned about his monster.

"You're a phoenix. What could your monster do to help?"

Graeden tries to laugh, but grimaces instead when the movement tugs at his wound. "Phoenixes are known for healing."

I narrow my eyes. "Only dragons, wyverns, and hellhounds can heal."

"Ah," Graeden slumps deeper against his bed. "Phoenix's can regenerate. If I can get the cuff off, I can be reborn from its ashes."

"Ashes," I say. "I am *not* burning you alive."

Stepping around Graeden, I toss the blossom onto a small table. "What do I do first?" I grumble.

Graeden's eyes roll toward me. For a moment I think he'll put up a fight, but the blood drains from his cheeks. He sighs. "Strip the blossom from the leaves. Crush them. The extract inside the petals needs to be poured on my tongue."

I tear the soft petals into small pieces and drop them onto a clay plate. Drawing my dagger from my belt, I flip it over and pound the rounded hilt into the torn blossom. My gaze slides to Graeden slouched against the floor. His chest barely rises, and his hand has fallen slack against his wound.

He didn't ask where I found the Jivanna or how. My chest lightens. Maybe he's starting to trust me… or maybe he doesn't care. Shaking the thoughts from my head, I grind the blossom until a fine sheen of juice coats the earthenware.

Before it can absorb into the porous plate, I scrape the petals and juice to the edge. "Open your mouth."

Graeden's eyes flicker open, and his gaze meets mine. It could be his exhaustion or perhaps his resignation to meet his end, but something softens in his eyes. Setting my jaw, I lift the plate to his lips and pour everything into his mouth.

He settles against his bed again and closes his eyes.

"How long will it take?" I ask.

Graeden hums as if he's about to drift off to sleep. "I have no idea."

Silence fills the space between us. Dragging my fingers through my hair, I lean against the opposite wall. I should leave. I'll leave as soon as I see some sign of improvement.

I cross my arms and stare at Graeden. Even in his restless sleep, he looks strong. Capable. My chest aches as my memory returns to the betrayal that had swathed his expression when he'd seen Tib and me. I've never seen him look so hurt. Of course, it was just after our conversation at the pub.

How can he not see the darkness in what the trolls force us to do? The way he looks at them... I wrinkle my nose, and acid crawls up my throat. I'll never see the trolls the way he does.

I glance at the closed door. We need to leave Eida, even if that means leaving Graeden and everyone else behind. This isn't my life. It never will be.

Graeden stirs. "Thank you for rescuing me," he whispers.

The acid in my throat curls over my tongue. I brought Graeden the Jivanna, but this changes nothing. Glancing at my feet, I shove myself away from the wall. I'm the last Fallen Graeden has left. What will he think if I choose to leave him? My stomach twists.

I don't want to hurt Graeden, but we aren't on the same side. We never will be. I don't want to think about it. Too much has happened in the past few days. Stepping quietly around his legs, I whisper a farewell and slip out the door.

My feet land too loudly to my ears as I stumble down his front steps and into the alley. Tib leans against a stone wall a good six paces from me. His frame has grown wiry, and dark veins twist from the corners of his eyes beneath his skin. He keeps his nose tipped to the ground.

"He took it," I whisper. "I think he'll be fine."

Tib doesn't respond. His arms tremble, and he nearly collapses at my side. He curls around himself as though trying to smother whatever is happening to him. His rasping breath is shallow, and sweat has dewed on his skin. I scan the length of him. No obvious injuries. Crouching near his side, the scent of decay barrels into me, and I'm thrown off my feet. I cover my nose with the back of my hand as the odor washes around me. What is that rank smell?

The Plague.

Inaara's answer weighs heavy on my heart. Tib has caught the Plague. Scrambling away from him, I put distance between us.

"Tib! Why didn't you say something?"

Not that he could. The Plague comes on so quickly. But had he, he could have used the Jivanna or at least part of it. He could have rested. We could have figured something out before he got worse. What has he done?

My racing thoughts slow. What have *I* done? I should have noticed the signs. I should have forced him to slow down. I should have looked beyond my own narrowed sight and *seen* him.

Tib's head lulls to one side, and he drags it back up the wall. His rough voice serrates my nerves. "Nothing in this realm can cure the Plague," he rasps. "Might as well die for a cause."

"The king." The words float through my lips before I can stop them. The Plague began within the last five years, only after he took reign of Eida. He started this disease by promoting so much death and carnage. He should fix it.

The rest of my thought tangles in my throat. The Troll King has the power to heal such illness, but he'd never use it on a Seeker… or a Fallen.

A terrible cough seizes Tib, and his shoulders hunch forward. Blood sprays across his dirt-encrusted hands as he wretches. I lean away from the scent of his rotting flesh. He's as good as dead. My eyes burn as pain stabs my heart. Was watching my father and sister burn not enough? Does fate have to destroy every person I care for?

When Tib finishes hacking, he wipes the bloody spittle from his chin and rests his head against the temple wall. "Your master needed the flower." The words sound like a serrated blade dragging up his throat. "I need you in safe hands."

I shift backward. Away from him. Away from death.

Survive. The thought races through my head as it has done thousands of times before.

I can't do this again. I can't watch one more person I love die. My stomach churns with Tib's rotting scent… *Flaming nights,* I'm going to vomit. Spinning on my heel, I race from the alley and disappear around the corner.

I empty the contents of my stomach against the stone wall. We're surrounded by Arautteve's lush florals, but all I can smell is Tib's death. My head swims, and a cold sweat slicks my skin.

Fate is a cruel beast you can never outrun. That doesn't mean I can't try.

Inhaling a withering breath, I force myself to focus. Tib is plagued. A barrage of memories slam into my head, the most recent of my blade cutting through the flesh of that Seeker as we'd made our way to the market.

Pressing the crown of my head into the wall, I understand one thing. I can't kill Tib.

The early morning air dries the sweat on my skin and softens my thundering pulse, but its embrace tightens like a noose. Father. Atarah. My entire life. Now, Tib. I've lost too many. Perhaps it's better I die than everyone around me.

Breathe. It's Inaara who whispers the thought into my mind and curls the warmth through my chest. The strands of heat unlace the binds, and I inhale a full breath.

I open my eyes, and the dark sky glints above me. The clouds rumble overhead.

Tib has the Plague. A tear slips from the corner of my eye, burning a hot trail over my cheek.

What's one more loss? The question settles numbly over my heart. *It's everything.*

Tib's death is on my shoulders. He only traveled to Eida to rescue me. He was only ever exposed to the Plague because of me. He only whittled his lifespan down to days trying to help me.

I might survive this realm, but at what cost? Guilt burrows into my stomach. Bridgewick stole everything from me. Now, it's Eida's turn. No more.

What's the point of surviving if I have nothing to live for?

I don't want to lose Graeden or Tib. My gaze wanders over the trail of faded magic still glinting in the dark sky. Graeden will be fine even if we are not. But Tib…

Inaara's heat flares in my chest, a radiating calm through my panic. She purrs, and my eyes widen.

Immune, she whispers. She's immune to the realm's most ferocious disease. Wiping a hand over my nose, I hope that means I am, too.

I glance toward the alleyway. I know what I must do. For once in my life, I'll look beyond myself and save Tib. Or die trying.

The only cure for the Plague is in the human realm.

He and I are going to escape with or without shifting into shadow.

CHAPTER THIRTY-EIGHT

T IB SLOUCHES AGAINST THE temple wall just as I'd left him. His chest barely rises, his skin so sallow it looks translucent. Purple veins crawl out from the neck of his tunic. He's getting worse with each passing minute, and I'm sure the wound at his shoulder isn't helping.

I drag my fingers through my hair before letting my hand fall onto one of my blades' hilts. My thumb strokes the round pommel, and my chest tightens. There's only one way to save Tib now, and that's in the human realm. I crouch next to him, shoving away the thoughts that scream of the Plague.

I bridge my fingers over my nose and shake my head. If all goes according to my rough plan, we'll be back among our people in a few days. The eagerness I once had has now burned into remorse. I belong in Bridgewick's world no more than a bird belongs in a cage.

Tib gasps at my side, and he sucks in a pained breath through clenched teeth. I may not belong in the human realm anymore, but he does.

"Tib," I whisper. His lashes flutter, but he doesn't acknowledge me. Shaded galaxies of mottled blood crawl over Tib's arm, curling from the wrist and stretching over the back of the hand. I drop to my knees and rock his shoulder. "Wake up."

His eyes slip open, but his gaze is far off.

"I'm getting you out of here. Can you stand?" I ask.

Tib pushes against the ground and rises on unsteady legs. I sling his uninjured arm over my shoulder. The putrid scent of decay sifts around my head, but I refuse to react.

I steer us southeast toward the bathing pools. He isn't safe in Araurteve. Honestly, he isn't safe anywhere anymore. At least the pools are bathed in foliage where he can hide safely. If he keeps his distance, no one else should catch the Plague, and I can figure out what in Eida's fury I'm going to do.

"How much magic do you have left?" I ask.

Tib frowns. "Not much. Enough for one, maybe two spells."

I haven't been able to shift into shadow once. It'd be a waste of what's left of his magic to even try. "I want you to use it."

Tib's body stiffens, but I don't stop lugging him toward the pools.

"What else can you do besides shift into shadow?"

This time when Tib withdraws from me, I let his arm fall from my shoulders. He pulls his blade from his belt and carves another rune into the ground. Instead of the sharp lines of the Winter rune, this one is a series of flowing swirls like a hand extended to greet you.

"The Summer rune," he whispers. "With magicked blood, it gives you strength."

My eyes widen. "Then do it!"

Tib hesitates before unwrapping the cloth pressed against his arm from our earlier sacrifice. He digs his blade into the barely scabbed wound and uses his sling-wrapped arm to sprinkle it with the powder. His blood drips over the rune. Closing his eyes, Tib tips his face to the sky as though waiting for rain. The change is subtle, a swell of pink in his cheeks and the slight straightening of his spine. His breathing becomes less haggard, and the violet veins recede into his hairline. Tib releases a full, cleansing exhale.

My own panic eases as the life slips back into Tib. With heavy arms, he replaces his dagger at his waist.

"It's only temporary. It'll strengthen me for a day at most." Tib glances into his satchel and frowns. "And I only have enough magic left for one more spell, if that."

I barely hear his words as a muddled idea takes form in my head. One more spell is all we'll need. Inaara could free us right here. My gaze whips to the distant light pulsing against the Well's portal. Hope churns through my chest, and I can taste the ease of a summer morning on my tongue. Tib would only need the strength to hold on.

My eyes wander back to Tib, and I frown. Blood still seeps through Tib's sling, and his shoulder slumps. The rune did nothing to heal his wound. With the first beat of Inaara's wing,

Tib would slide right off her back. He doesn't have the strength right now. But if he had a chance for the wound to heal first…

The most I can give him is a few days.

We fight again in two days' time—the third and final battle. The trolls will turn off the inhibitors and release my dragon to full capacity to ensure the battle doesn't move into a fourth round. If Tib can make it that far and allow his shoulder to strengthen, I think I can save him.

"I'll help you to the bathing pools," I say. "But you must stay hidden and away from everyone. Do you understand?"

Tib presses his eyes together tightly before nodding. Despite his renewed strength, he's still exhausted and contagious.

"We fight in two days." My voice wavers, lined with the panic thrumming through my chest. Loss is not new to me, but I can't lose Tib. I won't lose him. "Please make it to the arena. I'm taking you home."

Deep within Ghora lies the only path to the Well of Eida. I peek over my shoulder toward where the Well flashes dimly on the horizon. If Tib wants to live, he'll have to muster the strength to hold onto my dragon's back, and maybe we can force our way back out.

"Take it easy and rest. The morning of our battle, use the Summer rune and what's left of the magic," I say. "All of it."

Tib slumps, his gaze finding his feet.

"Tib," I hiss. "All of it. We're getting out of here. When the time is right, I'll take flight and offer you my wing. You must grab it and hold on for your life."

Tib wets his lips, his brow knotted with thoughts I don't understand.

I plant my hands on his shoulders. "We're leaving Eida. Forever."

Tib purses his lips but nods. "And here I thought I'd come to save you."

I brush my palm against his cheek. "You did save me."

For the past two years, I'd hoped to someday reach my pardon and leave this forsaken realm. Tib has given me a chance to take my life back on my terms.

"Let's go."

I lead Tib toward the bathing pools, though he already knows where they are. He slips into the lush florals surrounding the steaming water, and I turn my back on him.

In three days' time, Tib and I could stand on our home land's soil again. Breathe the dry air. Enjoy the Enchanted Wood's changing color and leave Bridgewick and Eida behind as memories. Or, if we fail, we could stand on a precipice above the beast's gaping maw.

My jaw flexes as I imagine those teeth against my skin. I give my head a hard shake to knock the image away. If we don't try, Tib will still die, and I'll be trapped forever as a Fallen of Eida. No matter how many I kill for them, they'll never let their dragon shifter leave.

I glance at the darkened sky again. Inaara has a better chance of forcing our way through the Well without a passenger. I'd be faster on my own. Stealthier. The idea warms my insides. Inaara knows it, too.

My gaze wanders over my shoulder to where Tib disappeared. He may not make it to the arena anyway. Resignation drenches my concern. I won't leave Tib behind. He came to Eida because of me. I'm responsible for him as much as he's responsible for me.

Magic crackles against the sky as dawn approaches, and I sigh. Some things are worth dying for.

Isla's innocent face untucks itself from the recess of my memory. I didn't stand up for her when she needed it. I won't make that mistake again.

A hollowness settles in my chest as I walk toward my death. Nerves weave through my stomach, and my fingers keep finding my sword's hilt.

I've kept my distance from Tib, from Graeden. The past two days slipped by in a blur, and I didn't bother training. Magic flares against the sky marking a new day. The day.

My nerves are frayed as I head to Badavaru for the last time. By the Well itself, I hope this works. I hope Tib has enough magic to give him the strength he needs. I hope Inaara can penetrate the magic in the Well. I hope I don't kill us both…

As I approach the arena, the crowded streets thicken, and the air grows ripe with body odor.

I don't try to hide from wandering eyes. In fact, I saunter toward the promenade hall. Today is my final battle for Eida—nothing anyone can do can stop me now. Inaara's fire ripples through my muscles with excitement. She's going to be free soon. I haven't decided what role she'll play in the human realm, but I won't keep her prisoner there.

Turning a corner, I skid to a stop. Graeden leans against the portcullis' entrance. His cheeks are flushed, and his brows hang low over his eyes.

I stand my ground, locking my gaze onto Graeden's angry stare. His ire crumbles, widening the curtain to his hurt and pain. Inhaling to calm Inaara's sudden fire, I stalk toward Graeden. I've done nothing wrong.

He remains silent as I approach, so I pass him, careful to avoid knocking into his shoulder.

"How did you do it?" he murmurs. His voice breaks, and his posture stoops. "How did you find a Jivanna?"

I slow my stride. Glancing over my shoulder, I say, "I didn't. Tib did."

"Ari." Graeden's voice is flat and monotone. "What you are doing with that Seeker is wrong. It's only a matter of time—"

"Don't talk to me about what's right and wrong," I snap. "You have no idea what's happening."

Graeden's brows sharpen. "I know more than you think. I know the other day was not the first time you've snuck off to be with him. I know he's dying. And I am not the only one who has his eyes on you."

"Is that a threat?" My own anger breaches, and hurt bleeds through its cracks.

"A warning." Graeden closes the distance between us with a single step. Woodsmoke with a hint of vanilla surrounds me, and my traitorous heart beats wildly. Graeden tilts his head down, the tip of his nose almost brushing my forehead. "As your master, I must warn you. Whatever you are doing here today, be done with it. Abandon whatever it is you are planning. It will only bring you pain."

An ache splinters through my heart, and its furious pattering drops into heavy thuds. "Don't worry, it won't be long before you can forget your duty to me altogether."

Sweeping past Graeden, I dart into the promenade hall. The sooner the battle begins, the sooner I can leave this place and everyone in it behind. I had thought there may be something more between Graeden and me—something beyond his ownership over a slave. I thought maybe a bud of friendship had sparked. And maybe that bud would one day blossom.

I'm a fool.

No matter what my master wishes, there's nothing he can do to stop me now. Turning my back on Graeden, I face the arena. There's nothing left for him and me here. There never was. And I don't belong in Eida—neither does Tib. I need to return him to the human realm so he can heal from the Plague.

I'm ready for this fight.

Energy ripples through the promenade hall, but I don't register the cheers and cacophony falling from the stands. I wait near the portcullis for the Troll King to call his Fallen forward. I bounce on the balls of my toes trying not to act too eager. The crowd silences, and my ears strain to hear the Troll King's grating voice.

"Seeker, enter," he snarls. Chains grind against wood as Tib's portcullis raises.

He shuffles into the stadium, his steps light and cautious. His arms are free from the mulberry-streaked veins, and his skin is only a tint paler than normal. He must have used the rest of the magic. I hope it's enough to get him through the next hour. My hands tremble, and I grip my sword to steady them.

I wet my lips, and an empty feeling grows in my stomach. Any minute now…

The crowd grows wild, their bloodthirsty jeers filling the air. I glance around to see why they cheer—my dragon hasn't been unleashed yet—and my blood runs cold. From the southeast end of the stadium, a lion slinks into view. Its tail whips through the air, and two large talons scrape at the hard earth where its front legs should be. Great wings unfold at its side. A gryphon. Another Fallen. Not me.

Tib draws his sword. His fingers grip and regrip the weapon's hilt. He isn't prepared for this.

Spinning on my heel, I race from the promenade hall around the colosseum's base. There's got to be a set of stairs somewhere—how else would the trolls get to their seats looking down on us inside? But not any set will do. I lock my eyes on the east side of the stadium where the Troll King's throne sits. I need stairs that lead to him.

And then I see it, a polished set of stone steps spiraling upward. I've never considered climbing into the colosseum with the trolls. Even still, my gait doesn't slow. Any monster would be terrifying to face in the arena, but a gryphon? On the brink of death, Tib must fight one of the most fearsome creatures. With the strength of a lion, one snap of its beak, and Tib is dead.

A heavy hand lands on my shoulder, jerking me away from the stairs.

"Ari, I warned you," Graeden says. "I won't let you throw your life away."

"You!" Anger flares through my chest. Graeden's hand tightens around my shoulder, and his spare hand restrains my free arm. "How could you?"

"You must listen," Graeden says. His voice is soft, guarded, but tension braids beneath his feigned control.

Inaara's fire burns through my veins, consuming all rational thought. I don't care what Graeden has to say. He has ruined everything and risked Tib's life. I swing a fist at his jaw, and Graeden blocks the blow easily. Releasing my shoulder, he catches my next swing in his fist. He pushes me toward the side of the colosseum paces away from the staircase.

My back knocks against the aged stone, and my breath expels in a huff. Our chests rise against each other's with furious breaths. Graeden's ferocity splinters through his eyes as they move between mine. My anger smolders as I hold my glare.

Graeden's grip softens around my wrists, energy buzzing between our skin. Suddenly I'm very aware of his thumbs' slightest caress against my skin, the way his lips curve in perfect form, the rich amber swirling like melted chocolate in his eyes.

Graeden leans in, his temple brushing mine. "The trolls plan to kill you. They already know of you and your Seeker." Graeden pauses, the energy between us electrifying, but I can't pull away. "There is no place in Eida for the Fallen to pity the Seekers. We cannot lose you. Please stop fighting for your past."

My eyes flutter shut as his words sink in. How natural it would be to lean into Graeden's arms and walk away, to leave Tib to the fate he came to Eida to find. But it isn't that easy. I can't abandon Tib. I can't let him die when I could do something to save him.

I shake Graeden's hands from mine and push him away from me. He steps back, his brows pinching as though hoping I'll change my mind. I shake my head and duck toward the stairs.

"I'm not fighting for my past," I say over my shoulder. "I'm fighting for a future where I don't have to kill."

Graeden lunges. I thrust my knee up toward my chest and twist my body to the side. My knee collides with Graeden's ribs, and he spins into Badavaru's dust, landing with a thud. He climbs to his feet, but I'm already sprinting up the stairs.

On the highest level, the Troll King perches on top of his throne, overlooking his Fallen. His seat is adorned with the bones of his victims. Skulls line his arm rests, and a large set of ribs flare across the throne's back. Another set of steps have been carved into the colosseum's stone itself, descending toward the arena. Where the steps stop, the platform drops into a cliff. The arena spreads far below.

My gaze falls onto Tib as he swings his war hammer through the air toward the creature. The move is sloppy and all over the place. The animal takes flight and dives toward Tib. Its talons snatch the straps on Tib's back where his weapon usually resides, and the gryphon drags him into the air. Tib hangs limp in its talons.

He's going to die.

I've got to get in that arena and get close enough to Tib. That's exactly what I'm going to do.

"Fallen!" The Troll King's voice creeps over my skin, and a shiver runs down my spine. The last time I stood this close to the brute, he ordered my lashings. "Get back where you belong."

Sweat coats my palms, and I tighten my hands into fists.

"How could you take this from me?" I growl at the Troll King. "He's mine to kill!"

The Troll King's eyes flash, and he rises, his thick feet thudding against his throne's footstool. He lowers himself from the altar. His steps are thoughtful, precise, and with each step, I grow anxious.

"You dare question me?" he snarls.

I swallow the tremble rising in my throat. "Not you. I question who put you up to this. Never in Eida's history has the Troll King refused his Fallen to finish her Seeker."

"You've had your chance twice, Fallen," the Troll King hisses. "You would have us let you fail again? Your monster is wasted on you. Return to your hovel while I still have the compassion to allow you to."

My nostril's flare, and Inaara's fire burns through my lungs. Her wings beg to release beneath my shoulder blades, and her fire scorches my throat. I bite back the heat. My attention falls to the arena. Tib is on his feet again, but his weapon hangs low in his grasp. He's fatiguing fast. The gryphon swipes a studded tail toward Tib, and it smacks into his war hammer, sending the weapon into the stadium seats in a shower of splintered wood and steel.

"While you're at it, Fallen," the Troll King says as he saunters back onto his skull-encrusted throne. "Stop by your master's house. Eight lashes might help you remember your place." His eyes gleam wickedly, and my back stings from the memory alone of those splintered cords.

My resolve is set.

I retreat from the Troll King, and my dragon's fire surges through my veins. My steps are confident as I put more distance between him and myself. The colosseum's polished stone is slick beneath my sandals, its edge curving down toward the arena.

That gryphon is all yours, I whisper.

Heat incinerates my body, and I tumble backward from the Troll King's platform and into the arena.

CHAPTER THIRTY-NINE

Badavaru's stale heat whips through my hair as I fall, but nothing is as hot as dragon's fire. Inaara's illustrious wings ripple out to the sides, and she catches the air. Her wide jaw opens, and a ferocious roar tears from her belly and crashes through the stadium.

The crowd's cheers lose their luster, and heads turn toward us with confusion. The gryphon stands on all fours in front of Tib, screeching as it lunges and swipes a talon across his arm. The poor man has no weapons and no defenses, and yet the gryphon toys with its kill.

Inaara targets the gryphon and plows into the monster's side. The world spins as we barrel across the hard ground in a heap of scales and feathers. The gryphon screeches and pecks at our claws. Its beak barely pinches through our thick armor.

Good, I think. *Now it knows we're here.*

Inaara retreats from the gryphon having drawn its attention. Gryphons are powerful, but they're drawn to that same power. They're drawn to fierce monsters like us.

Bring it on.

The gryphon surges toward us, its great feathered wings cutting through the air like a blade. Inaara roars again, a last warning before she'll need all her breath to win this fight. No, not win it. Get Tib out of it.

Remember why we're here. The thought is directed at my dragon, but it's more for me.

Inaara gnashes her teeth as the gryphon swoops into range, but the gryphon is much smaller than us and darts beneath our wing. We swivel, the ground thundering beneath our heavy footfalls, and the gryphon keeps to our back. Our tail whips back and forth, and the gryphon weaves around it and climbs the ascent up our spine.

It screeches again before its sharp talons latch onto one of Inaara's spikes. The gryphon flaps its wings and tears at the spike. Pain ripples through our back, and our vision hazes. A roar rumbles in Inaara's throat as she tucks her wings and rolls. The gryphon doesn't let go.

Instead, the beast hurtles in the opposite direction, flapping its wings with long, hard strokes. The gryphon tears at the spike just before being crushed beneath our weight, and a grotesque sound rips through the air. Agonizing pain lances through our body as the gryphon rips out the spike. When it does, Inaara roars an agonized, bone-grating cry.

The gryphon retreats and Inaara's fire surges through our throat. Her anger writhes with the heat. I center my consciousness inside her until the battle is only a flicker of time outside of myself. I hear the faint roar of Inaara's ire, feel the subtle movements of her charging the gryphon and the fresh limp that accompanies her gait. I ignore it all and focus on her body. Our body.

She can heal me, and I her. A flutter stirs the shadows around me. I've never tried before, and I'm not sure where to start. With caution, I sift through the darkness and seek out the pain. My mind swims through her body with no light, only thought. The darkness rivals Eida's beast's lair until a flame catches the darkness and shreds it. The light of our pain.

It's rather beautiful, cutting through the darkness as it does. Pain-filled light. It flickers—so small, so simple yet with so much strength. I imagine placing my hands on either side of the flame and absorbing it into myself. With the thought, the light fades until I'm left alone in the darkness again.

Returning my consciousness to Inaara's, I flinch as we attack the gryphon again. Tib stumbles against the arena's wall. The dark veins frame his face. He folds in half and wretches blood over the sandy ground.

"Get Tib," I order.

Inaara hesitates for a fraction of a second too long.

"Get him!"

We turn our back on the gryphon and soar to where Tib has all but collapsed. Please, please have the strength to hold on. Inaara crashes into the ground spraying the fine sand over the crowd and tips her wing to Tib.

He races toward us without hesitation. His feet slip against our scales, but Inaara compensates for his lack of strength and lifts her wing until he grips the spikes along our back. Pushing off from the ground, we launch into the air and rise higher and higher into the sky.

The trolls shout beneath us. "The dragon! It's taking the prisoner!" "Turn on the inhibitors!" "Shoot it down!"

I ignore them and focus on guiding Inaara to the Well of Eida. We can't see the portal from inside the arena, so I draw on my memory. Light swirls in a flat, two-dimensional disc. Violet morphs into azure waves in my mind as it had done when I'd traveled through the Well two years ago. Inaara's wings beat through the air in a rhythmic wave, and adrenaline courses through my body. We could do this. For once, I could save someone's life instead of taking it. My pulse races with the thought.

And then pain. Everywhere.

I gasp as Inaara's flight falters. Another stab of pain crackles through my side, it cuts through her wing and spasms through our entire body. Inaara's eyes roll back, and her wings fall limp. Tib's grip slips from our back, and he free falls with us.

A bolt of energy snaps through our body, and Inaara shifts her weight and turns. She catches Tib against her belly and, with her fading strength, braces him between her arms.

Thank you.

We plummet through the air, and a fading thought worries about what will come next. Our body crashes into the arena, catapulting dirt around us like a meteor, and we lie still.

I don't want to die.

The thought slips through my head. It's mine. All mine. My ears ring. I blink, and my vision has shifted from my dragon's red veil to my own. Lifting my head, a stabbing pressure swells behind my eyes. Everything is hazy, even the two arrows protruding from my abdomen, blood dribbling down my olive skin and soaking the clothes hanging over my body.

How? The question settles on my tongue for a spare second before I taste it in the air and feel it pulse through my blood: Magic. The arrows were laced with magic. That's the only way they could bring us down. My hands tremble for a moment as I consider pulling them out, but I can't. My head falls back against the earth.

Inaara? I search for her in my consciousness, but she has disappeared, leaving me to face the pain of death alone and at full force.

This can't be how it ends. Trolls rush from the stadium until they surround Tib and me. Tib's on his feet in a heartbeat, a sword in his hand. He shields me from the growing horde, but I fear it's too late.

"Nobody touch her!" Graeden bursts from the crowd and raises his blade against Tib. "She belongs to me."

Blades crash, and the clang pierces through my aching head. I clamp my teeth together. A haze settles over my vision, blurring Graeden and Tib's battle, their weapons locked in front of their chests. I catch the barest of words. A whisper. A breath.

"Can you heal her?" A vein protrudes from Graeden's neck, and his worried gaze falls on me.

Why doesn't he help? The thought flickers through my head uninvited. Even through the haze, I already know. Graeden's lack of concern for my injuries is the only thing keeping the throng from falling upon me.

The Troll King cuts a path through the crowd. He thrusts a wart-covered hand toward Tib, and Graeden slinks to the edges of the crowd. I blink, and my consciousness wavers. The copper tang of blood touches my tongue, and its metallic scent curls through my nose.

I force my eyelashes open.

A small rune is carved into the earth near my arm. One I have yet to see.

Tib smashes into the ground at my side. Blood pours over his face from a deep gash along his forehead, and the Plague's violet poison darkens along the back of his neck. Even still, he leaps back to his feet. I glance at the crowd. They roar and push, but none enter the fight. I wonder if they can't. My gaze falls to the rune again.

I inhale softly, and pain spiderwebs through my entire body.

Tib lunges toward the Troll King. My eyes slip closed again, and the world darkens. Steel scrapes against steel. A breath. Clash.

Open, I command my eyes. And they roll open, albeit to see multiple Tib's fighting several troll kings. I grit my teeth against the nausea that rolls through my stomach and splinters against my head. Vomit burns the back of my throat. The Troll King thrusts his hand toward Tib again, and magic launches through the air. Tib rolls beneath it. My head swims, and when my vision clears, Tib's sword is gone.

Tib retreats from the Troll King. A sword is raised. My eyes flutter closed.

Open! I force them open with dying embers. My fight is running out. *I'm sorry, Father. Sister. Mother.*

The Troll King swipes his blade toward Tib's chest, and Tib disappears. Shadow deflects the strike, and Tib shifts back to his human form and lands near the edges of the crowd next to Graeden, his fist planted against the dirt. My quavering gaze falls from Tib to a shimmer of light slipping from Graeden's grasp into Tib's.

A dagger. Tib grips the hilt.

My head lolls upward, and my breath hitches. Suddenly, Tib is at my side.

He loosens the pouch near his elbow. I thought he'd used all his magic. Tib kneels next to the rune and swipes his palm over his bloodied face. He presses the gleaming blood in his hand against his open satchel.

My eyes slip closed. When I reopen them, a glittering black fog floats around his fingers like his own personal storm cloud. Tib whips his wrist toward the Troll King, propelling the magic forward.

Midair, the glittering dust flickers, and a small crystal blade cuts through the air in its place. It plunges into the Troll King's shoulder. He screams, his face contorting with waves of fury. But another scream drowns his out, high-pitched and filled with terror.

My eyes loll toward the ever-growing horde in time to catch a tangled mass of dull, rose-colored hair. Isla slams against the thick mass of trolls, her face contorted with rage. She, too, has come to finish me off.

My vision blurs, and I squeeze my eyes shut to center my mind. When I reopen them, another crystal dagger plunges deep into the Troll King's chest.

He bares his decaying teeth, and his growl rips into the air. Tib drops to his knees near my side. Sweat drenches his leathers, and the purple veins have receded a bit. He holds Graeden's sleek, curved dagger.

The ground rumbles with the Troll King's thundering footfalls. He runs, but it's as though he's trapped in time. My head rolls to meet Tib's eyes as the world slows in my fading vision. Shallow breaths crackle against my lungs.

Tib wraps my fingers around the dagger's short hilt. We're both dying, cleaving to any hope when there's none. Tib's expression softens, and he gently brushes the hair from my face.

"Do you trust me?" he whispers.

The Troll King's expression recoils into a snarl, his belt gleaming with over a dozen weapons. The distance between him and us is so small. In a moment, we'll cease to exist.

I can't speak, and the world is darkening, but I offer Tib what I hope is a nod. Tib presses the dagger deeper into my slack grip.

"I made you a promise."

The Troll King rushes Tib, a rapier in one hand and a short sword in the other. He arches his arm backward aiming for Tib's head. As the Troll King bears down on him, Tib grabs my hand wrapped around the dagger and thrusts it into the Troll

King's chest. Tib twists the blade and forces it deeper, the blade puncturing the Troll King's heart.

CHAPTER FORTY

The Troll King's breath catches, and he stumbles off our blade. The life bleeds from his face until his entire form collapses to the earth in a heap.

Silence bears down in the arena—no cheering, no laughter. The usual celebration of one's death within these walls has turned to ash. If I must die here in Eida, I'm glad I'm taking the Troll King with me. My lashes flutter, begging for relief, but I can't give up so easily.

Graeden warned me. He told me I'd be killed. He had tried to save me, but I wouldn't listen and now...

A faint glow seeps from the Troll King's pale green skin. A growl rumbles in my belly, but it falls from my lips as a whimper. By the Well itself, the Troll King better not be taken to a heaven.

The glow hovers above his still form, every hue of this realm gravitating around him. His magic. It pours from his skin in streams, constantly swirling, gathering, strengthening. When all the light has left his body, the magic slithers across the ground toward me.

I'd back away if I could move. Instead, I'm prisoner once more to the Troll King's final kill. The magic travels above my slack arm, climbing toward my shoulder. It rolls over my collarbone and disappears into my chest, straight into my heart.

White hot pain bolts through my spine, and I gasp. It trickles from the bruises on my cheeks and pours from the puncture wounds in my stomach. But even more so, every pain I've felt since arriving in Eida is drawn from my cells and gathers in my core.

I clench my teeth as it slices through my body like a thousand knives. Pressure swells in my stomach, the magic churning at full heat. A scream builds in the back of my throat, and when I think I can't hold it in, all the pain evaporates. Just like that.

My body collapses against the earth, and I gasp. My skin is damp with sweat. Rolling to my side, I press my palms in the dirt. My fatigued muscles tremble, but I force myself to my feet.

The arrows clatter to the ground, and my bloody clothes hang over my body. I stretch my fingers, feeling the pull of muscle over bone, and close my hands into fists. How in Eida's depths am I alive? A subtle glow pulses against my bare stomach.

My gaze flickers to Tib. Blood streaks his face and drips off his chin. The Plague courses through his veins, a mulberry tinge hugging his skin. The Troll King's corpse lies in a puddle of blood at my feet.

I'm alive. Nausea rolls through my stomach, and dread fills my heart. I'm alive because he's dead. Because I killed him. The Troll King's power now flows through my veins.

Stepping toward Tib, I rest my hand against his head wound. Blood seeps between my fingers, hot and sticky. I have no idea what I'm doing, but there's no better way to find out if I'm right.

"Heal," I whisper.

The word lingers on my tongue, and my eyes skim over every facet of Tib's face. A tingle brushes through my chest, and my dread seeps in. I imagine the Jivanna flower against Graeden's lips. My thoughts recall the searing pain of Inaara healing my lashes.

"Heal," I whisper again. This time, light flares beneath my palm. It's hazy at first but it grows until it's blinding.

Tib shuts his eyes, his face swallowed in a grimace. I don't dare close mine. As quickly as it had flared, the magic fades. Tib blinks. His skin is whole, without even a scar.

I lower my hand, and a heaviness sweeps through my body. I step back. The dark circles beneath Tib's eyes, the veins crawling over his body, the bruises and gashes are gone. All of it.

"You're healed." My mouth dries, and I swallow thickly against it. I stare at my hands where Tib's blood has already begun to crack.

My gaze lifts to the frozen crowd. The trolls' expressions soften—some gasp and cover their mouths while others wear amused smiles. Regardless of their expressions, every one of them falls to their knee and bows.

Only one stands: Isla, her glare skewering through me like her own kind of weapon.

"You are Eida's Queen." Graeden rises from the crowd. His expression is painted in a myriad of colors, and I can't tell what he's thinking. He stifles a smile tugging at the corner of his lips, and though he forces them together, his eyes lift with pride. "You have been healed with his power—*your* power."

A tremor rolls through my stiff arms, and my gaze darts through the crowd. I lift my hands in defense and retreat like a trapped animal from the center of their attention. Tib's brow knits together, and his smile falters. The gathering of trolls at my back parts as I approach.

Thoughts surge through my mind, but I can't grasp onto any of them. Only three words penetrate the haze:

Alive. Queen. Trapped.

The queen of Eida cannot leave her people. Ever. I shake my head trying to clear the fog, but those three words circle my brain, and my pulse quickens. I may not belong in the human realm, but I don't belong here either. I murdered the Troll King and usurped his throne. This isn't what I wanted. What little hope I had of a future is gone. Obliterated.

Turning away from Tib and Graeden, I shove through the growing crowd. Heads follow me as I race through the portcullis and into the promenade hall. I don't stop to see what they do.

My feet slap against Badavaru's packed dirt. Instead of racing to Arautteve, I turn southeast and head straight toward Vasa. I don't stop until I've buried myself beneath my stars. Hours pass as I sit alone in the darkness trying to make sense of what's happened. How did it come to this?

I know how. Tib. I let him into my head with his stories of hope and ideas of life being more than survival. But in the end, I'll forever be a slave to this realm for that very reason: survival. But what's the point? Survive to what? To see more humans murder one another? To punish those who don't fall into line? To feed Eida's beast?

I would never allow such barbarity under my rule. The panic thrumming through my chest dulls. Graeden said that this realm was once a respite, a haven for the Starfallen rather than a people bathed in blood. I stare into the shadows. Maybe it could be that again.

A sour tang coats my tongue with the thoughts. The trolls would never allow it. They may have bowed in the moment, but they'll never serve a Fallen. Besides, I'd rather be dead than reign over the trolls who stole everything from me. To be their queen and protector.

An ember warms in my chest as though spreading comfort over my hopelessness. My chest collapses with relief.

"There you are," I whisper. "I thought I'd lost you."

A soft purr vibrates against my spine as more warmth seeps into my bones. I imagine Inaara curling up inside me, tucking her snout beneath her tail.

"Are you injured?" I ask.

The warmth continues to spread without unease. She's fine—or at least she will be. So long as we both are alive, we can heal each other. My gaze drops to my hands where Badavaru's orange dust clings to the lines on my palm. Magic had seeped from these hands. They had healed Tib. I wonder how it might heal Inaara and me.

A twig snaps in the darkness, and my attention jerks toward the tunnel's entrance. I'm not sure what I fear. I'm queen, right? I should be able to travel anywhere, do anything. Yet my palms sweat, and I finger the hilt of my blade.

"Are you in here?" Tib's voice cuts through the darkness. Releasing my blade, I slump against the leafy wall and frown. Graeden wouldn't have come even if he knew of this place.

"Yes," I croak. I clear my throat as Tib kneels at my side. I keep my gaze locked on the stars, afraid if Tib looks into my eyes he'll see the fear I'm trying so hard to hide.

Tib says nothing, though. He's content to sit by my side in the darkness for as long as I need.

Queen. It's such an unfathomable, unwanted notion. I just wanted to get out of here, save Tib's life… My breath catches. Did he know? My life was tied to his blade, the steel that bled out the Troll King's heart. Did Tib know he was shackling me to this realm?

Shifting my weight, I put distance between the two of us. I whisper so he won't hear my voice tremble. "I don't want to be queen."

A heavy silence fills the space I've made between our bodies. The silhouette of his chest rises in the starlight. One breath. Two. When he speaks, remorse rolls through his tone. "I'm sorry."

Sorry. So, he did know. "Why did you do it?" I ask. "Now I can never leave the troll realm."

"I know. It was the only way I could think to save your life if the escape went bad." Tib slips his hand into mine, and I flinch.

I risked everything to save Tib's life and return us to the human realm. I knew the cost and was willing to pay it for once. But Tib stole that from me, and instead he imprisoned me in Eida in a state where no pardon can release me, and no escape will save me.

I survived beyond my fate. My eyes slip closed, and I recoil farther from Tib. I understand he did it to save me, but this wasn't a price I had agreed to pay.

"Tib, you're free." I tip my chin to the stars and trace the design I'll never see in my own realm again.

Tension ripples between the dark space. "I'm sorry, my Queen," Tib says quietly. "I have neither claimed my wish nor killed my Fallen so until then, I'm a servant to the throne of Eida."

"There is no out for me," I growl. Shutting my eyes, I control the words roiling at the back of my throat. "You'll never claim your wish to bring me back. You're free."

Tib shakes his head, his close-cropped hair having grown shaggy and sweeping the edges of his face. "How many times have I said it? I'm not abandoning you here. Not before, not now. If you're trapped in Eida, so am I." I open my mouth to order him to leave, but Tib cuts in. "This is your life now, like it or not. You might as well give it a try. It might be fun being the one with all the power for once."

I peek at Tib from the corner of my eyes, and the stars reflect in his. Power. My tongue traces the edges of my teeth.

"What would you have me do?" Tib asks, catching the twinkle in my eye.

Finally, we have the power to do anything, to grant any wish. It seems fitting we thank the one person who put us on this path.

"Bring me Caelum."

EPILOGUE

Caelum

The dry wind hisses through the switchgrass. My ears fill with their mournful song. I cock my head to the side as though to hear it better. Dried sweat clings to my skin, Bridgewick's usually balmy air now desiccated. I close my eyes against the village, the pebbled ground digging into my bare knees. Pain. Focus. A slow inhale. The baked air scorches my throat with my haggard breath.

When my eyes open, my gaze falls to my hands curled in my lap. Bloodied.

I swipe a short nail beneath another, and the blood on my fingertips cracks. I flex my fingers, then curl them into a fist. The blood flakes off in patches.

It's not my blood. It's theirs.

I stroke my fingers in soft designs over my bloodied palm and glance at *them*. All of them. On the other side of the barren road lies an ever-growing mass of chilled bodies. Their jaws are slack, their eyes sunken. Their souls gone.

What a cruel world.

I swipe my thumb over my palm faster as my eyes rest on two bodies wedged into the center, awaiting their turn at the blazing pyre in the center of the village. This blood on my hands—chipped and aged—is their blood. It's my reminder. My atonement for failing to defend my village. My parents.

The blood has coated my hands for days now, and it will until I exact my revenge on our neighboring village. Rage curdles in my stomach. It crawls up my throat, ready to unleash itself on the people of Norgrave. Because of them, my parents are dead. My neighbors. Many innocent people who had no right dealing with Norgrave.

My gaze sweeps the unlit streets. Blood darkens our soil. And for what? Insurrection? Disunity?

Norgrave was bold. They were careless. Savage.

Our elders have sought unity among our village and those surrounding us for decades. But it wasn't enough. Until every soul in our village stands together, we'll never be strong enough.

I'll show Norgrave what real pain is. They will know of our suffering. They'll feel our loss. I'll get my revenge even if I must take everyone that's left in our village into battle.

A quiet scrape echoes behind my back and cuts through my thoughts. Silence. Then a long, lumbering step. Halt.

"Caelum from Bridgewick." It isn't a question. A tepid smile crosses my lips. I recognize that deep set timbre, the smell of decay. "Aribelle Decatour, Queen of Eida, demands your presence."

Aribelle. Her name buzzes behind my lips. It's been nearly eight and a half years since I've seen her, yet a day hasn't passed that I haven't thought of her. The rich tones of her skin, her long legs that I craved tangle with mine, those soft rose-colored lips…

I thought I'd never see her again. She was supposed to die. My jaw twitches, and my stomach hardens. She was my offering to the elders—the first real step on our path toward peace and unity in Bridgewick. They wanted unity. I wanted her gone.

"Cast out the agitators?" Montague had repeated, his brow crossed with concern. The elders always were slow to make change.

"Of sorts," I said. "Take them to the Well. Let me offer just one, and you'll see how quickly Bridgewick obeys."

The elders agreed, albeit reluctantly. I left their hut, my smile wide and growing. If I couldn't have Ari, neither would my brother. As I reached her window, I donned a sorrowful demeanor. She followed me to the Well of Eida like a cow to the slaughterhouse. I offered her to the Well in return for absolutely nothing. And they took her.

Fear swept through the village when news of Ari's disappearance spread. She'd broken Bridgewick's rules, snuck out at night, and was taken. My lips quirk. That's what we told everyone. And as fear snowed upon the village, the elders finally understood.

Yet, Ari's still alive. Heat burns across my neck. She's queen. She's supposed to be dead.

The temper crawling over my skin melts into a wave of ice. My gaze flashes to the flames in the distance where my people burn. We weren't strong enough when Norgrave attacked, but we will be. I stroke my thumb across my collarbone where the ink of the

White Knight stains my skin. I'm Bridgewick's protector now. If I play the game right, I can still finish the job and claim an army while I'm at it.

A cold smile curls my lips as I glance over my shoulder. Yes, a troll. The creature towers over me, a bludgeon holding a steady beat as he drops its end into his palm.

"Queen, you say?" My eyes roam over the shackles draped around the troll's neck. Iron and Callamar—the strongest of materials with which to escort me. So, it won't be a social call then.

Climbing to my feet, I brush the barren dust from my clothes. My parents' blood clings to my hands like the crisp leaves lingering at autumn's end. Eventually, we all must let go. I brush my fingertips over the blood once more and silently offer an oath.

I will kill you, Aribelle Decatour, and bring peace back to Bridgewick.

Flashing the troll a courteous smile, I lift my stained hands into the air. "Well then, let me wash my hands, and we can be on our way."

TO BE CONTINUED

A Message from Me

Thanks for reading Well of Eida! This project has been so close to my heart and has taken years to get to this point. I'm honored you chose to spend your reading time with this story.

Now, I need your help! If you enjoyed Well of Eida (or even if you didn't), please consider leaving an honest review on Goodreads and/or Amazon!

Did you know that reviews are the lifeblood for authors, especially indie authors? Your opinions can help Well of Eida find its way into the right readers' hands. Remember, reviews don't have to be long. It can be as simple as "I loved it!" or "It wasn't for me". Please share your thoughts!

Okay then, now to the fun part. If you'd like to join me and my books on this crazy adventure or just want to stay in the know about The Fallen Kingdoms and my other series, come hang out with me!

I'm active on Instagram where I share all the fun teasers, love to chat in DMs, and nerd out about all things fantasy. Just kidding, fantasy is *not* nerdy. You can follow me here: https://www.instagram.com/kb_benson_books/

If you want more than that including exclusive giveaways, freebies, first looks at new releases and opportunities to join teams, etc. come join my newsletter here: https://www.kbbenson.com/newsletter.html

All the important news goes out there and I would love to have you join!

Reign of Darkness

The Fallen Kingdoms, Book 2

Coming January 2024

ACKNOWLEDGMENTS

It was right after my son underwent massive open-heart surgery that I began exploring the world that is Eida and the characters that were sacrificed to it. I never imagined the story would have taken the turns it has or that I would be so incredibly proud of the book it has become.

And I never could have done it alone.

I firmly believe it takes a village to raise a child, and it takes a village to create a book baby. A huge, never-ending thanks to my village.

First and foremost, I'm so grateful to my Father in Heaven who wants to see me reach my dreams and strengthen my talents. I'm so grateful He never gives up on me as I try to find some semblance of balance in my life. I'm so grateful that He has somehow made it possible for me to be a busy SAHM while finding time to do this writing-publishing thing. I'm forever grateful for His guidance and for His miracle in maximizing my capacity. Storytelling gives me life and I'm so grateful for His love.

I absolutely need to thank my ever-supportive and amazing husband who encourages me to go for my dreams. Thank you for staying up late to listen to me ramble about exciting plot points or gripe about the frustrating plot holes. Thanks for being willing to offer me suggestions to fix them even though I rarely take them. Though, you did solve one of the biggest gaps in the overall story that readers will get to read in the final book. I'll give you that one. Thanks for taking the kids so I can go on writer's retreats, to writer's conferences, and to meet up with my writer's group. I love you!

To my amazing writer's group and critique partners: Courtney Millecam, Caitlyn Ainge, & Julie Janis. Thank you for reading the rough, long-winded, pile of words that was the first draft. And more than reading it, thank you for giving me your honest feedback so I could make this book the best I possibly could.

I'm so grateful for Write the # Book. It is a fix I need every month to hang out with my writing ladies, Leisa Wallace, Courtney Millecam, Amber Harrison, and Jess Prather. I did it! I wrote the d*** book.

Thank you to my amazing beta readers and street team. Merrit Townsend, Rachel L Schade, TM Ghent, Bethany Olin, Heidi Hiatt, Corey Grint, Danielle Williams, Erin Izatt, Crystal Balz, Tralyn Hughes, Katie Marie, Lauren James, Elianna Lucas, Caelan J Peters, Brittany Bateman, and Crystal Frost. I was so nervous to share Well of Eida, but your enthusiasm and excitement over my characters and the world left me feeling like I could do anything. Thank you so much for your endless support and excitement.

I'm grateful for Alyssa Stockwell. Thank you for always letting me brainstorm marketing strategies and plans with you. I always need to talk plans out, and I'm so grateful your door (aka, Marco Polo ha) is always open. You are also a wizard with photoshop, and even though you say it's easy, all the design help you give me at a moment's notice is HUGE! You are invaluable. Love you, sis!

To Heather Austin, my incredible editor, thanks for taking a chance on me and Well of Eida. You warned me you "weren't the nicest editor", but you were exactly what I needed to level up this book. You were invaluable, and I'm so grateful to have worked on Well of Eida with you.

To my wonderful proofreaders, Alyssa Stockwell, Justin Benson, Courtney Millecam, and Sharon Lender. Thank you for reading the whole book in such a short timeframe and catching all those pesky typos that STILL made their way through.

A huge thank you to Franziska Stern, the face behind the gorgeous cover on Well of Eida. I am in love with every cover you make, and you were so easy to work with and willing to help me get the perfect cover for this book. I'm especially grateful that after you made me a cover, you were willing to completely rework it so we could find the right fit. You're amazing! I'm excited to work with you again on the rest of the series.

And last, but never least, my readers. YOU! Thank you for taking a chance on me and my books. Thank you for reading the story that is so close to my heart and for being on this journey with me and my characters. It's because of you that I get to live this dream and do what I love. I can't wait for you to see how this story ends for Ari, Graeden, Tib, and all the others you'll soon meet. I'm so honored to have you as fans, but more than that, as friends. Thank you!

About the Author

KB Benson is a Young Adult Fantasy author who loves adventuring on the page and off it with her hubs and two littles. You'll often find her immersed in her fictional worlds or enjoying time with her family in the real one. KB is a huge advocate for following your dreams and loving the journey on the way. Each experience is a part of the beautiful story of your life. She loves escaping reality with readers and diving into action-packed fantasy so that we all can come back to reality a little stronger.

KB is the author of the Call of the Sirens series and The Fallen Kingdoms series. Connect with her online!
https://www.kbbenson.com/
https://www.kbbenson.com/newsletter.html
https://www.instagram.com/kb_benson_books/
https://www.bookbub.com/profile/kb-benson

Printed in Great Britain
by Amazon